ALSO BY MEGHAN QUINN

BRIDESMAID by CHANCE

MEGHAN QUINN

Bloom books

Published by Bloom Books, an imprint of Sourcebooks
P.O. Box 4410, Naperville, Illinois 60567–4410
(630) 961-3900
sourcebooks.com

Cataloging-in-Publication data on file with the Library of Congress.

Printed and bound in the United States of America.
PAH 10 9 8 7 6 5 4 3 2 1

HUDSON

"PULL HARDER... *HUSBAND.*"

"I don't want to hurt you... *Wife,*" I say on a grunt as the strings of her corset dig into the flesh of my fingers.

"How could you possibly hurt me any more than you already have?" Sloane counters with that telltale sass that I've grown to know very well.

A sass that grates on my nerves—like a rusty knife, spinning and twirling in my insides. I'll tell you one thing for certain: when I initially hired her as my assistant, there wasn't one telltale sign of that sass. But now... now it's all I fucking get.

I let go of the strings of her corset and take a step back, fucking irritated with this situation that I've gotten myself into because it's... it's... Sloane.

Sloane Galloway, thirteen years younger than me and sister to one of my best friends, brother-in-law, and business partners.

She's my assistant.

She's my biggest fucking secret.

What kind of secret? Well, she's my wife.

Yup, you read that correctly. My wife.

It happened so fast, I can barely remember the circumstances.

Shit. That's a lie. I remember every second of how it happened.

Every goddamn, intricate second when I felt my world shift.

When everything changed.

When vulnerability met need and I succumbed to the combination, falling like a leaf, barely putting up a fight.

It all started as a favor to a friend.

Jude's sister needed some help finding a temporary job to gain some experience straight out of college. Being the upstanding guy that I am, I offered her a job at the company. It was a win-win for everyone. I needed help. She needed help. A solution was formed.

What I didn't expect was to be...distracted.

And yes, it was my problem not hers.

The pervy fucking grandpa over here—that's me—couldn't stop feeling his heart beat just a touch faster anytime she was in the room.

Nor could I get rid of the florally addictive scent of her perfume in my office.

Her hair—long, sleek, brown—captivated me.

Her deep brown eyes that are so large, so doe-like, that I kept staring at her longer than I should have.

It got to the point that I could feel her...all around me.

I saw her all the time.

Her husky voice greeted me every morning.

Her tailored outfits hugged her body in all the right places.

Her attentiveness, the way she would look at me...the occasional brush of her hand.

I know, I'm pathetic.

So when she proposed marriage to me, I...I fucking folded.

Yes, me, Hudson Fucking Hopper, the billionaire business tycoon out to prove his dictator of a father wrong.

I folded.

I said yes.

But not only did I say yes to marrying her, I said yes to keeping it a secret from her brother.

I fucking know—I can feel your cringe from here.

Keeping a secret from my friend and business partner about marrying his sister is definitely not one of my smartest decisions ever...

"Hudson," Sloane says, pulling my attention to where she's standing in front of me, her arms clutching at the corset she's required to wear, looking all sorts of fuckable at the moment as those innocent eyes of hers stare back at me.

"What?" I ask, my voice coming out harsh.

"I need you to dress me."

I feel my Adam's apple bob as I swallow the saliva building in my mouth.

My skin itches from her proximity.

My hands beg me to reach out and touch her.

And when my eyes fall to her mouth, that sultry fucking mouth that has brought me to my knees on many occasions, I can feel myself slipping.

And she can see it as well.

Because when the corner of her lips tilts up, I know I'm in trouble.

"Or has your intent been to undress me this entire time?" she asks just as she drops her corset to the ground, putting her perfect tits on display.

Fuck.

Me.

She closes the space between us, pushes me back onto the bed, and then moves between my legs, kneeling before me.

Yup.

I'm fucked.

I'm so goddamn fucked.

CHAPTER ONE
SLOANE

HOW DOES HE DRINK THIS stuff?

I set Hudson's green juice on his desk and twist the cup, so the logo is facing him when he takes a seat at his desk. It's not required, but I think it's a nice touch. I've learned in life that appearances matter.

I glance at the watch on my wrist and note that he'll be here in five minutes, so I take the time to set up his pen and notepad, wake up his computer, and grab him a glass of water from the kitchenette in his office.

Once everything is set, I stand to the side of his desk, ready to greet him.

Yup, this is my life.

Sloane Galloway, twenty-two-year-old assistant to Hudson Hopper, making sure all of his wildest dreams and business goals are met, a.k.a. fetching him drinks and telling him people are waiting to talk to him on line one.

Fresh out of college, I was looking for any sort of job, an internship, or anything that paid and could give me experience in…well…in anything. I majored in business management with no idea what to do with that, interned at a dying newspaper for a few months, and then desperately pleaded with Jude, my brother, to help me find something where I make some money and earn more corporate experience.

Enter Hudson Hopper into the chat.

He needed an assistant.

I'm great at assisting—even better at listening and catering to your every need.

It was a match made in heaven.

I make decent money. He doesn't use and abuse the assistant role. And well…I'm learning quite quickly with every demanding email and phone call that business is a lot about slapping on a smile and being gracious even when it's the last thing you want to do. I can safely say executive assistant is not the future career for me. I'm not sure the corporate life is for me either.

Corporate jobs feel a bit soulless, and the emphasis on money and making more of it feels wrong as someone whose family struggled for years to figure out where our next meal was going to come from or how we were going to afford the roof over our heads.

What do I want to do?

That's yet to be determined and something that I hope I figure out along the way.

The door opens to Hudson's office and—just like every other morning when he strolls in wearing his bespoke suit, head down, looking at his phone—I feel my stomach flip, my skin break out in an acute sweat, and my pulse beat faster, because…

Oh.

My.

God.

He is so handsome.

No, *handsome* is not even the most suitable word to describe him. He's…ungodly.

Olive skin; full, light brown hair; and eyes the color of the sweater Andrea Sachs wears in *The Devil Wears Prada*…cerulean blue. His long legs are endless, his waist, thick but narrow, and his shoulders are broad, rounded in muscles that pull on his button-up shirts whenever he removes his jacket. Not to mention one of the best asses I've ever seen in a three-piece suit. And when he's in the state of full-on concentration with his sleeves rolled up—his brow pinched together as he stares down at his notes—he's stunning. It's hard to pull my gaze off him from where I sit at my desk, looking into his office, wondering if there is a way I can ease the tension for him, something more than just bringing him a drink.

Hudson pulls his attention away from his phone and looks up at me. The same mandatory smile he offers me every morning plays on his lips as he says, "Morning, Sloane."

"Good morning, Mr. Hopper," I answer, my hands folded in front of me.

And just like every other morning, he turns his attention away from me and brings it to his desk where he takes a seat.

Do I wish that he'd give me more than just his smile used for employees?

Of course.

Do I wish he noticed the outfits I spend a great deal of time putting together in an effort to impress him?

Obviously.

But that's wishful thinking because this is Hudson Hopper. Not only is he way out of my league, significantly older than me, and my boss, but he's my brother's friend, brother-in-law, and business partner, and there's no way Hudson would ever cross that line.

I know this from how upset he was when he found out that his brother, Hardy, was cross-pollinating with Everly Plum, who works for Maggie Mitchell.

Maggie owns Magical Moments by Maggie and is the official event planner for Hudson and Hardy's co-op. She's the owner of Bridesmaid for Hire as well, which is an emerging, booming business that rents bridesmaids to brides and grooms in need. Everly heads up the program and recently helped Hardy's friend, who needed someone to train the maid of honor. Long story short, Hardy fell for Everly, and Hudson had a conniption about it.

I heard him ranting about how you don't mix personal with business. It was a rough day in the office to say the least.

"Any meetings today?" Hudson asks in a gruff voice as he picks up his green drink and mumbles, "Thank you."

"You have three," I say while pulling my phone out to go over his schedule. This is where I transform. This is where I have an out-of-body experience.

Normally, I can be snarky, sarcastic, maybe a bit too sassy for my own good, but when I'm around Hudson, I'm on my best behavior. Again, I know the value of appearances.

I'm talking, *we're having dinner at the in-laws, do not say anything incriminating* type of behavior.

I'm polite.

I'm courteous.

I do the job, and I don't linger.

When I got this job, Jude pulled me to the side and told me that I needed to put my big-girl pants on and be professional, especially since I would be working for his friend.

And I do what Jude says.

So, yup, every time I'm in assistant mode, I feel like I'm having an out-of-body experience.

"The first meeting is with Maggie at Magical Moments. A check-in on the business and then right after that, a few blocks down, you're meeting with Archie Wimbach." Hudson's gaze falls to mine.

"Archie's today? I thought that was tomorrow."

I shake my head. "It's today. I sent you the notes yesterday about the possible property purchase."

"Jesus," he mutters and then goes to his email. He scans through his inbox, and when he sees my email, he mumbles something else under his breath and then pinches his brow.

"Is everything okay?" I ask.

"Fine," he says in a snappy tone, and I know it's not directed at me, more so at himself.

I've heard it a few times, the anger and irritation over something he's done or something not going his way.

Here's the thing about Hudson Hopper. He's incredibly intelligent, a diligent and hard worker, a kind, caring boss, but also vastly more intense than anyone I've ever known. Why?

Because he has something to prove.

Only a few months ago, together with his brother and mine, he formed a new business after parting ways with Reginald Hopper, Hudson and Hardy's dad.

But not only did they part ways, they started a co-op with Reginald's enemies, the Cane brothers, who own Cane Enterprises. It was the merger of the century. They invested in smaller businesses, such as Maggie's, and they're building up their philanthropic side by expanding affordable housing during a time when big companies are scooping up property and price-gouging. No one saw the co-op coming, not even Reginald, and now, he's out for blood.

Which has led to the intensity Hudson lives with on a daily basis.

Hudson blows out a heavy breath and leans back in his chair while pinching the bridge of his nose. "Sorry, I didn't mean to snap at you."

See? Kind. Caring.

Hot.

Just look at how the top two buttons of his shirt are undone, showing off his muscular pecs and bare chest. I saw exactly what was under those button-downs when we were at Jude's wedding in Bora Bora. God, he's so impossibly attractive that just looking at him makes me sweat.

Weak.

And panting like a dog—for lack of a better description. Although, I am quite feral when I see pec definition.

I've had the occasional thought of how I would motorboat in the ridges all over his body.

And sure, do I seem like a horny assistant drooling over her boss, obviously, can't deny it, but I swear I perform my job well.

"It's okay. I understand the stress you must be under at the moment."

He glances my way briefly, barely giving me a glimpse of those sultry eyes of his. "Thanks, Sloane."

He sits up again and takes a sip of his juice. When he sets it back down, he stares back at his computer. "This possible purchase is important. It could grant us access to low-income housing in the UK, an expansion that would impress the Cane brothers as it's something they've been looking to do."

"It seemed like a pretty big deal when I was writing up the notes for you, but I think you can make it happen. Mr. Wimbach and you definitely have something in common."

"What's that?" he asks.

"You both went to Stanford."

"Did he?" Hudson asks, turning toward me again, but this time, it's not just his head. He turns his whole body. His deliciously firm body.

"He did. He graduated a few years before you, but you were both Cardinals and he's a pretty big donor, which means he loves his college more than the average student. I think that's something you can easily play off. Not to mention, he's recently engaged. Your sister just got married in Bora Bora, so you can bond over that. Maybe discuss your sister's business while you're at it, pop in the idea that she could bring her vacation rental brand over to the UK."

Haisley started her own business a few years ago. Separating herself from her father and Hopper Industries earlier, she took some money from her trust fund and purchased a house in Nashville, which she completely gutted and renovated, then themed the whole house around Dolly Parton. She took the revenue from that house—because who doesn't want to vacation with Dolly?—and bought a house here in San Francisco, which she decorated based on the movie *Clueless*.

Hudson scratches the side of his cheek. "You know, that's not that bad of an idea."

I want to say that's a compliment, but why did he have to say it like that? As if he expected me to have a bad idea, but I surprised him with a good one?

"Thanks," I say, even though I still feel the slight burn of his comment. I might be much younger than him, but I'm also very perceptive; he might not know it yet, but I'm a good addition to his team.

"Okay. I'm going to get some work done before we leave."

"We?" I ask, surprised. "Before *we* leave?"

"Yeah," he says, looking at me again, this time his brow full of confusion. "You're coming with me."

"Oh. I've never come with you to meetings outside the office before."

"This is an important one. I'll need you to take notes. Is that okay?" He raises his brow at me.

"Sure," I say. "Not a problem at all." I glance down at my flouncy skirt and heels and then back at him. "Um, is what I'm wearing okay?"

His eyes travel down my legs, heating me up before they travel to my face. He clears his throat and turns away from me, focusing entirely on his computer. "Yeah, it's fine."

Fine?

Just fine?

I mean, not that he would compliment what I'm wearing, the man barely even looks at me, but I thought my outfit today was better than fine.

I worked hard on putting it together. I changed at least three times.

My lush skirt I found at the thrift store—which, by the way, shopping at the thrift store here in San Francisco, you can find some amazing designer clothing for so cheap. My maroon blouse I got on Poshmark for twelve dollars along with these matching maroon heels. I know how to make dollars stretch. There were several times growing up when we didn't have money for new shoes or coats, and people treat you different when they see your coat sleeves are too short or that your tennis shoes have soles that were obviously glued to last a bit longer. I'm not saying it's right, but we do live in a world where appearance matters more than it should. It's why I care so much about playing the part while I'm in the office. At most, I think I paid thirty dollars for this whole outfit, and when I was walking out of the house today, even Stacey, my twin sister, told me I looked like an executive—but that the skirt was too short.

Too short was also the perfect answer.

Hence why I asked Hudson about my outfit.

This is one of those instances where I slap on a smile and keep my mouth shut. If I wasn't trying to be professional and hold back, I'd tell Hudson to look again because I'm more than just fine.

He's a stoic man. I really shouldn't expect anything more from him.

"Okay, well, I'm going to go work on some emails. Let me know if you need anything."

"I will," he says with a nod, his eyes fixed on his computer.

I turn away from him and work my way out of his office, making sure to shut the door behind me, and then straight to my desk, where I take a seat and scoot my chair in.

From here, I look through the glass of his windows that frost when he wants privacy, and I stare at the crinkle in his brow and the sturdy grip he has on his mouse as he scrolls through emails.

He's always so tense I wonder if he ever does anything to relax.

Like, what does he do when he gets home from work?

He goes to the gym, that's extremely obvious. Through his suits, I can see his muscles, and when he rolls up the sleeves of his button-up shirt when it's late at night and he's been thinking hard…oof those forearms.

But there must be other things.

Like…what kind of shows does he watch? Does he even watch any?

What music does he listen to? I can't imagine him listening to anything honestly. In my head, he walks around this earth in complete silence, always thinking about business. He probably drives to work in silence and gets ready for his day in silence, although I bet he listens to the stock market and how well that's doing. Ugh, boring.

Does he do anything on the weekends?

Does he like sports?

Does he…go out on dates?

I once tried asking Jude about Hudson, but he quickly told me it was stuff I didn't need to know because I was working for him and anything personal was none of my business. Soooo that was helpful and also somewhat embarrassing.

Either way, I wonder about him. But I guess that's not my responsibility.

Nope, I'm here to answer emails, schedule meetings, and, apparently now, accompany him to meetings outside the office.

At least it pays the bills.

At least I'm learning what I don't want to do with my life.

And at least there's outstanding eye candy.

"We're here," I say to Hudson as the car comes to a stop.

Hudson looks up from his phone for the first time since we got in. "Okay," he answers and then exits without another word.

Sheesh, there's not an ounce of personality in that man. Which is weird because Hudson was a different man at Jude and Haisley's wedding. He was more carefree, he joked around, he played games with the family, and he smiled.

But this guy?

Mr. Business.

Sir Tightwad.

Lord Stick-Up-His-Ass.

He's all sorts of boring.

When I first started working with him, I assumed he'd at least talk to me in the car on the way to a work meeting. Nope, he types away on his phone while I play the Spelling Bee in the *New York Times* app.

The pangram was "publicly." My nipples went hard when I saw it. Nothing makes me feel more accomplished in my day than when I find the Spelling Bee pangram.

I exit the car as well, thank our driver, and then straighten out my skirt as I stare at the storefront of Magical Moments by Maggie. The window is covered in pink hydrangeas, inviting anyone and everyone on the street to take a picture. Such a smart idea. Then again, it's Maggie. She's an incredibly smart businesswoman.

When we reach the door, Hudson holds it open for me, and as I pass him, I thank him. He just acknowledges me with a nod before following me in. Wouldn't it have been amazing if he gave me a good spank to the ass instead?

A girl could dream.

"Hey, Hudson," Maggie says in greeting. She walks up and shakes his hand. "And, Sloane, it's so good to see you. I haven't seen you in a while. What brings you here today?"

"Taking notes," I say, holding up my pen and notebook.

"Can I get a copy of those when you're done?" she jokes.

I offer a wink. "Of course."

"Is that Sheridan?" Everly says as she walks out into the main space of the store.

Everly is Hardy's girlfriend, and she's so freaking gorgeous. Long, black hair that's always tied up in a tight bun when she's at work, the prettiest bone structure I've ever seen, and extremely luscious lips. Plus, the girl knows how to organize better than anyone I've ever met. She's actually helped me out on a few occasions, giving me tips and tricks on how to keep Hudson organized. She's been a real help.

"Oh, hey," Everly says, spotting us. "Sorry, I thought you were Sheridan."

"Sheridan who?" Hudson says, growing stiff next to me.

"Sheridan Soon-to-Be-Wimbach," Everly says. "Do you know her?"

Wait, isn't that Archie's fiancée?

"Yes, I have a meeting with her fiancé after this about a possible merger. Why are you meeting with her?"

"She had some questions," Everly answers. "I told her we were pretty booked up, though, and I wasn't sure if we would be able to help."

Hudson is about to respond when the door opens behind us and a woman with bright-red hair and a face full of cute freckles steps in.

"Hudson?" she says as a gentleman steps in behind her. "What are you doing here?"

"I have a meeting with Maggie." He shakes both of their hands. "Looks like we had the same idea, a meeting before a meeting."

It's so fascinating to me, watching Hudson turn it on when he's around potential business partners. He morphs into a completely different person. He's animated, smooth, and funny. He listens intently to the person talking to him, making direct eye contact. He's invested and charming.

I like this side of him even more, even though I don't mind the grump either. Because let's face it, the grump is sexy too.

Archie—a very tall man with dark-framed glasses, fluffy blond hair, and lanky limbs—takes Hudson by the hand. "Always being efficient. You know, I read that you've had a hand in creating Magical Moments by Maggie; that's why we're here actually." Ooof, what a rich English accent. Yummy.

Hudson shakes his head. "I didn't create anything. Maggie is the mastermind behind the business. I just saw how brilliant she was and invested. She has taken the reins and created something truly special."

I catch the smile that passes over Maggie's lips, because who doesn't like a compliment like that? I know I would.

"Well, we are impressed," Archie says.

"And in desperate need of help," Sheridan adds.

"Why don't we all take a seat at the conference table," Maggie says. "And we can discuss. Unless you don't want to discuss in front of Hudson."

"No, I think it might be good to have all hands on deck," Sheridan says as we move toward the conference table.

"Let me grab everyone drinks," I say as I set my notebook down. "Is water good?"

"We also have some sparkling waters and juice," Maggie adds.

"Water is good," Sheridan and Archie answer.

Because I've been in the offices before, I make my way to the kitchen and help myself to the fridge, where I pull out a few waters in aluminum cans and set them down on a tray. I then find a basket of snacks that I figure the ladies bring out for guests, so I set that on the tray as well and add some napkins. Then, for good measure, I pick up a milk glass bud vase with a pink flower sticking out of it and put it on the tray as well.

Satisfied, I make my way toward the conference table, where Sheridan's explaining her wedding.

"So yeah, she just called to say that she broke her leg and can't be part of the wedding. And of course, I don't have anyone to fill in."

I set the tray down and pass out waters. I finish by setting one down in front of Hudson, who whispers a thank you, before I take a seat next to him and open up my notebook to take notes.

Not that I need to take notes for this meeting, but it could be helpful if anyone needs things emailed later.

"That's when we heard about Bridesmaid for Hire," Archie says. "We thought it would be a good option since the wedding is coming up soon, and we don't have anyone else who could fill in."

"Plus, and trust me when I say I'm not proud of this, but we could pick someone who might fit the part a little better, you know?" Sheridan adds with a slight wince in her expression.

I write down in my notes *fit the part*, whatever the hell that means.

Seems like I cut out at the wrong time, when the tea was being spilled.

Something about someone breaking their leg, them needing what I assume is a bridesmaid, and needing someone who fits in. Doesn't seem like too big of an ask. If anyone can help them, it's Maggie and Everly.

What kind of wedding are they having?

"I don't think we have anyone who fits the requirements," Everly says, looking nervous at saying that in front of Hudson.

Orrrrr maybe not.

I glance at Hudson only to be met by an unhappy pinch in his brow, and yeah, I guess I would be nervous to disappoint as well when he's looking at her like that.

"Really?" Sheridan says, her voice falling flat.

"Oh, I'm sure we can find someone," Hudson says, stepping in, causing both Maggie and Everly to turn their heads toward him in shock. Yikes, don't think they were expecting him to jump in with such a strong commitment. But really, they don't have anyone who could help?

"Really?" Sheridan asks. "That would be such a huge help."

"Sure," Hudson says, not breaking a sweat. "What exactly are you looking for in a bridesmaid?"

Great question—that's why he's the boss.

"We would need someone well-versed in Regency ballroom dancing."

That's a new one. Regency ballroom dancing? What the hell is that? I write it down in my notes.

Is that like…what they do on *Bridgerton*? The fancy line dancing?

Good luck finding someone with that kind of knowledge, lady.

"Someone who can take time off and be in London for a couple of weeks."

Ooh, London, never been there but have always wanted to go.

Double-decker buses, telephone booths, tea, and *cheerio, mate*.

Not to mention, the possibility of stalking Harry Styles—sign me up.

"It would be convenient if she was married since it's last minute, though it's not a high priority. I'm sure Archie can get it approved with the club, but it would make things easier."

A club? Fancy. What kind of club are we talking about? Because my mind is wandering.

Imagine them looking for some Regency-dancing, unemployed, sex-club enthusiast to be a part of their wedding.

There's a request.

"And would love for her to have dark hair since all the other bridesmaids have dark hair as well."

That's easy. I write down in my notepad *someone willing to have dark hair*.

Looking over these notes, I can't see how impossible it will be to find someone. Perhaps—

"Not to be presumptuous but someone like her," Sheridan adds.

Like who?

I look up from where I'm making another note about dark hair when I see all eyes on me at the table. Because I'm very confused as to why people would be looking in my direction, I glance over my shoulder to see if there is anyone possibly standing behind me. When I come up short, a wave of anxiety washes over me as I bring my pen to my chest, pointing at myself and say, "Me?"

"Yes," Sheridan says with a smile. "You actually would be perfect."

"Oh, I—"

"She'd love to," Hudson says before I can even tell her I'm not quite sure what the Regency era really is.

Pardon me, sir?

"I...I what?" I ask.

Hudson nods his head. "Sloane would love to fill in for you."

Errr...what?

Fill in?

Let me clear my ear because I could have sworn Hudson just said I would love to be a bridesmaid for this person I don't know.

Umm, correct me if I'm wrong, but I'm not an unemployed, married, ballroom-dancing enthusiast with a penchant for sex clubs. I'm none of those actually. The only thing that I remotely check off the list is the dark hair, and that can't possibly be a good enough qualification...right?

CHAPTER TWO
HUDSON

DO YOU SMELL THAT?

The distinct scent of sweat and desperation?

Yeah, emanating from me.

The moment I saw Sheridan and Archie walk through the doors of Magical Moments by Maggie, I knew I was going to say something stupid.

I felt it in my bones.

I've been rocked the last few weeks with the pressure of growing the company and proving to everyone that not only did my brother and I make a good decision to step away from our father, but we made a good, life-changing decision for the people who depend on us. And when I got wind of a possible buyout with the Wimbachs to expand our low-income housing globally, I knew it was an opportunity we couldn't miss.

So seeing Archie and Sheridan in need of help, well, it prickled my ears.

I told myself to be cool, to not jump in with a solution to whatever problem they were facing. But do you remember that desperation I was talking about? Yeah, it grabbed me by the balls and started tugging, telling me I needed to leap in like a goddamn hero, arm extended into the air, ready to save the day. And before I could stop myself, I was offering up my assistant to Sheridan and Archie as a well-enthused Regency ballroom dancer without even blinking an eye.

Pretty sure I would have offered them my right nut if they'd asked for it—that's how desperate I am to make an impression.

Did I consider how this might affect Sloane? Maggie? Or even Everly? Not in the slightest.

Did I consider that she might not know anything about Regency ballroom dancing?

Nope.

Did I think to myself, *Oh, Sloane has brown hair and could get the time off because I'm her boss, so she'll do*?

Absolutely.

I absolutely fucking did.

I could not have made the decision in my head faster before I spat it out to the room.

"Really?" Sheridan asks, her hands clasped together now, so much hope in her expression.

"Of course," I say, even though I can feel the questioning stares of Everly and Maggie directed at me.

Well, not just questioning but concerned. I can't even look in Sloane's direction. Those fucking huge-ass eyes of hers are probably as wide as can be.

"Do you know anything about Regency dancing?" Sheridan asks Sloane.

Before Sloane can even open her mouth, I continue to dig my grave. "She was just telling me the other day how she's been partaking in some ballroom dancing in her spare time. More modern waltzes, but I'm sure it's the foundation for good footwork. I have no doubt she'll be able to pick it up quickly."

I also have no doubt she probably wants to stab me in the throat with her pen to get me to stop talking.

"Oh, that's wonderful. Yes, any experience is great," Sheridan says just as a phone rings and Archie pulls it out of his pocket.

"Sorry, I need to take this," Archie says and then stands from the table and walks toward the back of the store.

When he's out of earshot, Sheridan says, "Sorry about that. His father has been sick, and well, we're trying to speed this wedding along so he can be a part of it. Everything that we're doing for the wedding is really for him, hence having it in England with a Regency theme."

"That's really sweet," Everly says.

"I'm kind of in love with the idea of holding a Regency-themed wedding. Sounds dreamy," Maggie adds.

Sheridan smiles as I sit there, my skin prickling with the awareness that I just threw my assistant into a position I'm fairly certain she not only doesn't want to be in but that she has zero experience at.

Maggie asks Sheridan about the decor and what she plans on wearing. Sheridan gushes about the colors—iceberg blue and cream. She regales us about the flowers—lilies. And sings praises about the club where the wedding will be held—it has an ornate ballroom with painted ceilings where the reception will take place. All the while, I remain as still as possible, sweating and mildly panicking because I fear if I turn to look at Sloane, she'll be one breath away from chopping me in the esophagus with the side of her hand, cutting off all oxygen.

"Yeah, so it should be a great week of celebrating. We can't wait," Sheridan says just as Archie returns to the table.

He softly smiles. "Sorry about that. Darling, we're going to have to head out. Unfortunately, some tests came back for my father that were not what we were hoping for, and well, my father needs me in London." He looks at me and continues, "I'm going to have to cancel our meeting for today. My deepest apologies."

"Oh, we can meet anytime." I stand. "Business can wait. Please, focus on your family."

"Thank you, that means a lot to me." Archie helps Sheridan stand as well, both of them with concerned looks on their faces.

"So…where do we stand with everything?" Sheridan asks, looking between all of us.

Knowing I'm the one responsible for this mess, I jump in, "We'll get Sloane prepared for the wedding. Just send us the information, and she'll be ready."

"Thank you so much," Sheridan says, looking incredibly relieved.

"Of course," I say.

Archie turns to Sheridan and says, "Can you wait for me in the car? I need to discuss something with Hudson for a moment."

Sheridan smiles softly, places a kiss on his cheek, and then takes off with a wave to the girls. When she's gone, Archie turns to me. "May I have a moment?"

"Yes, of course."

"You can use my office," Maggie says graciously.

"Thank you." I guide Archie to the back, to Maggie's office, and shut the door once we're inside. He doesn't try to take in the space, getting right down to business.

"I need to make this quick," he says. "I don't want to stress Sheridan out since she's already stressed about her injured brides-maid and the wedding preparations, but that was actually her father on the phone."

"Oh," I say. "Is *your* father actually okay?"

Archie shakes his head. "Unfortunately, no. I received a text from my sister that he was asking for me. I told her we'd fly out tomorrow. Sheridan and I were already discussing that. But Sheridan's father, Terrance, has been adamant about not selling to you."

Fuck.

Why the hell not?

"Now, he owns about 10 percent of the shares in the company and doesn't have much of a say, but he and Sheridan are very close. I know that Terrance's approval of me matters a lot, and we have a good relationship, something I don't want to damage over a business deal."

"I understand that completely and respect it," I say. The words feel like gravel coming out of my mouth because—*10 percent. You're going to let a guy who owns 10 percent make a decision about your business?*

"So I have a big ask of you." He presses his hands together and continues. "Would you mind coming to London so my father-in-law could get to know you better? Come to the wedding, show Terrance that you're a good guy, someone he can trust? I believe you could be the right fit for us, especially with the business practices you've been engaging in with the Cane brothers and their business model, but I can't make the final decision with Terrance harping in my ear."

"I appreciate your trust in me." I shift my weight. "Can I ask why he doesn't entirely trust me?"

Archie nods his head. "Because of, as he put it, what you did to your father." Christ. "And to be fully transparent, he contacted your father, and well, now he's trying to work out a deal with him."

Mother.

Fucker.

I keep my face neutral as I absorb this brand-new information.

"I appreciate you offering up this information. Honestly, you need to choose what's best for your business, and if that's keeping your father-in-law happy with you, then I totally understand. If you are granting me the chance to show Terrance that I'm someone he can trust, I'll take you up on the opportunity."

"I'm more than happy to. I can have my assistant send you the schedule, but whenever Terrance is in the UK, he spends a lot of his time at the Mayfair Club, where we are having the wedding. It's one of his favorite places to be, so that would be a good place to start."

I nod, knowing exactly which club he's talking about. "Sounds good. I'll be in touch; looking forward to receiving the schedule. And hey, business aside"—I pat his shoulder—"I'm really sorry to hear about your father."

"Thank you. That means a lot."

"Please let us know if there is anything we can do for you. I know Maggie and Everly would be more than happy to help if anything comes up with the wedding. And if there's anything we can do to ease some of the responsibility, let us know."

"Thank you, Hudson. I appreciate it."

He shakes my hand and then we head out of Maggie's office. The girls are still at the conference table, and when they see us approach, they all stand.

"It was lovely chatting. We'll be in touch. Thank you, Sloane, for helping us out."

"Y-yes, of course," she says, stumbling over her words.

We say our goodbyes, and he takes off, meeting Sheridan at the car out front. Once Archie is gone, I turn toward the girls. "Fuck, I'm sorry." I let out a deep breath and take a seat at the conference table, feeling the weight of my decision resting like a fucking hippo on my shoulders, the heaviness of it all, tremendous. I scrub my hands over my face. "This account with Archie is a big one, and well, I was trying to be accommodating. I apologize for putting you in a tough spot."

Maggie looks nervous as she says, "Hudson, we are, uh, kind of full at the moment. We really don't have any time to take on any extra work and took the meeting just to be courteous."

"I know." I drag my hand over my face again. "I'm sorry."

"Um, just to be clear, since I'm taking notes," Sloane says from the other end of the table. "Did I hear it correctly that I'm going to be in their wedding? A wedding in London with ballroom dancing?"

"That would be a question for Hudson," Maggie says. "Care to answer that, Hudson?"

Not wanting to face her at the moment but knowing I need to, I stare down the length of the table and slowly nod. "Yes, you heard that correctly."

"Okay, great," she says, almost sarcastically. "Umm, think I can have a moment with you, Mr. Hopper?"

I hate when she calls me that.

Fucking hate it to my bones.

That's what my dad makes everyone call him, and for some reason, no matter how many times I tell her not to call me that, she still does.

Maggie clears her throat and stands from her chair. "Uh, I have emails. Yeah, emails I need to look at." Not subtle at all.

"Same," Everly says, standing as well.

"Wait," I say. "Everly, I need to talk to you about the Bridesmaid for Hire program. Possibly help us out here."

Everly winces. "Yeah, things are really tight right now, but, uh..." She glances over at Maggie. "I think maybe if we move some things around, we can possibly manage it without sacrificing the quality of the other projects we currently have scheduled."

And I know that nervous look, I've made that nervous look before. She's staring down the barrel of a large workload, but she's trying to keep her boss happy at the same time.

I don't want to put her in that position.

So, I say, "I don't want you having to move your schedule around; that's not fair to you."

Nervously, Sloane raises her hand. "Not to be the bearer of bad news here, but I have no idea what any of this entails."

Silence falls upon us as Everly and Maggie both exchange looks.

After a few seconds, Everly steps in. "I mean, I think maybe I could work some time in my schedule." Hell, I know she's just saying that to appease the investor in her boss's business. And I don't want to put that on her.

No, I'm just going to put all the pressure on my assistant instead.

Jesus, man.

"No, please focus on your work. I'll, uh...I'll train her myself."

"You will?" Everly and Sloane say at the same time.

Yeah, you will?

You are not fluent in the program, you have zero idea what Regency ball-room dancing entails, and for all you know, weddings in London could be vastly different than ones in America.

But sure, offer to train her.

"I have to go to London anyway, and I got her into this mess. It would be the right thing to do."

"You're going to teach me how to dance?" Sloane asks.

I rub my forehead in frustration. "We will learn together."

Do I know how to ballroom dance, let alone the dances from the Regency era? The answer would be no, but Sloane shouldn't have to wear this on her own. Plus, with money comes the ability to hire people.

"We can figure out the logistics. Right now, I think we should leave Everly and Maggie to get back to work, and we can talk about what's to be expected moving forward."

"Okay," Sloane says in an unsure tone. I don't blame her. I just put her in a shitty position, and it's not like she'll tell me no. Knowing her, she's going to find a way to be the best bridesmaid in the wedding, despite not having a personal connection to the bride. Because that's who she is. She's a hard worker, reliable, and good at what she does, even if it's sometimes as simple as getting me my green drink in the morning. Something I hated asking her to do at first, but I'd needed her out of the goddamn office, so I started sending her on errands.

But now, now it seems like I've gotten myself into a fucking pickle.

We offer our goodbyes to Maggie and Everly, I apologize once again, feeling like an idiot in front of the girls—not to mention we didn't even meet like we were supposed to—and we head out to the street where the driver's waiting for us. He opens the door, and I slide into the car first, Sloane following closely behind.

When our driver settles into his seat, I say, "Back to the office."

He nods and takes off.

I pull out my phone and shoot a quick text to Hardy.

Hudson: I think I just fucked up big-time.

I set my phone on my lap and stare out the window with the phrase *you're a moron* playing over and over in my head.

I can only imagine what Hardy is going to say...

After a few seconds of silence, Sloane clears her throat next to me. "Um, are we going to talk about what happened?"

"When we get to the office," I say as my phone buzzes with a text.

"Okay, sure. Back at the office. Marvelous. I wanted to wait until then too." She turns to look out her window while I answer my text.

Hardy: Jesus, you have my ass clenching. What did you do?

Hudson: To keep it short and simple, I told Archie Wimbach and his fiancée, Sheridan, that Sloane would be more than happy to fill in as a bridesmaid for them without her consent.

Hardy: Ummm...why the hell would you do that?

Hudson: Desperation.

Hardy: Is that what that smell was that passed by?

Hudson: I don't need your fucking jokes right now, asshole. I'm in some trouble.

Hardy: Yeah you are. Why the hell would you do that to Sloane? Is she okay with it?

Hudson: From her deer-in-the-headlights look, I would say no. But haven't talked to her yet.

Hardy: Dude, that's really shitty.

Hudson: I know! I feel fucking awful. Also, Archie told me that his soon-to-be father-in-law, who owns 10 percent of the company, doesn't trust us after what we did to Dad. So now

I have to go out to London for a few weeks and suck an old man's ass.

Hardy: Fuck, the visual on that. Take Chapstick.

Hudson: And the worst part, he reached out to Dad to see if he wanted to work with them.

Hardy: The fuck!

Hudson: Yeah. Not only am I having to deal with this business bullshit, but I also have to train Sloane in Regency ballroom dancing.

Hardy: Uh, wait, hold on a second. Where did the Regency shit come in?

Hudson: It's part of the wedding. Doesn't matter. I'm fucked. Oh, and the best part, Terrance, the father-in-law, loves hanging out at the Mayfair Club. Archie thought it might be good for me to hang out with him there.

Hardy: Did Archie get the impression you were married? Because pretty sure that's the only way to get into that club.

Hudson: I don't know, I didn't get into it. Either way, if Dad gets wind, you know he's going to want to join the club, especially if I'm not able to.

Hardy: He's tried to join before, never got in. It's one of the things that has plagued him for years and that I've relished.

Hudson: Really? Why didn't I know that?

Hardy: I don't know. But yeah, that was the club Dad was desperate to join. Imagine if you got in and he didn't. I think that would be the day hell froze over for him.

Hudson: Probably right about that. Either way, how fucked do you think I am?

Hardy: Well, the buyout situation sucks but nothing you haven't dealt with before. The Sloane thing, that's a different ball game because not only are you disrupting the peace in the office that you have with her, but you also know how protective Jude is of his sisters. A pissed-off Jude is not something you've faced before and I don't think it's something you ever want to face. I saw him crack an egg in his fist the other day. Made me shiver.

Hudson: I don't think Sloane will tell him.

Hardy: You don't? What about Stacey? If Sloane tells Stacey and Stacey tells Jude, I could see your face meeting his fist in the near future.

Hudson: Christ. Think I should tell him myself?

Hardy: Are you nuts? I'd talk to Sloane, feel her out. Does she seem up for the challenge?

Hudson: She seems like she wants to melt into the seat next to me.

Hardy: Could be worse, she could be making slicing motions across her neck with her finger while staring you down. You can work with melting into the seat.

Hudson: Yeah, maybe. Fuck, why did I have to be so goddamn desperate?

Hardy: Because you have daddy issues.

Hudson: Isn't that the fucking truth?

CHAPTER THREE
SLOANE

"HAVE A SEAT," HUDSON SAYS as he sits in one of the chairs in his office.

Instead of sitting at his desk like he always does when he addresses me, he's in his sitting area that consists of a brown leather couch and two matching chairs with a wooden coffee table in between.

I've never sat in the lustrous area before, but I've seen him have meetings here. Guess it only takes him offering me up as a bridesmaid to a business contact for me to get a serious meeting with him.

My mind is still grappling with that, by the way. The entire drive back to the office, I was replaying the moment he said I could do it over and over in my head. Did he panic? Sure. That was obvious, but he hasn't even looked in my direction. It's kind of...shitty.

And it took everything in me to hold my tongue while we were sitting in the car.

I took deep breaths.

I stared out the window.

I even tried playing *Toy Blast* on my phone to relieve the anxiety building in my chest.

And lucky for me, it worked, but now that I'm in his office...I have questions.

First: *How dare you?*

Second: *Have you lost your mind? I know I'm looking for a new career path, but this is not it.*

Poised, I sit across from him and hold my pen and paper to take notes because I don't know what else to do with my hands.

He leans forward, resting his forearms on his thighs as he clasps his hands in front of him. He stares down at the carpet for a few seconds before meeting my gaze, and I'm struck with just how handsome he is. It's rare when I get his undivided attention like this, when I get direct eye contact. Maybe I need to be grateful for the rarity because I could get lost in this man's eyes.

But then he reminds me why we're here. "Listen, Sloane, I need to apologize about what happened back there. It was extremely unprofessional, and I never should have put you in this kind of position."

Well, we must give the man credit for owning up to his mistakes. Well done.

"Thank you," I say, letting my professionalism guide me.

"And I know this is asking a lot, so I want to give you the option to back out because I'll never force something upon you. And don't worry about giving me an answer right now. I really want you to think about it. This would entail going to London for a couple of weeks, learning how to ballroom dance, and parading around to impress, which is a lot of pressure on someone, especially when they didn't ask for it."

"Seems like it," I say.

"It is," he says as he leans into the couch and blows out a heavy breath. He stretches his arms across the ledge of the couch and tilts his head back. "This is not how I envisioned the day going." He pinches his brow. "Your brother's going to murder me."

I mean, murder seems like a pretty extreme response. I'm not sure Jude would even get mad over this. And why bring up Jude? I'm a grown woman. I can handle my own life, thank you very much.

"Why would he murder you?" I ask.

"Because he told me to—" He stops, catching himself, and then shakes his head. "Nothing you need to worry about. Shouldn't have even mentioned it."

Uhh...yeah, not getting off that easy.

"No, what did he say?" I ask, setting my pen on my notebook now. Consider my interest piqued.

"Nothing you need to worry about." He nods at me. "Why don't you take the rest of the day off? I've put you through enough today. I think I might hit up the gym, relieve some tension."

The early dismissal, not going to work.

"You know, I'm a big girl. I can handle myself. I don't need you worrying about my brother and what he might think. This is my job, and what I do at my job is my business." There, that should put an end to it. Doesn't stop me from mildly shaking because it's the first time I've ever stood up for myself in front of Hudson.

And from the quirk in his brow, I'm going to guess he wasn't expecting me to say such a thing.

"You're twenty," he counters.

Twenty-two.

I'm freaking twenty-two.

"Twenty-two," I say, irritation creeping up my neck.

I hate when people discuss my age.

Despise it.

"Twenty-two? No, you're not the same age as Everly. She always said you were younger."

That's a problem I've had my whole life—I've always looked younger than what I actually am. Probably something I'll appreciate when I'm older, but right now, when I'm trying to be taken seriously, it's not ideal.

I'm about a year behind in my pursuit of finding a career. I took a year off between high school and college, when I worked odd jobs to help pay the bills while Stacey started taking community college classes. She was always the smarter one between the two of us, so I thought it would be best for her to get started while I attempted to find more grants to help me pay for college and started saving—and trying to figure out what I planned on doing with my life. Spoiler alert, still trying to figure that out.

"She was wrong," I say, keeping my poise the best I can. "I'm twenty-two."

"Either way, you're still young," he says.

Still young…

That stings.

Because that's not how I feel.

I feel like I've seen life, I've experienced it.

I lost both parents at an early age and had to be raised by a crotchety old lady who barely took care of us. There were days when Stacey and I were helping our grandma get in and out of bed before we went to school, while Jude was out working, providing for all of us. Housing wasn't stable all the time because there were moments when our grandma would make us fend for ourselves.

I've been forced to grow up much quicker than others.

I've seen more people exit my life than enter it.

I've worried about paying bills along with my siblings. I've known what it's like to not have running water for a few days, or electricity.

I've spent the night in a car, huddled next to my sister.

I know what it's like to make it to the soup kitchen just in time to get a warm meal for the night.

There is nothing young about my soul.

And the fact that all he can see is the number over my head, that's… that's insulting to me.

"I might be young in years, but I'm old in experience," I say, even though this is my first real job out of college. Experience doesn't always come professionally. Experience comes through the trials and tribulations of life, and a lot of the time, we have to grow up sooner than we expected. That was me and my siblings. We had no choice but to grow up quicker than we wanted. That's what happens when you don't have parents but rather a grandmother whose patience was lacking.

"Okay, Sloane," he says on a scoff.

That's all it takes.

That derisive look.

That huff in his voice.

That disbelief.

The professional veil has been lowered, and I can feel the real me crawl right out into the room, ready for a fight.

I set my notepad and pen on the coffee table, and I place my hands on my lap, staring him down. "I don't appreciate you talking to me like I'm a child, Hudson."

It's the first time I haven't called him Mr. Hopper in the office, and I think it throws him, because he blinks a few times, looking confused.

"I'm...I'm not trying to talk to you like a child."

"Well, you are, and it's insulting. If you want to make sure you don't piss off my brother, then don't piss me off. Don't act like I'm some young dick-around who doesn't know what they're doing, who can't stand up for themselves. Who can't make a decision about my work life without worrying it might make my brother mad."

He sits taller now. "Dick-around. I never called you a dick-around."

"You didn't have to. You're implying it."

"No, I'm not."

"Yes, you are," I argue, holding my ground.

"I was just saying you're young."

"Yeah, well you're old, but you don't see me handing you aspirin and Icy Hot every time your bones crack." The beast has been unleashed, and right now, all I see is red.

His eyes narrow. "I'm not that old."

"You're thirty-five," I counter, throwing his ageism right back at him.

"Yeah, that's not fucking old. Still in my prime."

"Well, didn't seem like it today," I say, the words flying out before I can stop them.

"Excuse me?" he asks, leaning forward now. Oops, kind of forgot for a second that he's my boss. "What exactly do you mean by that?"

Look what you've done now, gotten yourself into some trouble with that mouth of yours. It was bound to come out at some point. I've always been mouthy, speaking my opinions without consideration. When I took this job, I told myself I was going to tamp down that side of me, that I was going to keep it together and act professional. But consider me triggered because the real Sloane has arrived.

Now, I can either turn back into the demure girl that said yes to everything, or I can move forward with my true self and show Hudson Hopper who I really am—a strong, opinionated individual with quick wit and sass that can bring anyone to their knees.

What do I really have to lose at this point? He needs me more in this situation than I need him. What's he going to do? Fire me? Good luck finding a bridesmaid.

So chin tilted up, I say, "I'd hardly suggest you were a man in his prime today. You resembled a weaselly suck-up, looking to score a deal."

His eyes narrow, and I realize that maybe I could have left out the name-calling. Perhaps such ability to hold back will come with age... how ironic.

Looking perturbed, he replies, "That's not sucking up. That's what it takes to build business relationships, something you clearly have no experience in."

Oh, he went there.

"So what you're saying is that in order to succeed in business, you have to go around kissing ass? Let me write that down, since I'm learning from a real professional." I pick up my notebook and in giant letters, I write and say, "*Suck ass.* Got it."

He quirks his head to the side. "What the hell has gotten into you?"

Carefully and calmly, I set the pen and notepad down. "I don't appreciate you calling me young when you don't know anything about me or my life," I say. "I don't appreciate people judging me because of my age and assuming I'm inexperienced. Age means nothing in this world. Trust me."

"It means something, as no one in their right mind with experience would be talking to their boss the way that you are right now."

"Because they don't know how to stick up for themselves," I say. "Maybe they went to the same weasel school you went to."

Oh boy, now the tongue is flying, and there's no stopping it.

"Sloane," he says with such arousing command in his voice, which would normally make me feel weak in the knees, but something in my brain has switched, and I can't stop poking the bear. Yup. Poke.

Poke.

Poke.

I know I shouldn't be talking to Hudson like this, and if Jude ever found out that I did, he'd be livid with me. I do know better. I understand the value of playing the part I'm meant to play. But...I don't know, today has been a whirlwind. I've been thrown to the wolves, apologized to, and then insulted. And maybe this is further evidence that I'm not cut out for this kind of work. Holding my feelings in all day, getting walked on for the betterment of the company, just feels icky.

And if you know me, you know I don't take kindly to insults. I never have, and I've always stuck up for myself in those situations. Sure, can I be the polite girl who does what she's asked? Of course. But I also can be a rabid beast with gnarly fangs when I'm doubted.

"Yes, Mr. Hopper?" I ask, crossing one leg over the other.

His jaw ticks as he stares me down. I can see the wavering in his mind, wondering how to handle this situation. If I were any other person, he'd most likely fire me, but because I'm Jude's sister, there's no way—

"I think you should pack up your desk."

Wait…what?

I uncross my leg, pressing both feet into the ground. "Hold on, what did you say?"

Staring me down, he says, "I said, you should pack up your desk."

A nervous chuckle falls past my lips. "Oh my God, it…it kind of sounds like you're firing me?"

He works his jaw to the side. "Listen, Sloane, I can't have you talking to me like that and getting away with it. It's not professional, and if you don't learn now, then you're never going to learn."

Hold up…hold up…

"Wait. You're seriously firing me?" My eyes blink in disbelief.

"Yeah," he says. "I am."

Holy shit, he's really firing me.

I can't…I can't believe this.

After what he put me through only half an hour ago? He has the nerve to fire me when I stick up for myself?

And yes, the name-calling was out of hand, but what happened to a slap on the wrist and a carry on with business?

He's just going to up and fire me?

Okay, sir…

This is not going to go well for you.

Apologies in advance for what's about to come out of my mouth.

"Wow, okay." I stand from my chair and smooth down my skirt. "If that's how you want to play this, I guess good luck with your bridesmaid stuff. Seems like you're going to need it. Especially after you promised Archie I'd help out. Then again, you reek of desperation. I'm sure you'll have no problem finding a wig and stuffing a bra in order for you to play the part."

I move toward the door, and I can practically hear the regret in his voice when he says, "Sloane."

I glance over my shoulder, waiting to hear an apology. Yup, go ahead, beg and plead, apologize until your mouth is frothing for forgiveness.

He adjusts the sleeves of his shirt as he says, "I'll let Jude know."

I blink a few times, because he's serious. That's all he's going to say? No, *I'm sorry*? *Please come back*? *You're the apple of my eye and I need you*? He's...

He's really firing me.

Well...that's...that's just rude.

He really can't handle the truth?

How eye-opening. Facts are facts. He was a bit of a weasel in that meeting, and that's coming from me, the girl who worships the ground Hudson Hopper walks on with his fancy, expensive loafers.

I was just being honest, and if he can't handle that, then good luck. That's a him problem.

Yeah, that's right—that's a him problem.

Why should I feel bad about trying to help a guy out?

Why do I feel embarrassment creep up my back, slowly crawling to the nape of my neck?

Why are my cheeks heating?

Maybe because the man I'm infatuated with just fired me, and that's slightly humiliating. Maybe because he made it quite clear in a matter of seconds that, despite the hard work that I've put into this job that I hate, despite working effortlessly at making sure Hudson is taken care of—days full of meetings, demands, and decisions—that I'm fully and freely disposable to him.

And that doesn't settle well.

It hurts, actually, and there's only one way I know how to react when I'm hurt...

"Don't worry about telling Jude you fired his sister. I have no problem informing him of your terrible business practices. Maybe while I'm at it, I'll inform him of other things. Like...like..." I try to think of something revealing, anything, and then something snaps in my brain. Oh yes, I got it. "Maybe I'll inform him that your green drink you slurp up every morning actually has a ton of sugar in it, something you apparently never looked into. Might still taste like crap, but it's full of empty carbs."

His face falls flat. "No, it's not."

"Oh, yeah...it is. So much sugar. The most sugar. All of the sugar, Hudson. The wrinkles in the corners of your eye will only grow deeper if you keep filling your body with such filth."

He touches the side of his face, which nearly makes me laugh, but I hold it together as I continue with my rant.

"And just so you know, if you actually emptied your inbox, I wouldn't have to repeatedly send you the same email over and over again because it keeps getting buried. It's called organization, Hudson."

He straightens, looking perplexed and outraged at the same time.

"Not to mention the healthy snacks you request for the kitchen, no one likes them. Not one single person. We constantly donate them to shelters while Freida stocks up on snacks from Costco and divvies them up around the office for people to keep in their desk drawers. It's a waste of money and no one will say anything because they're too scared to hurt your brittle ego."

His brow pinches together. "The snacks are good."

"No one wants dried cucumber, Hudson. What's even the point?" I toss my arms up in frustration. "And since we're on the train of honesty, that brown suit you wear on occasion is hideous and should be burned."

"That's from Italy."

"Doesn't make it any less ugly. Just atrocious. I throw up a little in my mouth every time you walk into the office wearing it."

He folds his arms now. "Is that all?"

"No," I say, letting it rip. "I use your bathroom when you're gone because your toilet paper is softer. I once scraped ketchup on your back by accident before you went into a meeting and didn't tell you but watched you give a presentation to a room of twenty people with a bloodlike condiment staining your suit jacket." I take a deep breath and keep going. "You are negligent when it comes to compliments and my work ethic. You refuse to acknowledge the thought and care I put into looking professional every day. And I've spent countless hours sitting at my desk, staring into your office, wondering about all the ways I could help ease the tremendous amount of tension you carry on a daily basis. Sitting on your face is always the solution I come up with."

The moment the words fall past my lips, I know I've gone too far.

Oh shit.

The truths were supposed to be about him.

Not me.

His face grows serious. "Sitting on my face?"

"Uh, did I say that?" I ask, a flitty laugh falling past my lips. "I don't think that's what I said."

"That's exactly what you said."

I tap my chin. "Hmm, doesn't sound like me."

"Sloane," he says in that dangerous tone all over again.

"Yes?"

I wait for him to say something, anything, but when he doesn't, I take that as my sign to get the hell out of here.

With a quick 180 on my heels, I turn away from him and head for my desk, where I open my desk drawer, grab my purse, and then start shoving bags of fruit snacks inside. Freida just refreshed my supplies, and there's no way I'm leaving without them.

When I catch Hudson leaning against the door to his office, arms crossed, watching me, I take that moment to toss a fruit snack packet at him. "See? We don't like your snacks."

He catches it with one hand, and I don't allow myself to consider just how hot that was.

I straighten, grab the picture of me, Jude, and Stacey on the beach in Bora Bora from Jude's wedding, and hold it close to my chest.

The pens can stay. I have no attachment.

The Post-it notes that I would cut into hearts on slow days, they must be left behind.

And my notebook with every detail I ever wrote about Hudson's insufferable meetings can die in this office. Hopefully, he will flip through it and see just how boring he can be.

False pride trying to lead the way, I start my walk of unemployment toward the elevator when I think of one last thing.

I face Hudson again and say, "When you speak of this to Jude, please let him know that not one fruit snack was left behind in my retreat, but for the love of God, don't mention the sitting-on-the-face thing, even though I don't recall saying that—"

"So you're just going to lie like that?"

"Call it temporary amnesia. Either way. No thanks to that detail. Okay, well, great working with you, take care, 'kay, love you, bye." I pause, my eyes widening. "No, I mean, not *I love you*. I don't love you. I don't know why I said that. It was a slip of the tongue. There is no love and no…no sitting on the face. Got it?" He just stares at me. "Okay, looks like you got it. And just in case you missed it the first time, you look like trash in the brown suit."

With that, I turn away from him and head toward the elevator, a purse full of fruit snacks, a chest brimming with pride, and a stomach bubbling with embarrassment.

———

"Why is it so dark in here?" Stacey asks, walking into the living room where I'm perched on the corner of the back of the couch like an owl on a branch, leaning against the wall, empty fruit snack wrappers scattered below me. "Whoa, what's going on in here?" Stacey sets the mail down on the coffee table and takes a seat on the couch. "You realize the couch is meant to be sat on like this, not like what you're doing at the moment?"

"I know," I say, opening up another pack of fruit snacks and eating one while I stare off toward the wall.

From the corner of my eye, I catch Stacey looking over at what I'm staring at and then back at me. "Care to explain to me why you're acting like a parrot in the dark, eating fruit snacks?"

I pop another in my mouth and chew. "Just rethinking my life decisions today."

"And what life decisions would those be?" she asks as she picks up the mail and starts sorting through it. Between the two of us, Stacey is the one who likes to take care of everything around the house and then dictate to me what needs to be done. It only works out because I don't mind her bossing me around about chores, and she thoroughly enjoys being the leader of the household, especially now that Jude's living with Haisley.

"Umm, decisions," I answer.

She pauses sifting through the mail and gives me that look only a twin can give, where they can practically see into your soul. "Don't make me pry it out of you. I'm exhausted from work today."

She's exhausted? Sheesh, wait until she hears about the roller coaster I was on.

Although I don't want to discount her vicious days. Stacey works for Amazon. She's in charge of coming up with the Dog of the Day shout-outs on Alexa. Sometimes she does the Dinosaur of the Day as well, but mainly she works on Dog of the Day. Riveting work. Shocked AI hasn't taken her job yet.

"Couldn't find a good picture of a cocker spaniel?" I ask.

"Don't change the subject," she replies. "And it was a dalmatian."

"Those spots can be tricky."

"Sloane, stop avoiding the question. What's going on?"

She never puts up with my shit.

Ever.

"Um, well, you see…" I dump the rest of the fruit snacks in my mouth and then say in a garbled voice, "Something happened at work today—"

"Oh my God." She stares me down. "You nuzzled his crotch without his consent, didn't you?"

As you can tell, Stacey is very much in the know about the crush I've been harboring—hard to keep such a secret away from your twin, especially on Friday nights when we dust off the blender and make homemade margaritas.

"No, I did not nuzzle his crotch."

"Then you flashed him a boob? Your ass? Sat on his face and told him to feast?"

Well, face sitting was mentioned…

"No, Stacey," I say in annoyance and then slide down the back of the couch where I take a seat. "I got fired."

"Fired?" she screeches. "Hudson fired you? How the hell did you manage that?"

"Um, we don't need to go into the details." I wave her off.

"If our brother's friend fired you, we most definitely need to go into the details. What happened?"

I start brushing my hair nervously with my fingers as I say, "Well, we had a meeting, and the meeting was going well. I was taking notes, and then out of the blue, Hudson said I could be a bridesmaid for a business contact and—"

"What?"

"Please, Stacey, no interruptions. This is going to be long. I'll address all questions after. So anyway, he signed me up to be a bridesmaid, and I was stunned because I didn't know bosses could do that, and I mean, I would pretty much do anything that Hudson told me to do because, you know, I think he's the most attractive man to ever walk the planet, and well, I kind of blacked out for a moment, and then the next thing I know, he's apologizing to me in his office and telling me I can think about the whole bridesmaid thing and that it wasn't fair for him to do that, and I thought, that's so nice of him, and then this is where it gets tricky because I really don't remember how it happened, but he called me young."

Stacey winces. "Oh God."

"Yup, I can tell from the look on your face that you know exactly where this is going."

"You let loose." She presses her lips together. "Did you tell him off?"

"I mean, in a nice way. It started slow, respectable, with a light jab here and there, but then it built up and I think I called him a weasel. I know I told him his snacks sucked and that he was eating too much sugar and that's why he has wrinkles, and then one thing led to another and he fired me."

"Oh my God, Sloane," she groans.

"That's not even the worst part." The same embarrassment that I felt in his office takes root all over again.

"How on earth is that not the worst part?"

"In my ranting," I say, humiliation nearly choking me alive, "after he fired me, I grew ashamed and angry, and it all swirled together to the point that I said a whole bunch of things that I never should have said, something along the lines of marking him with ketchup and letting him give a presentation with a ketchup jacket, and then after that, I told him that I wanted to sit on his face."

Her eyes widen and she whispers, "Dear God."

"I know." I nod. "It's...it's bad. And then of course because I'm an idiot, when I was saying bye, I was on autopilot and said ''kay, love you, bye.'"

"You did not," she says, her voice rising.

"Oh, I did. Then in the midst of covering that up, I told him I never said I wanted to sit on his face and that he must have misheard me. There was a lot of rambling. I took all these fruit snacks and then left with my chin held high, but now that I've been sitting here in the dark, thinking about it, I am kind of on the side of maybe Hudson was right, maybe I am young. I think a more mature human wouldn't have brought up the sitting-on-the-face thing."

"You think?" she says on a sigh. "Jesus, Sloane. What the hell is he going to say to Jude?"

"I have no idea. I'm kind of hoping that he tells him we went our separate ways, because I know for a fact that if Hudson tells Jude that I said I'd sit on his face, Jude would disown me."

"Yes. Yes, he would. God, what a mess; where the hell did this all stem from?"

I lean my head back on the couch and stare up at the ceiling. "Hudson was trying to impress this guy, Archie Wimbach. Hardy and Hudson are attempting to purchase his property to extend their affordable housing project globally. I don't know much about the backstory. I caught some of his text messages though."

"You what?"

"He was texting Hardy in the car, and I was reading them."

"Invasion of privacy much?" Stacey says.

"Listen, the man signed me up to be a bridesmaid in the dude's wedding because the person that was supposed to be in the wedding broke their leg or something and can't perform the Regency dances."

"Regency dances? Like...*Bridgerton*?"

"Yeah, I guess they're knocking it back a century and putting on their petticoats. Anyway, I fit the look, and Hudson said I was available. Talk about shocked, pretty sure my chin hit the table." I lift my chin for her to examine. "Is there a bruise?"

"There is no bruise," Stacey deadpans.

"Lucky for him. I could have filed worker's comp. Anywho, the texts— Hudson was going off about Archie and this club and how he needs to get close to the father of the bride."

"What kind of club?" Stacey asks. "A sex club? Because I could be into that."

I roll my eyes at my sister. "I know you could, but I think it's one of those posh, rich clubs."

"What was it called?"

"Uh…what did he type?" I scratch the side of my head. "I think the Mayfair Club."

Stacey pulls out her phone and types it into her internet search.

"But do you know what I really found out today, Stacey? I'm not the kind of person who can put up with this kind of business. It's not for me. I mean, without even a second of thought for my well-being, Hudson offered me up to his business partner, and sure, it could have been worse, but this is not what I want to do with my life." I drag my hand over my face. "I want to do something that's more fulfilling. Something that isn't fetching drinks and answering phone calls. I want to make a difference."

"I know that feeling so well," Stacey says. "This, coming from the Dog of the Day girl. Maybe this is a good thing, maybe this is the wake-up call you needed to switch jobs. Perhaps you were so comfortable getting paid that you settled for something you didn't like."

"That's great and all but getting paid is the key to what you and I both need right now. We can't afford the luxury of pursuing a dream. Hell, I can't even imagine dreaming. My brain is too focused on paying the bills; dreaming isn't even an option."

She sighs sadly. "Isn't that the truth?" She taps on her phone a few more times and then says, "That club you were talking about looks like it has been around forever. *Posh* is the nice way to put it. This is for aristocrats. They even have debutante balls where young women come out to society." Stacey smiles at me. "When I came out to society, no one threw me a ball."

"Because we knew you were gay the minute you started talking. No need to celebrate."

"Uh, coming out is a big deal. There's always a need to celebrate," she humorously counters.

"Hey, I got you a vibrator in solidarity."

Stacey chuckles. "Yeah, wore that thing out."

"Okay, none of that," I say, flitting my hand at her.

"You can talk about sitting on your boss's face, but I can't talk about the adventures of pleasuring my partners with the vibrator you got me for coming out? How is that fair?"

"It's not, and I admit it. Now, back to me."

Stacey laughs and shakes her head while she plucks a piece of mail from the pile and opens it. "Either way, Hudson's not getting into that club. It's for the married folk only."

"Yeah, he's not married, or else what I said to him would have been exceedingly more inappropriate." I groan in frustration. "This is such a mess. I can't afford to not have a job. What the hell am I going to do?"

"Probably apologize." She unfolds a letter and starts scanning it. "Apologies can go a long way."

"Apologize? No way. I'm not about to apologize to him. That would be, for one, humiliating. Two, require maturity, which I think we found out today, I lack. And three, be humiliating."

"You said humiliating twice."

"Because it would be double the amount of humiliation, and I can't take that." I flick at her paper. "What the hell are you reading? Don't you see I'm in a crisis?"

"I do, but..." She pauses and her nose scrunches up. "Oh shit."

"What?" I ask, leaning over just enough so I can see what's in the letter.

"I think the landlord is selling the house."

"What house?"

She shoves the paper at me. "Our house, cement head."

"Hey, I told you not to call me that," I say, taking the paper in my hand

and reading through it. "Thirty days?" I mumble. "What the hell, they can't just sell the house."

"They can. They own it."

"Uh, yeah, but we live in it."

"We rent it. The owners can do anything they want."

"Well, they can't," I say, glancing around the living room of the quaint bungalow that we shared with Jude when he was still living with us. The house that he rented for us when our grandma passed and we needed a place to stay. The house that we formed a strong bond over when we had no family left but ourselves. This house...it was a light during a dark time.

A safe haven.

A place where we felt comfortable shedding tears and showing our emotions. A place that felt so incredibly safe that we started to come into our own. It's where Stacey came out to us, right here in this living room. It's where I slipped and fell in the kitchen and broke my wrist, only for Stacey to slide in and do the same exact thing. It's where Jude first told us that he was in love...and where he told us he was going to ask Haisley to marry him.

This house has been a possession that we've never been able to own but that we've worked hard at maintaining because it felt like ours either way.

"This is our house," I say.

"It's not. We don't own it, Sloane."

"I know we don't own it, but we've lived in it. We've made it a home. I mean...this is where...where we grew. Where we survived. We can't just leave because the owner wants to sell it."

"Well, we can buy it," she says absentmindedly. "The offer is in the letter."

"Really?" I ask and pick up the letter again. I scan to the bottom where it says we can rent to buy with a down payment of $40,000. Hope starts dwindling away. "Forty thousand dollars, fuck. Do you have that kind of money?"

Stacey gives me a get-real look. "I write about the dog of the day for a robot who informs pesky children. Do you really think I have forty thousand dollars?"

"I don't know. I thought maybe you were stashing cash away."

"Not so much."

"Damn it. I have nothing in my bank account. I'm nearly living paycheck to paycheck over here, because of the school loans."

"Says the girl who works for a billionaire."

"Used to work," I say on a groan. "Ugh, why did I have to tell him I wanted to sit on his face?"

"Because if you didn't, we wouldn't be in this situation?" Stacey shakes her head. "Face it, we have the worst luck. We're never going to find another place like this house. It's close to the park and walking distance from the restaurants we love. It's quiet and peaceful and just...feels like home." She pauses and then turns toward me. "Think we should ask Jude for some money?"

I shake my head vehemently. "No, we swore we wouldn't ask him for anything. He married into money and we're not about to take advantage of that. It's bad enough he got me a job with Hudson. When he left, we swore that we would make him proud. Not to mention asking for money negates the idea of us being adults and moving through life on our own without help."

"And what a great job we're doing at that. I write dog facts for a living, and you're apparently now a world-renowned fruit snack muncher." She shakes her head. "And here I thought I was the muncher in the family."

"This is serious, Stacey," I groan. "We need forty thousand dollars."

"Right, should I just start looking for spare change in the streets? Create an OnlyFans account? I heard I have nice feet."

"Think you can get forty thousand dollars off feet pics?" I say with hope and then take in her unmanicured toes and shiver. "Not with those talons."

"They're not freaking talons. They're just unkempt at the moment."

"Your pinky toe doesn't have a nail."

"Never grew one. I think it was a defect when I came out of the womb."

"Well, no one's going to spend big cash on your freaky, nail-less pinky toe."

"Never know, could be a demand for a nail-less toe. It's very niche."

"No one wants that, Stacey. No one."

"At least I'm coming up with ideas. You're the one getting fired. If you weren't so *young* and immature, maybe you could have said something along the lines of... *I'll be your bridesmaid for a forty-thousand-dollar bonus.*"

"Gah," I scoff. "That would have been such a good idea."

"Yeah, I know, but you can't do it now because you got fired, you idiot!"

"Think he would take the deal anyway?"

Stacey shakes her head. "He wouldn't have fired you if he needed you that much. No way he'd take the deal."

"Well, maybe I can offer him something else. Something he can't refuse."

"If you say your vagina on his face, I'm going to murder you."

"No, what if it's something he really needs? Maybe he'd be willing."

"And what exactly does a billionaire really need that he can't get himself?"

She's right. Hudson could pretty much have anything. What could he possibly need?

What could he possibly want?

What could he...

And then it hits me.

Strikes me so hard in the brain that I actually feel a headache coming on.

"Stacey," I whisper, a slow smile spreading across my face. "I've got it."

"You've got what?" she asks, doubt searing off her lips.

"I've got an idea that's about to make us forty thousand dollars."

CHAPTER FOUR
HUDSON

NOT LOOKING FORWARD TO TODAY.

Not only do I have to find a solution to being short a bridesmaid and an assistant, but I have to tell Jude that I fired his sister.

Not ideal.

To make matters worse, I didn't get a lick of sleep last night because all I could think of was what Sloane told me, that she wanted to ease my tension in a way that—I hate to admit—I've thought about several times.

Hell, I thought about it yesterday when I caught a glimpse of her in that skirt.

How easy it would be to slip off her underwear, bring her to the couch, and have her hover above me.

I pinch my brow.

What a fucking nightmare.

The elevator dings, and I head down the hall, nodding and putting on a smile for some of the early risers in the building. Since we began the co-op, we've been able to bring on fifteen employees, which is huge considering we just started a few months ago. The Cane brothers have assisted with the hiring and even moved some of their employees in Los Angeles up here to help train. I know for a fact that if it wasn't for the assistance of Cane Enterprises, we wouldn't even be close to where we are right now with our business. We would probably still be investing in a single idea and that's it. But now...hell, we have our hands in everything.

Hardy is in charge of our agricultural department, focusing on our almond farms and expanding distribution.

Maggie and Haisley are working closely together on the event and wedding business: Maggie with planning, Haisley with vacation rentals that are geared more toward bachelorette weekends.

Jude is heading up construction and engineering with the Canes.

And now we're moving into expanding the low-income housing projects that Cane Enterprises started here in San Francisco.

Not to mention Brody, Maggie's boyfriend, is opening pop-up shops in old storefronts around the city, giving another life to worn-down spaces.

It feels...fuck, it feels good to know that we have made meaningful and significant changes and so quickly. So why does it feel like such a nightmare walking into my office this morning?

I should be proud of everything we've accomplished and the plans we have in the works. But yesterday...yesterday felt like a giant leap backward, leaving me to schedule an awkward conversation with my brother-in-law/friend/business partner who, in all honesty, kind of scares me.

Jude is built different. Hardy and I are tall, muscular—in a swimmer's body kind of way—and we could hold our own if we needed to, but Jude...he's...he's as if J. J. Watt and Gaston from *Beauty and the Beast* had a baby together. Massive. Intimidating. But also has a real heart, which makes him extremely protective of the ones that he loves. Which I appreciate, since he's married to my sister, but something I don't appreciate when I have to tell him I fired his little sister.

Huffing out my frustration, I walk down the hall, making a note to DoorDash my green drink—which apparently has a lot of sugar—and when I reach my office, I open the door only to be greeted by Sloane, holding my green drink and smiling as if nothing happened yesterday.

"Jesus fuck," I say, startling back. "What...what the hell are you doing in here?"

She glances at her watch and then back at me. "You're later than usual. That's okay, sometimes we need that extra sleep."

Umm, what?

"Good thing I waited until the last minute to get your green drink, or else it would be warm." She hands me the drink, and I stare at her as if I'm in some sort of twilight zone.

I...I fired her, right?

I did that yesterday?

That was real...wasn't it?

"I already warmed up your computer for you and checked your schedule. It seems as though you don't have any meetings today, which is surprising, given what a busy bee you usually are." She nudges me toward my desk, and because I'm so fucking confused, I follow her direction.

"But not having meetings is a good thing because I saw your inbox, and you have a lot of emails you need to sift through." She pulls out my desk chair for me, and I take a seat, right before she pushes me into my desk.

What the hell is going on?

This is not normal.

I mean, the green drink is normal.

But the chattiness.

The maneuvering.

The... Wait, is she wearing pants?

I glance at her outfit, taking in the power suit sheathing her body. She's never worn a power suit. It's always dresses and skirts. I should know because I've averted my eyes from her legs at all costs every single day she's been in the office.

Yeah, this is not normal. Something is up.

I take a sip of my drink and immediately cringe.

Smacking my lips, I hold the drink away and say, "What the hell is this?"

Smiling, she leans forward. "Had them take out the sugar for you." She taps the side of my head and whispers, "Wrinkle patrol."

I knew yesterday was real!

I set the drink down, scoot my chair back, and stand. "I fucking knew it," I say, as if I've caught her red-handed.

"Knew what?" she asks, looking confused.

"I knew that yesterday was real."

"Um…yes, yesterday was real." She takes a step closer, her perfume filtering in between us, making me feel light-headed. "Are you okay? Did you hit your head or something?"

"No. I'm fine. The question is, are you okay?"

She grips her lower back. "A little sore after I attempted to do a backflip off the couch from a sugar high, but other than that, okay. Why?"

"A backflip?"

She nods. "Stuck the landing, but I didn't complete perfection without a little bit of a hit to the old lower back. That's what happens when you get older, not as nimble as we used to be. But you know all about that."

My nostrils flare, and I take a step back, giving myself some distance from her as I say, "Didn't I fire you yesterday?"

"I believe that you did." She nods as if it's no big deal.

"Okay, so…care to tell me why you're here, in my office, handing me a green drink with no sugar?"

"I chose not to take part in the firing."

"What the hell does that mean?" I ask.

And then to my surprise, she plops herself on top of my desk, crosses one leg over the other, and leans back on her hand, the pose incredibly too sexy, especially since the position makes the lapels of her suit jacket pop open, revealing that she's not wearing a shirt under that blazer. Just a bra.

Christ.

"It means I chose not to be fired."

"That's not a thing," I say.

"Oh, it is. You see, I've been taught to seize what I want, to take charge, and that's exactly what I'm doing. Therefore, I've decided that I'm not fired."

"You can decide that all you want, but that's not how things work. I'm the boss, you work for me; therefore, when I say you're fired, you're fired. There will be no point in coming into the office because I will not be paying you."

"Says who?" she asks.

I point to my chest. "Says me."

"And would you say that you're the one that makes all the decisions?"

"Uh, yeah. That's what the term *boss* entails. The decision-maker."

"And your choice is to fire me?"

What kind of fucking circus is this? Is this some sort of social media trend? Refusal to be fired?

Am I actually old and I don't realize it?

"Yes, my choice is to fire you; that's why I did it yesterday: I fired you."

"You did, but a part of me thinks that you might regret that decision."

I stick my hands in my pockets and ask, "What makes you think that?"

"Because I have a proposal for you." She hops off my desk and gestures toward my seating area. "Please, join me."

Skeptical but also intrigued by the fuckery, I follow her and take a seat on the couch as she does, only about a foot of space separating us, close enough to catch the lavender scent that clings to her.

"What's going on, Sloane? I have things to do."

"I know; this won't take too much of your time." She places her hands on her lap and looks me in the eyes. "I was thinking about yesterday and everything that happened. And I know the right thing to do would be to come in here and tell you I didn't mean any of the things that I said, but that would be a lie. I meant every single word."

Every single word?

Because I remember specifically one thing in particular that she tried to deny saying, but I'm not going to bring that up, not when she's sitting this close and smells this damn good.

"Okay," I say.

"And an apology is not why I'm here. I'm here on business."

"Sloane, I don't think I can give you your job back."

"Not looking to be your assistant," she says, and then, to my surprise, she gets down on one knee in front of me, takes my hand in hers, and continues. "I'm looking to be your wife."

My WHAT?

"Hudson Mitchell Hopper, will you marry me?"

She smiles up at me. Blinks.

Fucking winks…

She's kidding right?

I look for something, anything, to tell me this is a joke. I glance around the room. Are there hidden cameras in here? Am I on a daytime talk show where someone is going to come out, have a gotcha moment, and say to the audience that I've been lusting after my too-young-for-me assistant?

I wait a few seconds, and when I realize none of that is happening, I clear my throat. "Excuse me?"

"Look at you, in shock. How cute." She pats my hand. "Hudson, it's a simple question. Will you marry me?"

"Uh…" I shake my hand out of hers and slide back on the couch, putting space between us. "Not to sound like an obtuse ass, but why the fuck would I marry you, Sloane?"

She rolls her eyes. "And here I thought you were a smart businessman."

She gets off the ground and sits back on the couch. She straightens her clothes while I try to comprehend what the hell is happening this morning. This is why I need more coffee in the morning. Forget the green drink, I need a twenty-ounce cup of pure, unfiltered coffee, straight from the goddamn bean.

"I'll lay it out for you: you need a wife, and I'm the one for the job."

"I fail to see how I need a wife."

"Are you really that dense?" she asks.

"Uh, are you really this delusional?" I counter.

Another roll of the eyes. "Jesus, Hudson. You need to impress Archie's father-in-law, right? What's one way to do that? Slip into the Mayfair Club. And what is one of the requirements to get into the club? You must be married." She holds out her hand and points to her empty ring finger. "All you've got to do is put a ring on it."

Wow.

Okay.

She's lost it.

I think the conversation I need to have with Jude is going to veer in a different direction than I'd thought. More like *I think your sister might need some help.*

"You know, not really in the market for a wife at the moment, but thanks for the offer. Now, I think it's time that you leave."

She shrugs. "Suit yourself." She stands and starts heading toward the door. "By the way, your father called this morning. I took a message for you because I thought I might be helpful despite being fired. He said to tell you that he still plans on suing you, but he's currently working on another investment, so he might be held up at the moment."

And then she heads out of my office, leaving my skin prickling with irritation.

What the fuck just happened?

———

New day.

New start.

Today will be better than yesterday because yesterday was an absolute shit show.

After I was proposed to—still trying to understand that entire situation—Sloane told me about my dad and well, that sent me into a tailspin. He knew exactly what he was doing making that phone call. He found out that I was interested in the Wimbach property, which would give us the chance to expand the affordable housing market in the UK, and he's showing me that he has no problem stealing it away.

A part of me believes that Sloane knew exactly what she was doing by telling me about his message because last night, all I could think was, *What if I said yes to her proposal?*

Stupid, I know. There is no way I would say yes to marrying Jude's sister. That is just asking for trouble.

Which is why I'm walking into the office today with a freshly brewed cup of coffee, my head on straight, and—

"I thought I told you that brown suit is hideous," Sloane says as I walk into my office.

"Jesus Christ, Sloane," I say, nearly having a heart attack from her surprise appearance. "What the hell are you doing here?"

"Just came to see how you were. I could sense your tension yesterday, and I think you know how I'd help relieve it." She wiggles her eyebrows, and I swear on my right nut, it takes everything in me to look away and not think about *that* type of relief.

"I think you should leave." I move over to my desk, set my coffee down, and take a seat only to be greeted with a photoshopped picture of me and her in front of an altar. She's in a dress, I'm in a tux, and we're holding hands. I pick up the frame and flash it to her. "What the hell is this?"

"A subtle reminder of what could be."

I shove the picture into my desk drawer and say, "No reminder needed."

"Are you sure?" She walks up to my desk and takes a seat. Today she's wearing another power suit, but this time it's a short skirt instead of pants, and I'm pretty sure there's no shirt under that blazer, just like yesterday. "I could be a good wife, Hudson." She nudges me with her toe.

I turn toward her, my head tilted. "Why the hell would you want to marry me?"

Because that's the question I've been asking myself on repeat.

How would this benefit her?

"I'm so glad you asked." She stands up again and gestures to the couch. "Care to join me?"

Not this again.

With a huff, I stand from my chair, bring my coffee with me because I'm going to need it, and take a seat on the couch where she joins me.

Once again, she rests her hands in her lap and looks me in the eyes. "This could be beneficial for the both of us. You need me, and I could possibly need you."

"Possibly?" I ask. "I doubt someone who has come into the office twice despite being fired would use the term *possibly*. Looks like you need me."

"Semantics," she says, brushing me off. But I can see right through her. There is something she needs, and she's come up with a crazy-ass plan on how to do it. "Here's the thing, you want this property deal, right?"

"I don't discuss business with people who don't work here."

"Hudson." She levels with me, and hell, I like it when she says my name. "Just answer the question."

"You already know the answer," I say.

"So then, yes, you want the property. And you also promised Archie and Sheridan a bridesmaid, something I think you're forgetting about."

"Trust me." I drag my hand over my face. "I have not forgotten about that." That was the reason I woke up at two this morning and couldn't get back to sleep. I broke out in a sweat over the fact that I've gotten myself into a major mess.

"Well, it seems like you're in a bit of a pickle, and I could help you get out of said pickle. Here is what I propose. I will be the bridesmaid that you signed me up to be, and I will be your bride so you can get into the club."

"And what do you want from me?"

Sloane composes herself, swallows, then says, "Preferably, my job back and forty thousand dollars."

I feel my eyebrows raise because I guess I wasn't expecting that answer. The job, sure, but the money? She doesn't seem like someone who is desperate for money. I mean, if she needed anything, wouldn't she just go to Jude?

"In exchange for forty thousand dollars and my job, I'll sign a prenup, marry you, do the whole bridesmaid in London thing, and then we can amicably divorce later and be on our way. You'll have your property, everyone will be happy, and we never have to see each other again—after I find a new job of course."

"Other than the fact that your brother is married to my sister."

"Eh, I never cared for family gatherings," she says with a wave of her hand. "What do you say?"

I take a sip of my coffee and shake my head. "I'm not in the business of buying a bride, Sloane."

"You're not buying me. You're paying me for a service."

"Yeah, I'm not doing that either."

I stand and move back to the desk. My shaky legs nearly give out because...it would be a good solution. She gets what she needs, I get what I need—a simple solution to a chaotic few days.

Yet I can't fathom saying yes, not when I know *who* I'd be marrying. She's Jude's sister, and if he caught wind of the fact that I even considered her proposal for a mere second, he'd have my balls in the palm of his hand.

It's a good idea but a terrible, horrible one at the same time.

It's going to be a no for me.

———————

I peek around the door of my office and fearfully look around, scanning for a clingy brunette, most likely shirtless and in a power suit. When I come up short, not even a *sugar-free* green drink on the desk, I know the coast is clear. I meant to contact security last night and ensure her pass was revoked, but something about that felt so wrong. This is Jude's sister. She's not a threat to the security of our company.

Letting out a deep breath, I step inside the office just as the door shuts behind me and Sloane says, "Morning."

"Mother of fuck," I yell as I cover my ears and fly into the wall, turning to see her standing there in a pink suit. This one has shorts and a blazer with no shirt. "Fuck, Sloane."

"Aw, did I scare you?"

"What the hell do you think?" I ask as I straighten up and let out a deep breath.

"You know, I told you I could help you with that tension."

Yeah...I know.

I tried to assist with the tension this morning in the shower, imagining what's under that goddamn blazer of hers, and let's just say my imagination and my hand were lackluster at best.

"The answer is no, whatever you have to say today, the answer is no." I move toward my desk. "As I said before, I don't buy brides, and I'm not fucking marrying you."

"Hudson."

"What?" I say, exasperated as I look up at Sloane, standing before me, hands clutched in front of her.

A serious expression crosses her face as she quietly says, "I...I need this." The tone has changed, and I can almost feel her words as she says them.

"You need to marry me?" I ask.

She shakes her head. "I need this deal because I need the money."

The seriousness in her voice tugs me in as I take a seat at my desk and ask, "Why?"

She looks off to the side and from the droop in her shoulders and her timid expression, I can tell that this is not easy for her. "Stacey and I got a letter in the mail from our landlord. They're selling the house that we're living in, and we can either move, or we can rent to own. Rent to own requires a down payment of forty thousand dollars. Stacey and I don't have anything close to that, which means we'll have to move out if we don't find the money and…and we can't move out." Tears start to form in her eyes, which of course makes me move around my desk to her. "This was the house that Jude found for us once our grandma passed. It was our sanctuary, our comfort, and we've shared so many memories in it, we don't want to let it go."

"Have you spoken to Jude about it?"

She shakes her head. "I don't think he has enough capital, and it's also something we don't want to do. We said we'd provide for ourselves when he moved out, and we promised ourselves we wouldn't bother him."

"He's your brother," I say.

"Yes, which means he'd do anything to help us. He was wary of leaving us to begin with when he moved in with Haisley. The last thing we want is for him to worry again. We want to do this on our own because we are not children and don't need a handout from our brother. That's why I came up with this idea; that's why I came to you."

"Christ," I say as I tug on the back of my neck and start pacing the room. Well, this puts a much different spin on her proposal, one that I wasn't prepared for. It has me…hell, it has me thinking. "You think getting married is the solution?"

"It's the best one I could come up with, and I swear, I'll sign any prenup you want. I don't want your fortune or your business or your house. I just need the down payment, preferably my job back until I can find something else, and I'll help you secure the deal with Wimbach."

It feels doable.

Like it could all work.

But there's a small element holding me back: Jude.

Hell, that's not a small element, that's a big element.

I shake my head. "No, Jude would kill us both."

"He doesn't have to know," she says, walking up to me. "I promise, Stacey will be the only one that knows on my end. You can tell who you need to tell. I'll even sign an NDA. Please, Hudson. I know this is crazy, but it could work. And it's not forever."

Gone is the sarcastic girl who came into my office two days ago after being fired and in her place is a girl who reeks of desperation, the same sort of desperation I feel when I consider the shitstorm I've put myself in.

I pull on the short strands of my hair. Hell, I can't believe I'm even considering this. It's dumb.

Foolish.

A really bad idea.

Yet she's right. It has all the potential to work. It's only for a few weeks. We can go to London, she can be a bridesmaid, I can secure the deal, and then we can be on our merry way.

Feels simple.

Foolproof.

"You're thinking about it," she says, coming up to me and taking my hand. "Please say yes, Hudson."

In that moment, I do something really stupid, something that cracks me, breaks me, tears down the miniscule wall I had erected to keep her as far away as possible. I look at her, in her eyes, and it's my undoing.

Because how can I say no when she's practically begging, when I know that this could help her?

"Shit," I mumble.

"Is that a good shit or a bad shit?" she asks, tugging on my arm.

"Doesn't matter; it's a shit." I head to the couch and sit down, bringing my fingers to my brow. "You owe me an apology."

I see hope in her eyes as she joins me. "An apology for the other day? Not a problem. I'm sorry for the way I treated you. It was very immature, and I learned my lesson about inappropriate behavior in the workplace. That being said, I stand by my words about the green drink and the brown suit. The green drink is filled with sugar your machine of a body doesn't need, and the brown suit does nothing to highlight the contours of your well-carved frame." She clasps her hands in front of her. "Does that mean you're going to be my husband?"

Does it?

I look into her stunning eyes. I swear she doesn't know the power she could have over me if I truly gave in to her. She's too fucking beautiful. *Even when she's begging me to do something incredibly stupid.*

Something that will most likely come back to bite me in the ass, but I can see it.

In this moment, I can see it—I'm staring back at my future wife.

CHAPTER FIVE
SLOANE

"ARE YOU NERVOUS?" STACEY ASKS as I stick folds of toilet paper under my armpits in the private bathroom of Hudson's office, attempting to soak up the sweat that seems to be pouring out of me.

"I don't know," I hiss-whisper at Stacey. "I have toilet paper in my armpits, what do you think?"

"You know, you don't have to go through with this," she says as she pulls some toilet paper from the roll and starts dabbing my forehead and upper lip.

"Yes, I do. He's waiting out there with a reverend and his lawyer. And there's a check in an envelope in my purse made out to me for forty thousand dollars. I just need to...I just need to get it together."

And I thought convincing Hudson to say yes was going to be the hardest part. Little did I know actually going through the wedding ceremony was going to be the biggest hurdle.

Because this is...this is a real, genuine marriage.

Like, I belong to him, he belongs to me. I'm technically going to be Mrs. Hudson Hopper.

There is no make-believe.

There is no trial run.

This is the real deal. He's going to slip a ring on my finger, and we're going to...

"Oh God." All the blood drains from my face.

"What?" Stacey asks.

I turn to my sister and grip her shoulders, the toilet paper sticking to my sweaty armpits, and say, "Is he going to kiss me?"

Her nose turns up in disgust. "Why would he kiss you?"

"Uh, because that's what people do at weddings. They say 'you may kiss the bride' or each other or your partner or whatever! You may kiss thee! The couples kiss. There's kissing!"

"Oh…right." Stacey thinks about it. "You know, great question. That's not something you talked about?"

"I wouldn't be freaking out if it was."

Knock, knock.

"Everything okay in there?" Hudson asks from the other side of the door.

Oh God.

"Yes," I squeak. "Everything's great."

"Are you sure?"

"Ask him about the kiss," Stacey whispers, and I shake my head. She nods toward the door. "Yes, ask."

"No," I say through clenched teeth.

"Sloane?"

"Yup, everything's great," I say in a rush. "Can't, uh, can't wait to be your bride. Your beautiful, blushing bride. Just, uh, finishing up in here. You know, plucking things."

"Plucking?" Stacey mouths in disgust.

"I don't know," I whisper.

"Uh, okay," Hudson answers back, sounding perplexed. As he should. "Well, the reverend is getting tired, so if you can hurry up with the plucking, that would be best."

"Be right out."

I lean against the wall, pull the toilet paper from the roll and start dabbing and wrapping every surface of my body. The sweat, there's too much.

"What the hell would you be plucking right now?" Stacey asks.

"I don't know; I panicked."

"Panic about lipstick, not plucking."

"It doesn't matter," I say as I continue to dab myself. "Please, fan me. Do something. I'm sweating off my makeup."

She rolls her eyes, but like the dutiful sister that she is, she grabs the hand towel from the towel rack and starts whipping it in front of my face, shooting bursts of air in my direction.

"Don't get too close. I don't need you whipping me in the—"

Whack.

"Son of a bitch," I shout, grabbing my eye.

"What happened?" Stacey asks quickly as she lowers the towel to find me wrapped up in toilet paper, leaning against the wall, and clutching my eyeball that I have no doubt at any moment will fall right out of its socket and across the bathroom floor.

"You got me in the freaking eye."

"Ooof, really? What are the chances?"

"Pretty high, apparently."

"Hey." Hudson knocks again. "Are you sure everything is okay in there?"

My God, man. I said I was plucking! Leave a girl to pluck.

"Yup, fine," I groan and pull my hand away, trying to blink my eye back into its spot. "Just, you know, final touches. Have to look good for my husband."

There's silence, and then he twists the handle and thank God we locked it. "Sloane, let me in."

"Can't," I say. "Uh, Stacey is naked, from the plucking."

"What?" she whispers at me, murder in her eyes.

"Sloane, now." Hudson's voice grows tense.

And I'm about to try to reassure him that everything is fine when Stacey moves toward the door.

My lips purse and my eyes narrow. "Don't," I say. She moves even closer. "Stacey," I whisper-shout, pointing my finger at her. "Stop. Don't."

But it's too late. She unlocks the door, and Hudson charges into the bathroom, where he finds me looking like a toilet paper mummy, up against the wall, with my eyeball half hanging out of my head—not really, but have to play up the dramatics for the imagery.

"What the hell is going on?" he asks, taking me in and then looking over at Stacey.

Nervously Stacey backs away. "I think I'm going to introduce myself to the reverend and find out where he grew up," she says as she moves out of the bathroom, leaving me alone with Hudson.

When the door clicks shut, Hudson closes the distance between us and starts tearing off the toilet paper that's sticking to my sweaty skin.

"What are you doing, Sloane?"

"Isn't it obvious?" I ask.

"No."

"Yeah, didn't think so." I let out a pent-up breath and say, "Just nervous and sweaty and trying to combat the sweatiness with toilet paper and then my sister whipped me in the eye and now you're going to have an eyeless bride. So, sorry about that."

He continues to help me with the toilet paper and stays silent as I allow myself to give my future husband a good once-over. He's wearing a dark blue suit, not quite navy but not royal blue either, maybe a color in between. He's paired it with a black button-up shirt and a black tie. His full head of hair is styled off to the side but also sort of pieced in the front, making him exponentially more attractive. And because it's eight at night, his five o'clock shadow has come in, giving him a darker, more mysterious look.

And I'm supposed to be all casual and act like marrying this man is no big deal?

Afraid not.

The man is disgustingly attractive. No single human should be as good-looking as him.

"You know, I'm nervous too," he says.

"Yeah, I can tell. You're really shaking in your loafers."

He finishes removing the toilet paper and pulls me away from the wall. "I am nervous. I apparently just don't sweat as much as you."

I peel the toilet paper from my armpits and deposit it in the trash can. "Yes, well, you're missing out."

"Is your eye okay? It looks like it's bruising."

"Really?" I turn toward the mirror, and sure enough, that's a bruise forming in the corner. "Lovely. Just what I was hoping for on this precious day of marriage, a black eye." I let out a breath and turn toward Hudson. "Okay, let's get this over with."

"You can still back out," he says as I head toward the bathroom door.

"You gave me a check. I'm not backing out."

"You can keep it," he says, looking all kinds of serious. "Consider it a loan or a bonus. Hell, it could be for the bridesmaid work."

I shake my head. "No, this was my idea, and I'm going through with it. We're getting married."

"Sloane."

"What?"

"I'm not going to pressure you."

"You aren't." I take a deep breath. "I just needed a second to gather myself. Okay? Trust me, everything is fine. Let's get married."

I march out of the bathroom, where the reverend is talking to Stacey and the lawyer is sitting at Hudson's desk.

I clasp my hands together. "Sorry about the wait. Are we ready?"

"We are," the reverend says as he moves away from Stacey and holds his book in front of him.

I glance back at Hudson, who is standing in the doorway of his bathroom, studying me, and I fear that he might pull the plug—see right

through my facade and call this off. But then he adjusts his suit jacket and joins me in his office, determination set in his features.

Together, Hudson and I get into position in front of the reverend and awkwardly stand there as he starts talking about long, lasting love.

Yup, that's us, the couple bound for long and lasting love.

Eternal love.

The once-in-a-lifetime kind of love that so few find.

A knot of nerves forms in the pit of my stomach.

Hudson starts with his repeated vows, telling me to my face that he's committed to me through better or worse. He keeps his eyes on me but his hands to himself.

When it's my turn, I repeat the same words, my hands becoming slick as I watch his Adam's apple bob, the first sign of nerves that I've seen from him this entire time.

At least I'm in good company.

"May I have the rings," the reverend says, and the lawyer brings over a box. Hudson opens it, revealing a giant square-cut diamond ring.

"Holy shit," I say without a filter and steal it from his hand. "Is this for me?" When I catch the reverend from the corner of my eye, I say, "I mean, wow, darling, you, uh...you went all out. Mommy like."

Stacey snorts behind me while Hudson raises his brow. "'Mommy like'?"

"Err, I meant...Sloane approves."

Not any better, jackass.

"I'm glad," Hudson says and hands me a simple black band for himself.

We spend the next few minutes listening to the reverend talk about rings being the symbol of everlasting love and repeating after him while we place the rings on each other. Once all is said and done, the reverend says, "I now pronounce you husband and wife. You may kiss the bride."

Great.

I look up at Hudson, who pauses, seeming just as confused as I am.

So I move in with my hand, he moves in with his head, and I poke him right in the stomach.

"Oop, hello, Mr. Ab," I say. "Sorry about that."

He grumbles something and sticks his hand out just as I stand on my toes to offer him my cheek, but the sudden movement causes him to poke my breast.

"Nearly missed the nipple there, mate," I say in a horrible British accent.

"Dear God," I hear Stacey whisper from behind me.

Before I can say anything else, Hudson grabs my cheeks, bends down, and presses a kiss right to my...nose.

An old boop-boop to the nostrils.

I couldn't think of anything less sexy.

The poke to the breast was better than a nose kiss.

The reverend clears his throat and says, "Lovely."

"Thank you, we practiced," I say, my awkwardness showing up in spades.

"Well, I shall sign the marriage certificate and be on my way."

"Thank you," Hudson says in a more serious tone.

Silence fills the room as the reverend scribbles his signature. When he's done, he looks between me and Hudson, who are just standing there, not touching, not doing anything.

A concerned look crosses his face so to reassure him that this isn't a bought-bride situation—even though it kind of is—I wrap my arms and one leg around Hudson, holding him tight.

"Ooof, can't wait to climb this man tonight and really seal the deal, you know?" I wink at the reverend and that puts a smile on his face.

"Yes, well—"

"We'll be copulating; don't worry about us. Can't wait to climb this log or his log—"

"Okay," Hudson says as he shimmies away from me. "Let's sign the papers. Thank you, Reverend. You've been great and we appreciate you being patient with us."

We sign the marriage certificate in silence.

"Congratulations." The reverend packs the paper away and takes off, leaving us with Hudson's lawyer.

"Well, can't say that wasn't entertaining," Stacey says as she takes a seat in one of the chairs. "I really liked the vows. Touching."

Hudson ignores her and hands me the pen to sign the additional stack of papers the lawyer has for us.

"I thought the vows were nice. Very traditional," I say. "What did you think...Husband?"

"Can we not right now?" he asks, seeming testy.

Sheesh, you think he'd be happy after making an honest woman out of me.

We sign an NDA and then a contract about what's to be expected with our agreement. When I first arrived, I signed a prenup, not even bothering to look through it, because hell, I got my check. I'm telling myself that's all I care about.

Once everything is signed, the lawyer puts the papers in his briefcase, stands, and says, "I'll make copies and send them to you, Mrs. Hopper."

Oh yikes, he went there.

Mrs. Hopper—sends a shiver down the spine, doesn't it?

"Yup, thanks. I'll, uh, be sure to put them in a fireproof safe."

"We don't have one of those," Stacey says.

"I'll be sure to get one. Got to keep those documents safe."

The lawyer just nods, shakes hands with Hudson, and heads out the door, leaving it to just the three of us.

"So." I clasp my hands together. "I guess that's a wrap." I hold my hand out to Hudson. "Nice doing business with you. I shall see you in the morning. Oh, and thanks for the ring." When he doesn't take my hand, I stick it in the pocket of my white dress. "Well, uh, Stacey, shall we?"

"I think we shall," she says as she stands, and we start heading to the door.

"Where do you think you're going?" Hudson asks, stopping the both of us.

We turn around together, and I glance at my sister and then back at Hudson. "I believe back to the house, right?"

"I mean, I was kind of hoping you'd treat me to some ice cream," Stacey says. "After all, you made your husband believe that you were plucking me minutes before your wedding."

I chuckle. "Right, not my best moment. You know what, I will treat you to ice cream."

"The good ice cream, none of this grocery store bullshit."

"Lady, I got married today, we're getting the—"

"You're coming home," Hudson says, drawing both of our attention.

Nervously, I chuckle and pull on my ear. "Oh God, I thought he just said I was going home, like his home."

"No, I think he meant our home, like you and I are not getting ice cream. We're to just go home. Maybe it's a marriage curfew or something."

"Oh, is that a thing?" I ask.

We both turn to Hudson again, whose jaw is tight and who is looking none too entertained. Seems like someone lost their sense of humor when they said *I do*.

"You're coming home…with me."

I stand there, stunned, blinking as Stacey leans toward me, and from the corner of her mouth, she says, "I think he said you're going home with him, like to his home."

"I think that's what he said too," I whisper back, still staring at him. "I can't tell if he's serious."

"Dead serious," he says.

"Ha, okay." I chuckle. "Good, uh, good one, my man. But you know"—I yawn and stretch my arms above my head—"it's getting late, and that ice cream is not going to eat itself, so why don't we put this whole *Beauty and the Beast, you stay with me* act to rest because, frankly, it's slightly outdated."

"I told you to read the agreement," he says.

"I did. I skimmed it. The legal jargon was a little much, if you ask me. Like, why we so fancy? You can use regular English. Nothing wrong with simple sentences."

He takes a step closer to me and says, "In the agreement, it states that you are to live with me."

"Where?" I ask. "Where on earth did it say that?"

He picks up his copy of the contract that the lawyer left "for his records," brings it over to me, and points to the very sentence. I read it three or four times, mouthing the words before looking up at him, dread filling me. "Why on earth would you put that in the contract?"

"Because we need to get to know each other, and the best way to do that is to live with each other."

"Uh, hey, captor, I work with you. Remember, I'm your devoted assistant again? We can get to know each other here."

"This is the workplace, not a place for me to get to know and understand my wife on a deeper level."

"Wow, okay, the way you said *wife*, sheesh, it sounded like you really meant it."

"It did," Stacey whispers. I wouldn't be surprised if she were to pull a bucket of popcorn out of her pants and start shoving handfuls in her mouth as she watches the drama unfolding. And there is some good reasoning for that. We have known Hudson Hopper for a while now through Jude, and he's always been quite…intense. Add in what his father did to their family and that has simply made his gravity balloon. But living together? He doesn't mean—

"I did mean it," he says, his serious tone never faltering, his eyes never straying. "Our car is waiting for us downstairs."

Stacey taps me on the shoulder and whispers, "I think he means it. I think you're supposed to go home with him."

"That's what it seems like." I lift my chin in the air. "Okay, Husband, if I'm supposed to go home with you, then where am I supposed to sleep? Huh? What about clothes? A toothbrush? Going to tell you right now, I'm very keen on dental care. No way in hell am I going to go to bed without brushing my teeth. That's nonnegotiable."

"Everything you need is at our house."

Our.

He just said *our house.*

This entire situation just got a whole lot more serious.

"Stacey," he says, addressing her. "I have a car waiting for you as well. Tell the driver where you would like to go for ice cream. It's on me."

Then he walks up to me, holds his arm out, and says, "Let's go home."

I stare at his arm and then back at him. I point to his gesture and ask, "Am I supposed to just slip my arm in yours and act like this is all normal?"

He leans in and says through clenched teeth, "The quicker you realize just how real this is, the easier it will be for you."

Oh boy.

Okay.

So this is serious.

This man really thinks this marriage is real.

"You know, just for the record, I assumed this was going to be more casual."

He takes my arm and slips it through his. "This isn't fake dating, Sloane. This is a goddamn marriage. You're my wife. The expectations are different."

He guides me down the hall, my sister trailing after me. "Expectations." I swallow the lump in my throat. "Can you elaborate on those?"

He punches the down button and faces forward as he says, "Read the agreement. You will know."

The elevator doors open, and we step in. When he pushes the button for the first floor and the doors close, Stacey says, "Note to self, always read the document before signing."

No shit.

CHAPTER SIX
HUDSON

I FLIP ON THE LIGHTS to the entryway of my midcentury home and allow Sloane to walk in front of me.

"Wow, so this is where the beast dwells," she says, taking in the newly renovated open space of the dining, living room, and kitchen. Fresh oak flooring, dark gray walls, white furniture, and floor-to-ceiling windows that look out toward the bay. "Fancy."

I set my keys down and move to the kitchen, where I take a highball glass off the shelf and pour myself some water because my mouth is dry as fuck.

Ever since Sloane showed up to my office wearing that fucking white dress that squeezed every curve of her torso but flared out at her hips, hitting her midthigh, I needed a drink—something much stronger than the water I'm currently consuming.

I kept telling myself over and over again, *Don't do it.*

Leave.

Run.

But as the reverend checked the time and I sensed something was going on in the bathroom that didn't deal with any sort of plucking, I knew she was getting cold feet—like me. And internally, that fucked with my pride.

I'm ashamed to even admit it.

But something inside me, a protective side, told me I needed to soothe her. So that's what I did, which of course set me on the straight and narrow to holy matrimony. Because once I saw the trust she had in me, I was a goner.

And now...well, fuck, now what the hell am I going to do?

My lawyer, Frederick Steinfeld, the fucker, told me that I needed to put in that agreement that we would live together. The man didn't bat an eyelash about the entire thing; it was as if it wasn't his first time drawing up a marriage contract because he spoke from experience. He told me she needed to live with me, that if we were going to be married, we needed to go all in, in order to convince people. At first, I didn't think it was necessary because we were just doing this for business, but the more I thought about keeping it a secret, the more I thought: *What happens if it gets back to Jude?*

If he ever finds out, I want to at least be able to tell him that I treated his sister like a queen. That I was a model husband. That I never let anything bad happen to her. That I could look him in the eyes and say I took the vows seriously.

And that's what I plan on doing.

Sloane is my wife, plain and simple; therefore, she will be treated like my wife.

"You know, I never pegged you as a white furniture kind of guy." She sits down on the couch and bounces a few times. "More comfortable than it looks, still in pristine condition. Do you even sit in here?"

"Rarely," I answer and fill up my glass again. "Do you want some water?"

"Don't mind if I do," she says, coming into the kitchen.

I grab her a glass and fill it up for her. She takes the drink from me, then holds it up. "To wedded bliss." She clinks my glass with hers and chugs her water until it's all gone. "Ooof, that tastes good. Even your water is fancy."

She drags her fingers along the marble countertops, observing my place, while I stand there, dumbfounded, observing her.

Jude is going to murder me.

Decapitate me.

I will have no head.

No balls.

No dick.

He will rip me to shreds with his bare hands.

Yet here I am, not doing a damn thing about it.

"So, where is the room where all the magic happens?" she asks, twirling around just enough that her short skirt lifts in the air and I catch a brief glimpse of the bottom of her left butt cheek.

Christ, it's going to be a long couple of weeks.

"Upstairs, to the right," I answer.

"This girl is exhausted. Getting married really takes it out of a lady." She starts climbing the stairs, then pauses. "You know, we didn't get any pictures. We should have posed at least in front of your desk. Think of all the bonding memories we shared there while we were courting."

"We never courted."

"Sure felt like it." She winks and keeps walking up the stairs.

She's too much for me.

There is no way I'm going to be able to handle her, not this…this new side of her that I never knew existed. She used to be so quiet, so demure, so…*yes, sir*, and now she's mouthy, confident—which isn't a bad thing—and by no means ready to submit. Not that I need her to, but Christ, might be slightly helpful.

I set my glass down in the sink, turn off the lights, and head upstairs, where I find her in my bedroom—well, I guess *our* bedroom—making snow angels on the king-size bed.

This is what I'm talking about.

This is what I can't handle.

She has too much fucking energy, and I know I'm not a grandpa, but she sure as hell is making me feel like one when she does shit like that.

"For a place this large, I'd expect there to be more guest rooms."

"Can you stop that?" I say as she opens her legs and shuts them. I avert my eyes, trying not to see anything…too private.

She sits up on the bed. "Am I messing up your bedding?"

"No, you're flapping your legs open, and I…I don't need to see that."

"Yikes, not something a lady wants to hear on her wedding night." She hops off the bed and asks, "So this is what we're doing? Playing house?"

"We're not playing anything," I say as I move toward the closet, where I take off my suit jacket and tie.

She follows me and leans against the doorframe. "Okay, but you realize this marriage isn't real, right?"

I start unbuttoning my dress shirt and her eyes immediately fall to my chest. "Sloane, it's as real as they come." I untuck my shirt, finish unbuttoning, and then throw caution to the wind and remove it entirely.

Probably a big mistake because she has no shame eating me alive with her eyes.

Nope.

Her gaze roams up and down, from my shoulders to my pecs and all the way down my stomach. And when I think she's done, she goes for another pass while she very subtly wets her lips.

Fuck.

Me.

I clear my throat, which brings her attention back to my eyes. "Did you hear me?"

"Um, I want to say yes, but your perfectly proportioned nipple-to-pec ratio distracted me."

Got to give it to her for being direct.

"I said this marriage is as real as they come."

She folds her arms and takes one more gander at my stomach. "Sure, in the legal sense, but not on the emotional side. I mean, I'm not in love with you, although I could see myself falling after seeing what you're currently offering."

I unbuckle my pants and push them down.

"Oh my, tight thigh."

I pull my pants back up and stare her down. "Can you please not ogle me?"

"Says the man who wants this marriage to be real. That's what wives do; they ogle." Then she walks into the closet and plucks one of my T-shirts off my shelf. She turns to me and says, "Be a lamb and unzip me please."

"Can't you unzip yourself?"

She scornfully looks over her shoulder. "Sir, this is what husbands do. If you want to play the doting roles, then snap into character. Now, unzip me."

She's got me there.

Reluctantly, I move behind her, grab the small clasp of her zipper, and slowly pull it down, revealing a white lace bra and the top of white lace underwear.

Fucking help me.

My mouth goes dry as I step back, and I'm about to turn around, but she lets the dress slide down her shoulders and drop to the ground where it pools on the floor. My eyes travel back up her luscious legs and right to the curve of her thong-covered ass.

Mother.

Fucker.

Round, thick enough for me to grab on to and fucking ride. Jesus.

Then she reaches behind her and undoes the clasp of her bra, and I nearly go hard right then and there as she lets her bra slide off her as well, leaving her back completely bare to me. I envision my hand sliding up her spine, to the nape of her neck, where I press her head into the mattress and prop that delicious ass into the air.

Just as the fantasy starts playing out in my head, she slips my shirt over her body and turns toward me as she pulls her hair out of the collar. She must catch me staring because a smile crosses her face. "Performing your husbandly duties with a little ogle yourself." She walks up to me and pats me on the chest. "Well done, Hudson." Then she makes her way into the bathroom, where she spots the basket of toiletries I had put together for her and sent to the house.

I take a few seconds in the closet to calm my body down—the last thing I need is to walk in the bathroom with a half-stiff cock.

"You even have the right facial cleanser. How did you pull that off?" she asks from the bathroom.

I take my pants off again, adjust myself in my briefs, and then move into the bathroom, where I say, "Your sister."

"Huh, and she didn't even tell me. She acted like she didn't know I was going to sleep here."

"She thought it was a wedding gift."

Sloane's face turns to disgust. "She thought you were giving me facial cleanser as a wedding gift, and she still let me marry you? Wow, what a sister." She removes her toothbrush from the packaging, wets it, and places some toothpaste on it.

I do the same, and in silence, we brush our teeth. After we both spit, she says, "What a wedding night, right? Such magic, you and me, brushing our teeth in tandem. This is how I always envisioned it."

"Are you always this sarcastic?"

"Yes."

"You weren't when you first started working for me."

"Because I was trying to be a good girl."

Why did she have to say it like that? *Good girl.* Fuck, I bet she's a really good girl.

"So this is your true self?"

"Yup." She rinses her mouth. "Consider yourself lucky. I only show people my true self when I feel comfortable."

"Real lucky," I say.

We spend the next few minutes getting ready for bed. We both wash our faces and apply lotion. She goes to the bathroom. I go after her, and once we're all done, I shut the bathroom light off, and she stands at the foot of the bed.

"So this is really happening, huh? We're doing this whole sharing-the-bed thing?" So it seems, and it doesn't really make sense to me either. I have a large house. She could sleep in a different room. It's not as if anyone will know she's staying in my bed. I truly have no idea why I am subjecting us both to this. So I say the first thing that pops into my mind.

"You're my wife, so yes." *Idiot.*

"Mm-hmm, you keep saying that, so I want to be clear: Do wifely duties also include...other things?"

Fuck. No. Jude would make sure my body was never found.

"No," I say as I move toward the right side of the bed, the one that's closest to the door. It's not my normal side, but also, she shouldn't be the one that's closest to the door; it should be me.

"So I don't have to do any fondling or sucking or riding or faking—"

I snap my head around to look her in the eyes. "You wouldn't be faking it with me."

"Ooh, looks like I pressed a hot button."

"No, just making sure you have your facts straight."

She slips into bed and sinks down onto my pillow. *How is she not at all resistant to sleeping in my bed?*

"How do you know I wouldn't need to fake it? You might have been with girls with an easy trigger...or you might not have known if they were faking it because they were good actresses."

"They were not faking it."

She shrugs. "Okay, guess I'll just have to take your word for it. And if we're sharing, I'd like you to know that I'm amazing at giving head. It's my specialty."

Not something I needed to know.

"As for the orgasm department, I've only had one guy who could deliver. It was pretty good. Actually, I'm lying; it was really good."

Foolish jealousy rips through me because that's not something I want to hear. I don't want to know that she's been pleasured by another man. I don't want to even know she's been with other men.

"His name was Devin," she continues. "He had the smallest curve in his penis, and he knew how to use that curve to his advantage."

"I don't need the details," I say as I sink down into the pillow as well.

"I thought we were sharing." She turns toward me. "Want to tell me the best sex you've ever had?"

"No."

"Seems a bit harsh. I think a wife should know something like that."

"Why?"

She shrugs. "Because I think it's nice to know that my husband has been pleasured. I mean, what if you've never had an orgasm?"

I turn toward her and give her a look. "I came in the shower this morning."

Her eyes widen as a small smile passes over her lips. "Oh my God, Hudson, I came in my bed before I got in the shower. Look at us doing the hard work on our own. Coming buddies." She pushes at my shoulder, and I hate myself.

I hate everything about this.

Why? Why did I make this choice? I'm a smart man. I've been able to navigate life well up until this point, so why now? Why am I making decisions that are putting me in actual physical pain?

Some might say I'm a masochist.

Others might assume I've had a small crush on this girl the moment I met her and now I'm fulfilling a fantasy I have no right to even consider.

"So is that going to be part of your morning routine? A good stroke and scrub? Because if so, just let me know. I can be downstairs while you take care of business."

"I don't plan on doing anything like that while you're here," I answer.

"Oh God, is that going to be a rule? I sure as hell hope not because there is no way I'll last. Which reminds me, do you have any vibrators? If I have one of those, thirty seconds and I'll be good."

I press my fingers to my brow and say, "Can we just not right now?"

"I can sense this is painful for you. That's fine. We can come back to the topic when you're feeling a little more comfortable." She quiets, and I let out a deep breath because sleep—that's what I need. I need sleep. "Can I just say how magical our first kiss was? A total inspiration for romances to come."

I groan and turn away from her.

"I'm sorry. When I'm nervous I tend to talk a lot." She's quiet for a moment and then adds, "Did you mean to kiss my nose or was that a spur-of-the-moment thing? Bet it was the first nose kiss the reverend ever saw at a wedding. Should have told him it's how I like it to really sell the connection."

"You can stop talking."

"Sorry. This is just weird, and I don't do weird well." She pauses. "But, I mean, are we nose kissers? I need to know because I'm going to need you to bend farther down if that's the case. I'll kiss your nose, but I'm not kissing your nostril."

"Good night, Sloane."

"So…is that a yes on the nose kissing?"

"It's a *go the fuck to sleep*."

"Sheesh," she says as she turns on the bed. "Wasn't aware you were a grump outside of work too."

And I wasn't aware I married a smart-mouth chatterbox with the finest fucking ass I've ever seen. But here we are.

CHAPTER SEVEN
HUDSON

"GOOD MORNING," SLOANE SAYS AS she joins me in the kitchen, wearing a long dress that reaches her ankles. It's dark blue with a gold overlay of cutout flowers. The off-the-shoulder sleeves show off her shoulders and nothing else. I picked the dress out and assumed it wouldn't make me think about bending her over my desk, but as she floats innocently through the kitchen, I'm quickly realizing it's not what she wears. It's just her. "So from the lack of coffee machine, I'm going to assume you don't make coffee here."

"Nope," I answer.

"Okay, um, so is it a no on a coffeemaker? Because, you know, some people might like one."

"Tell me which one you want, and I'll get it," I answer as I finish my protein shake and rinse my cup out in the sink.

"Well, in that case, one of those espresso machines only baristas know how to work."

I eye her and she laughs, the sound so fucking heavenly. She reaches for a banana and starts to peel it, which is my sign to leave because I don't need to watch her eat that thing.

"I'm meeting Hardy for breakfast. I won't be in the office until later, so no need to get me my green drink."

"Sounds good," she says, and I glance over my shoulder, where I catch her taking a bite of her banana, but she's not eating it the way I thought she would. Instead, she's treating it like a piece of watermelon and eating it horizontally.

"What the hell are you doing?" I ask.

She pauses, ready to take another bite. "Eating a banana."

"I see that, but why the hell are you eating it like that?"

She looks down at the banana boat in her hand and then back at me. "Because I knew if I ate it the other way, you'd moan and groan and envision the banana as your penis and me as the sucker of said penis."

I nearly choke on my own saliva. "Excuse me?"

"Please, all men do it. Don't act like you're innocent. I was saving you just now." She takes another bite of her banana, and it splits in two. *The proper answer would be, thank you.* I stand there, stunned, so she continues. "You're welcome. Anyway, since you're not in the office this morning, think I could go to my place and pack up some things to bring over here? Maybe show my sister that I survived the night despite you constantly kicking me?"

My eyes narrow. "I didn't kick you, did I?"

She smiles and pops one of the banana halves in her mouth. "No, but it's nice that you're concerned. For a second there, I thought you were a robot." My face falls flat, which makes her laugh. "So is that a yes on gathering my items?"

"Yes," I answer and then head toward the garage. "I'm taking my car. Bart is out front, so he'll drive you wherever you need to go. After work, we'll go to dinner together."

"Oh, is that right?" she asks. "You're just going to tell me what we're going to do?"

"Yes." I pick up my car key, stick my wallet in my pocket. "See you at the office."

"Hey," she calls out and walks up to me. She pauses, then slips her hand behind my neck, pulls me down to her, and then, to my surprise, she kisses me on the nose. When she releases me, she says, "Nose kiss," as if it's a funny inside joke. "Have a great day, Husband. See you in the office." Then she twiddles her fingers at me and goes back to the kitchen.

Christ. Out of all the women…she's the one I married.

Great, Hudson.

Really great.

Think of the property purchase. This is only temporary. You can stick this out for a month.

"I swear to Christ, I keep unsubscribing, but no matter what I do, those fucking flamingo emails keep coming in," Hardy says as he stabs his eggs with his fork.

"It's because you keep donating," I say to him as I lean back in my chair, my food barely touched.

"It's hard not to when JP makes such a compelling argument about the damn birds." Hardy leans forward and whispers, "I donated to the pigeons too."

"Dude."

"I know," he groans. "Fuck, but the email had a picture of a once-domesticated pigeon, now looking into the window of a warm house, snow falling around him. It was devastating."

"It's a fucking pigeon."

"Trust me, I hate myself." He shakes his head and takes a mouthful of his eggs. "It's just so fucking cruel. Society takes these birds in, domesticates them, and then we're like, *nope, see ya, you fucking sky rats.*"

"You need help."

"That's what Everly told me this morning when I was bitching to her about the damn emails. Maybe I just need to change my email. You know how people are too scared to quit the gym, so they change their credit card altogether? Maybe I'll do that, change my email to stop getting those fucking sad bird emails."

"He'll find you," I say. "JP will fucking find you."

Hardy slowly nods and wipes his mouth with his napkin. "I know. I'm just fucked. Before you know it, you're going to see me on the pier with JP, talking to the damn pigeons."

"That's one way to get Everly to break up with you."

"You think she would? You don't think she'd see it as the sensitive side of me?"

"Not a chance," I answer and take a sip of my orange juice, something I know Sloane will tell me has a ton of sugar in it and will make my wrinkles deeper—which, is that even a thing? I make a mental note to look it up.

"So why aren't you eating?" Hardy asks.

"I ate."

He takes his fork and pushes at my half-eaten omelet. "I'm calling bullshit."

"Just not hungry."

"Also, calling bullshit. What's going on with you?"

I guess there really isn't a good time to tell your brother that you got married. That's why I brought him here after all.

"Uh, I have something to tell you," I say as I push my silverware to the side. His eyes follow my movements, specifically my hands, and I know the minute he sees my ring.

His mouth falls open and he slowly lifts his head. Pointing at the ring, he asks, "What the fuck is that?"

I clear my throat and shift on my seat. "Um, so I have something I have to—"

He yanks my hand across the table and looks at the ring closely. He taps it a few times. "That's fucking real. Dude, you know that's real, right?"

"Yes, I know it's real."

"Is that like…one of those decorative rings? You know, that people wear for style?"

"Do you think I'm someone who would wear a ring for style?"

He swallows and shakes his head. "No...no, you're not. But you're also not someone to wear a ring for...other reasons." He continues to stare at the ring and then he reaches for his phone. "I need to call Haisley."

"No," I yell, slapping his phone out of his hand, sending it to the ground and skittering toward the table next to us.

"What the fuck?" Hardy asks while an older gentleman picks up Hardy's phone and hands it to him. We offer our apologies and then Hardy leans forward and whispers, "Why can't I tell Haisley?"

"She can't know."

"Why not? You clearly got married. I think that's something our sister should know."

"She can't, Hardy."

"Why not?"

"Because," I say and steady my breath. "Because I married her husband's sister."

The look of shock on Hardy's face would be comical if I wasn't so fucking terrified out of my skin from announcing those words.

"No, you fucking didn't," he says.

I slowly nod. "I did."

He leans back in his seat, his hands resting in his lap, looking... defeated. "Well." He nods, staring off into space. "It was nice knowing you, Hudson. You've been a good big brother. For a moment, I thought it might be a heart attack that kills you because, well, you know, Dad and all. But no, it's going to be our brother-in-law."

I want to say he's overreacting, but I know he's not.

He's right.

Then he leans forward again and whispers, "She's like twenty years younger than you, you fucking pervert."

"She's thirteen years younger."

"Oh yeah, much better," he scoffs.

"Twenty years would make her fucking illegal, nimrod."

He starts to slowly clap. "Glad you did the math to make sure she was legal."

"Hey, she's the same fucking age as Everly."

"Yeah, but I'm younger than you, so should I do another round of clapping?"

"Can you not?" I shoot back. "I'm, I'm fucking struggling here."

"I can't believe you married Sloane. And here I was, bitching about flamingos and pigeons, and you're just sitting there with that goddamn ring on your finger. Jesus Christ, that should have been the first thing you said to me when we sat down."

"I was working up the courage."

"Because you know what you did was wrong."

"Of course I know that," I answer.

"Then why the hell would you marry her? Are you two in love? Jesus, have you been fucking this whole time? You were giving me grief about Everly, and there you are, in a secret relationship with your assistant, our brother-in-law's sister. The fucking hypocrisy."

"We were not in a secret relationship."

"Okay, sure, yeah, so you just got married?"

"Yes," I answer.

"Stop fucking with me. There's no way you would get married unless you were in a—" He pauses and tilts his head to the side, his mind working. Slowly, it hits him. "No." I glance down at my lap. "Hudson. Please, for the love of fuck, don't tell me."

He knows.

"Don't tell you what?" I say, still looking at my lap because I feel so fucking ashamed.

Speaking quietly, he says, "Did you marry her to get into that fucking club?"

I blow out a heavy breath and say, "It was her idea."

"Holy...fuck." He leans back in his chair, hand to his forehead.

"You're...you're dead. You are so fucking dead. You realize how bad this is, right? Like how incredibly bad this is."

"Yes, I know."

"And you still went through with it. I mean, did you? Well, clearly you did," Hardy says, his voice growing hysterical. "You're wearing the goddamn ring—unless you're just trying it on for size to see how you like it. Please tell me that's the case. Are you just playing pretend right now?"

I look up at my brother and level with him. "Sloane is my wife."

"Noooo," he groans out, dragging his hands over his face. "You fucking idiot. Out of all the stupid things we have done collectively, you and me, this has got to be the cream of the crop, the most idiotic decision either one of us has ever made."

"I know." I hang my head. "For what it's worth, I said no to her several times."

"Oh wow. Should I tell the town crier? Throw you a fucking parade?" In a whisper-yell, he says, "Hear ye, hear ye, Hudson said no to her several times; let's all praise his fortitude."

"I don't need your sarcasm right now."

"Yeah, well, I don't need your stupid-ass decisions right now. Christ, man. Why her? You know how protective Jude is. And he's...he's our brother-in-law, our business partner."

"I know who he is, okay? It's not like this is forever. It's just until, well, until the property purchase is over."

"Uh-huh." He nods, his tongue poking at the side of his cheek. "And when Archie later invites you and the wife over for dinner, what are you going to do?"

"Pay her to come to dinner."

"Jesus Christ." He shakes his head and then stops. "Hold on. Did you pay her to be your wife?" I wince, and he shoots straight up from the table. "I...I can't handle this."

"Sit the fuck down," I say through clenched teeth.

He sits and then practically lies across the table to get as close to me as possible. "You fucking paid her?"

"It was her idea. She needed the money to put a down payment on their house that they love, and she told me she would be the bridesmaid Sheridan needs and she would marry me. This was after I fired her of course."

"You fired her?" Hardy's eyes nearly pop out of his head before he sinks low in his chair. "This is too much. Way too fucking much. What the hell happened to you? You used to be smart."

"I was thinking the same thing." I twist my water glass on the table. "She slept at my place last night."

"Of course she did, because might as well keep digging your grave deeper and deeper."

"We didn't do anything, but Frederick thought it would be best if we treated this whole thing like a real marriage, so he wrote it in the contract that she was supposed to live with me and treat me as a real husband."

"That's just great. Wonderful actually. So excited to see that you're treating Jude's baby sister like a mail-order bride because your lawyer told you to. This isn't going to backfire at all."

"It'll be fine. And I'm making sure to treat her like my wife, with care and sensitivity. She's going to live like a queen—anything she needs or wants, it's hers."

He studies me for a moment. "Are you looking for an award? Because you're not going to get one from me. When Jude finds out, he's not going to care about that shit."

"He's not going to find out," I say, trying to convince myself as well. "As long as you don't say anything to Haisley or Everly."

"You think I'm going to keep this to myself? You've lost your fucking mind. No way I'm keeping this from Everly."

"Hardy," I say in a stern voice. "Jude and Haisley can't find out. Which means you can't tell Everly because she'll tell Maggie, who will tell Brody, and that motherfucker can't keep anything to himself. He'll end up posting on his social media about it because he's such an idiot."

"I agree, Brody is an idiot, but dude, you're leading in that category right now. The gold medalist with no one coming even close to challenging you."

"I'm being serious. You can't tell anyone. If this is going to work, we need to keep it sealed."

"Then why the hell tell me?"

"Because I'm going to need to consult with you when I'm in London. You're going to need to know that I've taken a wife."

"Taken a wife? What are you living in, the 1800s?"

Exasperated, I say, "Please just tell me you're not going to say anything to anyone."

"I'm telling Everly, but I'll swear her to secrecy. She's good at keeping secrets. She didn't tell me about the crush she had on me for a long time. So I know she can hold out."

I roll my eyes and then point at him. "If this gets out, it's on you."

He shakes his head. "No, man, this is all on you."

CHAPTER EIGHT
SLOANE

"SO NOTHING HAPPENED?" STACEY ASKS as she tosses some underwear in a bag for me.

"Nothing," I reply as I sift through some of my comfortable clothes, since Hudson seemed to have a variety of professional clothes for me. Although, I did pack some of my skirts because it seems like some of the things he picked out for me are on the prudish side. I mean, a dress that goes all the way down to my ankles? The nerve.

"Did you want something to happen?"

"I just wanted to make sure I didn't do something stupid like...fart in my sleep."

"God, the horror. Could you imagine?"

I shake my head. "I could not. I did wear his shirt to bed though and that felt amazing. Oh, and I changed in front of him, and he seemed to enjoy that. He saw my ass, Stacey."

"Your ass?"

I nod with a smile. "My ass."

"We have great asses."

"We do, and I think he noticed because he cleared his throat."

"Aw, telltale sign of him approving of your ass."

"That's what I thought," I say.

"So overall, what would you rate the night?"

"Hmm." I tap my chin. "I'd give the wedding a five, that nose kiss was a real downer. I'd give his house a ten out of ten. And then the sleep, well, maybe a six because I was too focused on the not farting."

"Is that something you normally do?" she asks.

"I mean, not that I can recall, but I remember watching a TikTok about a girl who farted in bed while with a new love interest and he asked her to leave. It was humiliating on all accounts, and I just couldn't fathom that happening, so I kept things tight. Anyway, overall I would rate it a seven."

"Not bad for someone who got married to someone they don't know."

"I thought the same thing. Like the people who get married on that show, *Married at First Sight* or whatever it's called, I lucked out big-time."

"I think so."

"What did you do last night?" We finish packing, and I bring my two suitcases over to the entryway of the house.

"I called Beth."

"You did?" I ask, excited. "How was it?"

She shrugs, but there is a smile playing on her lips.

"From the twinkle in your eyes, I'm going to guess good."

"Yeah, it was good." Stacey takes a seat on the couch. "She's really cool. We talked for two and a half hours, and then we both started yawning and figured we should get to bed."

"Two and a half hours. Not sure I've ever talked to someone for that long in my life."

"You've never had a real connection with another person."

"It's not my fault they've all been duds. Well, besides one. God, he was good."

"There is more to relationships than sex, Sloane."

I roll my eyes. "I'm aware. Just haven't found anyone I care enough to listen to."

And isn't that the truth? I've always avoided close relationships. I lost my parents, then my grandma. In some ways, I lost Jude when he found Haisley. I know Stacey will eventually find someone to be with too. I haven't ever opened myself up to the possibility of creating a close relationship because I figure it will hurt less when they leave.

She chuckles. "Well, that's one way to put it."

"So are you guys going to go out on a date?"

"I think so," Stacey says while twirling her hair. "I'm trying to figure out when the appropriate time would be to text her. I don't want to come off too desperate, but I also want her to know that I'm interested."

"Uh, just text her. Don't play games. I bet she'd love to hear from you this morning. And open with something smooth. Something like…*I had to get coffee this morning. I didn't sleep at all because I was thinking about you.*"

"That's lame."

I scoff. "No, it's not. I thought that was pretty clever."

She shakes her head. "No, it's lame."

"Oh yeah, watch this."

I pull my phone out and text Hudson.

Sloane: I had to drink a lot of coffee this morning. I didn't sleep at all because I was thinking about you.

"Did you just send that to Hudson?" Stacey asks.

"Yes, now watch him eat from my hand. The man is going to fill up with so much pride, he's going to regale me with his sleepless night as well. Now help me with these bags. I have to bring them to Bart." But the moment I open the front door, Bart is standing there, waiting for me.

"I'll take those, Mrs. Hopper," he says, grabbing the bags from me.

"Oohh," Stacey coos. "*Mrs. Hopper* has a nice ring to it."

"Funny, because it makes me feel slightly pukey."

"Really? Why? It's not like it's really real."

"That's the thing," I say as I move back into the house. I call out to Bart, "Be right there." Then I shut the door and grab Stacey by the arms. "He's treating this like it's real, and I'm trying to play along and act like I'm all cool and nonchalant about the whole thing, but I'm slowly dying inside."

"What do you mean he's treating it like it's real?"

"We're going out to dinner tonight."

"That doesn't mean anything." She waves me off. "You both need food, makes sense."

I shake my head. "No, there was something about the tone of his voice, how he said *we'll be going to dinner*, this was different. And he's serious about me living with him and spending time with him. He calls me *wife*. Like he's really into this."

Stacey thinks about it for a second. "Maybe he's, I don't know, trying to get into the right frame of mind because you have to be married around businesspeople? Maybe this is like…practice so when you're in the moment and you have to truly pull this off, it's easier."

I'm about to answer when my phone beeps with a text message.

Stacey and I stare at each other for a few seconds before she whispers, "I bet that's him."

"We know that's him."

"Then let's see how he's eating out of the palm of your hand as you put it." She nudges me with her hand.

I lift my phone and unlock the screen. I read the text out loud to her.

Hudson: Then why did I see you sleeping several times throughout the night with your mouth open and drool on your pillow?

Stacey lets out a howl of a laugh as the insult pulses through me. "I was not drooling," I say as I text him back.

Sloane: Staring lovingly, I see. Hope you got your fill.

"Oh my God, I can't breathe," Stacey says, still laughing.

"It's not funny."

"Uh…it's so fucking funny," she says, gripping her stomach.

My phone dings with a message.

Hudson: For a lifetime.

And he says I'm the one with the attitude.

Sloane: If you got your fill, then no need to meet for dinner.
Hudson: Miss dinner and hand me back the check.

"Gah!" I gasp, staring down at the text.

"What?" Stacey asks while wiping her eyes.

"He's being rude to me."

"Rude? Or is he calling you on your bullshit?"

"Rude," I say with a lift of my chin. "Absolutely rude."

"Hello, Husband," I say, arms crossed, staring at Hudson, who is wearing a forest-green suit and white button-up shirt. A far cry from the ugly brown that makes him look like a potato. Nope, this is tailored to fit every curve and contour of his tall, broad body.

"Why are you saying hello? We drove over together."

"Yes, but you're finally acknowledging me."

"I was driving," he says.

"But conversation never hurt anyone. I see you're just carrying over your rudeness from earlier."

He opens the door to the restaurant and presses his hand to my lower back, guiding me inside.

"How was I rude?"

"Uh, your text messages."

He offers his name to the hostess, and she immediately guides us through the restaurant as he leans his head next to mine and whispers, "Don't play with fire if you can't handle the burn, Sloane."

And then he pulls out my chair for me when we reach the table. I stare at him for a few seconds, studying those dangerous eyes before I take a seat and he scoots me in.

Unfortunately, he's right. I played with fire this morning and got burned.

Learned a lesson though, that's for damn sure. He might be a silent one, but he can be quick.

"Well, this place is nice," I say as I place my napkin on my lap and take in the opulence of the restaurant.

I will say this, coming from a family who had absolutely nothing and then sliding into the world of the Hopper family, it's been a bit of a shock. It started when we flew out to Bora Bora for Haisley and Jude's wedding on a private jet. I had never flown before, let alone on a private airplane. Then we had a dream vacation on a remote island in bungalows that sat over the water. Everything was paid for; all we had to do was watch our brother get married and hang out with the family. It was honestly amazing.

And working for Hudson has had its perks. When I have to run errands for him, his driver drives me around. And let me tell you, not having to worry about parking in San Francisco, that's a perk on its own.

And this restaurant. Yowza.

You don't get through the front door unless you have a reservation. The tables are far enough apart from each other where you don't overhear any conversation. The lighting is dim, the booths are high and private, and I swear you could get away with some fondling and no one would even know. Although the fanciness is rather high, so I'm not sure anyone would stoop to the level of fondling.

"It's one of my favorite restaurants," he says, not even attempting to look at the menu in front of us.

It's one of those one-sheet menus with a few dishes on it. If you put fifty of these together, you would have the menu for The Cheesecake Factory.

"Oh yeah, why's that?"

"I know the chef well. His food is well seasoned and expertly cooked, and the presentation is immaculate."

Imagine living a life where "the presentation" is something you rate a restaurant on.

I prefer a good old sloppy breakfast thrown together on one plate at a diner.

This though, this is one of those places where they use a cloth to clean any stray drips or steam from the surface before shipping it out to the tables. And don't get me started on the white gloves being worn by the waitstaff.

"Ah yes, presentation is key," I say just as he looks up at me, sensing my sarcasm.

This man has made it a point to avoid all eye contact with me up until we've reached this restaurant, and now all of a sudden he's going to act like I exist?

All day he barely spoke to me in the office. And when we were in the car, I didn't even know he realized there was a passenger on board. But here, now, he's giving me the time of day with those sultry eyes.

It's jarring.

Alarming.

Not something I'm used to because let's call a spade a spade, my husband is hot.

Capital H, hot.

Like, *wowza, this guy is not human.*

I always thought he was incredibly handsome with his suit on, but with it off—let me bite my fist because holy moly, I was trembling last night.

All I kept thinking about as I tried to go to sleep was *Will he accidentally graze my breast?* Sure, he was on the very edge of his side and there was no possible chance of any sort of midnight collision, but God, did I think about it. And I thought about what I would do too.

I would act all coy and be like, *Oops, was that my breast?* And then slowly roll onto my back, my shirt would ride up, and then oops, he'd touch my bare hip. He'd grumble, I'd grumble, and then I'd turn again only to have him tear off my shirt and suck my—

"Did you hear me?"

"Huh? What? I don't know about forks."

His brow creases. "I wasn't talking about forks."

"Oh, you weren't?" I nervously laugh and then adjust my silverware. "What, uh, what were you talking about?"

"I asked if you wanted me to order for you."

"Oh, uh, that's not necessary." I lift up the menu and my eyes focus in on the words that make absolutely no sense to me. "What does 'confit' mean?" I lower the menu back down and say, "Actually that sounds like a great idea. I trust you. As long as there are no raw tomatoes, then we're golden."

"Not a fan of tomatoes?" he asks.

"I mean, I like ketchup and spaghetti sauce and sun-dried tomatoes, but if you keep them raw..." I shiver. "Vile."

"That's pretty harsh."

"It's the truth."

Our server steps up to our table, and I watch as Hudson studies the wine list and orders some fancy wine I've never heard of—praying it's white—and then he continues with what I want to say is sea bass but couldn't be sure. He rambled about a lot of things, and I was so caught up in watching his lips that I got distracted.

Dinner should be a fun surprise.

"So," I say when the server leaves. "How was your day?"

"You were there," he says. "You should know."

"Was I really though?" I ask. "Sure, I was in the vicinity of your day, but I wasn't really in the room. So I wouldn't know how your day went exactly. Seemed pretty smooth, no big fires that you had to put out, right?"

"Right," he says softly, not elaborating.

"Okay, so should we say an average day?"

He adjusts the cuffs of his shirt. "I told Hardy about the wedding."

Did you just hear that?

The sound of something getting the life sucked out of it?

Yeah, that was my right nipple shriveling into dust.

Why? Because Hardy is attached to the company. Who else is attached to the company? My brother. And the more people who know about the wedding, the more likely Jude will find out.

"You...you told your brother?"

"I did." He lightly nods.

"Okay, sure, because you know, congratulations are in order." I nervously twist my hands together in my lap. "Did he, uh, did he say that he was going to get us a wedding gift? Because a coffee maker would be aces."

"He did not."

"Sure, sure. Shame though because we could really use—"

"He was pissed, Sloane."

"Ah, yes. Not surprised by that reaction. Now, was he madder at you or at me, just so I can gauge how to be around him?"

"What do you think?" he asks.

"I was trying to be polite. I know he's pissed at you."

"Correct," he answers.

"Well, did you, uh, did you tell him not to share the news?"

"I did," he answers. "He said he'll be telling Everly because he tells her everything."

"Respectful. Just like I should tell you everything since you're my husband. Which reminds me, I've been keeping a secret. You know the green drink I was getting you in the morning? It was just a Naked Juice that I kept pouring into the same to-go cup. I found that if I skipped the stop at the juice bar, I could get ten minutes of extra sleep." When he just stares at me, I say, "I'm realizing in this moment that revealing that might not have been the best timing." I motion to him. "Please, carry on."

I catch the flare of his nostrils, but to his credit, he doesn't say anything—which might have been great timing in reality because I'm not getting a lecture. Also, the green drink I did get him the other day, the one without sugar, that was from the actual juice bar. Given the situation, I thought the stop was appropriate.

"He believes it was the wrong move and that if your brother finds out, I'm dead."

I press my lips together, because yes, that is far too correct. Hudson will be hung by his balls. "Very true, which is why he's not going to find out. We won't be married for very long, and we won't even be here, in San Francisco, for very long either. Aren't we going to London soon? Do you want me to book those tickets? Because I can."

"In a week," he answers. "Until then, we need to lie low."

"Right, so going out to dinner at an intimate restaurant is a total no-go," I say, glancing around the quiet restaurant, where tables are lit up by a single lamp.

"You realize you don't always have to lean on sarcasm to have a conversation."

"I do realize that, but unfortunately for the both of us, that's not how my brain works, especially when I'm nervous. I would just accept that 80 percent of what comes out of my mouth is going to be pure shit."

"Great," he says on a sigh.

"Hey, consider yourself lucky."

"Why?" he asks.

"Because I'll keep you on your toes, so you might never know what's going to come out of my mouth."

"That's not something to feel lucky about," he says. "That's the exact opposite."

"Ehh, agree to disagree."

"Okay, what's in this sauce? Because if we were not in public, I would be licking this dinner off my plate like a freaking rabid dog." I lick my fork and glance over at Hudson, who has a not-so-pleased expression tugging on those thick, scary eyebrows of his. "What?" I ask.

"Can you act more civil?"

"Civil?" I ask, sitting up straight. "Shit, am I supposed to be sipping my wine with my pinky out?"

"Sloane," he chastises.

"Yes?"

"I'm being serious."

"So am I. The pinky question is a solid one."

"I'm talking about you licking your fork."

"Oh," I say, staring down at my fork. "I was just cleaning it off. Am I not supposed to be licking it? Because… Oh…hold on." A smile crosses over my lips. "Is it turning you on?"

He dabs his mouth with his napkin and shakes his head. "No, it's not."

I nudge his leg with my foot under the table. "Liar," I say. "It was. It was turning you on."

"It was not. It's just…inappropriate behavior."

"Are you afraid I'm going to turn on the people around us?" I look around the dining area. "Oh, I just caught a gentleman looking at me."

"Who?" Hudson says with such possessiveness that it makes me chuckle.

"I'm just kidding. Settle down, jealousy."

"That's not funny," he says, positioning his silverware in that fancy way that tells the server that he's done with his meal. Probably something he learned in finishing school. Not sure he ever went, but I would be surprised if he didn't, or if he at least didn't have a tutor that taught him all the proper ways to poise yourself in public when you have the last name Hopper.

"Do you ever think anything is funny?"

"I do."

"Uh-huh, do you ever think I'm funny?"

"No," he answers while taking a sip of his wine.

"You know, that's hurtful."

"Say something funny and maybe I'll laugh."

"Challenge accepted." I take the last bite of my sea bass and then set my fork down. "You know, you were a different person in Bora Bora."

"Yeah, so were you," he says. "You barely said two words on that trip, and now it's like I can't get you to be quiet."

"Ever consider that it was intimidating to go on a trip with a family I didn't know and having to be on my best behavior for my brother? Not to mention, it was the first time we'd ever been on vacation? We were just trying to fade into the background and enjoy ourselves."

He swirls his wine in his glass. "What about when you first started working for me? You were different then too."

"Because I was trying to impress. I didn't want to do anything to jeopardize my job."

"And when did that change? Because I fired you over that mouth of yours."

"You called me young. It's a trigger for me because Jude has always babied us, and I hate it. Don't get me wrong. I'm grateful for the way he protected me and Stacey, but I've hated the way he hasn't trusted our instincts. He's constantly hovering. I understand him wanting to protect us, but we're adults now, and he hasn't quite come to terms with that. Given the way I had to grow up pretty quickly, skipping out on a childhood most get to enjoy, the term 'young' aggravates me."

He slowly nods but doesn't say anything. Not sure if he's trying to take it all in or if he doesn't care, but either way, the nonanswer grates on me. I opened up; a reaction would be good, especially if we're supposed to be taking this husband-and-wife thing seriously.

"What about you?" I ask. "Why are you different? In Bora Bora you were more carefree. Now, for a lack of better words, it seems like you have a stick up your ass."

"Life was different then," he answers.

"Care to elaborate?"

"No."

"Well, that's not very husbandly. I thought we were supposed to share everything with each other."

"Sharing everything was never in the contract."

"Okay, so then what do I need to know, Hudson?" I ask, not liking this one-sided situationship.

"What you already know."

"Uh-huh." I lean back in my chair. "Well, I don't know very much."

"Exactly," he says just as the server stops by our table.

"How was everything?" he asks.

"Wonderful," Hudson says. "We'll take the check."

"Right away," he answers as he motions for someone else to come pick up our plates.

We spend the rest of the time in the restaurant in silence while he pays the bill and our table is cleared.

It's silent.

Tense.

And it's obvious that he wants to pretend this marriage is real without doing the work to make it seem real. He can call me *wife* all he wants, but that's not going to bridge the gap of creating a relationship where we can make this deal work and make it work well.

When he's done, we both stand from the table, and I grab my purse while Hudson waits for me. Once I have everything, he surprises me by placing his hand on my lower back once again and guiding me through the restaurant. For anyone else, it's a subtle touch that I'm sure is not thought of twice, but to me, it feels like he's palming a scorching-hot pressure point. A move that is sending my mind into a tailspin because I can feel just how large his hand is against my back, the length of his fingers, the pressure of his touch.

There's a hint of protection, of possessiveness.

He leads me to the valet, where he hands the man working the podium our ticket. As we wait, Hudson lowers his hand from my back, and I miss the feel of him—that is until he reaches down and takes my hand in his. My eyes flit between the connection and back up at him.

"What are you doing?"

"Holding my wife's hand," he says as he looks straight ahead, his posture tall, not an ounce of uncertainty to be found.

"I see that, but why?"

His eyes meet mine and he says, "You're my wife, are you not?"

"I am."

"Then that means I hold your hand."

"Uh-huh, yup, I understand that, but what I don't understand is—"

He leans close to my ear, his lips nearly caressing my skin. "We're going to be in London together, married, in front of people that matter. Consider this practice."

"Right," I say as he moves away and I'm able to catch my breath. So he's good with this kind of show of being married but not talking. "Got it."

When his car pulls up in front of us, he opens the door for me and helps me in before tipping the valet and joining me. He pulls out onto the road and holds the steering wheel with one hand while he slips his other hand so casually onto my thigh that, to him, it seems like second nature.

To me, umm...not so much.

Every muscle inside me starts twitching from the feel of his warm palm on my thigh. My stomach twirls and somersaults. My inner thighs tremble. And for a brief second, I consider lifting my long-ass dress up and letting him actually touch my skin.

While we drive through the streets of San Francisco, the dark night lit up by streetlamps, I have a million questions I want to ask him. So many about him, about his intentions, if he's ever thought about me the way I've thought about him, but I hold back because I know he won't answer them. Like I said, he's not the same man he once was. He's different.

He's subdued.

Focused.

Uninterested in conversation.

So instead, I stare out the window while he holds on to me, and I revel in the moment.

———

"You know, usually your assistant does tasks for you, but it seems as though you have your driver do things for you now," I say as I observe every last article of clothing of mine hung or folded in Hudson's closet.

"Corinne, my housekeeper, put away your clothes."

I open a drawer where I see my underwear and bras lined up neatly. Well, thank God for Corinne, because here I thought Bart was folding my thongs. Not sure I'd be able to look him in the eye.

I move past my pajamas and snag one of Hudson's shirts again because they smell amazing and are comfortable. Teeth already brushed, I go to the bathroom and change out of the long dress I don't ever plan on wearing again. I deposit my dirty clothes in the hamper and then walk into the bedroom, where I see Hudson, shirtless and looking through his phone while lying in bed.

The man never stops.

I move to my side of the bed and then stop short when I see my vibrator casually placed on my nightstand. Nothing discreet about it.

Yup, thank God Corinne unpacked.

I pick it up and open the nightstand drawer where I place it, something Corinne could have done, but you know, we're not going to be mad at her; she might have been worried that I might not know where she put it.

When I slip under the covers, Hudson sets his phone down on his charger and adjusts his pillow. "Don't use that when I'm around."

"Excuse me?" I ask, turning toward him.

"Your vibrator—don't use it when I'm around."

"Uh...do you really think I'm about to just pull it out and get myself off while I'm next to you in bed?"

"You're too unpredictable. I have no damn idea."

"Well, I won't," I say, feeling insulted. "And just for the record, if I wanted to get myself off in front of you, I would, because I'm your wife, and I have no shame in it."

"If my wife wants to get off, then she asks me," he says, looking all kinds of tense and irritated.

"Oh yeah? So if I told you, Mr. Nose Kisser, I was horny and needed desperately to come, you would do that for me?"

His lips purse and he doesn't respond.

"That's what I thought. Please save the lectures. I don't plan on letting you in on the pure pleasure of seeing how I can please myself. That's sacred to me and only the luckiest of people get to be involved. Like... ahh, like Devin."

"Who the fuck is Devin?" he asks as I lie on my back and stare up at the ceiling.

"Uh, we talked about this. The one guy who made me orgasm. I told you about him. You know, maybe when this farce is all said and done, I'll give him a call. I'll need the release after whatever hell you're going to put me through."

I can practically hear his teeth grinding, and I love every second of it. I know I shouldn't be poking the bear, but the audacity of this man.

When he talks to me, he insults.

When I talk to him, he doesn't answer.

I would say this marriage is off to a rocky start.

"He worked hard," I say. "Really hard, because he knew how good I was at giving head, so he wanted to return the favor and, God, was it good."

"Enough," Hudson says, which makes me smile. So he doesn't see me, I turn away from him and snuggle into my pillow.

"Sheesh, and here I thought we were sharing everything."

"You're goading me."

"How am I goading you? The only way it would be goading is if you felt the same away about me." I glance over my shoulder. "And I think we both know you'd never admit to having an attraction toward me, not even a hint. Unless..." I flip around to face him now and come face-to-face, unaware that he was looking in my direction. I gulp for a second when his eyes light up under the moonlit room. "Um, unless you do find me attractive."

"I find you annoying."

See? Insults!

"And too young."

I hold up my finger. "No, don't do that, don't use my trigger word. You should know better by now."

"It's fucking true," he says.

"Okay, so if I weren't eighteen years your junior—"

"Thirteen," he says with an edge to his voice.

"Okay, if I weren't thirteen years your junior, are you telling me that you wouldn't care, and you'd lift my shirt up and over my head right now and have your way with me?"

"It's my shirt to begin with...and no."

"And why not?"

"Because you're Jude's sister."

"Which makes me off-limits. What if I weren't his sister?"

"I'm not playing this game with you, Sloane. There's a multitude of reasons why this will never happen. Those just being a few."

"But none of them are because you're not attracted to me."

His jaw clenches, but his eyes never falter as they stay locked on mine.

"Interesting," I say. "Well, good to know where you stand. Now if you don't mind, I think I might use my vibrator now." I turn and reach for it when his hand quickly wraps around my waist and stops me. He pulls me in close to his body, my back to his heated chest.

He whispers into my ear and says, "Don't even fucking think about it."

I can feel my heartbeat in my throat.

He's so close, my body pressed against his.

His lips nearly tickling my ear.

His hand splayed across my stomach.

"You're...you're not being a very good husband," I say, my voice shaking. "Happy wife, happy life."

"You're not being a very good wife, tempting your husband like this."

"Maybe if my husband weren't such a stuck-up snob, I wouldn't need to tempt him."

"What do you want from me?" he asks, his thumb gliding over my stomach. The intensity in his voice is anything but teasing.

Hell, I feel like if I say the wrong thing, I very well might get spanked. Although that's not a bad thing.

"I want you to not be an asshole," I answer.

"I'm not trying to be an asshole. I'm under a great deal of stress."

"And I've told you, let me help you ease that stress," I say, shifting my ass so I press directly into his crotch.

"Don't," he says, his grip on me growing tighter. "Just...fuck, don't."

And there it is—a microcrack in his otherwise strong facade.

That break in his voice.

That stutter in his sentence.

A part of me wants to push him, to see how far he'd let me go, but the other part of me, the one where I see this man struggling, knows that maybe if I push too far, he'll shut down altogether. And I don't want that. He's already teetering on barely talking to me. I don't want to make it worse.

So I let out a deep breath and quietly say, "Sorry."

Then I lift his arm off me and scoot away, toward my side of the bed. I keep my back toward him to avoid any awkwardness. And for a moment, as I get comfortable, I half expect him to pull me back toward him, to wrap his arm around me, but when he doesn't and just turns away, I know it's for the best.

This isn't over though. I need to find a way to make that connection with him. Because if we're going to sell this marriage, then I need to be more comfortable with him than just on the physical side. I need to be mentally there too.

CHAPTER NINE
SLOANE

"SHOULDN'T YOU BE WITH YOUR husband right now?" Stacey says as she opens the door to our house.

"He has a meeting," I say, lumbering into the living room, my purse hanging off my shoulder.

"Why does it seem like you're no longer living in wedded bliss?"

I flop on the couch and drop my purse to the floor. "I was never living in wedded bliss. Ever since this ring has been slipped on my finger, I've been living in purgatory."

"That seems awfully harsh," Stacey says as she takes a seat next to me. "It can't be that bad. You're living with a billionaire."

"It is for someone who likes to talk. Who enjoys conversation. For someone who is attempting to get to know the other person. For him, I'm sure he's having a ball of a time."

"I see," Stacey says. "He's all clammed up?"

"Yes." I glance down at the coffee table and notice paint samples. I pick them up and start sorting through them as I continue. "He wants to take the marriage seriously, but when I ask him things about himself, it's as if he doesn't know how to use words. He just stops talking. And how am I supposed to act like this man is my husband when I couldn't tell you what his favorite color is?"

"Why does it matter?"

"Because," I say, handing her a green that I really like, "he's acting like this marriage is real, hence why I'm currently living with him rather than here." I toss another green at her. "Are you picking colors without me by the way?"

"Just perusing. I wouldn't make any final choices without you."

I sink into the couch and stare up at the ceiling. "What am I doing, Stacey? I should be here, helping with the house. I mean, this exciting thing is happening for us, we are working to purchase this place, and here I am, attempting to play wifey with my boss."

"It's only temporary," she says. "It's not like it's going to be like this forever."

"Feels like forever." I turn toward her. "At dinner last night, we sat in silence for over five minutes. I know this because I checked my phone. Five minutes, Stacey—that's unheard of with me. But after a while of him not responding, I just kind of gave up. It's not healthy. This situation is not healthy."

"Five minutes, wow, I'm surprised you didn't explode."

"I know." I toss my hands up in the air. "And the worst part is that on the drive home, he put his hand on my thigh." I grip her arm. "My thigh, Stacey. I can't remember the last time my thigh was touched. It made my insides flip upside down. Then of course I went into a perpetual state of horniness, and let's just say it wasn't pretty after that."

"Yeah, no need to get into the details."

I groan. "And I have a whole week of this, and then God knows how long we'll be in London. I can't...I can't live like this. The silence. It's going to eat me alive."

"Then keep trying to talk to him. If anyone can break him, it's you, with your constant chatter and nonsense."

"I would take offense to that if it wasn't so true." I sit up taller. "Enough about my sham of a marriage. Tell me what you're thinking about for the house."

"Well, before I pull out my binder and show you every little thing that

I've thought of, let me end with this: Don't let yourself be uncomfortable with him. If you're going to make this work and pull it off, he's going to have to meet you halfway. So keep pushing, okay? Don't let him dictate how this relationship will work."

"You're right." I sigh heavily. "He's not the boss of me. I'm the boss of me."

"Well, technically, he is your boss, but I understand what you're saying. Take charge."

I slam my fist into the couch, feeling reinvigorated. "Take charge. That I can do. Now…show me this folder. We have a house to work on."

"Thanks for bringing home dinner," I say, as I help Hudson with the take-out bags.

He texted earlier and asked if I liked Thai food. It was an immediate yes for me. While he was gone, I pulled out my phone and started writing down conversation starters, things I thought he would answer without realizing that he was opening up to me.

Not just a hat rack, my friends.

"I'll grab plates," he says as he heads into the kitchen while I take the food to the dining room table. I will say this: Thank God I know Hudson well enough to move around in his space like this without feeling too awkward. If this arrangement was with someone else, I don't think I would feel as comfortable.

While he grabs plates and silverware, I fill up two glasses with sparkling water for us and take two lime wedges out of a Tupperware bin and place them on the side. When I make it back to the table, he's removing his suit jacket and rolling up the sleeves of his dress shirt.

I avert my eyes from his forearms. I've stared at them long enough before to know the effect they have on me. Tonight is about business and getting him to open up. Simple as that.

We pull out the cartons of food and start digging in together, filling up our plates with a plethora of noodles, steamed veggies, and curry chicken.

"Smells amazing," I say. "Is this where you order from normally?"

Question number one. Simple but hopefully effective.

"Yes," he answers, falling for it.

I wait for him to say more, but when he doesn't, I feel an edge of defeat. Okay, it's fine, it was just a warm-up.

"Where did you find it?" I set down the steamed veggies and pick up my fork.

"On my way home," he answers and squeezes his lime into his water.

On his way home. Well, that tells me that he's observant while driving and that this place is near him. So...that's a whole lot of nothing.

"Wow, this chicken, it's so good. Is this what you always get?"

"Yes," he answers and then sticks a piece of chicken into his mouth and chews without looking at me.

Creature of habit. Got it.

Think I wore out the food talk, so I let him sit in silence for a moment while I casually pull up the notes on my phone and look at the next question I can ask.

Clearing my throat, I say, "How was your meeting?"

I know it's an easy question and I shouldn't need a reminder in my notes, but I have a process, a slow process to get him to open up. Watch me peel him like an onion.

"Fine," he answers.

"Talk about everything you needed to talk about?"

He glances up from his food for a moment to look at me, and I nearly lose the air in my lungs from that one quick flash of his baby blue eyes.

"Yes."

"Great." I swallow. "That's really great. Don't you love it when meetings are successful?"

He eyes me for a moment. "What are you up to?"

"Nothing," I say. Oh God, is he catching on to me already? "I'm up to nothing."

"Why are you acting...weird?"

"You think this is weird? I'm just having a conversation. Nothing weird about that." I stab a piece of broccoli with my fork. "Just normal conversation is all." I chew my piece of broccoli, panic surging through me as he stares me down. "So, uh...do you want to talk about the biggest disappointment you ever experienced in your life?"

"Jesus," he mutters just as his phone rings in his pocket. He pulls his phone out, looks at the screen and says, "Excuse me." Then he takes off to the balcony where he answers the phone, leaving me alone in the dining room knowing damn well I failed.

"So, this is nice, isn't it?" I say as we walk together a few blocks from the office for a meeting. I suggested walking since it was close, thinking it would be a great time to try to talk to him.

"Hmm?" he asks as he stares down at his phone.

"Do you think you could put the phone down for a second?" I ask. "You know, watch where you're going so you don't get run over by a vehicle. I'm not ready to be a widow."

"Is anyone ever really ready to be a widow?" he asks, slipping his phone in his pocket.

"Maybe if they're not a fan of their spouse." I nudge him with my elbow. "Are you a fan of me?"

He quickly glances in my direction. "What are you doing?"

"Why do you always ask me that when I'm trying to make conversation? Isn't it obvious what I'm doing?"

"It's obvious that you're trying to do more than you have to."

"Some might say having a conversation with another person is a basic human right. Would you not agree?" I ask.

"I think we can just walk to a meeting without having to engage in any conversation at all. We can walk in silence."

"That is not ideal for me. I like to talk."

"So I've noticed," he says.

"So why don't you indulge your wife and answer her question? Are you a fan of me?"

"Jesus, Sloane."

I stop, causing him to stop and turn toward me. "I'm being serious, Hudson."

He tugs on his neck and says, "If I wasn't a fan of you, do you think I would have married you?"

I shrug. "I don't know. I was pretty convenient."

"With a whole lot of baggage if certain people were to find out about us. I wouldn't risk everything over someone I wasn't a fan of."

Well, when he puts it like that...

Coyly tucks hair behind ear

"That might be the nicest thing you've said to me since we got married."

His expression falls. "That's sad."

"Says the guy who can't give a compliment to his wife. You want to take this seriously, but any chance of me getting close to you, you back away."

"I'm not backing away," he groans. "Just...drawing a line."

"Not a fan of the line."

He walks up to me, takes my hand in his, and then leans in. "The line won't change."

Then, continuing to hold my hand, we walk down the sidewalk, him not saying another word while I contemplate if this was a small win for me or not.

I mean, he's holding my hand; I'm going to call it a win.

———

"I need to find out what kind of laundry detergent you're using on your clothes." I sniff his shirt that I'm wearing. "God, it smells so good."

He sets his phone down on his charger and turns out the light.

I settle on my pillow and turn toward him. "Want to play rapid-fire questions?"

"I want to go to bed," he says.

"Okay, Grandpa," I tease. "It's just past nine. You can spare a few questions."

"Go to bed, Sloane."

I'm met with the normal grumpy answer. It's the same thing over and over again, but he hasn't worn me down yet. It's a battle of wills, and I want to be the one who wins.

"Hey," I say, poking him in the chest.

His eyes open and they fixate on me. "What?"

"How was your day?"

"Fine," he answers.

"Want to ask me how mine was?"

His jaw grows tight as he says, "How was your day?"

"Well, I woke up early this morning thinking I was beating you to the shower, but then I noticed you weren't even in bed. Come to find out, you were out for a run. I enjoyed seeing you all sweaty in the kitchen. Sorry I missed you doing push-ups though."

"Are you going to recount your whole day?"

"Yes," I answer. "Thank you for asking. I appreciated you making breakfast for me. It was sweet, and you make some really good oatmeal."

"Thanks," he says, the anger easing a little.

Okay, I might have him hooked. Keep talking.

"Even though we ate in silence, I saw you stealing glances at me, and I thought that was a sweet, husbandly thing to do."

He clears his throat and says, "I liked your outfit today."

Well, holy shit, color me shocked. A freaking compliment. Maybe he does listen to my constant chatter and suggestions.

Be cool.

Be freaking cool.

Don't scare him away.

"Thank you," I say. "Once you were ready for work and we were driving over to the office, I appreciated that you let me pick the music. I also liked that you kept your hand on my thigh the entire time."

"Just getting you used to my touch," he says.

"Well, I liked it. Anyway, the day went by slow. Lots of emails and scheduling, which is never fun. Somehow started receiving these weird pigeon emails from JP Cane. Do you know what that's about?"

"Don't even ask," he says as he grows even more relaxed.

I take a risk, and I allow my hand to travel to his chest, where I carefully drag my thumb over his skin. When he doesn't shoo me away, I remain in the same position and keep talking.

"Lunch was kind of boring, since you didn't talk to me again but ate in silence. That seems to be a thing with you." When he doesn't have a response to that, I keep going. "Then I read an article today about how to please your husband because, you know, we're doing this for real, and one of the things was to tease him. So I tried teasing you."

"How did you tease me?" he asks.

"Remember when I was in the closet, about to change, I kept flashing my leg in the doorway."

"That's what you were doing? I thought you were trying to get out of your pants."

Well, that's one way to pee on my parade.

"No, that was me being teasingly seductive."

"Didn't get that," he says as I continue to rub my thumb over his chest.

"That's...depressing. Maybe it needs to be my breast next time."

"Please...keep your breasts to yourself."

"Can't hear that enough," I say, and then for a brief moment, a very brief moment, I swear I see his lip turn up in humor. But it's too fleeting for me to confirm. "Dinner was fine, watching a show with you was fine as well, and now that we're here in bed, I like that you're allowing me to talk to you."

"Is that all?" he asks.

"I think so. Do you have anything to add?"

"No," he answers.

"Not even a little something, like...like how you enjoy me touching your chest right now?"

"I don't enjoy it."

My thumb pauses and I feel my hope fall flat as I say, "You don't enjoy it?"

He wets his lips. "What I meant to say was, I shouldn't enjoy it."

"Oh." I feel a smile tug on my lips. "Just like I shouldn't enjoy your hand on my thigh?"

"Yeah," he says, letting out a heavy breath. He then takes my hand, removes it from his chest, and places it next to me, but he doesn't let go right away, instead his thumb rubs over the sensitive part of my wrist. "I'm sorry, Sloane."

"Sorry for what?" I ask, butterflies erupting in my stomach with every pass of his thumb.

"Sorry for not being the type of partner you want in this."

"You don't need to apologize. I just, I just wish that you would open up a little."

"I can't," he says.

"Why not?"

"Because." His Adam's apple bobs. "Because I just can't."

Then he releases my hand and turns away from me, scooting to his side of the bed and shutting down immediately.

Internally, I'm screaming no because I felt like I had him, he was right there with me, in the moment, but then he just snapped out of it, and that is infuriating.

So infuriating.

CHAPTER TEN
HUDSON

I STARE AT MY COMPUTER in front of me, but my eyes blur, my brain fuzzy. Nothing makes sense. I can read email after email, but it doesn't stick because all I can think about is the last few nights and how close I was to giving in to the temptation that is my wife.

How easy would it have been to slide my hand under her shirt, to glide her underwear down her legs, and then just fucking feast.

It would have been so simple, and I know she would let me. She would have let me do whatever I wanted, and that's the problem. I have that knowledge in my head—I have the knowledge that she wants me.

She fucking wants me.

And if I didn't have one ounce of willpower, I would have taken advantage. I wouldn't have stopped; I would have kept going, taking and taking and taking, until there was nothing left for her to give. And then in the morning, she'd regret it.

Hell, I'd regret it.

I would feel guilty and like I used her, even though I know that's not the case.

But now, as I attempt to get work done, it's all I can think about.

And it's fucking painful.

Knock. Knock.

I look up at the door where Sloane is standing, looking gorgeous with her hair curled and floating over her shoulders. A shade of pink lipstick stains her plump lips, and a thick coat of mascara highlights her very innocent eyes.

This morning, she was nonchalant, charming, cool as a goddamn cucumber, acting as if nothing happened last night. She jabbered on about what fruit she likes best, strawberries and pineapples, and how she thinks they're the ultimate fruit pairing. I just listened because I really had nothing to say. I did ask Corinne to grab some fresh pineapple and strawberries at the store for me, you know, just to have them on hand.

For no other reason than just to have them.

Not because I want to make my wife happy.

Not because I'm trying to flirt with my wife.

Sloane also chose to wear one of the outfits she brought from home. A black skirt with a white shirt tucked in. She paired the outfit with black high heels, making her legs look impossibly long. And even though I was itching to touch her in the car, I kept my hands to my fucking self. Smart move on my part.

"Can I come in?" she asks, hesitant.

Fuck, look at her. She's so fucking beautiful.

So innocent.

"Yup." I lean back in my chair and press my finger to my cheek and my thumb under my chin. "What's up?"

"Well, first of all, are you sure you don't want your green drink? I can do the Naked Juice, or I can go to the juice bar and get the gross one."

"I'm sure," I answer, trying to keep my eyes off her legs.

"Okay, but if you change your mind, you just let me know. I'm aware how much you enjoyed your green drink. I don't want you changing your habits because now we're married."

"Shhhh," I say, looking over her shoulder toward the hallway. "Don't mention that shit here."

"You don't want me to mention that we're married?"

"No. Christ."

She glances around my office and says, "You do realize that this is the exact place where we tied the knot. If you didn't want people to know, then why did we perform the ceremony here?"

"Neutral zone, less intimidating, and I was able to do paperwork at the same time."

"So romantic," she says, clutching her heart. "I'll always recall the moment I said I do, with your stapler watching the magical moment. Or the way your computer hummed in the background. A true backdrop of love."

"You done?" I ask with a lift of my brow.

"Not to mention, the nose kiss. Ahh, I'll never forget the nose kiss."

"It wasn't on purpose," I say, hating that she keeps bringing it up. It's truly something I wish I could forget about.

"What were you thinking? Were you trying to make a memorable moment? Because I'll tell you right now, I would remember—"

Movement from behind her catches my eye and just as I see who it is, I sit up straight and call out, "Hey, Jude."

Sloane's eyes widen, and I watch her smartly slip her ring-covered hand into the pocket of her skirt. Panic courses through me as I slowly slide my ring off my finger and casually stick it in my pocket as well.

"Hey, Sloane," Jude says. "Haven't seen you in a while."

Jude is at least a foot taller than his sister, and even though they look alike, they also look very different, if that makes any sense. Where Jude is rough around the edges, with a bit of a bite in his voice despite not meaning it, Sloane is softer, sweeter despite being a constant ball of sarcasm.

"That's what happens when you marry," Sloane says. "You don't make time for your sister." Jude's brow knits together, which makes Sloane chuckle. "I'm kidding, relax. It's okay to have a life with your wife and to have time to yourselves."

"I'll talk to Haisley about having you and Stacey over."

"Might just have to be Stacey," Sloane says. "I'm going to be very busy with work. Very, very busy." I study her, watching for any tell that she's nervous, that she's holding something back.

She shifts on her feet.

She fidgets with her hair.

She avoids eye contact.

Fuck, I hope Jude doesn't notice.

Jude glances in my direction and then back to his sister. "Do you have new responsibilities?"

"Uh, yes. I mean no…I mean…I have taken on a new role."

Jesus Christ.

"What kind of new role?"

"A personal one," she says, her eyes cutting to me briefly.

Fuck, don't look over here!

I can practically feel the sweat drip down my back while I hang on every word Sloane says, hoping and praying she doesn't slip up and give away the knowledge that we are currently betrothed.

"A personal one?" Jude turns fully toward his sister. "What are you up to?"

"Nothing." She waves at him. "Absolutely nothing. Well, I mean…not nothing. Of course I'm up to something. But not like a tricky something. Just a regular something. Figuring out life, making changes, nothing you need to worry about at the moment."

"I don't like you hiding things from me, Sloane."

She nervously chuckles. "Now, now, can't tell a brother everything." She pats his arm. "Anyway, you have a call with London?"

"Do I?" I ask, confused as to where that came from.

"Not sure. Let me go check." She turns on her heels and heads out of my office, leaving me in a pool of sweat. Aw, it was her escape route.

"London? Would that be Archie?" Jude asks, still sporting a scowl.

"Yes," I answer, my voice surprisingly steady. "Trying to secure the deal."

"Smart." If only he knew what exactly was going into it to seal the deal, he wouldn't think it was that smart. "Well, I came in to get some blueprints of the building on Seventh. Hardy said they were delivered here."

Sloane comes back into the room and says, "No call. Silly me."

Jude's scowl grows, probably disapproving of her current...flakiness.

"Anywho, anything I can help with?" she asks, looking between us.

"Blueprints," I answer. "Jude is looking for blueprints for the building on Seventh."

"They must be up front because we don't have anything back here," Sloane says. "Unless you have them?" she asks me.

I shake my head. "Nope, don't have them."

Jude's eyes flit between the both of us, and I can't tell if he's just listening intently or trying to connect the dots. Either way, I feel like there is a giant billboard over my head, pointing at me and saying, *I married your sister and almost slipped my hand under her shirt last night.*

Finally, he says, "Okay, I'll check up front. Hardy made it seem like they were back here."

The idiot probably sent Jude back here on purpose just to make me sweat. Well, job accomplished because I'm going to need a new shirt after this.

"Hardy doesn't know what he's talking about a lot of the time," I say.

"Okay, well, are we still on for our meeting this week to catch up?" Jude asks.

Fuck, I forgot about that.

There is no way in hell I'm going to be able to sit through an hour-long meeting with Jude, just me and him, without looking like something is bothering me. I'm smooth, but not that fucking smooth.

"Shit, I was actually going to call you about that," I say, lying through my teeth. "I'm going to have to cancel. There's a lot I have to prepare for, and I don't have a lot of time."

"Not a problem. I didn't have much of an update. I just wanted to make sure we kept up-to-date on everything. How about I shoot you an email with the few things I wanted to discuss, and you can take a look at it when you get a chance?"

"Yeah, that works. And then we can resume our regular meetings once I, uh, get everything under control."

"That works," he says with a nod. He then turns to Sloane and says, "Dinner at my house soon. Got it?"

"Sheesh, a formal invitation would be nicer than a demand."

"But it's not an invitation," he says. "It is a demand."

"Lovely," she replies with a playful eye roll. "Always enjoy accommodating my older brother's demands."

"Good, because they're not going to stop." He moves toward the door. "Good luck with Archie."

"Will do," I call out, and then he gives his sister a quick hug and is out the door.

Sloane and I just stare, watching, waiting, not saying a goddamn thing until...

"He's in the elevator. Coast is clear," she says and then flops down on the couch in my office. "Mother of God, you made me nervous."

"I made you nervous?" I ask, pointing to my chest.

"Uh, yeah, because you became all squirrely and scared."

"I was not squirrely and scared. You were the one rambling on about nothing."

"Because he can smell a lie on me. I could see it in his eyes." She shakes her head. "You did not prepare me for this."

"How could I possibly prepare you? You just needed to act like nothing was going on."

"Uh, we could have come up with a story."

"What kind of story?" I ask.

She shrugs. "A *why am I so nervous around my brother* story."

"Jesus," I say while rubbing my brow.

"This is why we need to talk more." She motions between the two of us. "We need to have better communication." She pats the couch. "Let's chat."

I scoot my chair into my desk. "We have work to do, Sloane."

"You don't consider our marriage work?"

"No," I answer, causing her to groan in frustration.

"You know, I have a check in my bank account that begs to differ."

"Get back to your desk, Sloane." I take my ring out of my pocket and slip it back on my finger. I can feel her eyes on me, but I keep my gaze fixed on the screen in front of me. I'm not going to get into it with her here. Not when anyone can drop in and listen.

After a few seconds of silence, she rises from the couch and heads out of my office, shutting the door behind her. When the coast is clear, I lean back in my chair and let out a deep breath.

Fuck, what the hell did I get myself into?

"Sloane," I call out. "What is this noon meeting I have on the calendar?"

Silence.

I lean forward, attempting to look out my door.

"Sloane?"

There's some rummaging of bags and then she appears at my door, holding carryout in one hand and drinks in the other.

"The noon meeting is with me." She brings the food into the office and sets it out on the coffee table—two salad bowls, some bread, and iced teas.

"What do you mean it's with you?" I ask as she walks over to the door, shuts and locks it. Then she heads over to my desk, where she presses the button to frost my windows, giving us more privacy. "Sloane, what—"

She takes my hand in hers and pulls me over to the couch where she pushes me down and then takes a seat next to me.

Turning in my direction, she says, "Thought I would have lunch with my husband."

"This is not a good idea," I say.

"Why not?"

"Because the door is locked and the windows are frosted and you are in here. People are going to think that we're...doing something."

"Please, no one is going to think that. I think everyone in the office believes you're celibate."

"Really?" I ask, my brow knitting.

"I honestly have no idea. I don't really talk to anyone."

"Then why say that?"

"You make me nervous. I just say things."

"Not a good quality to have." I grab my salad and start to move off the couch. "I can eat at my desk and work."

"Wait, hold on," she says in protest. "Have lunch with me, Hudson. Get to know me. We can play twenty questions, or...or we can talk about goals. I really don't have any at the moment, trying to figure them out actually, but maybe you can help me—"

"We're not doing this, Sloane." I stand and take my salad over to my desk, leaving her to sit alone on the couch, and a part of me feels bad, ditching her, but I also...I don't want to know things about her. I don't want to be sitting that close to her. I don't want to be the one that becomes fucking attached.

I'm not worried about her.

I'm worried about me.

I've never had someone look at me the way that she does.

Nor have I ever had someone as persistent in wanting to know me like she does.

She's different. She wears an air of innocence that's addictive. And I know that if I open up to her, if I let her see a piece of me no one else has seen besides my siblings, I'll open myself to getting hurt.

And I can't get hurt.

Not by her.

There are too many connections between us.

She lets out a heavy sigh and says, "Why am I even wearing this?" I look up just in time to watch her pull her ring off and set it on the coffee table. My eyes narrow in on the diamond.

"Put that back on."

"Hudson, this is stupid." She crosses her arms over her chest. "This whole thing is stupid. You act like you want this to be real, but then you won't even spend time with me."

I stand from my desk and walk up to her. I bend over, pick up her ring, and then pull her up from the couch. Looking her dead in the eyes, I say, "You're wearing your ring."

"But what if—"

"You're wearing it," I repeat, my body now thrumming with the need to claim her. "You're my wife, and you will wear the ring I put on your finger."

Her expression falls. "You realize how possessive that sounds, right?"

But it's as if I want her to take this seriously and I fear that she won't unless pressed.

"You realize that you made a commitment to me and these rings will be worn."

"Oh my God, Hudson, it's not—" She blows out a frustrated breath. "You know what? You're right, I made a commitment to you, therefore I will honor said commitment. Thank you for the reminder." She gathers her food, and without another look back, she storms out.

And for some reason, that doesn't settle well with me because I can see something brewing behind those eyes. Something brewing that I know will come back to bite me in the ass. The only question is, when exactly is that going to happen?

———————————

I place the key to my car on the side table next to the garage stairs, and that's when I smell something.

Something…cooking.

Sloane left early from work today, claiming she needed to run some errands and because she seemed to be testy after she left at lunch, I thought that maybe it would be good to let her get some air and time away from me.

I had no clue what kind of errands she had to run, but I didn't care. I enjoyed the reprieve from her. Instead of constantly peeking out my office window to catch a look at her, I was able to get some work done. Answered a ton of emails, went over a few spreadsheets, and even looked over some résumés that Jude sent my way for another construction manager that the Canes approved of as well.

And now that I'm home, I'm reminded of exactly why I was able to get all of that work done.

I turn the corner into the kitchen, where I see two pots on the stove, flames beneath them, a chopped salad on the counter, and what seems to be garlic bread ready to be put in the oven.

Confused, I glance around the room, and when I don't see anyone, I start to worry that Sloane might have begun cooking but got distracted and pulled away. I wouldn't put it past her.

Clearing my throat, I say, "Sloane?"

"Is that my sugar dumpling?" a voice calls out from the pantry. And then all of a sudden, her head pops out and a large smile spreads across her face. "Daddy's home!"

Daddy?

Uh…no.

She steps out of the pantry wearing a frilly white-and-pink apron… and a pair of heels. That's it, nothing else.

I can feel all the blood drain from my body and pool in one certain area as she walks toward me, her tits barely contained by the top of the apron, copious amounts of side boob peeking out. Her hair is down, curled, and she's wearing bright red lipstick as she walks up to me and places her hand on my chest.

Instinctively, my hand falls to her hip, where I feel the waistband of her thong.

Her hands grip my face, and she stands on her toes and lightly presses a kiss to my nose.

The fucking nose.

When she releases me, she says, "I'm so glad you're home. Dinner is almost ready."

Then she turns away from me and goes to the oven, where she turns off the burners and lifts the lids off the pots.

My eyes travel up and down her body, taking in her sexy curves, the thickness of her thighs, her perfectly round ass. Her tits spilling out of the apron. Christ…

I clear my throat and attempt to take my eyes off her, but I can't. Not when she's…hell, not when she's dressed like that. It's every kitchen fantasy come true, and she knows it, because she's strutting around, bending over, showing off her ass.

"Sloane," I say, my voice coming out rough.

"Yes, darling?" she asks as she wipes her cheek with the back of her hand.

"What the fuck are you doing?"

"My wifely duties of course," she says as she moves around the counter, coming right up to me. She pats me on the chest and says, "That's what you want, right? A wife?"

Yup, I knew something was brewing when she left my office earlier. It was clear as day—I just didn't know she was going to go this far.

"Which reminds me, you didn't say if you liked my outfit."

She turns me to face her and then conducts a small spin, showing off her apron.

"Normally, when a husband comes home and finds his wife in an apron, cooking dinner, he slides in behind her, caresses her bare ass, and then spins her around to lift her up onto the counter to take advantage of the lack of clothing. Imagine my disappointment when my husband doesn't even compliment me on my outfit."

"This is not what I'm talking about when I claim you as my wife," I say.

"But this is what a wife does," she says, stepping in close. "They like to please their man, and what's one way to a man's heart?" When I don't answer, she says, "Foods and nudes."

"We don't do nudes."

"And why not?"

"You know why not. We can't cross that line, Sloane."

"Mm, shame," she says as she turns around and my eyes go directly to her ass again. It's impossible for me to look away, especially when she saunters like that. "Can you set the table please?"

"Can you put some clothes on please?" I ask, just as she whips a T-shirt off the counter, turns away from me, and undoes the apron. She fits my large T-shirt over her body and then turns toward me when it's firmly in place.

"Happy?"

No.

I don't answer her. Instead, I gather plates and silverware and then grab us both waters and set the table. Once everything's in place, I help her bring the food over, while she monitors the garlic bread in the oven.

Unsure of what else to do, I connect my phone to the Bluetooth speaker and play some subtle music so it's not completely quiet in the house. I can't imagine the conversation is going to be flowing tonight.

She removes the garlic bread from the oven and then slices it up, putting it in a bowl. She sets the bowl down and gestures to my seat.

"Go ahead, sit down."

"I can serve—"

"I got it," she says, moving my chair away from the table now so I can sit.

Unsure what she has up her sleeve, I timidly take a seat and then scoot my chair forward, but she stops me midway and sits down on my lap.

"What are you doing?" I ask.

"Serving you some dinner," she answers as she starts dishing some noodles on my plate, followed by some sauce.

"Do you have to do that on my lap?"

"You can hold my thigh in the car, so I can sit on your lap at the dining room table. After all, just getting comfortable with each other, right? We're a married couple, Hudson, we need to act like one."

And yup, my words are coming back to bite me in the ass.

Seeing that she's in the mood to prove something to me, I decide to go with it and allow her to sit on my lap.

She sprinkles Parmesan cheese onto my noodles and sauce, adds some salad on the side, and then loads up the plate with some pieces of bread.

I stare down at the plate, taking in the mound of food. "I don't eat that much."

She turns on my lap so her legs are between mine and she's sitting on one of my thighs. She wraps one arm around my shoulder, picks up the fork, and loads on some noodles. "This is for both of us."

"So you're going to sit here the entire dinner?"

"Yes," she answers. "The guy who gave me the best sex of my life used to let me sit on his lap like this when we ate cereal, although he never asked me to put a shirt on like you did."

She brings the fork up to my mouth and I part my lips despite her bringing up that fucker again. I know I shouldn't be jealous, and I know that she's probably talking about him on purpose to make me crazy and, Christ, is it working.

"Would you rather be naked right now?" I ask her.

"You know how I feel about foods and nudes," she says with a wiggle of her brows before she sets the fork in her mouth and slowly pulls off the noodles. After she chews and swallows, she asks, "Do you think we'll ever see each other naked?"

I nearly choke on the water I'm swallowing. I set the glass down and dab my mouth with my napkin. "What kind of question is that?"

"An honest one," she says. "It's obvious that you find me attractive. You know I find you attractive, and we're married, so it's inevitable, right? Like what if I just happened to walk in on you while you were showering?"

"You'd see me showering," I simply say.

"So you wouldn't care?"

"What are you trying to get at, Sloane?"

Frustrated, she blows out a breath and says, "You're all about treating this as a real marriage. But you won't talk to me about who you are as a person. Therefore, we can go to option two, and that's the other thing married couples do. They fuck. So don't you want to fuck? Don't you want to get rid of this tension? It's...it's getting in the way, and I feel like if we just fucked, then it wouldn't be a big deal. We could be the married couple we're supposed to be and then we can go on our merry ways when it's all over."

"No, Sloane."

"Why not?" she asks as she pushes the food away and takes a seat on the table in front of me to really get a good look.

"Because it would complicate things."

"Things are already complicated," she says. "They became complicated the moment we got married."

"This will make it that much more complicated."

She folds her arms at her chest. "Then how the hell am I supposed to treat you as my husband if you won't open up to me and you won't fuck me? This is like being in jail. You want to take this seriously, but you're making it impossible to do that."

She has a very valid point, one that I have no counterpoint to. All I have is, I don't want to open up to her because I don't open up to anyone but my brother and sister. I don't want her knowing the shitty side of my life because, in the grand scheme of things, it's going to come off as the whiny rich boy who didn't get the parental attention he wanted.

And fucking her? That's completely off the table. I know the minute I give an inch, I'm going to take a fucking mile from her.

"You realize you're not being a hero by denying me, right?" she continues. "Like, I don't think that you're some white knight, swooping in and saving my vagina from complication."

"That's not what I think."

"Then what is it?" she asks, exasperated. "Is it Jude?"

"Yes, it's Jude," I say as I place my hands on her bare thighs. "I married you. That's bad enough as it is, but if he knew I fucked you? Christ, Sloane, it could kill the business. Okay? It could hurt everything my brother and I have put together. It could hurt the relationship with Cane Enterprises. It could hurt Maggie and Brody, tarnish my relationship with Hardy. There is so much at stake, and I can't be the selfish one here and think with my dick. I have to be smart."

I watch as she processes what I said, her mind working overtime.

And to reassure her, I say, "If I had it my way, my actions would be different." That's when her eyes find mine, hope in her gaze, so I add, "But it's not up to me. My dad spent his life being selfish, and I refuse to be the same person."

She slowly nods and then exhales. "I can see where you're coming from. I don't agree with it because I'm a big girl, and I can make my own decisions. I don't base my life around what my brother will think and how he will react. But sure, if that's the way you want to handle this, then so be it."

She hops off the table and goes to her side, where she picks up my plate and dumps half of the food onto her plate. When she starts digging in, I attempt to read her body, which is giving pissed-off vibes.

Just great.

"Sloane," I say while I pick up my fork.

"Hmm?" she asks, her mouth full of pasta.

"Don't be mad."

She chews, swallows, and then says, "I'm not mad."

"I can tell you're mad."

"How? You haven't given me the time of day to get to know me."

I work my jaw back and forth, not appreciating the slight jab. "The tone in your voice, your body language, your response to what I said— that's how I can tell you're mad," I say, naming a few.

"Well, you know, Hudson, maybe I am mad." She sets her fork down. "I'm irritated with the situation. You're giving mixed signals. One moment you're keeping me at arm's length, the next you're pressing your hand to my upper thigh while we drive around. What the hell am I supposed to do with that? You want to be married, but you don't want to be married. It's confusing."

Because it is fucking confusing. I'm stuck between a rock and a hard place here. I can't give in and take what I want from her at the risk of hurting her, because Jude would kill me. But I also can't just use her; I need to treat her with care, with affection and respect. It's a fine line I'm trying to walk, and apparently, I'm doing a real shit job.

"I'm not trying to give you mixed signals, Sloane. I'm trying to be honest," I say, imploring her to understand. "As I said, this isn't a simple case of whether or not I'm attracted to you. This is about my business. The people who count on me—"

"You say that, but I don't really believe that's what's going on here. I think you're afraid that I'll get attached. That if we 'complicate' this situation with sex or with getting to know each other, you're afraid you're going to break the young girl's heart. Trust me, I can handle my feelings. I don't need anyone looking out for me."

"I know you can look out for yourself," I say.

Annoyed, she pushes away from the table and picks up her plate. "If you truly thought that, then you would have no problem spreading me across this table and having me for dinner or sitting on that couch and telling me all about your childhood," she says. "Because you'd know that I could handle whatever I got myself into. Instead, you're protecting me—"

"I'm protecting me," I say, pointing to my chest. "I'm protecting myself from...from being the one that gets attached. You're different, Sloane. I'm aware how different you are, and if I allow myself to explore just how different, then I know I'm going to be crossing a line I shouldn't be crossing. I'm protecting the people around me by keeping my distance."

"You're not keeping your distance by sleeping in the same bed, holding my hand, running your thumb over my wrist."

"Because you deserve affection," I say before I can stop myself. "Because you deserve the kind of care that comes with being a wife. This has nothing to do with attachment on your end."

She shakes her head. "No, because if you truly believed that, then you wouldn't think twice about everyone else because you'd know that whatever we did wouldn't cause me to fall apart in the end. But the trust isn't there, which is fine, because why would it be? You don't know me. As your assistant, you haven't taken the chance to get to know me, and now that I'm your wife, the pattern continues. I thought we could have some fun, get to know one another on a deeper level, but I get it. I understand the assignment."

Plate in hand, she heads toward the balcony when I stand and stop her, my hand to her stomach. "Sloane, I trust you."

Her eyes connect with mine, and she smiles sadly. "You don't."

And then she moves out from under my touch and toward the balcony, where she eats dinner alone.

CHAPTER ELEVEN
SLOANE

"NO SEX FOR ME," I say as Stacey takes a seat on Hudson's bed.

"Uh, should I be upset about that?" Stacey asks as she smooths her hand over the fluffy comforter. "Jesus, this is rich."

"You should be upset about it," I say as I fold my laundry on the floor in front of her, preparing for the trip to London. We leave tomorrow, and after living like zombies who don't speak to each other for the last two days, I'm looking forward to getting the hell out of here.

"Why would I be upset about it? Isn't it good not complicating things between you and Hudson?"

I fold one of my lace bras and look up at my sister. "We're married. Pretty sure it doesn't get more complicated than that."

"The marriage is a piece of paper. It really doesn't mean that much. A true marriage is built on love and the life you form together. You guys haven't built anything together other than a fantastic lie."

"I understand that, but I'm just...I'm frustrated."

"Why?" Stacey asks. "I thought the whole point of getting married was to buy the house." She picks up her phone and says, "Which we need to leave now if we're going to get to our meeting about said house on time." She flashes me her phone, showing me the time, and she's right. We don't want to be late.

I stand from the floor, leaving the laundry where it is. I grab a pair of jean shorts from the pile, slip off my sweats, and pull those on before tucking in my shirt. I finish the look with a hat and then slip on my Birkenstocks.

"Ready," I say and move out of the bedroom, Stacey following me.

We head down the stairs and I'm about to respond to her when I see Hudson walk through the garage door, surprising me. It's early. He's not supposed to be home yet.

"Uh, hi," I say. "What are you doing here?"

The tension between us immediately sucks all the air from the room as his eyes travel up and down my body, like they always do, as if he needs to mentally approve what I'm wearing.

When I say we've been walking around like zombies the last two days, I'm not kidding. We haven't spoken to each other, we've barely acknowledged one another, and when we have, it's been curt sentences.

There's anger simmering.

Irritation.

A lack of understanding.

It's a recipe for disaster for two people who are attempting to act like they're in love.

Hudson tears his eyes off me when he notices Stacey to the side. "Hey, Stacey."

Stacey looks between us, clearly sensing the awkward and uncomfortable tone as she says, "Hey, Hudson. How's my favorite brother-in-law?"

Leave it to Stacey to push the limits.

Hudson visibly looks uncomfortable as he says, "Fine."

"Why are you here?" I repeat.

His eyes move back to mine as he says, "I live here."

"Yes, but you work in the office. Shouldn't you be on the phone, ignoring me?"

Hudson's eyes narrow. "I'm meeting Hardy and wanted to change because I'm going to the gym after. That answer good enough for you? Or do you need more of an explanation?"

"Ooh," Stacey whispers in the background.

"That explanation will suffice."

I head toward the front door, and he calls out, "Where are you going? Shouldn't you be packing?"

"I should," I say and keep walking toward the entrance.

"Are you done?" Hudson asks.

"You'll find out when you go upstairs." I nod toward the door. "Come on, Stacey."

I'm about to exit the house when he says, "Want to be treated like an adult, Sloane? Then act like one."

That pauses me midstep because where the hell did that come from? As far as I know, I'm the one actually communicating, unlike him.

"What did you say?"

"You heard me," he says.

Did this man really come into this house guns blazing, ready to pick a fight?

I forget that my sister is even here as I march right up to Hudson and stand toe to toe with him. "We have a very long trip ahead of us, Husband. I suggest you try to get along with me, rather than start more turmoil between us, because if anything, I'm the one trying to grow this relationship, not you."

His jaw grows tense as he stares down at me, a comeback on the tip of his tongue. Finally he says, "When will you be home?"

"I don't know." I turn away from him, but he grabs my hand and spins me back, right into his brawny chest.

"Will you be here for dinner?"

My mouth goes dry as his eyes zero in, those beautiful, sultry eyes of his. And I hate this. I hate that he has this power over me. That in an instant, he can steal all the air from my lungs.

"Don't plan on it," I say, my voice going shaky.

His hand connects with my neck and then slowly works up to my jaw, where he tilts my chin up with his thumb. "Make sure you come back."

"You're making that less and less likely," I respond right before he leans down and presses a kiss to my nose.

The mark of death of this relationship: the nose kiss.

With that, he takes off up the stairs, leaving me in an irritated state.

As I approach Stacey, she says, "That was...intense."

Tell me about it—my legs are feeling like Jell-O at the moment.

"Come on." I take off down the front stairs to the street, where Stacey has the car parked.

"I mean, the iciness in there, combined with the obvious sexual tension, I mean wow. And for a second, I thought he was going to banish you from the house, but then he threw me for a loop and did that nose-kiss thing. Is that like...something special?"

"No," I say as I get in her car, and she does the same. As we buckle up, I continue, "It's a sarcastic gesture that is a subtle way of reminding the other that what we have means nothing."

"Uh-huh, from the tension and anger, I can sense that you want something with him."

"No," I say, folding my arms.

"From the way spittle flew out of your mouth on that no, I'm going to assume you mean the opposite."

Groaning, I lean my head back while Stacey pulls into the street. "I mean, I wouldn't be opposed to it, but that tempting and teasing, that's more to just...I don't know, get him to break."

"He's not breaking."

"I know, Stacey." I groan and sink into my seat as she starts driving. "You know, when I decided on all of this, there was a part of me that thought maybe he would rub off on me."

"Eww, gross."

"No, not like that," I say with a roll of my eyes. "I mean, he's so business-minded, smart, knows what he wants with his life, has a direction. And I don't know, a piece of me thought that I would learn from him. I mean, I did this big risky thing, and I'm no further along in my life than where I started."

"It's been a week."

"Yeah, a week of nothing," I say. "I hate to admit it, but I really don't think I like myself at the moment. This…this isn't the person I normally am. I'm all thrown off. I never should have suggested we get married."

She brakes at a stoplight and turns toward me. "You have a lot going for you, Sloane."

"Yeah, name one thing."

"You get to go to London. We are about to sign the paperwork for the house. Things are happening."

"Still feel unsettled."

"I can sense that." She pauses for a moment and then quietly says, "We can always go back. We haven't used the check yet. We can return it and, well…move on."

I shake my head. "No, we're not giving the check back. I'm still married. I'm going to see this through."

"Okay, but it seems like you're a little crazed right now."

"I am," I say, feeling all kinds of unwell.

"Maybe you tell me about it then."

I tug on my hair. "I'm just…" I press my lips together, irritated with my feelings. "I don't think I'm mature enough to handle this situation."

And that truth causes Stacey to let out a roar of a laugh. "Oh, the irony."

"Can you not?" I stare out the window, unable to look my sister in the eye. "It's bad enough I'm realizing it. I don't need you laughing at me."

"And there you were, bitching that he's calling you immature, too young, your hot-button words, and you believe him. Wow, that's really rich. Are you going to tell him?"

"Have you lost your mind?" I nearly yell at my sister. "No, I'm not going to tell him. God, the gloating, I wouldn't be able to handle it. I need some help. I need like a crash course on handling this kind of situation."

"I don't think they make a book that gives you a rundown on how to handle a situation like this. I mean, we can go to the bookstore after the bank and see if there is a self-help section, but temporary marriage of convenience isn't a very popular everyday life choice."

"I don't need a book. I just need...I need to talk about it, get in the right frame of mind. Isn't there some wisdom you can impart on me?"

"This is kind of out of my wheelhouse, but you know"—she taps her chin—"I actually might have someone you can talk to."

"Who?" I ask.

She smiles. "You'll see. Let's sign the papers first, and then I'll have them meet us at the house. This might be incredibly helpful."

"Should I be scared?"

"Maybe a little."

───────────

"Is this weird?" I ask.

Stacey stares up at the living room ceiling with me, both of us with champagne in mugs, a pizza between the both of us half-eaten, her crusts waiting to be composted, mine fully consumed.

"Is what weird?" she asks.

"That we are technically lying here, in a house that we somewhat own?"

"Maybe a little," she says as she rolls over to look at me. "I didn't think we would ever be in this position."

"Of buying a house?" I ask.

"Yes, and where Jude actually left us to live his own life. Where he did something for himself, rather than always thinking about us."

"He still thinks about us."

"He does, but he also has given us freedom from his protection, not always keeping track of us. When Gran passed away, he was adamant about making sure we were always taken care of, and now that he's living with Haisley, it feels weird but wonderful. I'm happy for him, I'm happy for us."

"Same," I say as I pick up one of her pieces of crust and take a bite. "Do you think Gran would be proud of all of us?"

Stacey shrugs her shoulders. "I want to say yes, but her feelings about us were always complicated in a way."

"Like that we were a burden she had to take on when Mom died?" I ask, saying the words out loud that we've never really spoken about before.

"Yeah," she says softly.

"We might have been a burden," I say. "But I still think there were moments when she was proud of us."

"Maybe," Stacey says and then smiles at me. "Remember the first time Jude brought us here and the carpet was maroon and looked like several people had died on it?"

I laugh and nod my head. "He ripped the carpet out immediately, then went to Walmart and bought us all slippers to wear while walking around on the plywood floors. That roll of carpet lived out on the back patio for months because he didn't want the landlord to know."

"And the first night, that scratching noise."

"Mr. Whiskers," I say, remembering the rat that was rummaging through the walls at night. "And the hole Jude plowed through the wall trying to punch the thing dead. It's a good thing he was into construction and home repair." I look around the renovated space that we created ourselves.

It took a while and some growing pains along the way, but we put a lot of love into this home, a home that wasn't officially ours but one we made our own—one Stacey and I didn't want to let go.

"You know, this feels really big. We need to do something special with this house," I say.

"What do you mean?"

I shrug. "I don't know yet, but I feel like this is more than just buying the house. There's more to this story."

"Well, when you figure it out, will you let me in on the plot?"

"Absolutely."

Stacey sighs and says, "You know, *I'm* proud of us and your whore-ish ways."

"Whore-ish ways?" I laugh. "Where the hell did that come from?"

"Well, without you selling your body for us, we wouldn't be here right now, on a track to own our house."

"I did not sell my body. I sold my soul. There's a difference. If I sold my body, I'd at least be satisfied right now. Instead, I'm cranky and irritable, with a husband who likes to push my buttons."

"Please, you push his more. Dressing up in nothing but an apron was evil. May as well have worn devil horns with the getup."

"I had a thong on."

"I don't see how that makes a difference."

"Makes a little bit of one, as I can say I wasn't fully naked."

Stacey rolls her eyes. "Either way, you're both pushing each other's buttons."

Knock, knock.

"Ooh, that must be her, right on time," Stacey says.

"Care to tell me exactly who it is?" I ask.

Stacey gets up from the floor and moves toward the door, not answering me. When she opens it, a blond with short, early 2000s Kate Gosselin–type hair walks in. Her purple glasses are huge, covering nearly half of her face, and her vagina-shaped earrings are both fascinating and somewhat off-putting at the same time. The realism is a bit much.

Why all the folds?

"Melva, it's good to see you," Stacey says, pulling her into a hug.

Melva? When did my sister ever become friends with a Melva? What has she been doing behind my back?

"So good to see you," Melva says, squeezing Stacey tight. When she slowly—and I mean slowly—pulls away, her hand grazes over my sister's shoulder and down her arm, and Melva smiles lovingly at her, as if...as if there is history there.

Umm, what's going on here?

Stacey turns toward me and says, "Sloane, this is Melva. Melva, this is my sister, Sloane."

I step up to the eccentric woman and take her hand in mine. "Nice to meet you."

"Such a pleasure. I always love being in the presence of twins."

That's...that's a weird thing to say.

"Well." I clasp my hands together. "Glad I could make a lifelong dream come true."

She chuckles. "Ooh, she is funny." She touches my sister's face. "Funny and sweet, what a nice combination."

Uhhh, what's going on here? What kind of lady of the night is Melva? Because she's giving off those kind of vibes.

"Don't pump her up too much," Stacey says. "She'll run with it."

"Very true," I say, humoring my sister but then getting down to business. "So how do you two know each other?" I motion my finger between the two of them.

"A mutual friend," Melva says as she walks up to the pizza box on the floor, picks up a piece of pizza, and takes a bite before sitting on the couch, crossing one leg over the other.

Help yourself, wasn't planning on eating that.

"Mutual friend, that's fun," I say. "So, uh, can I ask why you brought Melva here, to eat our pizza and touch you in interesting ways?"

"Sloane," Stacey chastises, but I don't even care because this lady is weird. Not to mention, she's older.

Like…thirty years older than us, easily.

She's at least in her fifties.

"What? Just pointing out the obvious."

"I hear that you're in a marriage of convenience," Melva says.

"Yes."

"So am I," Melva says with a smile.

"Oh, I thought…Stacey, you said you didn't know anyone in a marriage of convenience."

"With my characters," Melva continues. "You see, I'm an author, and I know all about the marriage-of-convenience trope. Quite popular."

My expression falls, and I turn toward my sister. "You're kidding me, right? You brought someone who writes fiction for a living to tell me how to handle my very real situation?"

"Fiction is always the child of some sort of reality," Stacey says. "She might have some really good advice. At least you can listen—she's the closest thing we have to advice."

"I discuss personalities and human characteristics on the daily," Melva says. "I can very much help." She takes another bite of the pizza and smiles broadly.

"At least hear her out," Stacey says.

This is stupid, but do I really have any other options at the moment? Not really, so looks like I'm about to take some advice from Melva with the vagina earrings.

"Okay." I take a seat in the chair across from Melva and say, "Impart your wisdom on me."

"First, please tell me more about this man you married."

"Well, is this confidential? Because it's very important that this stays here, in this house."

"You have my utmost discretion," Melva says, her hand to her chest as Stacey takes a seat next to Melva on the couch.

"It's appreciated," I say, almost feeling like I'm making some sort of weird deal with her. "Um, so his name is Rossell." Stacey's nose quirks to the side, but luckily, she doesn't say anything. There's no way I'm giving away real names to Melva. Can't trust anyone with that kind of haircut.

"Rossell, a solid, strapping name."

"Very," I say. "And that's what he is, solid, strapping, extremely attractive. Maybe one of the most attractive men I've ever met."

"Ahh, I can see where this is going. You're married, and you want to push the boundaries of the original agreement."

"I mean, yes, why not have a little fun with it? The marriage was for a business deal, and I assumed that we would grow closer, get to know each other better. But he wants nothing to do with that. So I thought we could at least have some fun while in this purgatory, since I find him attractive and he finds me attractive. But he refuses to partake in that as well. Won't even budge on his decision no matter how hard I try, but then he does things like puts his hand on my thigh when we're in the car, and it's all very confusing."

Melva nods her head. "Let me ask, what do you want to get out of this?"

"I got money," I answer.

"No, what else do you want to get out of this? I understand the initial trade that occurred, but is there more you want?"

"I mean, we are going to London together. We have to act like we're married in front of a lot of people. He can be very affectionate in a way that I wasn't expecting, and it's...it's going to be hard sharing a hotel room with him where I'm not allowed to play around, even though I'm going to desperately want to. I just want to...enjoy myself while I have the chance and, when this is all over, just move on."

"Do you think you can do that? Move on?" Melva asks.

"Of course," I answer. "I've never been really emotionally attached to anyone besides my family. I don't think it'll be a problem at all. Plus, as much as I think Rossell is hot and I want to see him naked, I know for a fact that he's also not the relationship type. So there're no feelings there."

"This is purely carnal?"

"Yes," I say.

Melva nods. "And what's the holdup?"

"Our brother," I answer. "They're friends and well, he doesn't want to ruin that relationship. Not to mention, he thinks I'm too young."

"Aww, good plot, good plot." Melva nods her head, as if she's seeing a book come to life right in front of her. "And what have you done to try to get him to break?"

"Nearly everything short of actually making a move, and I fear the way he's been acting, he might ask me to put clothes on, and I don't think my confidence can take that hit."

"And he's still not budging?"

"Nope," I say.

"Well then, there's only one thing left to do."

"What?" I ask, feeling like I'm about to be blessed with the golden key to all answers.

"Nothing," Melva says and then bites her pizza.

My hope for an answer tumbles to the ground.

Nothing?

That's her grand plan? Her smart idea? For me to do nothing?

Did she mention if she was a bestselling author? Because I would not read that book.

So glad Stacey brought her here to eat our pizza and offer nothing of value.

"Wow, solid advice," I say with an edge to my tone. "Stacey and I never would have thought of that."

Stacey turns toward Melva and says, "You'll have to excuse my sister. She can be an ass when she's horny."

"I can sense her aura." Melva waves her hand at me. Motioning to my head, she says, "Very red in the brain." Then she moves her hand to the southern part of my body and says, "Very blue in the crotch."

I place my hands over my lap. "Please don't call my crotch blue...or say *crotch*. It's a gross word."

"Sorry, your vaginal walls are very blue."

"Okay, wasn't looking for a gynecological exam here." I go to stand. "It was nice meeting you, but I should get back to my husband."

"So you can continue to be frustrated? You realize if your vaginal walls turn purple, it's the end for you."

"You realize that what you're saying is not actually a thing?" I look at Stacey and say, "I love you, but this was weird."

"Sit down, Sloane. Let her explain," Stacey says in an exhausted tone.

"She did explain. She said I should do nothing. How is that helpful?"

"If you let me elaborate, then you would understand," Melva says, examining her pizza before taking a bite. "So sit. Let me turn your vaginal walls from blue to burning red."

Wow.

Out of pure curiosity to see what this nutcase has to say, I take a seat. "By all means, please, heat up my vaginal walls."

Smiling, she tosses her crust on the pizza box, brushes off her hands, and then folds them in her lap. "You're doing too much, trying too hard. This will only lead to frustration on your part, and why should you be the one who is frustrated over the male brain? It's not fair to you."

Okay, yeah, I can agree with that, so I let her proceed.

"You're trying every trick in the book, and nothing is working, which means, he's a different kind of breed. You need to try the *less is better* approach. You need to play along, so he's looking for affection, begging for you to pay attention to him. You've almost primed him at this point, to want to wait for you. Now he needs to see you disinterested. He needs to know what it's like when you don't pay him attention, when you're indifferent to the situation."

Shit...that's a good idea. I don't want to admit it, but God, it's actually really smart.

"You will break him because, if I know men like I know my heroes, they're not going to appreciate going unnoticed. And when you must be together, when you need to put on a show, that's when you give him a taste of what he's missing out on. But when you are alone together with no onlookers, you are unengaged, offering him nothing of your personality. Give him very little."

Stacey looks my way with a smile in her eyes as I think about this intriguing advice, something I never would have thought of—hell, my next move was going to climb into his lap at night, completely naked, and just start dry humping him, probably only to be rejected. But this...this feels genius. This feels mature.

Might I say...demure...mindful...

"Okay," I say, trying to hold back my conniving smile. "This feels... this feels brilliant."

Melva picks at her front tooth. "It's why they call me the plot fairy. I know how to twist and turn the lives of my characters."

"I guess so." I stand again. "Well, I guess I should go try it out, see what the husband has to think about my negligence."

Melva shakes her head. "No, dear, you are not."

"What do you mean?"

"I mean, you are not to rush home to him. You owe him nothing. You stay out as late as you want. Make him wait, make him wonder, make him wish that you were home with him."

"That is...that is even more devious."

She taps the side of her head. "Not just a rack for vulva earrings."

"Not even a little. Which I must say, love the earrings, very...labia-like."

"Thank you. I saw you eyeing them."

"How could you not," I say to my new best friend. "They're vaginas."

"You're right, and who doesn't love a vagina?"

"Not me," I say, raising my hand. "Sheesh, where are our manners? Can I get you a drink?"

Stacey rolls her eyes, probably hating my change of tune.

"No, but I would love some ice cream."

"Ooof, we don't have any," I say.

"Doesn't mean you can't order some. We have time."

A large smile crosses my face. "You are right. We have plenty of time."

CHAPTER TWELVE
HUDSON

I GLANCE AT THE CLOCK for the twentieth time in an hour and grumble under my breath.

Where the fuck is she?

Is she not coming home?

She hasn't packed yet, we leave tomorrow for London, she's not answering her phone, and it's past eleven at night.

I pace the living room, trying to keep it together, but Jesus, it's hard to not flip your shit when your wife is so...so erratic.

Lights flash past the window, and I quickly walk up to the curtains and pull them back slightly to see Sloane step out of a car and thank the driver.

I move toward the front door and open it just as she reaches the top step, scaring her.

"Jesus, what are you doing?" she asks as she makes her way past me and into the house, as if nothing is wrong.

"Waiting for you," I say. "Where the hell have you been?"

"With Stacey," she says and keeps walking up the stairs, no more explanation to that.

I quickly lock up the house and follow her up the stairs. When I reach the bedroom, she moves past the laundry I folded for her and to the bathroom, where she grabs a pair of pajamas from the dresser, not opting for one of my shirts. And that is just wrong. It's become my new normal to see her in my shirts, so what is going on?

"Uh, care to explain?"

"Explain what?" she asks.

"Where you were," I say.

"I said I was with Stacey. We were at the house, enjoying ourselves." Then she moves into the toilet room and shuts the door. When she comes out, she's dressed and puts her dirty clothes in the hamper before walking over to the sink, where she starts washing her face.

"Sloane," I say, irritated.

"What?" she replies as she suds up her face with facial cleanser.

"Are you going to ignore the fact that I was trying to get in touch with you and you weren't answering?"

She rinses her face and then towel dries it before picking up her lotion. "Why were you trying to get in touch with me?" she asks with such a blasé attitude that it grates on my nerves.

"Because I wanted to know where the fuck my wife was."

"You knew I was with Stacey."

"Were you though?" I ask, feeling jealousy pulse through me as my imagination runs wild with other possibilities.

"Yes," she says in an annoyed tone. "And before you suggest I was with anyone but you, you better check yourself. Because I might be horny, but I gave you my word. You're my husband, plain and simple. I won't be searching for anything else."

I'm annoyed that her reassurance puts me slightly at ease because I shouldn't care that much, even though I do.

"Why did you come home late?" I ask, not able to drop this.

She lotions her face and answers, "Because I don't need to answer to you. You made it clear that nothing in our arrangement extends past what is required of me, so that's what I'm going to stick to: what is required of me in this marriage. And frankly, Hudson, I'm done trying. I spent a week attempting to get to know you, to lean on you through this situation, and you've given me nothing. So I'll do what you want but give the bare minimum." She lines her toothbrush with toothpaste and starts brushing.

The bare minimum.

I don't like that.

And I have no right to complain about it because she's right—she's done a lot in the last week, and I've kept her at arm's length. I've shut her down, made sure to not get tempted, to not fall into the trap of her charm, because fuck is she charming.

This distance? The lack of joy in her expression?

The defeat in her shoulders?

Hate it.

But I can't do anything about it. I just need to accept it and move on because, like I said from the very beginning, I won't go there with her.

"Sloane, we leave for London tomorrow." She nods. "And it would have been nice to have discussed our plan for when we're there."

She spits her toothpaste out and says, "Type up a memo. I'll read it on the plane."

Then she walks out to the bedroom.

Well, fuck, she wasn't kidding about bare minimum.

A memo?

No. I'm not about to communicate with my wife through a memo.

I finish getting ready for bed, mulling over her new attitude, wondering if something else happened tonight that really made her change. I mean, it had to. The question is, how am I going to handle this?

I turn off the bathroom light and move into the bedroom, where she's lying on her side of the bed, turned away from me. She's scrolling on her phone, looking at Instagram, when I slip in behind her.

There is one thing I did promise myself when I put a ring on her finger: I would treat her like a queen, like a wife, like how she deserves, so I try to soften my approach.

"I'd prefer to talk to you about London, not write it up in a memo."

She sets her phone down and sits up in bed. The matching set of white-and-pink-striped pajamas are cute on her, but I got used to her wearing my T-shirts to bed.

"Fine, what are your expectations?" she asks while she rests her hands in her lap.

That mouth, those lips, pursed and ready to fire a comeback at me within a drop of a hat. It's one of the things I have come to appreciate about her—not that I should be counting up all the reasons I like her, but it is. She's spunky, doesn't take shit. And yeah, she might be young, but she's right: she handles herself well, makes me forget just how young she really is.

None of that matters now, though. She needs to know what to expect when we get to London.

"We'll have to share a hotel room."

"Well, since I'm currently sleeping in your bed, I don't foresee that being an issue. Also, I booked the travel; I know what kind of room we're staying in. Does this really need to be something we have to discuss?"

The fucking attitude.

"I thought it would be appropriate to let you have a voice in the matter."

"Oh, so if I told you I didn't want to share a hotel room with you, you'd get me my own?"

"No," I answer. "But I could at least plan to sleep on the pull-out couch."

She rolls her eyes dramatically. "Don't be a drama queen. I share a bed with you now. I can share a bed with you in London. What else?"

"I've secured dancing lessons for us, so that you can be trained in the dances that Sheridan requires for the wedding."

"Sounds enjoyable," she replies. "But what do you mean by us? You're not part of the wedding."

"I said I would train you."

"As far as I know, you're not versed in Regency dancing. How can you possibly train me?"

"You're going to need a partner," I shoot back.

"I'll just use whatever dancer they have available. I'm sure there will be a single man, ready to whisk me off my feet."

My eyebrows turn down. "I will be your partner."

"Stop, Hudson. I'm sure you have better things to do than to learn some dances with me."

"I'll be your partner," I repeat. "No discussion."

"Okay," she says with a roll of her eyes. Christ. "Anything else?"

I clear my throat, unsure of how to handle this side of her. "There'll be a lot of meetings and dinners we have to attend. You'll attend as my wife, not my assistant."

"Okay."

"And pack light, because I'll be taking you to Harrods when we arrive to make sure you have the appropriate wardrobe for the different events we will be attending."

"Okay."

I purse my lips to the side, annoyed with her one-word replies. "And I've set you up for a class in etiquette before any of the meetings or dinners we have. I want to make sure you're prepared to eat a meal among dignitaries. Not to mention how to speak to people in a higher position."

"Okay," she says, grating on my nerves.

I was sure she'd be insulted about the etiquette classes. I would be. And yet, she hasn't tossed back any sass. "If that's all, I'm going to sleep." She lies down again and turns away from me.

I slide my hand over my jaw and try not to let my discomfort get the best of me, but of course it does. Tonight has been one long night of irritation. She wasn't home. She wasn't texting me back. She got home very late. Didn't seem to care that I was...well...concerned. She's not treating me the same. She's lost her spunk. And she's not wearing my goddamn T-shirt.

As I list that all out, I know it's fucking ridiculous to be annoyed by, because in the grand scheme of things, she's doing nothing wrong. This is what she should be like in this type of arrangement. Detached. Distant. And yet somewhere in my sick fucking brain, I want more.

She turns off her light, and the room clouds in darkness as I sit there on the bed, staring at her back.

"There's one more thing," I say as I slide under the covers.

"What's that?" she says as she stays turned away.

So I move in closer and glide my hand over her waist. She doesn't move, doesn't even flinch.

"We're going to have to be intimate in front of people."

"And your point?" she says, as if this is no big deal.

My hand curls into a fist around the fabric of her shirt. "My point is, if I touch you, hold your hand, press a kiss to your cheek, you need to not be surprised."

"Hudson, unless somehow your tongue finds my pussy in public, I'm pretty sure we're not going to have a problem."

"I'm being serious, Sloane."

On an irritated sigh, she rolls to her back and looks up at me. In the moon-lit room, I take in her soft facial features and the rounded curve of her jawline. She's...she's so damn beautiful. I wish that circumstances were different.

"If I thought this was a joke, I'd be laughing. I know you're being serious."

"Then...then why are you acting like this?" I ask.

"Like what?"

"Like...like you don't care?"

"I do care," she says. "But I'm exhausted with this, with us. I'm kind of over it. So let's just get through the next couple of weeks, and then we can move on with our lives."

My brow creases because I don't like what she said, that she's kind of over it. Over what, exactly?

"Is this about the other night?"

She shakes her head. "No, it's not."

"Because I'm sorry," I say. "I'm sorry if...if I hurt your feelings. I know I can be an ass when I'm stressed, but you know I can't do anything about us."

She pats my chest. "It's fine, Hudson. Don't sweat it. Now, unless you have anything else to say, I'm going to bed."

Don't sweat it?

Oh, I'm going to sweat about it because this Sloane roller coaster I've been on has not been the easiest. The moment she walked into my office, ready to be my assistant, I knew I was in trouble, but I never thought it would turn into something this intense.

It's already beyond complicated because I feel the need to take care of her, to treat her well, to make sure she has everything she needs, yet I need to keep her at arm's length. I need to set a boundary because there is a great possibility that if I let her get too close, if I let her break down my walls, I could become attached.

And I can't be attached.

Not with who she's related to.

Not when I'm carrying around a load of baggage.

Not when I just need to stay focused on the business.

And, fuck, we haven't even gotten to the heart of what we need to do when we're in London. We're at the tip of the iceberg. If we're already irritated with each other now, imagine what it's going to be like when we're knee-deep in dancing and meetings. Not to mention, what happens after this? Is she...is she going to continue to work with me? The thought of her not coming back to the office when we return makes my stomach hurt. I know I can't have her. I know she's not mine, but I don't want her to leave either. I've realized I've become comfortable having her close, seeing her every day.

Jesus, what has come over me?

With nothing else to say, because what really is there to say, I release her and turn to my side, getting comfortable with my pillow as I feel her turn away.

I've done some pretty dumb things in my life—like hiring Sloane to work for me in the first place—but this...marrying her, yeah, I earned the gold in the "dumb shit to do" Olympics.

I stare at my watch on my wrist, watching the seconds tick by as I pace the airport, next to our gate, waiting for Sloane to show up.

I fucking knew taking two cars to the airport was going to bite me in the ass, but I forgot my computer at the office like an idiot, so I told her I'd meet her at the airport.

And now that I'm here and she's nowhere to be found, nor is she answering her phone, I'm starting to fucking panic.

What if she decided not to show up? This morning, when she was finishing packing, I gave her a hard time for waiting until the last minute because I was stressed watching her. And then I ended up being the one that forgot something. Did I push her too hard?

Of course you did, you fucking idiot.

You put her in this mess and now she's not going to come because you can't handle your stress appropriately.

And you're the one calling her young...

I drag my hand over my face, visibly stressed as I check my phone again.

I'm going to have a heart attack. That is exactly what that feels like, a heart attack.

I stuff my phone back in my pocket, and I'm about to ask the gate attendant to call her name over the intercom when I hear the sound of her laughter. I turn around to find her arm linked through another man's, heading right toward me.

What.

The.

Actual.

Fuck.

Tall with black hair and dark-rimmed glasses, the man looks like a knockoff Clark Kent.

"There you are," Sloane says with ease as she releases the other man, walks straight up to me, slides her hand up my chest, and presses a kiss right to the corner of my mouth. I feel my breath hitch as she pulls away and then slips her arm around my waist and leans her head against my chest. "Devin, meet my husband, Hudson. Hudson, this is Devin. We went to college together."

Devin holds out his hand, and I reluctantly take it. "Devin, nice to meet you," I say as I keep a firm grasp around Sloane.

"Nice to meet you." He looks me up and down, assessing. *Assess all you want, you fuck, she's married to me.* "I had no idea Sloane was married, nor did I know she was going to London to be in Sheridan's wedding."

"Do you know Sheridan?" I ask.

"Yeah, she's my childhood neighbor. Our families go way back."

Fucking great, which means...

"Devin is going to be at the wedding. Isn't that fun?" Sloane asks.

"Yeah," I say, swallowing back my animosity for a man I don't even know. "Are you in the wedding party?"

"I am," he says. "I was telling Sloane, I know all of the dances. I have no problem showing her."

Oh, I have a fucking problem.

A real fucking problem.

"Even showed her a little bit of one at the bar."

"Bar?" I ask.

"That's where I ran into Devin," Sloane answers.

"Flying sort of freaks me out," he says with this boyish charm that I don't appreciate. "I always like to grab a beer or two before I board." He glances at the gate and then adds, "Shit, we actually need to get on the plane."

"Yes," I say through clenched teeth. "They're about to do last call."

"Well, might as well get on." Devin nods toward the gate. "Shall we?"

"I think we shall," Sloane says sweetly as she heads toward the gate, following behind Devin.

Devin steps up to the gate agent and scans his ticket. He steps off to the side and waits for us, which grates on my nerves. We're not a threesome; move the fuck on.

I scan our boarding passes on my phone and then take Sloane's hand in mine, marking my territory as we head down the jet bridge.

"Remember that party we went to at the football house our senior year?" Devin asks as he walks in front of us, turning just enough so he is able to engage in conversation.

"Yes." Sloane chuckles. "That was a good night."

"A really good one," he says, wiggling his eyebrows.

The fuck? Do that again, motherfucker, and I'll rip your goddamn eyebrows right off your forehead.

"Are you guys heading back to economy?"

Heat rips through my body as I answer, "First class."

"Nice." He nods. "Me too. I'm guessing you got the middle pods together."

"We did," I answer as we move toward the front of the plane.

"Well, I'm right here," Devin says, finding his seat that's right across the aisle from ours. "If you want to come hang out, you know where to find me."

Yeah, over my dead body.

"Maybe I'll pop on over," Sloane says. "Have a good flight."

"You too," Devin says and then gets settled in his seat while I shuffle us over to ours. Thankfully, we have pods that are connected with walls that rise, blocking us off from everyone around us.

I guide Sloane into the pod and immediately put up the wall before sitting her down and taking a seat as well.

"Oh, this is roomy—"

"What the hell were you doing with him?" I whisper, getting extremely close to her.

"Pardon me?" she asks, leaning back.

"You were dancing in an airport bar with him? While I was fucking waiting for you, worried that you weren't going to show up?"

"You were worried?" she asks, a crinkle to her brow.

"Yeah, I was fucking worried. I was texting you, calling, you weren't answering, and then you show up with that fuck, hanging all over him."

"Uh, first of all"—she holds up her finger—"I was not hanging all over him. Second of all, he was the one who stopped me. We got to talking, and I just lost track of time. I guess it was good we were on the same flight, huh?"

"I don't like him," I say.

"You don't know him."

"I know him enough that I understand the way he was clinging to you, the way he was looking at you. And that bullshit about the football party, he brought that up only to make me jealous."

"Yeah, and it seems like it worked."

"Sloane, don't test me," I say, my irritation at an all-time high. And here I was, thinking I scared her away.

"As if I would want to poke the bear." She rolls her eyes and gets comfortable in her seat. "Trust me, the last thing I want to do is get this"—she motions to my body—"all riled up." She plucks the complimentary headphones from the hook and plugs them in before putting them over her ears.

I'm quick to remove them.

"We're not finished here."

"We sure are," she says. "I'm not playing this game with you. There's nothing to be upset about."

"So…if you saw me dancing with an ex—"

"He's not an ex, just a guy that…you know." She shrugs and then starts scrolling through the movies on the screen in front of her.

"That you what?"

"Come on, Hudson, use your brain. It's the thing that's causing you to be jealous right now."

"Were you fuck buddies?" I ask.

"If it needs a label, sure."

"I thought there was only one guy who…" My voice trails off as realization hits me. "Is that the guy? That's the Devin you mentioned?" I ask.

"Yup," she says and that just pushes me right over the goddamn edge.

He's the guy who has a choke hold on her orgasm.

The one and only guy that's ever made Sloane come.

She taps on the comedy genre and then chuckles when she sees *Anchorman* as a choice. She goes to click on it, but I stop her.

In a low, almost desperate voice, I say, "Sloane, how would you like it if—"

"Can we not do hypotheticals?" she asks. "Come on, Hudson." She shakes her head and sticks her headphones back on. I realize then that there isn't going to be a fighting chance that I can get through to her.

There wasn't last night, and there sure as hell won't be today.

She has shut me out.

Completely.

Stoic, uninterested, she wants nothing to do with me, and you know what? I can't even be fucking mad about it. I was the one who wanted this distance. I was the one who told her no time and time again. She's given in, and there's no reason why I should be this mad.

This irritated.

This itchy to have her back.

At least when she was walking around the house naked and in an apron, she was still herself.

Sassy.

Mouthy.

Keeping me on my goddamn toes.

Now she's...hell, she's slipping away. But maybe...maybe that's a good thing. Because don't I need to focus on the business? Don't I need to focus on maintaining all the relationships involved? The distance should be good. The distance will make the end of this journey easy.

At least, that's what I'm trying to convince myself of.

Instead of attempting to get her to pay attention to me, I let her turn on *Anchorman* as I pull my phone from my pocket and text my brother.

Hudson: I'm losing it.

While I wait for him to text back, I adjust my pillow and kick up my feet on the footrest in front of me. I glance at Sloane, who already has a blanket covering her and is looking extra cozy. I consider talking to her again but know there's no use, at least not here, on the plane where Devin the Douche can hear us.

My phone buzzes in my hand, and I immediately read the text.

Hardy: Let me guess, Sloane?

Hudson: Yes. We're on our way to London, and I've managed to make a complicated situation exponentially more complicated.

Hardy: Sounds about right. Didn't you know, happy wife, happy life?

Hudson: Apparently not.

Hardy: What did you do this time?

Hudson: The better question is, what didn't I do? Christ, man, I'm not cut out for this shit.

Hardy: What's going on?

Hudson: She's detached herself, which I should be happy about, but I'm not. She has zero need to talk to me, interact. She plays the part when she needs to, but fuck, when we're alone, it's as if I'm nothing.

Hardy: Umm…shouldn't that be a good thing?

Hudson: Yes! But I don't fucking like it and then she ran into an old friend in the airport who happens to be on the same flight and in the wedding, but he's also the one guy that's ever made her orgasm. The way she talks about him, you would think he's a goddamn hung horse.

Hardy: Well, is he? Have you looked inside his pants?

Hudson: Don't be a jackass.

Hardy: How do you know he's not hung?

Hudson: He wasn't walking like he is.

Hardy: Maybe he rolls and tucks it.

Hudson: If I rolled and tucked my dick, I would be waddling around like a goddamn penguin.

Hardy: Shhh, for the love of God, don't mention penguins. JP went on a rant the other day about them. I swear, if you talk about it too much, he'll sense it. I can't get on another one of his donation trains, man. I can't.

Hudson: You have issues.

Hardy: Says the guy who's mad that his wife, a wife he's not supposed to be attached to, isn't attached to him.

Hudson: Seriously, what am I supposed to do?

Hardy: Job one, forget about Sloane and any sort of attachment. It's best this way. You and I both know that. Two, find out if Orgasm Boy is hung like a horse. Inquiring minds want to know.

Hudson: You're not fucking helpful.

Hardy: Could have told you that from the start of this text thread.

Hudson: You know, when you were going through shit, I was helpful. Where's the return?

Hardy: When I was going through shit, you were yelling at me for falling for a girl that works with our sister. You're falling for a girl who is our sister's sister-in-law and the sister of our fucking business partner. Awkwardness and sarcasm are the only reasons I'm not gnawing my leg off from nerves at the moment.

Hudson: And this is why being the older brother is more difficult.

Hardy: That and the age, your back is always going to hurt more than mine. Although I say that now, but you should have seen the position Everly had me in last night. I thought I was going to snap my spine.

Hudson: I don't want to hear it.

Hardy: Jealous, I know. Probably been a while since you've had sex.

Hudson: Too fucking long.

Hardy: Shame you need to keep it in your pants.

Hudson: Yeah, trust me, it's not coming out.

Hardy: Just the answer I wanted to hear. Good thing you have more self-control than I did. Although, my situation seemed to work out for me. Think Jude would take kindly to you messing with his sister?

Hudson: What the hell do you think?

Hardy: I think he'd sit on your head until you stopped breathing.

Hudson: Exactly.

Hardy: Well, glad we got that covered. Hey, serious question.

Hudson: What?

Hardy: Have you ever had your balls tickled by a feather? Everly did it to me last night and I pre-ejaculated.

Hudson: What the actual fuck, Hardy?

Hardy: What?

Hudson: Don't fucking say shit like that.

Hardy: You're my brother. Who the hell else am I supposed to share that with?

Hudson: No one! Keep that shit to yourself.

Hardy: I can't stop thinking about it. Dude, I could not refrain, my dick was dancing all across my stomach. Like a fucking Magic Marker, decorating my abs.

Hudson: Bye.

Hardy: No wait, come back. I might have taken it too far with the Magic Marker thing. I can recognize that.

I set my phone down in the cubby just as a flight attendant comes by with a tray of champagne and water.

"Champagne? Water?" she asks.

I grab a champagne, thank her, and down it quickly. It's going to be a long-ass flight…especially with that fucking Magic Marker visual stuck in my head.

———

"Sloane," I whisper, tapping on her shoulder.

The cabin is dimmed. The meal service is over, and everyone has settled in to grab some sleep.

I, on the other hand, have made some bad choices.

Some very bad choices.

"Sloane." I tap again.

Her sleep mask is over her eyes, her whole body is turned away from me, and her blanket is up to her chin.

"I see you in there," I say, tapping again.

She snaps up, slips her eye mask up, and whispers, "What do you want?"

When her eyes meet mine, I smile. "Hi."

Her expression falls flat as she stares back at me.

I wave.

And then realization hits her. "Are you drunk?"

My smile grows wider. "The flight attendant has been heavy-handed with the champagne."

"Jesus, Hudson," she says as she turns toward me now. There's a partition between us, nothing too big but big enough to annoy me. "Sleep it off."

"I can't sleep. I'm not tired."

"Here you go, sir," the flight attendant says, bringing me another mini champagne flute.

Sloane sits up farther and holds her hand out. "Actually, can you take that back? He doesn't need another one."

"She doesn't know what she's talking about," I say. "I'm thirsty." I reach for the champagne, but Sloane pushes my hand down.

"Seriously, can you bring him water?"

The flight attendant eyes me for a moment, then to my annoyance, takes my champagne back to the galley.

"That was fucking rude."

"Hudson. Why are you drunk?" Sloane asks.

"I'm not."

"Yes, you are."

"I don't feel drunk."

"Well, you are."

"Prove it," I say.

She sighs and then picks up my phone and, unbeknownst to me, takes a picture of me, nearly searing my eyes with the flash. She turns the screen toward me, but I have to blink a few times before the picture comes into view.

And yup, there I am, looking drunk as can be with my eyelids heavy and my face sagging, almost in defeat.

"It's your fault," I say, pointing at her as the flight attendant puts a mini bottle of water next to me.

"How is you getting drunk my fault?" she asks.

"Because you're not being nice to me."

"I'm not being nice to you. How so?" she asks, fully turning toward me now.

"You're not...you're not yourself, and I don't like it."

"Uh-huh, and what would that entail?"

I shrug and sway to the side. "You're not wearing my T-shirt to bed."

"And that makes you..."

"Sad," I say.

"Mmm, but why should that matter?"

"Because I like when you wear it. Actually, why don't you wear my shirt right now?" I reach behind my head and start to tug on my shirt, but she quickly stops me.

"Do not take your shirt off on the plane, Hudson."

"But I want you wearing it. And why don't you care about me?"

"I do care about you."

I shake my head and reach over the partition to take her hand in mine. She lets me. "No, you don't. You don't talk to me anymore or look at me or...or...get naked."

"I never got naked for you," she says, the smallest of smiles tugging on her lips.

"Yes, you did. The apron." I blow out a breath and lean my shoulder against the back of my chair. "I can't stop dreaming about your ass in that thong."

Her smile grows. "Oh yeah?"

I slowly nod. "Yup. I wanted it so bad."

"Shame you couldn't take what you wanted."

"I know," I say, and I link our hands together. "If I had it my way, you'd never remember that Deacon guy."

"Deacon? You mean Devin?"

"Yeah. Devin the Douche. You wouldn't even be thinking about his dick."

"What would I be thinking about?" she asks.

I bring our connected hands up to my lips, and I press a gentle kiss to her knuckles. "You'd be thinking about my dick."

"Pretty presumptuous, don't you think?"

I shake my head. "No, you would." I pause and then lean closer. "Does he roll his dick?"

"Huh?" she asks cutely.

"Douche, does he roll his dick up?"

"Uh…no."

"So he's not hung like a horse?"

She chuckles and leans in closer, the smell of her perfume clouding my thoughts even more. "He's pretty big."

"Fuck." I exhale and lean my head against my chair now. "I didn't want him to be big."

"Why?"

"Just don't like that you've been with a big dick."

"Because you're…small?" she asks.

"No," I say. "Because I want to be the only big dick you know."

"Can you be quiet?" the lady next to us whispers. "You're being rude while people try to sleep."

"Sorry," Sloane says with a wave of her hand. Then she whispers to me, "Drink your water and get some rest."

She lets go of my hand and turns back around.

Not satisfied, I pick up my phone and text her. I know she signed on to the airplane Wi-Fi because I caught her texting her sister earlier.

Hudson: I want to be the only big duck in your life.

Shit.

Hudson: Duck.

God dammit.

Hudson: Not duck. Duck.

Growling, I slowly type out the word *dick*, and when I'm satisfied, I send it.

Hudson: Dick.

Sloane picks up her phone and reads the messages, a cute smile passing over her lips.

Sloane: Go to bed, Hudson.
Hudson: No. I want to talk.
Sloane: There is nothing to talk about.
Hudson: Did you suck him off?
Sloane: We're not doing this.
Hudson: When you saw him today, were you excited?
Sloane: Hudson, GO TO SLEEP.
Hudson: When he touched you…did you like it?
Sloane: Do you really want to know?
Hudson: Yeah, I really want to know.
Sloane: If I tell you, will you go to sleep?
Hudson: Yes.
Sloane: Promise?
Hudson: Promise.
Sloane: Fine. When I saw him today, I felt familiarity. When he danced with me, I felt special. When he linked my arm through his, I felt cherished. When I saw you and kissed the corner of your mouth…I felt butterflies.

I stare at her words, my heart racing a mile a fucking minute.

Because that's what I wanted to hear, that's what I wanted to know.

My phone buzzes again.

Sloane: Now go to sleep.

She sets her phone in her cubby, flips her eye mask down, and brings her blanket back up to her chin, shutting me out.

CHAPTER THIRTEEN
SLOANE

"YOU OKAY?" I ASK HUDSON, who is standing at baggage claim, looking practically green.

"No," he says curtly.

"Can I get you anything?"

"No."

"Hey, guys," Devin says as he comes up to us with a wave. "Customs was fun." He eyes Hudson up and down. "Dude, you don't look so good."

"I think he's feeling a little airsick," I say as I rub Hudson's back. "And it was hot over in customs. I think he just needs some fresh air and—"

Hudson takes off running before I can finish my sentence. I watch him throw up into the garbage can as Devin winces next to me.

"Yikes, that's not an ideal way to start a trip."

"Yeah, not so much," I say, watching Hudson heave into the trash can. The champagne was a bad, bad choice on his part.

Did I ignore Hudson to the point that he was actually asking me to talk with him? That was the plan, right? Melva plotted it out, it worked like a charm, and he was begging to have a conversation—and let me tell you, it took everything in me not to fall into the trap of conversing with him.

But now...now that he's clearly not feeling well...I feel bad, because no matter how many times he shooed me away, cut me off from digging deep with him or flat-out just trying to form a connection, I still don't like seeing him like this, and I feel responsible. I know the whole point was to get him to the place where he's acting...well, like this, but now that he's getting drunk, throwing up, because he's upset on account of me? Yeah, it makes me feel two things. For one...awful. I don't like putting people in that kind of situation. And two, he's tugging very hard on my heartstrings.

Hudson lifts up from the trash can, takes a few deep breaths, and then heads into the men's room, where I'm sure he's going to freshen up.

"Tough day," Devin says.

"Yeah, I'm sure he'll be better soon," I say while the bags start flowing down the carousel, our driver looking out for our luggage.

"I'm serious about the dance lessons," Devin says. "I don't mind helping you out. We might even end up being partners in the dancing at the wedding, so it could help to practice with you."

"Oh, uh, thanks," I say as I glance over to the bathrooms.

I know what Stacey and Melva would tell me to do in this situation. They'd say take him up on his offer. Make Hudson eat his words, turning me down over and over.

But for the life of me, I can't fathom doing that to Hudson.

Not after I read those texts and not after the state I saw him in.

He'd lose his mind.

Not to mention, he'd probably be sad, and let me tell you, when he's sad, it does something to my heart. Like a rusty fork, stabbing me over and over again. I can't take it.

The bottom line is: I do like Hudson. Yes, he can be brusque and, to quote him, an asshole. But I do know he's a man of substance and honor. Devin was...well, he was fun when we spent time together. And even though it wasn't that long ago, I honestly can't imagine fooling around with him again now. Not since I've met Hudson.

Not since I married Hudson and committed my time and loyalty to him.

"Thank you for offering to help me with the dances, but I think I'd like to learn the dances with my husband," I answer.

"I get it." Devin nudges me with his elbow. "Looking to add some romance to your marriage?"

"Yeah," I say absentmindedly as I stare at the bathroom, waiting for Hudson to return.

"Should be a fun time, though. Are you excited about the wedding?"

"I am," I say.

"How do you even know Sheridan?"

"Uh...huh, you know. I don't."

"What do you mean you don't?" Devin asks.

"I'm just a filler for her."

"What do you mean a filler?"

"One of her bridesmaids broke her leg, and she needed someone to fill in, and Hudson is an investor in a company called Bridesmaid for Hire. I was available, and the rest is history."

"Oh, wow. I had no idea you were doing that kind of work."

"I'm not. I actually work for Hudson's company," I say. "But I guess I was in the right place at the right time."

Finally, Hudson appears from the men's room, and he's looking rough. Like really rough.

"Excuse me," I say and take off toward him as he walks incredibly slowly toward the baggage claim.

When I reach him, I put my arm around him and whisper, "Are you okay?"

"Not even a little," he says.

"Okay, uh, why don't you take a seat on this bench, and I'll tell the driver that we're going to wait here for him?"

"Okay," he answers as if he's in pain. He takes a seat on the bench, and I go back to the driver, letting him know where we will be.

He goes off to get a trolley to help with the luggage while I wave bye to Devin and tell him I'll see him later. Then I head back and sit next to

Hudson, where he lays his head on my lap and I gently run my fingers through his hair.

It's the same position we take in the car to the hotel.

And it's the same exact position we find when we make it inside our hotel room after the quickest check-in process I've ever seen. Our bags were brought up for us, and when we reached the room, the bellman shut the drapes and had water and saltines brought to the room as well.

Hudson booked us a suite, so not only do we have a living room with a separate bedroom, but we also have a terrace that looks over Hyde Park. We're on the couch with a trash can in front of us and a clammy Hudson on my lap.

I sift my hands through his hair and ask, "Think you can have some water?"

He threw up three times in the car, and I'm starting to think it wasn't the champagne that's causing this, more like food poisoning.

"No," he croaks.

"The bellman was saying they could send a company up that administers IVs. Think you could manage that? Get some electrolytes pumping back into your system?"

"Maybe...in a bit," he says.

"Okay, well, do you want me to give you some space? I can get you set up in the bedroom."

"No," he says quickly and then clings to my leg. "Don't leave."

"Okay," I say softly, a smile playing on my lips—not because I'm happy about him being sick but because...men are such babies.

Hudson doesn't give off needy vibes, especially when he's wearing one of his suits and making multimillion-dollar deals happen in his office, but the moment he doesn't feel good, he becomes the clingiest man I've ever met. I continue to run my hands through his hair, hating this quiet moment but also loving it at the same time. This is a problem, because I'm getting a taste of his softer side, the side he doesn't want to show me.

It's breaking down my defenses.

It's causing me to...feel things.

"I'm sorry," he says quietly.

"Sorry for what?" I ask.

"Ruining the first part of your trip to London."

"You don't need to apologize. I'm sorry you're not feeling well."

"You know...if you want, you can leave. I don't want to keep you here against your will."

"You're not holding me against my will."

"You sure?" he says in the groggy voice. "After the last few days, I would have thought this wasn't for you."

"I believe I vowed to be with you in sickness and health, so this is me performing my wifely duties."

"You're good at it," he says.

"Funny how flattering you can be when you're not acting like an ass."

"Yeah...I know. I'm sorry you have to deal with me."

"It's also surprising how many times you apologize. Maybe you should be sick more often."

"I'd rather not."

"Thank you. He's in the living room," I say as I let the nurses in. We took the hotel up on bringing some IVs up here because, even though he's stopped throwing up, he's not looking great. He hasn't been able to keep anything down.

I follow the two nurses into the living room, where Hudson is stretched across the sofa with the TV on in the background. We found reruns of the UK version of *The Office*, and we've been watching that as Hudson has been switching from throwing up to sleeping. Now he's transitioned to dry heaving, so we think he's got it all out of his system.

"I'm going to take a quick shower while they hook you up, okay?"

He glances up at me, and I can see it in his eyes that he doesn't want me to leave. Which is hilarious to me, because here is this man, this strong alpha man, brought to his knees by some food poisoning.

He's needy, clingy, and flat-out pathetic.

Yet here I am, at his beck and call. Can't say that I'm proud of what I'm about to say, but I like the neediness. I live for his clingy arms. And I enjoy watching just how pathetic he is when I shift away. Like I said, not proud of it, but it's true. It's nice to be wanted.

"Or I can stay here with you," I say while I take a seat back on the couch and let him rest his head on my lap.

"Can you please turn to your back?" the nurse asks, and he does, very slowly. I rest my hand on his chest and gently run my thumb over his pec, while my other hand continues to run through his hair, something I've found he really enjoys.

The nurses get to work finding a vein, poking him, and setting him up with some fluids. Once they hang the IV bag up, they tell us they're going to step outside and come back to check on us in a little while. I give them a key card, so they can come in easily.

Once the door is shut, I ask, "You doing okay?"

"Yeah," he whispers, his eyes drifting shut.

"Tired?"

"Yeah."

"Well, I can let you sleep if you want."

"Why do you keep trying to get away from me?" he asks, his eyes peeking open to look up at me.

"I'm not, just wanting to give you your space."

"Isn't it obvious, Sloane?" he says in his delirium. "I don't want space from you."

"What do you want?"

"I don't know," he says on a sigh. "All I know is I can't have you."

"Something you don't seem to want me to forget."

"You can't forget," he says. "Because when I slip up, I need you to remind me."

"Slip up?" I ask.

He nods and closes his eyes. "It's bound to happen. No way in hell I can hold out. You need to remind me."

Slip up? Remind him?

Is he insane? As if I would ever stop him from making a move. Melva's plan be damned.

"And if I don't?" I ask as my fingers stroke his luscious hair.

"Then we're fucked. So...you need to be the moral compass."

"I don't like that responsibility."

"Someone needs to be responsible."

"I don't know, you're doing a pretty good job," I say.

"I hate it. I don't want to be responsible."

Neither do I.

I run my hand over his thick pecs, and I notice that his nipples have gotten hard, pointing against the fabric of his shirt.

"It's best that you are," I say. "Because I can tell you right now if you ever came up to me, walls down, defenses turned off, and ready to take me up against the wall...there is no way in hell I would stop you."

His teeth roll over the edge of his lip. "Not the right answer, Sloane."

"But it's the correct one."

———

I cinch my robe around my waist and step out of the bathroom and into the bedroom, where Hudson is freshly showered and wearing a pair of briefs, looking better than he was this morning. He's still moving slow, but he said the IV helped a lot, which is great. Especially since he's been able to keep water down.

"I love that shower," I say as I dry my hair with my towel.

Hudson glances over at me. "The water pressure is perfect."

"It is. I could have stayed all day, but the timer they put in the shower made me think about my water choices."

"Yeah, I saw that. Made me move faster too."

"I love this hotel. I think it's one of the nicest I've ever stayed in, well, besides the St. Hopper in Bora Bora, but not many hotels can beat bungalows over water."

"Or Hopper Hotels," he says reluctantly.

"I'm assuming you refuse to stay in one now."

"You would assume right," Hudson says as he makes his way to his side of the bed and slowly sits.

"Do you need anything?"

"No," he says softly, then lies back on the bed. "I have water. I should be good."

"Do you feel nauseous anymore?" I finish drying my hair and pick up my brush from the counter and start getting the tangles out.

"No. Feeling better, just exhausted." He lets out a sigh. "Never having chicken on an airplane again."

"Don't blame you. Chicken and champagne, I'm sure you'll regret the combo for a very long time."

"Yup." He checks his phone, and I take that moment to finish getting ready for bed.

It's early, around 6:00 p.m., but we're both so exhausted and jet-lagged that we decided to call it a night.

When I'm finished in the bathroom, I turn out the light and head over to the closet, where our clothes have been hung up and put into drawers. I find my pajamas in one of the drawers but also spot a stack of Hudson's shirts. And I tell myself not to remind myself of what Melva said about making him think I'm completely uninterested, but after the last few days, I just don't think I can do it anymore.

Not when he's acting the way he is now.

Appreciative.

Affectionate.

Like he can actually stand to look at me.

Who knows, maybe this could be the start of a friendship at the very least. So I grab one of his shirts, slip out of my robe, and pull it over my head. For a second, I bring the collar to my nose and take a big whiff. God, he smells so good. I could be happy just wrapped up in this.

Pleased with my choice, I exit the closet and enter the bedroom, where I round the bed and turn on the light on my nightstand. He's still on his phone when I climb under the covers. I kind of wish he saw what I was wearing, but then again, he's lost an entire day of work, and I'm sure he's wanting to catch up on running his empire.

I plug my phone in to charge and turn off my light.

I let out a large yawn. Unsure what else to do, I turn away and adjust my pillow.

"Tomorrow," he says in a distant, distracted voice. "Etiquette classes."

"Okay," I answer hesitantly.

"Then Harrods. Do you have something nice to wear to class, or do we need to go to Harrods first?"

I mean, I could use less of the condescending tone that just appeared out of nowhere.

"I brought a few dresses," I answer.

"Appropriate ones?" he asks.

Okay, sir. No need to be rude.

"Yes, they're quite appropriate."

"What's appropriate to you, Sloane, might not be appropriate to others."

Excuse me?

Hold on a freaking second.

What's with the insults?

Have I done something wrong to warrant them? Because the last thing I remember, I just nursed this man back to health. Here I was feeling bad for the doof when I should have known his golden-retriever attitude was only temporary. It's as though opening his email reminded him of the walls he erected earlier, reminded him of his thoughts about me, Jude's sister—too young. Look at him asking me questions about whether I can dress myself. *Uh, pretty sure the reason why you aren't still feeling like death is because I took care of you.*

God, he's infuriating.

With a less nurturing tone, I say, "They're appropriate, Hudson."

"I'll approve of them in the morning."

He'll take a look at them in the morning?

As if I need his approval?

Uh, that's not how this is going to work.

"Hey," I say, turning toward him and slapping his phone down. "Insensitive prick. Maybe instead of second-guessing my ability to dress myself appropriately, you could show some appreciation for the shit I did for you today."

He blinks a few times startled.

Yeah, that's right, you can't treat me like that.

"I'm...sorry."

"That's right you're freaking sorry. Christ, Hudson." I tug on my hair, my frustration getting the better of me. "You get your phone back, and in seconds you become the biggest douche in the world."

His brows knit together. "I had things I needed to check up on, Sloane."

"I get that, but also, you're being a dick to me, and I don't appreciate it. Did I or did I not lie with you for the past few hours? Did I or did I not make sure you were well-hydrated and taken care of? Even when you were dry heaving into the trash can, I was rubbing your back. Did I not show you how capable I am of managing this, nursing you, making sure you had everything you needed? And then you go and question my outfits? Treating me like some adolescent who has no idea how to act in society. Jesus. That's being a dick."

"I'm...I'm sorry."

"Damn right you are. Jesus."

With that, I turn back around and line up as close to the edge of the bed as possible because the last thing I want is to slide another inch closer to him.

God, what a freaking ass.

Do you have an appropriate outfit?

Guess what, just because you asked, I'm going to go find some titty tassels to match with a pair of leggings to wear to etiquette. And when they tell me to put clothes on, I'm just going to shake my tits at them. I'm going to let those tits fly. Let them bounce up and down, side to side, flick them in the face with the tassel. Teach them a freaking lesson on payback.

They want to show me how to drink tea with my pinky out? Well, I'll show them how to seek revenge on your husband/boss/man-child who can't handle his champagne and salmonella-infused chicken.

Do I have an appropriate outfit?

I inwardly scream.

What a freaking tool!

I hear Hudson set his phone down, and he turns off the light. Internally, I wish him the worst of nightmares, possibly one more dry-heaving session out of nowhere just to remind him of his humility. What I wouldn't give to hear him at the toilet tonight. Come on, second round!

He shifts on the bed, bumping around like an inconsiderate klutz until he finally settles in.

I half expect him to say good night, but the room falls to silence, and I can see that I've been taking care of an ungrateful—

His hand slides over my waist and right to my stomach before he tugs me right into his bare chest.

A gasp falls past my lips from the surprise attack, and I'm about to ask him what the hell he's doing when he settles his arm around me and snuggles into my body.

And let me tell you, at first, it's not the most romantic scene.

I lie like a dead fish just washed up by the ocean, stiff as can be, mouth agape, and eyes wide because this, my friends, is confusing.

He is big-spooning me.

Yup, he's the soupspoon that no one ever wants to use, and I'm the baby teaspoon that people pull out for their charcuterie boards when serving jelly with their Brie.

This is new.

This feels awkward.

But then...

His thumb glides over my stomach as his mouth inches close to my ear. "Relax."

"Relax?" I laugh as chills spread over my skin. "You want me to relax?"

"Yes, Wife...relax."

"Well, *Husband*, it's hard to relax when I'm harboring a decent amount of animosity toward you. You can't just swoop in here and act like everything is okay."

"I know," he says solemnly.

"You know? Then why are you trying to do that?"

"I...I don't know how to navigate this, Sloane. I appreciate you. I appreciate everything you did for me today. But I fear that if I speak up about how I feel, I might slip up; I might forget what's holding me back. And I can't forget."

"Hence why we don't do things like this."

"I'm well aware."

"Then why?" I ask. "Why now?"

He clears his throat and his thumb slides over my stomach as he says, "Because I just want a piece of you. Even if it's a small piece, I want a piece."

"That's pretty self-serving. You're running hot and cold with me. How is that fair?"

"It's not," he admits.

Feeling the weight of the words, I turn onto my back so I can look him in the eyes. His hand remains on my stomach. "This is not what—"

"You're wearing my shirt."

I glance down at my attire as if he's surprising me with such information. "Yes, I'm aware. I'm also aware that it was a mistake to put it on."

"Why?" he asks, his thumb still rubbing my stomach.

"I wish I weren't wearing your T-shirt because we're not connected in a way that would result in me wearing your clothes. And for a second, for a *minor* second, I thought that maybe you had a change of heart, that you were possibly going to be different. But then I was reminded of your behavior. Now I'm thoroughly regretting my decisions. Actually, I think I might go change right now." I start to move, but his hand clamps around my side, preventing me from going anywhere.

"Please don't change."

The heaviness in his voice nearly breaks me, because this is the man who brought me to putting his shirt on in the first place. Not the man with the phone, but the man who seems to wear his heart on his sleeve on occasion. "Why not?"

"Because," he carefully says, "I like you in my shirt."

"That's obvious, given how possessive you've been with me. But can you explain to me why it matters?"

"Can we not do this right now?" he asks. "Can we just let it be and sleep?"

"Always skipping out on the real talks," I say, feeling sad he won't go there.

"Sloane…"

"No it's fine." I wet my lips. "Just so I know that we're on the same page: You want to sleep like this, with your arm around me?"

He studies me for a few seconds, his eyes searching, before he finally says, "Yes."

"And I'm supposed to just be okay with it?"

"No," he answers, his gaze steady on mine. "It's your choice."

"Well, my choice is we don't do this; we shouldn't do this," I say and then pluck his hand off my stomach. "My choice is to draw the line because I can't keep riding on this roller coaster." I slide to the side a few inches, waiting for his response.

The unhappy expression on his face tells me that he doesn't approve, but to his credit, he doesn't press me. Instead he lies down on his pillow, facing me.

"If that is what you want, Sloane."

No, that is not what I want.

"What I really want is for things to be different between us, for you to always show kindness, to not treat me like some kid, to have confidence in the fact that I know what I'm doing, but I know I won't get that with you. So yes, this is what I want. This separation. You don't know what you want, you're muddying the waters, and I think it's best that we keep our distance."

He just nods his head.

"Because you don't want sex. You don't want to grow a friendship or a relationship of any sort. You want distance from me. You've made that very clear, so I'm just running with the rules you set from the very beginning."

"I know."

And I hate that response.

I sort of wished he would say something along the lines of *What if I want to change the rules? What if I don't want distance from you?* But that's not Hudson. He's stubborn, he's going to stick to what he said, and I think he would die trying before he ever changed his mind on the true relationship we're supposed to have as a married couple.

"Okay...good night."

He's quiet, so I take that as he's done with this conversation. Disappointed, I turn away from him and attempt to get comfortable, but I can feel his eyes on me. Even though the room is dark, the curtains shut besides a sliver that's letting in the light of the moon, I can still feel those eyes on me.

"Sloane?" he says, cutting through the silence.

"What?" I say, exhausted.

"I still want to hold you."

I squeeze my eyes shut because fuck!

There it is, that voice, those words, they're like a drug I never knew I needed but that I crave.

"Please," he says softly. I clamp my mouth shut, my frustration rocking through me, because why? Why does he have to be like this? When Melva wrote out this plan, did she expect him to show this softer side? I don't think she did. This is a major flaw, a flaw that is eating away at my self-control.

Second by second, I feel myself falter.

I feel myself give in.

And before I can tell him to fuck off, I scoot a few inches back.

And then a few more...

And a few more until his arm wraps around me and tugs me into his chest.

I can feel myself holding my breath as he snuggles in close, as his head goes to my hair, as his hand clamps around my middle, bunching the shirt up.

"Relax," he says. "Stop thinking."

"You realize that you're the reason why I'm thinking so much. You're the reason why I'm second-guessing all of this. You are the reason why I'm a neurotic mess."

"I know." He turns me on my back, and I'm forced to look up at him again. "And I'm sorry. I'm sorry that I don't know how to handle this. And I'm sorry I've made a difficult situation even more difficult. I don't want you to feel like—as you put it—a neurotic mess."

He's so close, so sincere, that once again, he pulls me back in.

I know I should give him hell.

I know I should tear myself away, but for the life of me, I can't.

Instead, I quietly nod and say, "Thank you for apologizing."

"Thank you for taking care of me today."

Needing to break the seriousness of this moment, I say, "Just doing my wifely duties."

"It was appreciated."

"Should be, given how you were on the airplane."

He shrugs and then lightens the mood as well. "I didn't like that Devin fuck."

The levity in the moment makes me chuckle as his hand presses against my stomach. This is what I've wanted. Hudson talking, chuckling, joking. Him being comfortable, it's all I've been hoping for when he calls me wife, when he says he's taking this marriage seriously. I've wanted this appreciation. "You didn't like him because he's the one man who has ever truly pleasured me."

"And as your husband, I don't appreciate that."

"Because as my husband, *you* have yet to pleasure me."

His expression falls flat, which makes me laugh even harder. "Not fucking funny."

I press my hand to his cheek, staring into his sultry eyes. "I agree. It's a real problem. We might need you to see a doctor."

"Yeah, to make sure my blue balls aren't about to fall off."

Oh.

My.

God.

I press my hand to my chest. "Hudson Hopper, was that a joke?"

"I do know how to make them."

And when he does, I feel a huge weight being lifted off my shoulders. I see sun peeking through the dark clouds because this is the side of him I've always wanted, I've always craved.

"Really? Because the only other time I've seen you lighten up was when you were at Haisley and Jude's wedding."

"That's because the rest of the time you've seen me has been in the office, and I don't fuck around in the office."

"That much is obvious," I reply. "You know, you could lighten up after hours, though."

"You're still part of the business," he admits.

"Not as your wife."

I can see his mind working on that one, like he wants to tell me differently. He could look at this two ways: he can feed into this not-so-realistic situation where we marry for convenience but sink into the roles, or he can play this off as just another business transaction.

Given how he's been, I have a good guess on how he's going to react.

"Being my wife is business," he replies, not surprising me in the least.

"Is that what you truly think?" I ask, pressing for him to think about it a little bit more. "Do you truly see me as a business transaction, or do you see more?"

He wets his lips as he shifts, his hand slightly moving over my stomach. "I don't think I can answer that. I don't think it's safe to."

A small smile tugs on my lips, because I'm starting to read him so well now. "Your avoidance of the question is all the answer I need." I lift up and kiss the tip of his nose. "Night, Husband."

CHAPTER FOURTEEN
HUDSON

"MORNING," SLOANE SAYS AS SHE walks out on the terrace where I'm sitting with a glass of water. "How are you feeling?"

I glance to the side, catching her smooth legs stretching out from the bottom of my shirt. Her toenails are painted white, her hair a beautiful mess.

"Better," I say and take a sip of my water, my mouth suddenly dry.

"I'm glad." She leans against the terrace wall.

She waits, not saying anything, which is unlike her, makes me think that she still might be giving me the cold shoulder—then again, she's out here talking to me.

Wanting to break the building tension from the past few days and from last night, I say, "Thank you again for yesterday."

"You're welcome." She's toeing the ground, but then she looks up at me. "You held me all night. Any time I tried to move away, your grip on me grew stronger."

I push my hand through my hair. "I'm aware."

"Why?"

I look away, out toward the rising sun. "I'd rather not examine it," I answer honestly.

She nods and then quietly says, "You know, some might say it's because you find yourself becoming attached to me."

Yeah, I fucking know.

I keep my gaze away from her because I fear what I might do if I catch those big eyes staring back at me. I have a feeling I might stand, slip my hand around the back of her neck, and pull her in close where I can explore…

"That's okay. You don't have to admit it," she says as she pushes off the wall and then walks up to me. She slides her finger under my chin and urges me to look at her. "For what it's worth, the feeling is mutual."

Then she winks and turns back into the hotel room.

I press my hand to my forehead. "Jesus Christ."

Hardy: You think it was the chicken?

Hudson: I have no fucking clue, but I still can't look at food.

Hardy: Humiliating that you not only threw up in front of her several times but also in public. Nothing screams wet blanket on the sexual tension than seeing someone dry heave repeatedly.

Hudson: Probably was needed.

Hardy: I mean, no one looks good retching and clinging to a toilet as if it's a lifesaver, keeping them afloat.

Hudson: I wasn't clinging to the toilet.

Hardy: Can't be sure of that. In my head, you were playing koala and gripping it like a eucalyptus tree.

Hudson: Why do I even text you?

Hardy: I honestly don't know. Don't you have any other friends?

Hudson: I do, but I'm currently married to his sister and trying to make sure he doesn't find out. And we already discussed why Brody can't be trusted.

Hardy: That dude is so unreliable. The biggest gossip among all of us.

Hudson: Also, he's a goddamn hot mess. I was in a meeting with him the other day and he happened to spill his coffee all over his lap. Thank God it was just me and him because he whipped his pants off so fucking fast. The dickhead was wearing a pair of briefs with Maggie's face on the crotch. I can't unsee it.

Hardy: Maybe that's why you were throwing up so much.

Hudson: Probably.

Hardy: I saw him yesterday, and he was showing me his scar from when he had his appendix removed. Why does he think that's something I want to see?

Hudson: He's fucking weird, but I still like him. Maybe there's something wrong with me.

Hardy: I think there's something wrong with the both of us because when he showed the scar to me and said I could touch it…I fucking touched it.

Hudson: Touching another man's scar…dude, that's weird.

Hardy: I know. Afterward, I thought, why the hell did I do that? He's rubbing off on us.

Hudson: He's rubbing off on you, not me. I wouldn't have touched the scar.

Hardy: You can't say that. You weren't there. You would have touched it. Guaranteed!

Hudson: We are not debating this. I have more important things to worry about. I'm slipping, man.

Hardy: Yeah, I know. Next text I get from you is that you had sex with Sloane and don't know what to do.

Hudson: I'm so fucking worried that's going to happen. I spooned her last night.

Hardy: Noooo, why?

Hudson: I couldn't stop myself. I needed to hold her.

Hardy: This is not fucking good. Seriously, Hudson. You are acknowledging your poor decisions. Which means you need to stop making those poor decisions.

Hudson: I know. But...there was that Devin fuck and she took care of me and I didn't like that she wasn't herself around me. I'm just so fucked in the head that I really don't know what the hell I'm doing.

Hardy: Well, I'm here to tell you to press the reset button. It's the spot just behind your balls.

Hudson: Grow up.

Hardy: YOU grow up. This is business, start acting like it. Get the job done, divorce her, and move the fuck on.

Hudson: I know. I know. Fuck. Why does she have to be so... interesting?

Hardy: Interesting? Sheesh, good thing you're not waxing poetic to her about your feelings, because that would be a real doozy. She wouldn't be able to keep her hands off you.

Hudson: I don't know how else to describe it. She's interesting.

Hardy: Yup, keep saying it, that makes it better.

Hudson: She's unlike any woman I've ever met. She has no filter and for some reason, I really like that.

Hardy: Probably because you've been surrounded by people your entire life, besides me and Haisley, who have always had a filter on.

Hudson: Yeah, probably. She's also beautiful. Like...fuck, you should see her in one of my shirts.

Hardy: Okay, we're not going there. Forget what she looks like wearing one of your shirts, make her wear a turtleneck to bed, also...STOP SHARING A BED.

Hudson: She's my wife.

Hardy: For fuck's sake. You know what, I can't deal with this fuckery anymore. She's not really your wife, you nimrod. She's...

she's an associate who happens to be wearing a ring you put on her finger. Nothing else. This is business.

Hudson: She's still my wife.

Hardy: Jesus Christ. Okay, well, I can see that we are still delusional. Please don't text me when you fuck. When Jude finds out, I want to be able to tell him that I was an innocent bystander in all of this.

Hudson: You are far from innocent. You're in deep.

Hardy: I fucking know!

"Is this really necessary?" Sloane asks as she fixes her hair in the mirror. "I'm not going to do anything embarrassing."

I take in the robe she's wearing and how it slightly parts in the front while she curls her hair. I know she's not wearing anything under it, which I shouldn't care about, but for the life of me, I can't stop thinking about it.

"It is necessary," I say. "I want you to be prepared. Sheridan's wedding will require you to act a certain way. And the Mayfair Club is full of pretentious rich people who will eat you alive if you're not prepared."

"You know, I have watched *Titanic*."

I'm sitting on the bed leaning back on my hands, looking into the bathroom and watching Sloane's every move. She can be random and different but *Titanic*? Where the hell did that come from?

"How does that have anything to do with what we're talking about?"

She finishes her last curl and sprays some hair spray over her hair before turning toward me and leaning against the doorframe of the bathroom. "Umm, I studied the class difference between Jack and Rose. I get it. You're Rose, and I'm Jack. You're trying to get me all gussied up and ready to hang with the wealthy, while I'm dragging you down to the cargo room and trying to fuck you in the car."

"That's...no. That's not what is happening."

"Isn't it though?" she says as she moves toward me, her leg peeking out from the slit of her robe. "You were born with wealth and expectations. I'm just a lowly soul, looking to have a good time Irish dancing."

"Jesus," I mutter as she moves in even closer.

"I know what it takes to hang with Rose," she says as she presses her hand to my shoulder and pushes at me until I'm lying flat on the bed.

Please don't climb on my lap.

Please don't fucking climb on my lap.

She takes a seat on the bed, right next to me, but leans down on her elbow and then dances her hand over my bare stomach. She's more playful this morning, almost back to her regular self, and even though I'm happy about it because I couldn't stomach the cold shoulder from her, I know I need to be hyperaware.

How I react when she's around.

What I say.

How I touch her...

"What do you think, Hudson? Think you'll let me draw you like one of my French girls?" Her fingers flick over my nipple, and I can feel myself start to go hard.

"No."

She smirks. "Mm, shame. Your wife would love to see you naked."

"Sloane."

"Hmm?"

"Stop."

She smiles again and slides her hand down my leg, causing me to lift right off the bed and away from her.

"Get...get dressed," I say as I attempt to hide my half-hard dick.

"You're no fun."

"What the hell do you expect me to do?"

"Get into the role. Be Rose. Speak with an English accent and tell me things that you would never tell Billy Zane."

"Get. Dressed."

She rolls her eyes. "Ugh, you're so annoying. Always business. That's you. Business, business, business. What happens when you're on your deathbed one day looking back at your life? Are you going to be happy with all of your business-focused choices? Or are you going to think back and say, remember that time I married my business partner's sister and had the time of my goddamn life? Don't you want *those* memories?"

"The reason I'd be on my deathbed is because I decided to have those memories with my business partner's sister and he was the one who put me in the hospital."

"Oh, it would be worth it," she says as she stands from the bed. "Because I'm worth it." She winks and turns away from me, dropping her robe right before she heads into the closet.

Fuck.

Me.

Hands on my hips, I try to clear that image of her perfectly round ass out of my head. I try to calm my racing heart. Tell myself not to fucking fall into the trap. Remind myself that this is what I wanted. I didn't want her being cold to me. I hated it, actually. I like this side of her; I just wish that it wasn't slowly eating away at my willpower.

"This class will be good for you," I call out as I push my hand through my hair. "It will prepare you for what's to come."

She pokes her head out of the closet and asks, "Did you say come?"

My expression falls. "Sloane, come on."

"Come on what? Come now? Husband, you can't just demand it. You have to work for it."

Jesus.

Christ.

"What kind of etiquette class is this?" Sloane whispers to me, leaning in close so her breath tickles my neck.

I glance over at her, my eyes falling to the immense amount of cleavage she has on display today. She chose a white-and-blue toile dress that's fitted up top but loose at her hips. If it wasn't for her tits nearly popping out the top, it would be the perfect dress to go get tea.

"I don't know," I say as I tear my eyes away from her cleavage. "I thought it was—"

"Shh," Madame Lori says with a snap of her finger in our direction.

Both Sloane and I straighten up.

So when I decided Sloane needed to go to etiquette class, I was thinking that it would be more of what utensils to use at a fancy dinner, things like that so she wouldn't feel so...out of place when we are out on business.

But this...this is not what I was expecting.

First of all, I wasn't expecting to be in the class.

Second of all, I wasn't expecting there to be not a single table in sight, but rather just a line of chairs with an instructor toting a riding crop in her hand. When she entered the room, she slammed it against the wall, scaring everyone right out of their goddamn shoes, me included.

"You have come to me for help," Madame Lori says. "And from the looks of it, you all seem to be in desperate need."

I glance around the room at all of the couples. I mean, we look like a decently posh group. How could she be a judge of that? The guy in the bow tie, for instance, looks more than ready to take on a business function that includes petty small talk and low-hanging quips.

A woman to the right, who is wearing a flower fascinator in her hair, raises her hand. "Yes?" Madame Lori asks.

"Is there time to go to the bathroom?"

What a dumb-ass question. Don't you know you always pee before entering an event? Maybe I was wrong; maybe these people do need etiquette training.

"You should have gone before," Madame Lori says with a snap, and I inwardly applaud myself. Might have been a while since I learned the rules, but this guy still has it. "Now, I need you all to take your chairs and move them to a distinct part of the room, find your own quiet section."

Odd but okay.

I stand up and just as I'm about to grab my chair, a resounding snap shrieks through the room, pausing all of us. We turn to look at Madame Lori and she yells, "Sit down!"

Shocked, we all sit and I can feel Sloane move in closer to me.

"When I offer you direction, you must say 'Yes, Madame Lori.'"

Jesus. Okay.

"Now"—she moves around the room again, tapping her crop in her hand—"please, pick up your chairs and find your own distinct area in the room."

Together as a group, we say, "Yes, Madame Lori."

Then we grab our chairs. I take mine and Sloane's and carry them to a corner off to the left near the closed curtains.

"Do we sit down?" Sloane whispers to me.

"I have no fucking idea," I whisper back.

"You should know; you've been through this kind of class before."

"This is different. Must be a more modern version."

"Now, line up," Madame Lori says, motioning for us to all line up in the middle of the floor. We do as we're told because I don't think anyone wants to see the markings of that riding whip on our skin.

Once we're in position, she walks up and down the line, examining every participant in the class. When she gets to me and Sloane, she studies Sloane's dress, and I inwardly plead for Sloane not to get picked on. Her breasts are nearly spilling out, and I know that's not what a teacher would be looking for in an etiquette class.

"Does she belong with you?" Madame Lori asks me.

"She does. She's my wife," I say.

"I see." Madame Lori steps back and looks Sloane in the eyes. "Join me."

"Shit."

Sloane steps forward and Madame Lori puts her into position, so Sloane is facing everyone in class.

"Take a look at…what's your name?"

"Sloane."

"Yes, take a look at Sloane." Madame Lori motions her crop up and down and then carefully drags it over Sloane's cleavage, which of course raises the hairs on the back of my neck. "Do you see this dress?" Here we go. "This dress is exactly what all of you women should be wearing."

Umm, what?

"Raise your hand if you have not looked at this woman's breasts since she's walked into the room."

I glance to the left, looking down the line of attendees, and not a single one of them raises their hands. What the fuck? The guy at the end is even wetting his lips and staring at Sloane. This is going to be a fucking problem.

"The silhouette is formal with the skirt hitting just above the ankles. The print is posh. And yet, her breasts are a promise of what she's not afraid to show off."

I scratch the back of my head and wonder what the hell is going on. Did etiquette classes change in the last few years? I thought I'd have to tear down one of the curtains and fashion Sloane a scarf to hide her breasts.

Madame Lori walks up to me and slides her crop over my chest. "Very well done."

Sloane joins me and smiles with a fist pump. "Passed the first test."

How?

Madame Lori then goes down the rest of the line, pointing out how each participant could have enhanced their outfits while I rack my brain to try to figure out what the hell I'm missing.

"Did you see everyone's been looking at my boobs?" Sloane mutters to me. "Even you, you didn't raise your hand."

"Hard to miss them," I mumble.

"I'm glad you approve, Husband."

I want to roll my eyes, but I'm still so fucking confused.

"Please, take your seats," Madame Lori says, with a snap of her crop. Why the hell does she have that thing in the first place?

I press my hand to Sloane's lower back and guide her over to her chair. We both take a seat so our knees are knocking together and we're facing each other.

"One of the first things we need to learn when it comes to etiquette in the bedroom"—in the what?—"is giving yourself over to your partner."

Uhhh.

Sloane leans in very close and says, "What the hell is she talking about?"

"Fuck if I know."

"Please raise your hand if you are the Dom in your relationship."

The couples around us offer their hands up, and when I look at Sloane, she has her hand raised with a giant smile crossing her face.

"What the fuck are you doing?"

"Clearly I'm the Dom between us."

"The fuck you are," I say just as Madame Lori walks up to us and smiles.

She slides her crop over Sloane's neck and says, "I knew you were just like me." Then she slaps the crop against the window and says, "Subs, on your knees."

Sloane points to the floor between us. "That would be you, Husband."

"Clearly we're in the wrong class." I clear my throat. "Madame Lori."

She whips around to look at me, the devil in her eyes. Christ, I don't know if I would want to be caught in a bedroom with this woman. She terrifies me.

"Yes?"

"Uh, I think we might be in the wrong classroom."

"This is the only classroom in this building. This is Etiquette 101."

"Yes, that's what we signed up for."

"Then on your knees, sub," she says, pushing at my shoulder and forcing me down to the ground.

When she walks away, Sloane covers her mouth and laughs. With Madame Lori's back to us, I quickly take out my phone and search my email for the confirmation of this class. That's when I read the name of the school under Madame Lori's name.

Madame Lori: a school of etiquette for the kinks.

"Jesus Christ," I say. "I booked the wrong school."

"Really?" Sloane says as she slides her leg over my shoulder. "I don't know, this feels like it might be the right school."

"We're getting out of here, Sloane."

"Did I just hear you correctly?" Madame Lori says. "Are you trying to dominate your Dom?"

"No, there's just been some—"

Madame Lori pushes me forward, bending me at the hips just enough for her to slap her riding crop across my ass.

"Motherfucker," I yell, causing Sloane to snort and cover her mouth again.

"You listen to your Dom." Madame Lori releases me. "Good thing you brought him to this class, Sloane; it seems as though he needs the training."

"Could not agree more," Sloane says.

"Now, submit." Madame Lori waits for me to move.

"I... What?"

Squatting down, Madame Lori gets right in my face and says, "Bow your head to your Dom and submit to her."

Not wanting to get whipped in the ass again, I look up at Sloane, who can't keep it together, and I slowly lower my head, bowing to her.

Her hand finds my hair as she says, "Such a good boy."

"That's it," Madame Lori says as I feel like the biggest asshole in the world, bowing to my goddamn assistant while her leg is draped over my shoulder. "Tell me, Sloane, does he listen to you in bed?"

"It's why we're here," Sloane says. "He has yet to make me come."

I'm going to kill her.

"Well." Madame Lori stands. "We're going to change that. Don't worry. We will give him all the tools he needs to give you everything you deserve."

"Thank you," Sloane says.

"Now," Madame Lori says to the class. "Subs, I want you to look your Doms in the eyes and tell them that you are there to serve them."

I lift my head and look at Sloane. "I'm not saying that."

Sloane's hand glides over my cheek. "Oh, Hudson, when will you learn? You will receive pleasure once I start receiving pleasure."

"Cut the shit, Sloane."

"Hmm, that doesn't sound like you want to serve me. Maybe try again, this time with less anger."

"I'm not fucking saying it."

"That's a shame because now I'm going to have to raise my hand and get Madame Lori to come over here and spank my naughty boy again."

She starts to raise her hand, and I quickly say, "Don't even fucking think about it."

"Say it, Hudson, or I raise my hand." I don't say anything. I remain still, and she drops her leg from my shoulder and leans forward, offering me the best view of her tits. "Say it, my good boy."

"Sloane…"

"Say it or I'm raising my hand." She starts to raise it again. When I don't say anything, she raises it fully and calls out, "Madame Lori."

Panic ensues because I don't want to be spanked, and despite not knowing what the hell is going on, I mutter, "I'm here to serve."

"A problem over there?" Madame Lori asks.

Sloane looks at me, eyebrow raised.

So I say it a little louder. "I'm here to serve."

"Here to serve…who?"

"Is there a problem?"

I glance at Madame Lori and that riding crop and then look Sloane in the eyes. "I'm here to serve you."

"Not a problem," Sloane says, keeping her eyes on me. "Such a good boy," she says and then leans forward and kisses me on the nose.

I don't think this could get any worse.

———

"His balls are really sensitive," Sloane says as she rubs my back while I'm positioned on all fours, tied up with rope, and feeling like a goddamn hog ready to be roasted over a fire.

"If that's the case, you don't have to tie his balls. You can leave those free," Madame Lori says, also rubbing my back. "It's a shame they're so sensitive. Ball play can be very pleasurable for both parties."

"I know, that's what I've been telling him, but anytime I go remotely near them, he comes."

"Oh," Madame Lori says. "So they're very sensitive."

You'd think I'd be defending myself at this point, but nope. Coming from her being near my balls is barely a blip in what I've been through today…during this three-hour-long fucking class.

She has told Madame Lori, who has paid extra special attention to us, that I squeal—yes, she said *squeal*—when she plays with my nipples and that I kick my legs when I go down on her, which is why she's had a hard time coming because the kicking has been distracting.

Madame Lori said she had a solution for that, hence why I'm tied up at the moment.

I've also been labeled as the early ejaculator of the group, the man with the large boner, and finally, Baby Blue Eyes by one of the other Doms in the class.

I've been rolled on my back, on my stomach; I've had my head tucked, lifted, my ass spanked several times; and I've watched another man come in his jeans because of how hard Madame Lori was spanking him.

Legit his eyes rolled in the back of his head as he groaned and moaned.

Easily the most uncomfortable situation I've ever been in, and yet, there's Sloane, fucking thriving, asking questions, getting into the spirit of the classroom.

"Would you mind if I touched him there?" Madame Lori asks.

"I mind," I nearly yelp. "I mind if you touch me."

"Silence," Madame Lori says. "That is not your choice to make. You gave yourself over to your Dom. Best you remember that."

I swear on my left nut if Sloane allows Madame Lori to touch me, I will hand her divorce papers today and ask for my money back because this is not the bride I purchased.

"Actually, I think I want to be the only one touching him," Sloane says, finally making some good choices.

"I respect that. Can I guide your hand, then?"

"Of course," Sloane says.

What? There should be no guiding. Also, guiding where?

"If you want to avoid him ejaculating so quickly and taking the fun out of a session, have you tried rubbing down his crack?"

"I haven't," Sloane says.

"Well, it's a great way to tease but not tease him where he's more sensitive. Place your hand on his tailbone."

Sloane, don't do it.

Don't fucking do it.

Her hand lands on my tailbone.

Yup, she's doing it.

And I'm regretting not wearing jeans right now, because these chino shorts are not the thickest material.

"With your middle finger, slowly slide it down his crack."

I clench and hold my breath, not wanting to be turned on—

Smack.

"Mother...fucker," I yell as the riding crop hits me in the ass.

I learned about two hours ago, when I asked whether the spanking was allowed, that I signed off on it when I registered for the class. I chastised myself for not reading the fine print.

"Unclench," Madame Lori snaps at me.

Breathing heavily, I unclench my ass and wonder what the other students are doing. I hear a little bit of moaning in the background, but my ears are ringing from the onslaught of emotions and feelings pushing through me.

"That's my good boy," Sloane says as she reaches around and squeezes my nipple. "Squeezing his nipple is like giving a dog a treat for a job well done."

"My sub loves when I play with his nipples," Madame Lori says.

Seriously, when I get out of this classroom, I'm going to have a really long conversation with Sloane.

"Okay, now slide your hand down his crack, but stop right before you reach his balls."

Sloane slides her hand down my shorts, and I stare at my hands holding me up, attempting not to feel anything. Just a normal day on the job, nothing to worry about here. Just working with my assistant, learning things that won't apply to us in the future, but gaining life experience.

Yup, that's it.

There is no way I'm going to get turned on—

"Now drum your fingers close to his testicles, so close, he can feel the vibration."

Sloane starts drumming and Madame Lori praises her.

"Yes, just like that. Continue to drum until he gets hard. I'll be back to check on you."

"Thank you," Sloane says.

When Madame Lori walks away, I mutter, "What the hell are you thanking her for?"

"Uh, this is good information."

"We don't do this shit," I say as she moves her fingers closer to my sack. Christ, that...that feels a little good.

"I know we don't do this, but that doesn't mean when we get divorced and I start my new life in the house I own with my sister that I'm not going to want to drum another man's perineum. As you know, I've only been with one man who's been able to give me pleasure. I don't want to risk another disappointment. If I go into my next relationship knowing how to drum, it could be the key to unlocking pleasure with my new partner."

"Can you stop talking about other men?"

"Jealous?"

"No."

"Liar." She leans forward so I can see her pretty face and asks, "You hard yet?"

"No, Sloane."

"Damn it." Then she lifts up and shouts, "He's not hard yet."

"Get closer to his balls," Madame Lori calls out.

"Must do what the doctor orders," Sloane says and then moves her hand right over the base of my balls and starts tapping on them.

Fuck.

Fuck...me.

I squeeze my eyes shut, and I feel my ass lift in the air without my permission as my cock starts to grow.

"Stop," I say.

"Stop?" she asks, coming in close to me.

"Yes, fucking stop."

I can hear the smile in her voice as she says, "Getting hard?"

"What the fuck do you think?"

"That my work here is done...Husband."

CHAPTER FIFTEEN
SLOANE

HAVE YOU EVER REALIZED IN real time that maybe you're taking something a little too far?

I have.

Today.

In the middle of our kinky etiquette, when I had Hudson lying flat on his back, me hovering over him, my breasts right next to his mouth, I realized that maybe things had gone too far.

Yet I couldn't stop.

I was way into the process of it all, and Madame Lori was a very good instructor. I didn't think etiquette class was going to be that fun, but wow, it was way better than I expected.

Now, did Hudson have fun? That would be a no. After I made him hard when he was tied up, he stopped talking to me.

I know sliding my finger down his crack was a choice I probably shouldn't have taken part in, but then again, he's the one who has said he's my husband. He's the one initiating all of the touching, the hand-holding, the cuddling. So this is an extension of that. Plus, I really liked the drumming. That was a new technique to put in my arsenal. Who knows when I'm going to use it, but when I do, whoever the lucky recipient is will be like, *Wow, this girl, she knows how to drum the dick to full-staff potential.*

Anyway, now that class is over and Hudson and I are driving in silence through the streets of London, I truly question what's going to happen next. He said we were going to Harrods, but after what he just went through, is that still the plan? Or is he taking me back to the hotel, where I'm certain he will pack my things and send me back home?

Sure, he's mad at me because I was the Dom in class, and sure, I engaged, but we can't forget that he was the one who booked the class for us. It would be one thing if *I* had stupidly booked the wrong class, but it was him. If he needs to be upset with anyone, it should be himself. Also seems pretty hypocritical to be mad about intimacy when he's the one who's been creating intimacy between us recently.

I look over at him and the clench in his jaw. Seems like he only wants it to be a one-way street.

Trying to bring light to the situation, I say, "For what it's worth, Madame Lori said I aced the class, so…you're welcome."

He flashes a death glare in my direction, and I shrink in my seat.

Maybe I shouldn't have talked about his nipples.

Or how he has yet to pleasure me. But it was the truth. The drought is big over here, and it's not like it's getting any better. He even said yesterday how he has blue balls.

I think I might have to take matters into my own hands because this is stupid. Us not having sex, it's just…stupid. We're about to enter some high-stress situations, and I think fucking will help with that. Then again, after what we went through this morning, maybe stepping back and not pushing it like I used to might be best.

I think I'll have to roll with what he wants to do now that I tied him up and drummed his balls.

Pulling my phone out of my purse, I shoot off a quick text to Stacey.

Sloane: Might have drummed on Hudson's balls today. Don't ask. But he's not happy.

Thankfully she's awake and texts me back.

Stacey: Umm, what?

Sloane: Long story, but the car right now is really cold. Like frigid.

Stacey: I thought you weren't making a move anymore.

Sloane: I wasn't but then he got sick and I helped him and he was so sweet and then we spooned and here we are now, me drumming on his balls making him hard only for me not to finish it off because we were in public. One guy totally came in his pants but Hudson is too good for that, despite me telling the teacher that he was quick on the trigger.

Stacey: What? How can someone ramble in real life and in a text message?

Sloane: That's not rambling, that's the truth. That really happened.

Stacey: I'm going to need some coffee to understand this.

Sloane: All you need to know is that I made him hard.

Stacey: I'm sure it's not the first time given what you told me. Why is now different?

Sloane: Because things are different. He talked to me last night, made a joke actually. I think he's cracking, and I don't think he likes that he's cracking, and now that I think he's cracking, what do I do? Do I keep pushing?

Stacey: Honestly, Sloane, I don't know if cracking him is a good idea. I thought you were there for business, not to see if you can get your boss to fuck you.

Sloane: I know, same, but don't you think we should fuck?

Stacey: I don't think you should have even married him.

Sloane: You know, you are more agreeable with coffee in you.

Stacey: Facts. When do business things start?

Sloane: We're going to Harrods to get clothes, and according to the schedule, tomorrow is our first business event. We're going to a fancy club.

Stacey: Oh, that should be interesting. Never been to one of those.

Sloane: We have not. I think he wants to get me an outfit that I can wear to it.

"We're here," Hudson snaps, pulling my attention away from my phone and out the window, where an ornate brown building with green awnings comes into view—a stack of letters that spell out *Harrods* lines the building, making this moment feel...magical.

As someone who admired Nancy Meyers's *The Parent Trap*, with Lindsay Lohan, Harrods has always been stuck in my head as a must-see place while in London. And here I am. With a grumpy husband, ready to go on a shopping spree.

Fun.

The driver opens my door for me, and I slip my purse over my shoulder as Hudson walks up next to me and takes my hand in his.

Well, at least he's holding my hand. I've got that going for me.

Together, we walk up to the entrance, where a bellman dressed in green opens the door. I'm immediately struck by just how beautiful the store is. I've seen videos and pictures of the Macy's flagship store in New York City, but this, this doesn't even seem to compare. The opulence, the architecture, the noticeable smell of wealth.

This is far beyond anything I've ever experienced.

"This way," Hudson says, leading me toward a back corner where we're greeted by a worker wearing white gloves. Yes, white gloves. Hudson gives the guy his name, and we are ushered into a private elevator, taking us to a more secluded floor.

"Hudson Hopper," a lady in a pencil skirt and cream blouse says as she walks up to us in her modest kitten heels. "It's nice to meet you. I'm Lorraine, and I'll be your personal shopper today."

"Lorraine, nice to meet you," Hudson says. "This is my wife, Sloane."

"Hi, Sloane," Lorraine says with a kind smile. "We have a lot picked out for you. Please follow me."

Personal shopper…fancy.

We follow Lorraine into a room encased by glass with a couch and a few chairs. There are mannequins sporting some of the latest fashions poised around the room and flutes of champagne on the coffee table for both me and Hudson.

Doubt Hudson will touch it after what happened to him on the plane.

"I've pulled quite a few outfits. Mr. Hopper, if you'd like to take a seat, I can start getting your wife into the selections—"

"I'd like to help her into the outfits," Hudson says, his grip on my hand growing tighter.

Uh-oh.

Why do I feel like that's not going to go over well for me?

"Oh, are you sure? Usually, I help the clients into their outfits and then we bring them out here and take pictures if it's something you like."

"I'm sure," Hudson says. "No one sees my wife naked but me."

"Of course. My apologies," Lorraine says, looking positively terrified at Hudson's authoritative, dark voice. "Allow me to show you to the room so you can get started. Right this way."

She takes us to a dressing room in the back, off to the right. The door is open, so when we step in, I'm not only surprised by the amount of clothing on racks but also by the size of this room. There's a settee in the corner, three mirrors in the other corner, and the rest of the perimeter is lined with clothes ranging from formal wear to everyday casual to… is that lingerie?

Um…sir.

My underwear is fine, thank you very much.

Hudson releases my hand and walks up to the racks of clothing. He pulls out a brown dress with polka dots and hands it to Lorraine.

"No," he says and then snags a few more. He picks up a short cocktail dress and says, "We need this in a different color. Something that will make her eyes pop." *Oh, well...thank you.* "And this, another color. These pants, I want them in black. No prints." He moves over to the lingerie, and I half expect him to pluck it all and tell Lorraine to remove it, but instead, he says, "I want her in ice-blue lingerie, as it will look perfect against her skin."

"Of course," Lorraine says, arms full of clothes. "I'll be right back."

"Please knock before coming back," Hudson says, his eyes on me, and yup, I know I'm in a whole lot of trouble. I might have had my fun earlier, but now it's time for Hudson to have his fun.

Lorraine shuts the door behind her, and Hudson takes a seat on the settee. With a nod, he says one single word. "Strip."

I clear my throat, feeling weary. "Um, what's that?"

"You heard me," he replies, that dark tone almost menacing. "Strip."

I set my purse down and say, "I know that you're a little—"

"I said strip, Sloane. We don't have all fucking day."

Yikes. Okay. So he's angry. I get that. I mean, I did just hog-tie him and play with his ass crack in front of a woman wielding a riding crop. So maybe I need to just do as he says.

I walk up to him, turn around, and ask, "Can you unzip me?"

He stands and moves behind me, his body so close that I can feel the heat pouring off every inch of him. He takes the zipper and slowly pulls it down my back until the dress is loose. Then he pushes the straps from my shoulders, revealing my white push-up bra underneath. He sends the dress to the floor, and I step out of it before bending over and giving him a view of my lacy briefs as I pick up the dress.

"Turn around, Sloane," he growls.

I turn around and set the dress on the settee next to him. His eyes feast on me, devouring me inch by inch as he takes me in, slowly making his way up and down my body until his eyes find mine again.

Legs spread, he says, "On your knees."

"What?"

"On. Your. Knees."

A shiver races up my spine as my body gets sucked in by his command. I lower to my knees in front of him, waiting.

Then he says, "Hands on my thighs."

I slide my hands over his thighs and scoot in a little more. He lifts his hand to my cheek and runs his thumb just under my eye. "Submit to me."

He can't be serious.

Back there, at the class, that was kind of a joke.

But right now, here, this feels nothing like a laughing matter.

This feels real.

"Sloane, as my wife, you will submit to me."

"Hudson."

"Submit," he says, sitting up now and leaning forward so our faces are nearly nose to nose. "I need you to remember who calls the shots here. Not you. Not your little quips or your sarcasm and wit. Me. I'm the one in fucking charge, so this is a reminder, one that you're not going to forget. Fucking submit...now."

If I weren't so turned on, I might actually be terrified.

And this possessive behavior is what I was looking for from Hudson when it comes to intimacy, that I knew was deep within him—that I knew wanted to come out. Between this side of Hudson and the fun-loving side of him that I saw in Bora Bora, it's hard not to get wrapped up in him.

Eyes on him, I say, "I'm here to service you."

"Good...girl." He tips my chin up with his finger and then places the softest of kisses right on my nose.

God, what I wouldn't give to have that kiss anywhere else—my fore-head, my cheek, my mouth, my body. Because I know the nose kiss means nothing. I know the nose kiss is his way of putting me in my place.

I hate the nose kiss.

Despise it.

There's a knock on the door. "Mr. Hopper, I have that lingerie you asked for."

Hudson stands from the settee and moves over to the door, where he cracks it open and takes the hangers from Lorraine.

"Thank you," Hudson says and then shuts the door again. When his eyes meet mine, he commands, "On your feet, face the wall."

I get up and walk over to the empty wall, turning to face it. He hangs the lingerie on one of the racks and walks up behind me where, to my surprise, he unclasps my bra.

"Don't fucking move," he says in his rich, velvety voice.

My heart rate increases as he slides my bra off my shoulders and lets it fall to the ground. His fingers play along my bare back before he lifts an ice-blue lace bra in front of me. With my back toward him, I'm not sure he can see anything, but if he could, he'd see exactly how hard my nipples are. How they're begging for his touch, for his palm, for any amount of pressure from his dexterous fingers.

He slips my arms into the bra and brings the straps to my shoulders. "Adjust yourself," he says.

Sad he's not going to do it for me, I lift my breasts into the cups, and when they're secure, he clasps the bra. Goose bumps spread across my skin as he slides his hands in my underwear and drags them down until they hit the floor. I step out of them, my ass on full display, and toe the underwear to the side. He then stands back up, trailing his fingers up my legs, over my rear, and to my back, where he grips my hips and speaks softly into my ear. "Don't move."

"I'm...I'm not," I say as I feel myself start to get wet as a dull throb erupts between my legs.

This teasing, it feels like torture, but it also feels like everything I've been wanting—everything I've been asking for and needing when it comes to him.

He walks back over to the rack, and I hear him unclip something, a pair of underwear I'm assuming.

He then squats back down and says, "Step in."

I look down to see a matching ice-blue G-string at my feet. Again, no price tag. *Because this is personal shopping.* I step into the leg holes and then he slides the soft material all the way up until it's secure around my waist. "Turn around," he commands.

I turn around to face him and watch as his eyes once again devour me. He wets his lips, his hunger clear in his eyes as he lightly pushes me against the wall. He takes both of my hands in his and pins them against the wall above me. Then with his other hand, he trails a finger over my collarbone, then across the swell of my breasts.

"You will not wear any color but this, understood?"

His finger travels between my cleavage, down my stomach, and right above the waistband of my G-string. My breathing becomes labored, my core so freaking wet and ready for him that if he doesn't take me in this dressing room, if he doesn't give me what I want, I very well might perish on the spot.

"Touch me," I say.

"I am."

"No," I say. "Touch me where you know I want it."

His teeth pull on the edge of his lip as he lowers his hand between my legs and hovers. He then sticks out one finger and lightly grazes my slit. "Here?"

My eyes roll in the back of my head as a quiet moan falls past my lips. "Jesus, yes."

"Or..." His finger glides up my stomach to my breast, where it circles my nipple over the fabric of my bra. "Here?"

I pull at my pinned hands, but he doesn't let them move.

"Answer the question, Sloane."

"Both," I say. "I want both. God, I'm so wet right now. Give me relief, Hudson."

A sardonic smile passes over his lips. "You're wet?"

"Drenched," I say.

"Good," he responds and then releases my hands. "Then try on the dresses."

And with that he leaves the dressing room, leaving me horny and extremely frustrated.

Well played, Mr. Hopper, you asshole.

If you thought the atmosphere in the car was icy on the way to Harrods, that's nothing compared to what it is right now.

It is positively arctic.

We have not spoken a word to each other, other than Hudson nodding his approval to outfits he liked on me and me thanking him for the clothes when we checked out—because I do have manners despite how pissed I am.

While they packed up the clothes, he was off in a corner on the phone talking to someone, leaving me sitting there, waiting like some disregarded housewife. Nothing about the interaction at Harrods was what I thought it would be. And I could tell that Lorraine felt bad for me—and awkward—because after Hudson left the room, she was the one in charge of dressing me, despite Hudson saying no one saw me naked besides him. Talk about mixed signals.

I know that entire situation in the dressing room was his way of getting back at me for the drumming, but his felt more malicious.

Perhaps because she felt bad about the disconnect Hudson and I were suffering through, Lorraine slipped a complimentary bottle of perfume into my bag that she told me would make Hudson wild for me. As if I needed the help. I thanked her kindly despite wanting to throw the perfume back at her and tell her I didn't need it, that the stupid ice-blue lingerie should do the trick.

Guess who won't be wearing the lingerie though. This girl. That's right, if he thinks he can control me, he is sorely mistaken.

When we arrive at the hotel, the bellman opens our doors and fishes out the bags from the trunk. Hudson moves to my side, takes me by the hand, and together, we walk into the hotel and straight to the elevator that's waiting for us. I will say this, money gets you a lot of things, service being one of them. It's wild to me how many people are willing to be at your beck and call.

As we ride up to our room, Hudson's hand remains glued to mine, but his attention is on his phone. I understand he has to work, but Jesus, it's all he ever does.

When the elevator doors part, we head to our room, a trail of bellmen holding bags behind us. Hudson opens the door and lets me in first before the bellmen. I stand there and watch them set the bags on the dining room table before Hudson tips them, they leave, and he shuts the door.

I'm about ready to go off on him when he says, "Get ready. We're leaving in an hour and forty minutes."

"Excuse me?" I ask.

He peels his eyes off his phone and looks at me. "We have dinner... with Sheridan and Archie. They want to welcome us to London. Wear the black sequin dress. We're going somewhere nice."

I work my jaw to the side and cross my arms at my chest. "Anything else, your majesty?"

"No," he says, dismissing me.

I have never loathed someone so much in my entire life. Like absolutely despise. If I could throw one person to the wolves, it would be my husband. Straight to them, no regrets, please have a meal on me.

Frustrated, I move into the bedroom and head toward the bathroom, where I pause for a moment.

You know what? I'm frustrated because this man is getting me horny as hell and not doing anything about it. It's about time I take care of things. I march into the bathroom, draw myself a bath with some of the lavender bath salts the hotel provided, then slip out of my clothes, walk naked to my nightstand, and grab my vibrator from where I noticed the staff placed it when they unpacked.

Already feeling relaxed from the possibility of taking care of things, I walk back into the bathroom, test the water, and slip into the tub. Thankfully, it fills up fast, and the jets help as I settle in and make myself comfortable.

Glad my vibrator is waterproof, I lean my head against the tub, spread my legs, and turn it on. I take a second to run the vibrator over my breasts, making my nipples hard for me to play with before bringing it down my stomach and between my legs, where I rest it right against my clit.

"Fuck," I draw out as I sink deeper into the water.

Yes, this is what I want; this is what I need.

This release.

"God," I moan as the vibrator does its work. Always takes me seconds. My body is already warmed up, my nerve endings all pulling toward my stomach. To slow down the process, I slide the vibrator inside and let it vibrate against my inner walls, keeping me excited but never pushing me over the edge as I continue to play with my nipples.

"Fuck, so good," I whisper as I pull the vibrator out and bring it back to my clit. "Fuck, yes," I say, my voice carrying through the bathroom. Was that too loud?

Then again...

What if I am too loud?

What if he hears me from the other room? What if he hears me as I come?

The thought of that only turns me on more.

So I close my eyes and let myself feel, let myself get lost, let my mind drift to the moment in the dressing room where he had me pinned against the wall, his finger trailing all over me, when I was so needy and aching for him that I thought I'd burn up on the spot.

"Yes, God, yes," I say, my legs spreading wider. "Fuck." My lips clamp together. My body starts to shake, my fingers pinch my nipple. "Oh fuck," I yell. "Yes, fuck." My voice becomes breathy, my pulse hammers in my throat, and every sensation in my body pools in the pit of my stomach as my orgasm reaches its apex. "Fuck, I'm…oh God, oh God," I yell, my entire body on fire just before my orgasm hits me, tipping me over the edge. I squeeze my legs together, pressing the vibrator into my clit as I come over and over again until I can't take it anymore and release.

"Fuck," I mutter as I open my eyes and turn to set my vibrator down, only to find Hudson in the doorway of the bathroom, leaning against the frame, staring at me.

My cheeks go red from embarrassment even though there was nothing embarrassing about what I just did. No, what I just did was exactly what I needed to do. It was exactly what I craved.

"Get a good show?" I ask him as I grab a bar of soap and start lathering up. I'm not sure how much of me he can see from there, but I don't bother to cover up.

Without a word, he turns away and shuts the door behind me.

Well, I think I got my answer.

CHAPTER SIXTEEN
HUDSON

I SIT ON THE BED, facing the bathroom, as my leg bounces up and down, waiting for her to be done as the sounds of her coming echo through my head.

The first moment I heard her moan, I knew what she was doing. How could she not be? I've been dying to get here and take a shower ever since the goddamn etiquette class. But when she started getting louder, I knew exactly what she was trying to do. It was her counterattack. It was her tempting me to join.

And I swore I wouldn't, but that didn't stop me from watching.

I had no problem standing there, watching her get lost in pinching her perfect little nipples, seeing her find the right spot to use her vibrator, watching her mouth fall open, her cheeks redden, and seeing her lose all control while her orgasm rocked through her.

Fuck, was it breathtaking.

Addicting.

So fucking bad for me to witness that I've had to mentally lock myself to this bed to not try to replicate the same sounds and looks myself.

What I did to her in the dressing room, that was conniving, evil, but I couldn't stop myself. I wanted her to feel as tormented and tortured as I'd felt. And I know she did, I could see it in her eyes, but she came back with a vengeance, making matters even worse.

The bathroom door slides open, and she walks out in a black lingerie set, clearly trying to piss me off.

"What the fuck is that?" I ask.

"What?" she asks, looking down at herself and then back up.

"I said ice blue."

She struts up to me, her hair still wet and pushed to the side. She places a hand on my shoulder. "I know, but guess what: until you fuck me, I'll be wearing whatever lingerie I want." And then she places a kiss on my nose and struts toward the closet, her beautiful ass swaying away.

Grumbling, I pull my shirt off and leave it on the floor before making my way to the shower, where I flip it on. I don't bother shutting the door. I don't even care at this point. My dick is so fucking hard, so goddamn desperate for her, that I just need release. I slip my shorts and briefs off, letting my cock spring forward, and step under the warm water. The water sluices down my body before I grip the base of my cock and start pumping it.

Christ, the first stroke feels phenomenal, like the last stroke right before you come. It's powerful and claws at me, skyrocketing my body to another dimension where everything around me fades to the back, and it's just me and this pleasure that has been building at the base of my cock, yearning to come out.

I press my hand to the tile wall for support as my mind races with images of Sloane, the last being of her in the tub, masturbating, taking control of her own pleasure. Jesus, I wish she were doing that right now, giving me a goddamn show as I pump my cock. What I wouldn't give to be able to do this in front of her, to make her watch me pleasure myself, and then tell her to open her mouth so I could decorate those pretty lips.

"Fuck," I grumble as my hand moves faster, my legs starting to wobble.

I imagine what it would feel like with her kneeling before me, licking my balls as I stroke myself, watching her tits bounce, seeing those beautiful eyes stare up at me, her body soaking wet.

"Ahh, fuck," I say as precum falls down the head of my cock.

I bet she's tight.

I bet she's warm.

I bet she has the best fucking cunt, made just for me.

I squeeze my cock tighter, continuing to stroke up and down.

Everything about her makes me want to come. From her lips to her sultry mouth, to her perfect tits, to that ass. Jesus, I want to mark her with my mouth, with my cum. I want to see her coated in it.

My balls tighten from the image.

My mind set on what that would look like.

"Jesus," I say, my stomach hollowing as my cock grows tighter, my body tensing, my orgasm at its precipice. "Fuck...fuuuuck," I drag out just as my cock swells and I finish all over the shower floor.

I give myself a few more pumps before I push off the tile and take a few deep breaths. When I turn around, I catch Sloane standing in the bathroom, staring at me.

Her eyes drop to my cock, which is still fully hard. Her tongue peeks out, wetting her lips, and I swear to you, in that moment, from that little movement, my cock twitches, wanting more.

When her eyes move up my wet body, to my face, I get the privilege of seeing those cheeks fully red now. So I take that moment to say, "Never see a real man make himself come?"

She clears her throat and slowly steps away, out of view. Looks like we're even.

"Stay there," I tell Sloane as I get out of the car and walk around to her side. I button my suit jacket, then hold the door open for her. Her lotioned, glistening leg pokes out first, and then she stands from the car and takes my hand in hers. She looks fucking stunning.

The black sequin dress drapes over her body, molding over her curves, a waterfall of black. The dip in the neckline offers a small view of her cleavage, but not too much, and the back clings around her ass, making her rear end look plentiful, like two handfuls, ready to be grabbed. She paired it with black high heels, her hair parted to the side and slicked back behind her ear with a clip, and a red lipstick that is making me nuts.

But the thing that is really driving me crazy, that is making me lose my goddamn mind, is the perfume she's wearing. I don't know what it is, but I find myself getting closer and closer to smell it. To run my nose along her neck, to bury my face in her cleavage. She has always smelled good, but this—this is something else. This is unlike anything I've smelled before.

"Ready?" I ask, the tension between us at an all-time high even though we both took care of business.

"Yes," she says.

I take that moment to bring my head to her ear, where I take a deep whiff, letting my eyes roll to the back of my head. "You smell fucking incredible."

She turns her head just enough to look at me as she whispers, "Your cock is huge."

And that...that breaks the tension. Just like that. Four words and she has me smiling and chuckling.

"Thank you."

Her teeth pull on her lip. "Like...massive."

"I'll remember that," I tell her as she starts to head toward the door, but I stop her and turn her toward me. "First, I just...I want to acknowledge that things got tense earlier, and I didn't handle it well. I was embarrassed about booking the wrong class and then took it out on you. I'm sorry."

Her brow lifts. "Wow, uh, wasn't expecting an apology," she says in a teasing tone. "That's really...not like us."

"Yeah, I know, but I just want to make sure you're okay. I promised I would treat you well, and teasing you in the dressing room, that wasn't treating you well."

"I don't know. I wouldn't have minded if you kept sliding your finger across my slit."

I press my lips together and quietly say, "You were wet."

"I was."

I tug on my neck and look away. "Doesn't matter. I shouldn't have done it, and I'm sorry."

"I'm sorry for drumming your balls."

That makes me chuckle. "Apology accepted. Now, I know you don't need me to say this, because as you've reminded me, you're capable, smart, and know what you're doing, but this is our first real outing as a married couple with businesspeople. I just want to make sure that you're comfortable."

"I am," she says.

"Are you sure?"

"Positive. Let's do this."

"Okay," I say, and then I guide her into the restaurant where I hold her hand just a little tighter.

The hostess leads us back to a private Scotch room, where the walls are lined with bottles, a large table situated in the middle of it all. "Your party is waiting for you," the hostess says as they open the door.

Sheridan and Archie stand from the table and are about to greet us, revealing another person behind them at the table, also moving to stand and sending my good mood right into the fucking shitter as Devin comes into view.

The motherfucker.

Now, not only do I have to convince Archie and Sheridan that Sloane and I are very much in love, but I have to do it in front of a guy who actually has more physical relationship experience with Sloane than I do.

"Hudson, Sloane, it's so nice to see you," Sheridan says as she gives us both hugs. "Wow, Sloane, you smell incredible."

Tell me about it.

"Thank you. I'm so excited to be here."

Archie gives us a hello as well, and then fucking Devin steps up and offers me a handshake that I reluctantly accept. Then to my horror, he presses a kiss to Sloane's cheek before telling her how beautiful she looks tonight.

Keep the compliments to yourself. She doesn't need them from you. She gets them from me, you douche.

"So good to see you," Sloane says to Devin. "I didn't know you were going to be here."

Yeah, neither did I.

"Oh, I squeezed in at the last minute when I asked these two what they were doing." We all take our seats, and I make sure to sit between Devin and Sloane, keeping my chair close to hers. "When I heard that they were going out to dinner with you two, I told them how I knew you and that we used to date."

"That's so crazy. What are the odds?" Archie asks.

Pretty great, actually.

"I know, I thought the same thing," Devin says. God, he's so annoying. And I hate how his hair bounces.

You know that viral video of the guy arguing with another guy about the Wicked Witch? The guy yelling and losing his shit when he says *"the Wicked Witch of the East"* and his hair bounces back and forth? That's Devin.

That's Devin's fucking hair.

Use some product, dweeb.

"I had no idea that you two were married," Archie says, motioning to me and Sloane.

"Yeah, since we work together, we don't really mention it," I say as I press my hand to her thigh. To my surprise, she places her hand on top of mine.

"Did you two meet in the office?" Sheridan asks.

Oh fuck.

We didn't discuss that. I guess I tried to, but we weren't really talking before we left for London, then I got sick. Shit.

I feel the back of my neck heat up as I turn to Sloane, ready to make something up when she swoops in with a response.

"No," Sloane says, surprising me. "We actually met in Bora Bora."

"Oh wow, what an exotic place to meet," Sheridan says.

"It was. Breathtaking. Too bad when I met him, he was running from a snake, screaming his head off."

Excuse me?

"Come to find out, it wasn't a snake. It was just a branch."

The entire table erupts in laughter besides me.

When I turn to look at her, I can see her wince. Well, at least it seems like she regrets her response.

"Are you afraid of snakes?" Archie asks as his laughter dies down.

No, Brody is. That exact thing happened to him in Bora Bora.

"Uh, I was just startled. I mean, who really likes to come across a snake out in the wild?"

"But it wasn't a snake, it was a branch," Devin says.

Trying not to lash out at the prick next to me, I say, "At the time, I thought it was a snake."

"It was very lifelike," Sloane says. "So lifelike, that I actually screamed a little too, startled backward, and fell into a pool of water. One of those rapids, you know?" And there she takes a hit to the ego, but she does it with class and an adorable self-deprecating tone.

"Oh wow, seriously?" Sheridan asks.

"Oh yeah, took me right under."

"Oh no. Did you have to be rescued?" Archie asks.

"Yup, by this big old lump of man," Sloane says while leaning her head against my shoulder. "Once he realized that the snake was a branch, he leapt into the water, rode the rapids until he was able to snag me, and dragged me up on shore to safety, where he gave me mouth-to-mouth. I always like to say our first kiss was a lifesaving one."

Sheridan presses her hand to her heart. "Oh my God, that's so sweet."

"Because I had to be resuscitated, they took me to the hospital, where I stayed for a few days, just for observation since I took in a lot of water. And this guy sat by my side the entire time."

"I wasn't going to leave her," I say, even though the story is not true— pretty convincing though. "I wanted to be there for her."

"And you were." Sloane turns toward me and cups my cheek. "You're always there for me."

"Well, you two are the cutest," Sheridan says. "And I'm so glad you could help us out for the wedding. It works out that you and Devin know each other. He actually suggested that you be partnered up for the dancing."

Oh, I'm sure he fucking did, that goddamn weasel.

What is with this guy? He can clearly see that Sloane has a ring on her goddamn hand, that she's happily married, so move the fuck on and stop clinging to someone else's wife or I will fucking end you.

"Oh, that's nice," Sloane answers.

"That's why I suggested we practice together, so we can get used to each other," Devin says. "And of course, so Hutton over here doesn't have to waste his time."

Oh that motherfucker.

He did that on purpose.

He knows my goddamn name.

"It's Hudson," Sloane says.

"Right, my mistake. Sorry, bro."

He knocks on my shoulder, and it takes everything in me not to plow my fist right through his skull, but I hold my composure. "Honest mistake, but listen, any time spent with my wife is not wasted time. I'm looking forward to dancing with her. We took dancing lessons before our wedding."

"You did?" Sheridan asks as I lift Sloane's hand to my mouth and press a kiss against her knuckles.

"We did. It was just for us. We had our own elopement and then danced privately together, but it was nice, to have my wife in my arms and to be able to dip, twist, and turn her around our living room."

"Remember that time you dipped me and your back gave out?"

Why, Sloane?

Why?

"Happens to the best of us, man," Archie says while placing his hand on his back in solidarity.

"He said it was because he lifted three hundred pounds in the gym that day." Umm, okay, can't lift that much. "But I said it was because he's thirteen years my senior."

"Thirteen?" Sheridan asks. "Wow, that's quite the age gap."

"It is, but the only time we notice it is apparently when he's trying to dip me after working out so hard in the gym. But in the bedroom, oh my God, the man is sensational."

Okay, not the crowd. I squeeze her thigh, letting her know to drop that.

"I mean, he can really rattle a headboard. One neighbor thought there was an earthquake, but nope, just my husband's hips."

Jesus, Sloane.

Archie takes a sip of his drink and then smirks at me. "Congrats, man. Always great to know you have good working hips."

"Ones that might need a replacement if you keep trying to show off," Devin says, making my nostrils flare.

This guy is on my last fucking nerve.

Pushing me.

Poking me.

"It's not showing off," I say. "It's just the way I fuck."

The moment the word slips past my mouth, I realize just how unprofessional it is.

"I mean, shit, I'm sorry," I say to Archie and Sheridan, who both have red cheeks.

"Oh, we're all adults here." Sloane waves me off and then whispers to the group, "Some older than the others." They laugh, thankfully. God, she's charming. "But he's correct, that is how he fucks and it's okay to say that, because I'm sure you're the same way." She gestures toward Archie. "I've seen you stand, quite the powerful rump you have."

I squeeze Sloane's thigh again, trying to get her to stop, because we don't need to go into detail about others' sexual encounters. But she doesn't stop—instead she attempts to overcompensate for my mistake.

"I'm sure you can scoot a California king bed across the bedroom floor with one powerful thrust, Archie, which of course leads me to send my congratulations to you, Sheridan. Always nice to find a man who can tickle the old uterus." Fuck, she's losing it. *Abort! For the love of God, please stop talking.* "And, Archie, you also look quite healthy, like you don't lose your breath very quickly. Another positive." Archie smiles but you can tell that it's forced. "Not to mention it helps to have such a beautiful lady to drive into." And here I thought things were going well for a moment.

"It does help," Devin says with a wink, which nearly makes me come out of my goddamn seat.

"I think we're both lucky," Sheridan says with a lift of her water glass. "To powerful hip thrusts and tickled uteruses." Well…thank Jesus for that.

"Here, here," Sloane says with a raise of her glass.

I raise my glass but keep my eyes on Devin…as he keeps his eyes on Sloane. I'll tell you right now, over my dead body will he be dancing with her.

———

"Do you like your meal?" I ask Sloane, leaning in close to her ear.

Her eyes meet mine, our noses nearly touching. "I do. You order so well."

"Because I know what you like," I say, even though that's not really the truth.

She smiles, and I'm so tempted to kiss her, so tempted to continue to lay my claim on this woman in front of Devin, but I know the minute I do, the minute I touch my lips to hers, I'm done.

Cooked.

No way I would be able to stop myself, so I keep my distance in that regard.

She scoops up some of her mashed potatoes and brings them close to my mouth. "Want to try?"

Keeping my eyes on her, I open my mouth, and she slips her fork past my lips, slowly I pull the mashed potatoes off her fork. I swallow and say, "Delicious."

She smirks and then turns toward the rest of the table. I almost forgot there were other people here. "How is the steak, Devin?"

"Fantastic," he answers before taking a sip of his red wine, which I wish were staining his teeth, but I'm not that lucky tonight.

"And the beef Wellington?" Sloane asks Sheridan and Archie.

"Unbelievable," Sheridan says. "I don't think I've ever had anything better in my mouth."

"I think you have," Archie says with a wink that has Sheridan's cheeks blushing again.

She then points her fork at me and Sloane and says, "Look what you did, you corrupted him."

Sloane and I chuckle. "It was Hudson, not me."

"He was corrupted way before them," Devin says.

"Not in business meetings," Sheridan says.

"Ah, I would hardly say this is a business meeting," Archie chimes in. "This is a gathering of friends."

"It has to be, especially if you're talking about the things that have been in my mouth," Sheridan shoots back, causing Archie to chuckle.

"Not even sorry. Although, given what we've discussed, I doubt we should even talk about the property purchase at this point."

I smooth my hand over Sloane's shoulder. "Yeah, probably not the best time."

"Maybe we can tomorrow...at the Mayfair Club."

The Mayfair Club.

Why does it feel like I just passed the first test, and all it took was for Sloane to talk about powerful hip thrusts?

"I'm available," I say.

"I can get you an application and in front of someone who can help with your membership."

"The Mayfair Club, huh?" Devin says, eyeing me up and down. "Can you afford that?"

The fuck?

This fucking guy.

He's got to be kidding me right now.

"Devin," Sloane says, leaning forward. "Hudson is one of the heirs of Hopper Hotels."

"Ah." Devin nods. "So Daddy's money."

Yup, I'm going to kill him. I'm about to tell him off when Sloane turns toward him.

"Actually, he doesn't work with his father anymore. He is in a co-op with the Cane brothers. They focus on admirable investment projects that are not only great for the cities they work in, bringing life back to old buildings and neighborhoods, but that assist those who have less with affordable apartments that are often partially self-sustainable. They make smart business choices, which is why they're working on a merger with Archie." I can sense the tension as Sheridan and Archie look between us.

"Thank you, baby," I say and then press a kiss to the side of her head, keeping it very innocent but also showing affection. "You don't need to prove anything to him, though."

"He is quite the astute businessman," Archie says.

"Is that right? Well, good for you," Devin says, his voice dripping with disdain.

"Thank you, and what exactly do you do?" I ask.

"I'm in medical school, studying to be a cardiac surgeon. Lost my dad at a young age to heart failure, so this is my way of honoring him."

Well, fuck, can't make fun of that, so looks like I'm going to have to take the high road on this one.

"That's very commendable. What year are you in?"

"I'm in my fourth year of medical school."

I nod. "I'm sure you have a long road ahead of you. I wish you the best of luck." It pains me to be this nice.

"Thanks," Devin says awkwardly, which is fun, because without the snark, he's forced to play nice in front of everyone.

"Devin is really smart," Archie says. "Top of his class."

"Which will make him top in his field," I say, the compliment splitting me in half.

Sloane leans into me and her hand slides along my thigh, I think a reward for playing nicely. Not that she needs to reward me; this is technically my business meeting. But a reward nonetheless.

"Thank you again for dinner," I say. "We'll see you tomorrow." We say our goodbyes to Archie and Sheridan, who found a friend at the bar on our way out.

Devin took off for the bathroom, and I secretly hope it's food poisoning.

Hand in hand, Sloane and I make our way out to the front of the restaurant, where I text our driver that we are ready.

I would say, despite Devin getting on my nerves, tonight was a success. Sloane was remarkable, even with the rocky start. She was charming, graceful, and poised. It was as if she transformed right in front of my eyes, and I feel a little ashamed for doubting her in the slightest.

"Can I ask you a question?" Sloane says, breaking the silence between us.

"Yes."

She turns toward me, those beautiful eyes of hers connecting with mine. "When you and Archie were talking about business, you touched on the project housing for a little bit. Would that be the same thing that you're doing with the Cane brothers in San Francisco? I mean, I know it is, but we haven't talked about it much nor have I been involved with the project, so I guess I just find it fascinating."

"It is," I say, wondering where this is coming from. "It's part of the philanthropic side of Cane Enterprises that Hardy and I really liked, one of the things we wanted to jump on board with when we formed the co-op. They purchased a few buildings in the city that were not at full capacity of use, or abandoned, and they turned it into low-income housing for those who may struggle more living in the city. It's a great way to give back to the community, especially when housing can be so expensive."

"It can be," she says, looking off to the side.

"Why do you ask?"

"I don't know, it just had me thinking."

I lift my hand to her chin and bring her focus back on me. "Thinking about what?"

"About my situation. The house Jude found for us, that Stacey and I are buying. We were lucky in a way that the landlord didn't keep raising our rent every year. I think he saw that we were a struggling, low-income family and gave us a break. It makes sense why he went to sell it if I think about it. He probably saw it as a loss and didn't have the heart to increase the cost of living."

"From a business perspective, yes, to shed the weight of a house like that when you're not increasing the cost or receiving tax benefits from the government, that's something you don't want to hang on to."

She nods her head, her brain spinning.

"What's going on in that head of yours?"

She shrugs. "Just thinking. We were lucky someone helped us out. Makes me think I want to do the same thing."

"There you two are," Devin says, walking up to us. Fucking great. No food poisoning for him. "I thought you were going to slip out before I could say goodbye."

That was the intent.

"Such a fun night. I'm so glad I could join in." That makes one of us. "Hopefully I'll see you in dance class."

"Yes, that would be great," Sloane says, being polite.

"Aw, here's my ride." He points to a car pulling up. "I'll catch you guys later." He holds his hand out to me, and I reluctantly shake it. "Hudson, great seeing you."

"Yup, have a good night." It's the best I can do. This man has been on my last fucking nerve all night.

The staring.

The ogling.

The memories he tried to share with Sloane.

It's as if he had zero grasp of the concept that when someone is married, you back the fuck off. At one point, I caught him wetting his lips as he stared at Sloane's cleavage. Seriously, he's lucky I didn't take my knife and stab him in the eye.

He turns to Sloane and slides his hand up her arm before gripping her shoulder. "Sloane, it's been so long. I'm so glad I got to spend the evening with you." *Move it the fuck along, man.*

"Yes, it was a lot of fun catching up."

"I'll see you soon." Then to my goddamn horror, he leans in, cups her cheek, and then presses a kiss to the other one.

When he leans back, he winks, fucking winks, then takes off.

That motherfucker.

He's dead.

He's so fucking dead.

CHAPTER SEVENTEEN
SLOANE

I DON'T KNOW HOW TO read Hudson right now. He seems charged, irritated, ready to possibly rip one particular person's head off...ahem.

Dinner was awkward and uncomfortable, no thanks to Devin.

The food was amazing, the wine even better.

The conversation was...intriguing. It got me thinking about things. About what Stacey and I could possibly do with our house. Almost gave me a vision of what I should do with my life. Still working it out in my muddled brain, but there's something there.

I would say, overall, I did a good job presenting myself and representing Hudson. Although Hudson is fuming, and I can't be sure if it's because of the accidental sex talk I brought to the table or if it's because of Devin. Either way, the moment we stepped into the hotel, he went straight to the closet and started undressing without saying a word.

It's late, we're both jet-lagged, and I can only imagine him wanting to wash away this dinner. So I slip into the closet as well just as he sets his clothes on the hanger for dry cleaning.

"Can you unzip me?" I ask, pulling my hair to the side.

He doesn't say anything, just walks up behind me, places his hand on my hip, and slowly tugs the zipper down until the fabric is loose on my shoulders.

I turn around and look him in the eyes. "Thank you."

He nods and is about to step aside but then pulls a shirt from one of his shelves and hands it to me. He doesn't have to say anything for me to know what he wants me to do.

I slip out of my dress and put it on a hanger next to Hudson's suit. I remove my bra and underwear and slip his shirt over my head. The soft, rich cotton feels like a warm blanket, wrapping me up in the best way possible. Seriously, nothing is better than wearing one of his shirts, especially after having to wear that dress all evening with the sequins poking my arms.

Once dressed, I move into the bathroom, where Hudson is brushing his teeth. In silence, we get ready for bed together, me taking longer because I have to remove my makeup and go through my skincare routine. The difference in time between men getting ready for bed and women is entirely unfair. Once I put on my last bit of lotion, I turn off the light and head into the bedroom, where Hudson is typing away on his phone.

I ignore him, go to my side of the bed, and slip under the covers while turning out my nightstand light. With my back to him, I adjust my head on my pillow and shut my eyes, trying to rest my head after the insane day I've had. Too much happened—too much for someone who hasn't been in London very long.

And a lot is going on tomorrow; before we left the restaurant, Sheridan asked if we could go to tea tomorrow at the Mayfair Club, so while the boys are in the cigar room, I'll be partaking in a spot of tea.

Rest is key, especially so I don't slip up again and start saying something like...how big Hudson's dick is.

Spoiler alert, massive.

Did I hear him in the shower? Yes. Did I tell myself not to look? Absolutely. Did I look anyway? How could I not? I walked into that bathroom like I was handed a private invitation to a show. And I watched. I watched that man masturbate like my life depended on it, and it was easily the sexiest thing I've ever seen, especially knowing that I was the reason he was doing it.

The man is ripped, head-to-toe muscle wrapping around every limb and his entire torso. And when he's turned on, when he's ready to come, the veins in his arms get thicker, more prominent. His expression, tense yet sexy. His hand so large, pulling on his long, thick cock…

God, I'm getting turned on just thinking about it.

I will never get over the sight of him in that shower, wet and pleasuring himself. That will stay with me forever. And whenever I go to pleasure myself again, I know exactly what I'll be thinking of—

"What are you doing?" Hudson says, startling me.

"Sl-sleeping," I say.

His hand wraps around my stomach, and once again, just like last night, he pulls me across the cold bed and right up against his body.

"You sleep here," he whispers.

"Oh, I wasn't sure, you know, because of how quiet you've been."

"This is where you sleep at all times. Understood?"

"Yes," I answer, feeling the frostiness of his voice against my ear.

"Good." He rests his hand on my stomach like last night and tucks his other arm under his pillow.

"Um…is everything okay?" I ask.

"Fine," he says, his hand curling around the fabric of my shirt.

"Are you sure? Because you seem agitated. And if it was because of what I said at dinner, I just want you to know that I was nervous and—"

"It wasn't you."

"Was it Devin?" I ask on a wince.

He lifts up to look me in the eyes. "What the hell do you think?"

"He's not that bad of a guy, Hudson."

His eyes widen. "Are you really defending him right now?"

Yeah, what the hell are you doing, Sloane?

"I just don't want you thinking—"

"I'll tell you what I think, Sloane. I think the guy is a dick and has no respect for the fact that you're wearing my goddamn ring on your finger.

I saw the way he was looking at you. I saw the way he said goodbye. The asshole is trying to make his move."

"Hudson, he's not trying—"

"You're mine," he nearly growls. "Do you hear me, Sloane? You're mine, and I don't fucking appreciate that man sniffing around you. I don't want him anywhere near you."

"I mean, I don't want to purposefully seek him out, but if I'm going to be part of the wedding, then I'm going to have to dance with him."

"No, you're not, and I'll make sure of it."

"Hudson, you don't want to make this a thing. Remember this is business, and you want to make sure Sheridan and Archie are comfortable."

"We are doing them a favor with you as a bridesmaid. They should make us comfortable."

"Are you forgetting all rules about business?" I ask. "That's not how—"

"Do you know how many times I caught him staring at your tits, Sloane?"

"I... Was he?"

"Twelve times. I caught him twelve fucking times. As your husband, I don't fucking appreciate that." His hand moves down to the hem of my shirt, and then to my surprise, he slides his palm against the skin of my stomach. My breath catches in my throat from the touch. "You're mine; this is mine. I don't want him thinking he can just fucking look at you, undressing you at the table anytime he wants." His thumb strokes my skin. "You're mine, not his."

I roll my teeth over my bottom lip. "I...I know."

"Do you?" he asks. "Do you realize how important this is to me? I might not be able to have you, Sloane, but the fuck if someone else is going to while we're together."

His hand slides higher up my stomach and my body lights up as his thumb inches closer to my breasts. What I wouldn't give for him to play with me, to touch me, at least give me something to help with this itching need I have for his touch.

"I don't want anyone else," I say.

"Promise?"

"Promise," I say. "I'm married to you, Hudson. You're the only one I want, the only one I think about."

In fact, it wouldn't matter if Devin made a move, if I'm honest. This man in the bed next to me, holding me captive as if I'm really his, is who I want. Sexually, at least. His new territorial nature is only turning me on. Devin doesn't hold a candle to this man. Even though I know Hudson will never be really mine. I'm his for now. If only he'd take me.

He wets his lips.

I spread my legs apart.

"I want you so bad, Hudson. So fucking bad. Not him. You."

His breath becomes labored as he stares down at me. In my head, I keep saying, *Break. Break.*

Fucking break!

Please, for the love of God, end this sexual tension.

His hand moves another inch up my stomach, just below my breast now.

"Touch me," I whisper. "Please, Hudson, just touch me."

His eyes flit back and forth between mine, his mind working a mile a minute. I can see that he wants it. I can see that he is teetering on the edge of giving us both relief, but then he says, "Touch yourself."

"Hudson—"

"Hand between your legs, Sloane. Touch yourself."

"I don't want that. I want you."

"And I want to see you touch yourself, so fucking listen."

The command in his voice is so intense, so freaking sexy, that I can't do anything but listen to it. I move my hand between my legs, where I slide my finger along my clit.

"Oh God," I moan as I sink into the mattress.

"Are you wet?" he asks.

"So wet." I bring my hand up between us and say, "Want a taste?"

"I fucking do, but I can't."

Hope slams hard in my chest as I realize that he might not break at all, that this is all I might get from him. If it is, then I better soak up every second of it.

I press two fingers against my clit and start circling it, giving it just enough pressure and movement to heighten the pleasure that's already tripping through me.

"I wish this were you. I wish you were playing with my clit while driving your huge cock inside me. God, I want it, Hudson. I want you to fuck me so hard. I want to feel you bottom out and touch me places no man has ever touched me before."

He wets his lips and his thumb inches upward, just underneath the swell of my breasts.

"Take a swipe," I say. "You know you want to feel me. Just one brush, Hudson."

He lets out a deep breath and I wait patiently to see if he will do it, if he'll listen. I hold my breath, hoping that he will until...his thumb barely caresses my breast.

"God, yes," I say, scooting down just enough to make the back of his hand touch me. "Play with my nipples, Hudson. Please."

"No," he says, still holding strong. "I fucking can't. Just...fuck, just let me see you come."

"And when I do, what are you going to do?" I ask as my hand that's not pleasuring me finds his erection.

His hips buck back. "Don't, Sloane."

"Don't what? Help you finish?"

"Focus on you."

"I am, but I just can't...hit the right spot."

I need that right spot.

I feel crazed, teetering on the edge. Desperate for more contact. One swipe of my breast isn't going to cut it.

It's not going to make me lose control like I want to.

So taking a risk, I sit up on the bed, push at his chest so he's lying flat on the mattress, and straddle his lap before he can do anything about it. I'm met with a surprised expression from him while I grip both of his wrists and pin them just above his head.

"Sloane...fuck...we can't."

But that's the problem. We are two consenting adults.

We can.

Wanting to prove that, I find the hard ridge of his cock and glide my center right over him—it's one thrust, one gloriously delicious thrust.

"Fuck," he breathes out as I wait.

I wait for him to move me.

I wait for him to tell me to stop.

I wait for him to bolt out of this bed, but when he doesn't move, doesn't even attempt it, I rock against him.

"Jesus Christ," he whispers.

"God, you're so big. This is what I want; this is what I need. You."

"Sloane, this... Fuck." His jaw clenches and his hips thrust up into mine. "Fuck, I want more." I reach for the hem of my shirt to pull it off, but he quickly says, "No. Don't."

"Why not?"

"Just...don't. Just ride me."

Seeing that he's given me an inch, I'm not going to take a mile. But I am going to ride out what he's willing to offer and take full advantage of it. I place my hands on his chest, propping myself up, and then start thrusting over his erection, loving the friction and how quickly I can get myself ready.

"So good, baby. So fucking good," he says, his eyes on me the entire time. "I can feel how wet you are through my briefs."

"Because I've wanted this for so long. I've wanted you. And I want more. This isn't good enough. I want your tongue, your cock, your hands. Just, fuck, touch me, do something, Hudson."

"I can't," he says, keeping his hands in place. "Just fucking use me to get off."

"I want more."

"This is all I can give."

Frustrated, I dig my fingers into his chest and pump my hips over him, riding him harder, grinding into him with more intensity, trying to fill the void he keeps making.

The entire time, he doesn't touch me, doesn't even lift his hands to my hips to help. He just lets me use him for my own pleasure.

"Fuck," I say as I feel my stomach start to twist, my clit throbbing, looking for that last push.

Frustration rips through me because I want more. I need more, and he won't give it to me.

"This...this isn't good enough." I slow down my hips. "I want to come, but I—"

I don't get a chance to finish as I'm tossed onto my back, my legs are spread wide, and his hands fall to either side of my head right before he starts thrusting his brief-covered erection against me.

"Oh my God," I say as I claw at his shoulders. A whole new wave of pleasure rushes over me. "Yes, Hudson. Oh my God, yes."

His eyes fixate on where he's humping me, only the thin layer of his briefs between us. But it's all I need. This is what I needed, for him to take control, for him to want me just as much as I want him.

"Don't stop. Please don't stop. Yes, yes, Hudson. Oh my God..." My body starts to seize, pleasure pools into my stomach, and then a burst of light surges through me as I tip over the edge and my orgasm rocks through me as such a hefty spiral that I'm clinging on to him, legs wrapped around his waist, holding him tight until my orgasm slows. "Oh my God," I say breathlessly, my legs relaxing.

Hudson pulls away, lifts my shirt up so my stomach is showing, and then he pulls his cock out and right in front of me, starts stroking himself. It takes only a few before he groans and then busts all over my stomach. Drop after drop until he's completely done.

He hovers over me, breathing heavily before he swipes his hand across my stomach and leans forward, his lips right next to my ear as he whispers, "Mine."

Chills break out all over my body as he gets off the bed and goes to the bathroom.

I lie there, thrumming, his cum hot on my stomach, my mind swirling with what we just did as my body settles.

Jesus, that was...that was really hot.

That was unexpected.

That just fucked with me big-time because if I can experience an orgasm like that with him when we're just dry humping, then what the hell would he be able to do with all clothes off?

I push my shirt down and then stand up just as Hudson walks back into the room with a washcloth.

"Let me," he says, but I shake my head.

I take the washcloth from him and then go into the closet, where I pluck another shirt from his pile. I then walk into the bathroom, shut the door, and remove my shirt. I stare down at where he marked me, fascinated.

The whisper of that one singular word pulsing through my veins.

Mine.

Mine.

I believe him.

I fully believe everything about the one single word.

I'm his. Right now, in this moment, as I wear his wedding ring, I'm his. And he might not give me all of him, but he sure as hell is claiming all of me.

I set the washcloth down, and instead, I turn on the shower. I tie my hair up into a bun and slide into the shower, where I rinse off using the delicious-smelling soap that the hotel provides. When I'm done, I dry off, throw on some lotion, and slip his shirt over my head. I take a moment to stare in the mirror. My cheeks are still flushed, but that's the only sign that I just felt Hudson Hopper, felt how close he could be, felt how good he could make me feel.

I nibble my lower lip, envisioning what his five o'clock shadow could do to my skin, what his mouth and teeth could mark.

I need it, desperately.

And if I have to wait, if I have to keep taking these small steps to get there, I will. Because he's what I want. Everything about him. I need him in my life, and I won't rest until I have him.

I turn off the light and open the door. His light on his nightstand is on, but instead of looking at his phone, his hands are behind his head, and he's waiting for me.

I feel his eyes track me as I round the bed and then slip under the covers. He turns off the light and turns toward me. I keep my back toward him and wait…

And wait…

And then his hand wraps around my stomach and he pulls me in close to his chest.

"I thought I fucking told you this is where you sleep."

I smile to myself. "Sorry, must have forgot."

Sloane: OMG OMG OMG we dry humped last night and it was the greatest thing I've ever experienced and I will forever and ever and ever want to dry hump with him.

Stacey: I'm about to go to bed and this is the freaking text you send me?

Sloane: I'm sorry but I couldn't keep it in. I went down to the lobby for some coffee so I could get away from him. I swear he's stalking me like prey now. He had a little taste and now he wants the main course.

Stacey: What do you mean?

Sloane: I mean he woke up this morning and he has not taken his eyes off me. He's always on his phone, always typing away, but it's different now. It's like he's waiting to pounce and it's thrilling. And the dry humping, omg! Gah, and I saw his dick and I know you don't like dicks, but Jesus, Stacey, even you would like this one. So big and long and thick and I rode that cock hard last night, through his briefs, and it brought me to completion.

Stacey: This is all…too much. I don't think I want to know about thick dicks.

Sloane: Stacey, this is HUGE! Just like his penis.

Stacey: Dear God. You realize this is bad, right? You weren't supposed to cross this line?

Sloane: I know but I can't even remember how it happened. Oh yeah, he wanted me to masturbate in front of him and I was trying but then I wanted so much more. And that's when I started riding him but I couldn't find the right spot and then he flipped me to my back and pulsed into me. I'm surprised he didn't plow a hole through the wall from the force. Oh, and then he came on my stomach and whispered "mine" in my ear. My nipples are hard just thinking about it.

Stacey: God, that's the great thing about being with a woman, you don't have to worry about a man marking you up with his freaking semen!

Sloane: I love it. I want him to mark me all over my face.

Stacey: And I'm done with this. Good night.

Sloane: Wait, I'm not done. I have questions, I have stories. I want to tell you how great my orgasm felt.

Stacey: Night.

Ugh. What good is having a twin if you can't tell them about your orgasms? I grab my coffee from the half wall I set it on and then start toward the elevators only to stop when I see Hudson waiting by them, arms crossed, waiting for me.

Dear God in heaven.

Is it possible to have an orgasm just from the sight of someone?

Wearing a pair of expertly ironed black dress pants and a matching button-up shirt, he looks dark and dangerous, like a CIA operative ready to take down anyone who comes in his path.

Coffee in one hand, phone in the other, I walk up to him and say, "What are you doing down here?"

"Looking for you," he says as he presses his hand to the nape of my neck and guides me toward an open elevator.

"Oh?"

When the doors shut, he closes in on me, pressing me against the wall.

"Was there anything in particular you were looking to talk about? Anything that you felt needed to be discussed?"

"I don't like it when you leave and don't tell me where you're going."

"Ah, I see, the whole possessive thing is still carrying over from last night, and I guess…the day before that and the day before that." I hold up my coffee cup between us. "Just getting some coffee. Not running away or being taken."

"I could have had them bring the coffee up to you. That's why we have a staff for our every need." His hand strokes my cheek, and it's such an intimate touch that I nearly melt right here in the elevator.

"I wanted to give my legs some time to loosen up. Cramping is never a good thing."

The elevator dings and we step off it and into our room, which he opens with his key card. When we're inside, he asks, "Who were you texting? Is that why you went downstairs? You wanted privacy away from me?"

"No," I say with a shake of my head.

"Then who were you texting?"

"That's, uh…that's private information."

His brows narrow as he moves in closer to me. "Sloane, who the hell were you texting?"

I take a step back. "If you think it's Devin, then you are mistaken."

"Then who was it?"

"Do you really not trust me?"

"I don't trust him," he says, closing the space between us again.

I press my hand against his chest. "You don't have to trust him, but you can trust me and the fact that I know who my husband is."

His jaw ticks as he thinks about it. "Okay."

"Okay?" I ask, surprised he's dropping it like that.

"Okay," he answers as he takes a seat on the couch. "Fuck, I'm sorry." He blows out a heavy breath, and I can see just how complicated his thoughts are by the way his brows bounce around, ranging from concern to passiveness, to a more relaxed state. I don't think I've ever seen a man war with himself as much as Hudson does.

I sit next to him and curl my legs under me. "It was my sister. I was texting her."

"Why did you need privacy for that?" he asks, his hand landing on my thigh.

"Because I was telling her how huge your dick is and how I got to dry hump it last night, and it felt amazing. And if it felt that amazing with clothes on, I can only imagine what it would be like with clothes off, you know, stuff like that."

The smallest of grins turns up the corners of his lips but is quickly washed away when he looks down at his lap. "I...I shouldn't have done that last night. I'm sorry."

"God, please don't with the morning after apology. Nothing hurts worse than an apology after an orgasm."

"I'm serious, Sloane. That never should have happened."

"I hear you loud and clear," I say. "And yet I'm glad it did happen."

"I'm not," he says softly, then leans back against the couch, blowing out a heavy breath. "Fuck, I'm getting distracted. I honestly can't even remember why I'm out here, why I'm doing this. All I can think about is you."

"I'm flattered." I press my hand to my chest. I know he's feeling slightly tortured at the moment, but I like seeing him not bent over his phone. I like hearing him speak to me, telling me about his feelings. "Thank you. It's not very often you hear of someone constantly thinking about you. Now, in your thoughts, am I bent over a lot?"

"Sloane," he grumbles. "I'm being fucking serious."

"So am I. A girl wants to know what positions you're drawn to. More than that, a wife wants to know what her husband loves sexually."

He slides his hand over my hip as he looks me in the eyes. "You're torturing me, Sloane. Fucking torturing me. Last night should have never happened, you and I both know that."

"And yet you came all over my stomach and claimed me as yours." I tap my chin. "Seems like you kind of wanted it to happen."

"Why are you making this hard?"

"Because I like it when you're hard."

He drags his hand over his face. "This is why age gap doesn't work."

"Mm, or is this why it does?"

"Christ." He starts to get up, but I push on his chest.

Easing up on him, I say, "How about this? Last night was amazing, I fucking loved every second of it, and even though I want so much more, I won't ask for it. The next move is on you."

"There won't be a next move."

I shrug. "Okay, if that's what you choose, then that's okay with me." I stand up and head toward the bedroom. "I'm going to get dressed." Since I took a quick shower already this morning, I slip out of my shorts and shirt and then reach for my underwear, where I find the ice-blue sets Hudson got for me.

Smiling to myself, I slip them on, adjust the cups of the bra, and then with all the confidence in the world, I walk out into the living room where Hudson is typing on his phone. I lean against the doorjamb and ask, "Anything in particular you want me to wear to tea?"

He looks up from his phone to answer, only to take in what I'm wearing. His expression immediately morphs into hunger, and a rush of female satisfaction pulses through me. Because I did that. In a matter of seconds, I was able to change his mood.

He tosses his phone to the couch and walks up to me. I continue to lean against the doorway as he closes the space. He places his forearm above my head and leans forward, his other hand landing on my hip. "Why are you fucking with me?" he says in a tortured voice.

"You claimed me; therefore, I wear what you want."

"Fuck," he says as his finger traces the waistband of my thong. "This looks so fucking good on you."

"I'm glad you like it," I say. "Anything for my husband."

His finger trails up my stomach, the sensation turning me on immediately. When he reaches my breasts, he traces the lace for a few seconds but then drops his hand, only for his eyes to meet mine.

"You need to wear a dress and a hat for tea."

"Okay, anything else? Do you want to pick it?"

He shakes his head. "Surprise me."

"That I can do." And then because I can, I lift up on my toes and kiss him on the nose. When I pull away, his eyes meet mine again, but he doesn't move. He stays there. "Anything else I can help you with?"

His eyes flit down to my mouth and then back up to my eyes. His head moves in even closer, our foreheads touching now.

"What do you want, Hudson?" I ask as his hand travels up my side, to my back, and to the clasp of my bra. "Tell me what you want."

He wets his lips and I can see him wavering, fighting with himself.

"Do you want me naked?"

"Fuck," he breathes out. "I do. I really fucking do."

I reach behind me to undo my bra, but he stops me, his eyes opening to mine.

"Don't."

"Do you want to do it?" I ask.

"No, I don't...I don't want you doing anything. I want you to get dressed."

"Hudson," I say in disappointment. "Just take what you want."

He shakes his head and then lifts away. "No. I won't." He then leans forward and kisses the tip of my nose, but instead of pulling away, he lingers, his mouth moving what feels like a centimeter south, right above mine.

I won't do it. I won't close the distance—it has to be him.

He has to be the one that makes the move.

"Do it," I whisper. "Kiss me."

He wets his lips again, and I swear, when I feel him lean forward just a little more, my heart stops beating and my breath seizes in my lungs. I wait.

I wait for that moment.

For the one both of us has been waiting for.

Just kiss me.

Please.

End this misery and kiss me, Hudson.

He sucks in a sharp breath and then leans away, pushing off the wall and taking two steps back. He tugs on his hair and stares me down.

Jesus, I've never seen a man with such strong willpower.

Got to give him credit.

"Dress and hat it is, then," I say as I slip back into the bedroom.

CHAPTER EIGHTEEN

HUDSON

HEAD ON FUCKING STRAIGHT, HOPPER.

You have things you have to accomplish.

Deals to be made.

Businesses to grow.

There is no need to be doing anything but that.

With Sloane's hand held tightly in mine, we walk up to the Mayfair Club's front doors, which are managed by a bellman.

"Good afternoon, sir, ma'am. How may I be of assistance?"

"Hello. We're meeting with Archie Wimbach."

"Right this way," he says as he opens the door, revealing mahogany walls, green-and-blue-plaid carpet, and the smell of old books combined with pine. This is exactly what I expected it might be like inside the Mayfair Club. An old parlor club.

We are led into a study where books from what seems the eighteenth century line the walls. Not a speck of dust on them, yet they look like they haven't been touched for years. A secretary desk is positioned catty-corner to the window, and a seating area of antique furniture rests in the middle.

"Mr. Remington will be right with you."

"Thank you," I answer as the man shuts the door behind himself.

Sloane turns toward me and whispers, "Uh, I feel like I don't belong here. It's extremely fancy."

"This is what money will buy you."

"Musty walls and furniture that was built in medieval times?"

"Exactly." I chuckle just as the door opens and in steps a man in a suit. He's bald except for a whisp of hair on either side of his head and clean-shaven. His glasses barely hang on the tip of his nose, and his bow tie matches his pocket square.

"Mr. and Mrs. Hopper, thank you so much for making it in today. It's delightful to meet you. I'm Mr. Remington, and I'll be your advisor regarding your club membership. Please, be seated."

With Sloane's hand still in mine, I bring her over to the couch and we sit. She chose a white dress with thick straps that cover the ice-blue straps of the bra I know she's wearing. She paired the dress with a white hat with a pink ribbon around the base. Her hair is down, and she looks every bit the part she's here to play.

She crosses her feet at her ankles and sits tall next to me.

"Thank you for having us," she says. "The club, from what I can see, is breathtaking."

"Thank you, we take great pride in maintaining the building's original structure. We were forced to make some renovations after the kitchen fire back in 1942, but other than that, everything else is original, besides some flooring that has suffered wear and tear from heels over the years."

"Very impressive," Sloane says as she looks around.

"Thank you. And I must say, your application into the club came with a very high recommendation from Archie Wimbach. His family has been members of the club for generations now."

"We are very grateful for the recommendation," I say. "Archie and his family are very good people. We're honored."

"They are, and wonderful donors. I've seen that you've put in a dona-tion amount as well." Sloane glances at me, but I ignore it as I nod.

"Yes, earmarked as well."

"I see that. For the Brothers and Sisters program, correct?"

"That's correct."

"Wonderful, and I've read your reasoning, which was touching. I've brought your membership request to the board, and they've all agreed that you would be a superb fit for the Mayfair Club. We'd like to welcome you as members."

I feel a wave of relief release through me as I say, "Thank you. That means a lot to us."

Mr. Remington stands, so we do as well. "It's an honor. And I believe the Wimbachs are waiting for you upstairs. In the Sherry Room. Mr. Wimbach said he'd be delighted to give you a tour."

"Thank you." I shake his hand and so does Sloane before we both head out of the room and up the curved staircase.

"What's the Brothers and Sisters program?" Sloane asks quietly as we make our way up.

"They focus on matching children with mentors, it's like the Big Brothers, Big Sisters program in the States."

"How much did you donate?"

"Does it matter?" I ask.

"No, but I'm curious." Of course she is. She's always curious. But there is a very good reason I chose this charity, and although I can share part of that with her, the rest? Well, that's deeply humbling. My brother and sister saved me from becoming like *my father.* The money to support this cause was not just a means to an end.

"One million," I say, causing her to gasp. "And before you ask, I chose the program because I know that both of us wouldn't be where we are today without our siblings in our lives. Our childhoods were different but also very similar in some ways. We lean on those relationships, and I want to give disadvantaged kids the same opportunities."

She pauses at the top of the stairs and looks up at me with those doe eyes of hers. "Are you trying to get me to fall in love with you? Because I will. Keep doing things like that and I very much will."

"Shouldn't my wife already be in love?" I ask in a teasing tone, which I know she loves. She's made it quite clear that she likes the lighter side of me, and in all honesty, I like that side of me too. It's just harder to show around her since we're always involved in business.

And I'm always trying to avoid her.

Always trying to keep my guard up to protect her. To protect the both of us. To protect the business.

"She should, but I don't think you paid her enough."

"Shhh," I say on a laugh. "Jesus, trying to give us away?"

"The marriage is real. The rest, well, that's up for discussion."

Shaking my head, I lead her to the room on the right that is marked *Sherry Room*. We walk inside and find Archie and Sheridan talking to a few people. Okay, time to tighten up and put on another show.

When they spot us, large smiles spread across their faces. "Hudson, Sloane," Archie says, "so glad you could join us. We were just talking about you two. Please tell me you were accepted."

"Largely in part due to your generous nomination," I say.

"Ah, well, it was an easy one to write." Archie shakes my hand. "Welcome to the club. First, can I steal you away for a signature smoke in the cigar room while Sheridan takes Sloane for some tea?"

"Would love that."

"Let them get all stinky and we shall dine on tea and scones," Sheridan says.

"Sounds like we have the better end of the bargain," Sloane says with a little shimmy of her shoulders.

God, she's cute.

Before she takes off, she comes up to me, presses her hand to my chest, and then, on her toes, kisses my cheek. Whispering, she says, "Your ass looks stunning in those pants." Then she pulls away and winks. My eyes trail after her as she walks away, sauntering in those fucking heels and looking so damn good that I'm going to have a really hard time keeping myself in check.

"How long have you two been married again?" Archie asks.

"Not very long," I answer and then turn to him. "But she's always captured my attention."

"I can tell. When we were meeting at Maggie's office, I felt like there was something going on between the two of you, but you maintained professionalism well. I admire that. I don't think I could be the same way with Sheridan."

Something going on? Jesus, maybe I wasn't as sly as I thought I was.

"We make it a point to keep things professional while working. But when we're home, that's different."

"I like that." He claps me on the shoulder. "Come this way."

Archie gives me a brief tour of the upstairs portion of the club. Basically, it's just room after room of parlor spaces where members congregate and talk, drink, smoke cigars. In one of the rooms, hors d'oeuvres are passed around by servers wearing white gloves, while in the courtyard—a lawn space carved out in the middle of the city—members are playing croquet.

Don't think I've ever seen anyone play croquet.

Archie brings me into the smoking parlor, and honestly, I'm not much of a cigar person, never liked them, but that doesn't mean I won't join him.

We walk toward the far end of the room, where there are shelves lined with cigar boxes and a man at a cigar bar, ready to assist.

"What are you thinking?" Archie says.

"Not to burst your bubble, man, but I'm not much of a cigar guy."

Archie pauses and then turns toward me. "Seriously?"

"Yeah, but please, feel free. I don't mind at all. My dad always smoked cigars. I have a time or two, but it's just not my thing."

Archie chuckles and says, "Mine neither. I just do it because of my dad."

That makes me laugh. "Did your dad make you smoke during casual business meetings?"

"Yes," Archie says. "And it was not the end of the world, but I don't know, Sheridan is not a fan, and I just don't have a strong penchant to smoke. I was offering because, well, that's what I've been told to do."

"You don't need to with me."

"If that's the case, I have the perfect thing for us. Do you like sparkling water with lime?"

I chuckle. "Sounds great."

Archie flags down a server, tells them we will be out on the terrace, and to please bring two sparkling waters. Then we head down the hall and out two French doors to a terrace that overlooks the courtyard. A bistro table is off to the right, which Archie snags for us.

When we both take a seat and get settled, I look around and say, "I can see why this is such a hidden gem and an exclusive club. Having a piece in the city like this, where it's calm, it's truly breathtaking."

"It is. I'm excited to be over here full-time."

"Is that happening after the wedding?" I ask as our drinks are set down at our table, along with some cookies—or biscuits as they call them here.

We both thank the server and Archie says, "Yes. We're going to Fiji for our honeymoon and then headed back to the States to wrap up some packing, but after that, straight to London to be closer to my dad and family."

"How is he doing?"

Archie looks out toward the sky. "He's hanging on."

I can tell how uncomfortable he is talking about it, so I quickly move on, not wanting to make him upset. "I'm glad to hear it. I'm assuming you've already secured a flat?"

"We have," he answers, looking grateful for the quick change in subject. "It's currently being renovated, so we're staying with my parents, but we were able to take a peek at it yesterday, and they just finished installing the wallpaper." Archie smiles to himself. "Sheridan was brimming with excitement."

"That's great." I sip my sparkling water.

"Hey." Archie nudges me. "Yesterday, with Devin, everything okay there?"

"Yeah," I say, trying to be nonchalant. This is business; I shouldn't be inserting my personal grievances, but then again...this is the perfect segue into making sure Devin stays as far away from Sloane as possible. "Why?"

"Just seemed tense between you two."

I take another sip and then set my drink down. "Can I level with you and you not hold it against me?"

"Of course."

"Devin and Sloane used to date casually, and he had an impact on her life that I don't care for—not a bad one but...just an impact, if you know what I mean."

"Ah, yes," he says in understanding.

"I've received the impression from Devin that he has zero boundaries when it comes to Sloane being married."

Archie nods "Yeah, I get that. He's always been that way. Flirtatious and pushing the limit. I had a sense that he was doing that last night."

"He was, and I didn't appreciate it, but I tried to remain calm and collected at dinner."

"But inwardly you wanted to bash his brains in?"

"Pretty much."

Archie laughs. "I'm impressed, mate. You held it together. You're a better man than I am, because if it were me in that position, I don't think I would have taken too kindly to what he was saying."

"I didn't want to cause a scene, mainly for the both of you but also for Sloane."

"That's very dignified of you." He picks up a biscuit and takes a bite. "If you want me to make sure they're not dancing partners at the wedding, I can do that."

"It would be much appreciated."

Archie laughs. "Consider it done."

_____

"Have you ever played before?" Sheridan asks, handing Sloane a wooden mallet.

"Never." Sloane lifts the mallet to examine it. "Why do I fear I'm going to hurt someone?"

"Why do I fear it's going to be me?" I say as I lower her mallet below her waist. "Keep that thing there."

Sheridan laughs and says, "There's no reason to be hurting anyone if you're doing it right."

"Hear that?" I say to Sloane. "You don't need to be hurting anyone if you're doing it right."

"I heard her," Sloane says in a teasing tone.

I don't want to jinx anything, but fuck, today has gone incredibly well. Archie and I bonded more than I thought we would, talking over business, the pressure of being the oldest sons; we even talked about Stanford and our college days. He opened up a little more about his dad, which brought us to Sheridan's father and how he has been hard to navigate for Archie but Archie also values his opinion for the most part.

Archie explained some of the history of the Mayfair Club as he showed me around. I was interested in the philanthropic work that has become the main focus of the club. They didn't want to exist only as a place for rich people to congregate; they wanted like-minded people with big hearts and open wallets to discuss the good they can do in the world.

It made me think of my father and how he so desperately wants to be a part of this club but how he doesn't have the charitable heart to fit in.

Put a smile on my face for a moment, because this is something I have over him. This is something I can say I did not inherit from him but established on my own. Sure, I had to weasel my way into the club by marrying Sloane, but I know I will do good here.

I vow I will.

"Okay, the object is to get your ball through the hoops, or wickets. You start at the pole here." She points to a stick in the ground. "And then you pass through hoops one and two, then over to three off to the right. We go in a W-shaped pattern until we get to the other pole, and that's when we turn around. Every time you get a ball through the hoop, you get a bonus hit. If you hit an opponent's ball, that's also a bonus hit. First one to get through all the wickets and back to the starting pole, wins."

"Seems simple enough," Sloane says.

"I'll start, then you can follow," Sheridan says as she adjusts her straw hat and sets her purple ball down. She taps her ball through the starting hoop, then through the second, and then shoots it over to the third, where her turn ends. Archie does the same, following right behind, and I follow suit as well.

When it's Sloane's turn, she sets her yellow ball down and says, "Looks like this won't be too hard." She lines up her feet to shoulder width, adjusts her hands on the mallet, and winds back like she's about to tee off at a par five.

"Whoa, whoa, whoa," I say attempting to stop her.

And from here, it's unclear what happens. Not sure if she doesn't hear me, doesn't see me, doesn't care...but as I approach, all I see is her down-swing and my body merging right in the strike zone.

The world around me slows down as everything happens in what feels like minutes rather than seconds.

She downswings, and I leap to avoid being chopped in the ankles.

But it's the wrong move because I lose my balance and somehow tumble on top of her.

We fall to the ground, limbs tangling, as a resounding rip sears what feels like a deafening silence.

The mallet winds up between our bodies, Sloane clearly loses all the air out of her lungs as she exhales from my large body flinging on top of her, and people around us gasp.

"What are you...doing?" Sloane muffles.

"Fuck, sorry," I say as I start to get up but then feel a very cool breeze shoot right up my backside. Oh fuck, what's that?

The sound of fabric tearing.

The breeze...

Did I rip my pants?

"You're suffocating me," Sloane says as I grip her and roll us over in a state of panic so I'm on my back and Sloane is on top of me.

"What on earth are you doing?" she asks, her arms clamped to her side, her hat poking me in the face.

"Fuck," I mumble. "I felt a breeze."

"Yeah, so do I and I'm the one wearing a skirt with a thong."

"Shit," I mutter as I see the skirt of her dress getting blown by the wind.

"Let go of my hands, Husband," she grinds out.

I release her, and she presses her dress down, but it's too late because we have caused quite the commotion as everyone out in the courtyard has their eyes on us, including Archie and Sheridan, who are both covering their mouths and chuckling.

Fuck, this is not how it was supposed to go.

Embarrassment stains my cheeks because, sure, Archie and Sheridan might be chuckling, but this is still business. This can still hurt me. We have very few chances to make a positive impression, and this is one that I don't want to make.

"Was your ass out?" I ask her.

"What the hell do you think? I'm wearing a dress, and you just flopped me around like a fish out of water. My ass is definitely imprinted in the minds of every human out here. All because you felt a breeze. What is wrong with you?"

"Sloane."

"I mean, if you feel a breeze, don't make it easier for people to see that breeze take flight up my skirt."

"Sloane…"

"Especially in such a place of high society. Thank God I lotioned my ass cheeks today, imagine everyone seeing them all dry and pasty."

"Sloane," I say in a sterner voice.

"What?"

"I…I think I tore my pants."

"You ripped your pants? Like in your knee? Big whoop. Sure, it's less than dignified, but it's not your entire ass waving hello to the courtyard."

"Not in my knee. In my butt."

"Your butt?" She looks down at me and then back up. "So?"

Clenching my jaw, I add, "And I'm not wearing any underwear."

"You're not… Oh." A smile tugs on her lips.

"Don't. Don't you fucking dare."

She covers her mouth, her shoulders shaking in laughter.

"Stop. Don't you dare laugh."

She leans in closer and asks, "Why don't you have underwear on?"

"Because the pants were too tight. You could see the outline of my briefs."

She nods. "Panty lines are a real thing. But have no fear, I can check if you have a hole."

"Everything okay down there?" Archie asks, stepping up to us.

Sloane waves him off. "Thinks he split his pants. I'm just going to check."

Fuck, Sloane, don't announce it!

"No…don't check."

But it's too late. She has my leg in the air, examining between my legs as if I'm at my very own gynecological exam. What the hell is she doing? Has she forgotten where we are?

"Sloane, put my leg down."

But she's determined, because to my fucking surprise, instead of putting my leg down, her finger snakes between my legs and pokes me dead on in the balls.

"Motherfucker," I yelp as I sit right up, shooting my leg down to the ground. But because of where she was positioned, examining me, my leg knocks her to the ground and lands across her back as her face buried into the ground and her ass sticks up.

"What the hell?" she mutters.

"Jesus Christ," I say as I move my leg, and she sits up, a mud smear across her face and a murderous look in her eyes.

"You just ostriched me."

"What?" I ask.

Archie now squats next to us, tears falling down his cheeks. "Uh, if you two don't get it together, they're going to revoke your membership."

"You saw that, he just ostrich-ed me." Sloane gestures toward me.

"I don't even know what that is."

"Mate...you most defiantly ostrich-ed her."

Sheridan squats down too and says, "I saw the ostrich, and it most definitely was a deliberate attempt to collapse her."

"See." Sloane gestures toward the two on her side. "I think I have fertilizer in my mouth."

Jesus.

"You do not."

"I most certainly do." She shakes her head. "All because you didn't want me to beat you at croquet. The audacity." She stands and adjusts her dress. "Way to ruin a perfectly delightful lawn game."

"I wasn't scared of you beating me," I say as the courtyard starts to go back to what they were doing before this monstrosity of an occurrence. "I didn't want you to hurt anyone. You had too big of a backswing."

"I was going for two hoops, a double pointer. Of course I had a big backswing."

I press my hand to my brow and say, "How about we don't argue about it now, not in front of our gracious friends who recommended we join this club."

"I'm grateful they are here, as witness to the ostrich-ing."

"There was no ostrich-ing," I whisper-shout.

"There was a little bit of ostrich-ing," Archie says as he lends me a hand to help me up, but I don't take it. Not because I'm irritated but because there is still a breeze down below.

Sheepishly, I look up at Archie and say, "Umm, so, I definitely ripped my pants."

"Oh, he for sure did," Sloane says as she picks at the dirt on her face. "Tailbone to ball sack, those pants are done." Leave it to her to give a description.

"Ah, okay." Archie stands straight and looks around. "Want me to find you a towel or something to cover up?"

"It's fine," Sloane says nonchalantly as if she deals with this kind of thing every day. She takes her hat off her head. "I'll just cover him up with this, but suffice to say, our time at the club is done for the day."

"I would say so," Archie says on a chuckle.

"Go ahead, stand up. I'll protect your modesty due to your lack of underwear."

Why does she have to put it like that? Does she not remember where we are? That maybe there should be an ounce of class coming from her?

Just wanting to get the hell out, I stand and quickly take the hat from Sloane, covering my backside with it.

"That looks normal," she says.

I give her a death glare and turn to Archie and Sheridan. "So incredibly sorry about all of this. I promise, this isn't the norm for us."

"I kind of wish it were," Archie says, clearly having a good sense of humor. "Let me call you a car to take you back to your hotel."

"That would be much appreciated," I say.

And with Sloane's hat attached to my ass and a light breeze puffing up between my legs, we shamefully walk through the club, all eyes on us.

Not the best first impression.

CHAPTER NINETEEN
SLOANE

TO SAY THE HOTEL ROOM is frosty would be an understatement.

In the car, not a word was said.

You could have heard a pin drop in the elevator.

And now that we're in our room, the only sound filtering through the space is the heavy breathing of a very pissed-off Hudson.

And I don't know why he's mad at me. I'm not the one who started this entire thing.

Actually, I killed it at the club before he tackled me like a three-hundred-pound linebacker looking for his fiftieth career sack. I had a very enjoyable tea with Sheridan, where we discussed the dress fitting I needed to schedule. She showed me pictures of her gown and the flowers and the venue. It all looked so dreamy. We ate scones; she introduced me to clotted cream and taught me how to make the proper cup of tea. Note: As per the English, add milk *before* the tea is poured. Very important to protect the china. Apparently.

When we met with the guys out in the courtyard, it seemed like they'd had just as good of a time, not to mention, neither of them smelled like cigars, so a plus for the ladies.

It was all good...until it wasn't.

And if he expects an apology from me, he is sorely mistaken. If anything, I deserve an apology because my ass was the one that was on full display.

I was the one who was mooning the courtyard, giving them a bit of an afternoon delight.

A little bit of crumpet with their tea, if you know what I mean.

And that was humiliating.

It was like he reverted back to his old ways again, didn't trust that I knew what I was doing and tried to fix a problem before there was even a problem to fix.

So...yeah, he should not be mad at me. He should be—

"That was humiliating," Hudson says from the bedroom doorway, looking pissed and ready to fight.

Well, join the club.

"That was humiliating? Uh, yeah, I know. I was the one ass up, waving my pasty butt at the club."

"Because of your own doing."

"My doing?" I say on a scoff. "My doing? You're being serious? You thought that was all from my doing? Sir, that started with your mediocre tackle."

"Because you were about to hit your croquet ball into Buckingham Palace."

"Uh, exaggerate much? Buckingham Palace isn't that close to the club."

"Yes, I know; that's how hard you were about to hit it."

"Oh my God, drama queen. I was not. I was going for the double hoop," I say.

"Why? There was no need. Everyone did the single."

"Yeah, amateurs. I saw the potential of the bonus swing. I wanted two swings to get to hoop three."

"This wasn't a fucking prize competition, Sloane. This was a friendly game of croquet."

"Yeah, well, that wasn't in the description. I wanted to represent the Hoppers. I do recall your competitive spirit while in Bora Bora." I tap my chin. "I believe you were the one dry humping your brother to pop a balloon on the beach."

"I was not dry humping him. I was sitting on his lap."

"Thrusting your hips to get the balloon to pop."

"Don't act stupid."

"Excuse me?" I say from the bowels of my stomach as I stand from where I've been sitting on the couch. "Did you just call me stupid?"

"No, I said you were acting stupid."

"Explain to me how that's better."

"I'm not questioning your intelligence, just your personality."

"Umm, not better," I shoot back.

"Well then, don't act stupid," he says without an apologetic tone.

"Wow, you really are trying to get kicked in the penis in the middle of the night, aren't you? I'll have you know, my donkey kick is powerful and precise, not something you're going to want to mess with."

"Once again, the maturity is really showing."

My mouth falls open as I watch him spiral into an ass right before my eyes. "You're kidding me, right?" I ask. "You're really going to bring that up again? I thought we moved past that, Hudson. And for your information, I showed more maturity than you back there. You were the one knocking me to the ground. I was trying to help. I was the one being the good wife."

"You poked me in the balls in the middle of a courtyard. That's you being immature."

I shake my head. "Don't freaking test me, Hudson. Do not test me."

"What are you going to do?" he asks, looking so unimpressed.

I get into a fighting position, arms in front of me, ready to strike. "I'm nimble, quick, and can sting. Also, not afraid to bite."

"I like biting," he says, his eyes going dark.

The motherfucker.

"Don't." I point at him. "Don't you dare start with that bullshit. No sexual innuendos. Talk about maturity. You're over here yelling at me and then turning it sexual."

"I just said I like biting. That's it. You're the one who turned it sexual."

I fold my arms over my chest. "Please, if you didn't mean it in a sexual way, then how the hell did you mean it?"

"It doesn't matter," he says, taking a step closer. "What matters is that what happened at the club was a disaster, and we'll be lucky if we're invited back."

"They'll invite us back. They didn't seem to care. People were laughing."

"Yeah, because that's what I want, people laughing at us."

"Jesus, Hudson, pull the stick out. Have a sense of humor. Won't hurt you."

Deadpan, he says, "I walked out of there with your hat covering my ass. There's nothing funny about that. They're not letting us back in."

"Maybe you should have thought about that when you chose to wear such tight pants then, without freaking underwear! It was a recipe for disaster from the beginning. Ever think about that? Or maybe you shouldn't have tackled me."

"You were going to hurt someone. Maybe you shouldn't have tried to send the ball into orbit. Not to mention, you touched my balls in public. Fucking poked them."

"I was confused at what I was looking at," I shout back. "I thought it was gum or something."

"Jesus fuck, you didn't think it was gum."

"I don't know." I toss my hands up in the air. "I had no clue what happened back there; I blacked out." I touch my head. "I honestly feel concussed after you ostrich-ed me."

"If you say that one more goddamn time," he says, exhibiting a great deal of irritation.

"It's true," I shout. "You ostrich-ed me, sent my head right into the dirt, ass out. I'm wearing that thong you just had to buy, and now everyone at the club has seen my ass in that thong. Everyone. Lucky that I'm the only one that saw your bubblegum balls."

"Do not fucking call them that."

"Well, that's what they were. Do you wax down there? Jesus they were bald."

His jaw ticks, his teeth clenched together. "I'm trying to have a conversation with you, Sloane."

"No, you're trying to blame me for what happened."

"Because it is your fault," he shouts, his arms thrusting out. "It all started with you."

"It started with you," I yell back. "You could have just let me hit the ball. You were trying to ride in like some hero, and you fucked it up. This is on you, not me. Don't try to blame me for this shit. It's insulting that you think you can."

Fed up with him, I head toward the bedroom, attempting to move past him, but he stops me with his hand to my stomach.

"Let me by," I say. "I don't want to play these games with you, Hudson."

"I'm not playing games, Sloane," he says, his voice dark and dangerous. "This is my livelihood, and not just mine but my brother's and my business partners."

"Then maybe think about your actions before you act on them," I say.

"You're really not going to take any blame on this?" he asks.

"Why should I? You anticipated something in your head that never happened and created a scene. You embarrassed me, you embarrassed yourself, and now you're trying to figure out a way to place blame elsewhere."

"You were not innocent in that entire situation, Sloane."

"Sure, I didn't handle myself well as my thong-covered ass was flapping in the breeze; excuse me for being awkward and uncomfortable, but I never would have been in that situation if you didn't try to stop me from swinging in the first place. It started with you. So you can fuck off."

I move past him and head straight into the bathroom, where I shut the door and stare into the mirror, feeling angry and disappointed. Just when I think we have a moment of clarity, a moment where things are moving along for us and we are actually sort of becoming friends, something like this happens. Hudson spirals, and the man I can't stand shows up.

It's not fair, and I'm not going to stand for it.

———————

The bedroom is dark when I finally remove myself from the bathroom. I took another shower because, well, I felt dirty after that conversation with Hudson. I spent a good deal of time brushing and braiding my hair and went to the bathroom once more.

I move around the bed, where my phone is plugged into my charger—looks like the husband did something nice—and I pull back the covers and slide under them.

I will tell you right now, if that man attempts to come over here and snuggle into me, he's getting the donkey kick right to his bald balls.

Once I'm settled, I hold my breath, waiting in anticipation for the scoop of his hand to my stomach, but when it doesn't happen, I feel equally disappointed and relieved.

I didn't want to snuggle awkwardly with him, but I also sort of love it when he pulls me into his chest.

But tonight my anger might just outweigh any interest I have in snuggling.

I close my eyes and attempt to relax my body, not letting our argument or the arrogant man next to me make me lose any sleep.

Tomorrow is going to be a better day.

Tomorrow we're going to learn how to dance, and when I say "we," I mean "me." I will dance with myself if I have to. I refuse to be in this man's arms more than I need to be.

Nope, not after today. Not happening.

I adjust my head on my pillow, happy with my plan.

Now to just fall asleep—

"I'm not happy with myself," Hudson says, the soft tone of his voice breaking over my skin.

No, do not feel sorry for him.

Do not feel emotions toward him.

Let him be unhappy with himself. He should be.

"This is not how I envisioned things going when we left my dad's business."

Still not paying attention.

Still just trying to go to sleep on my own terms.

"We grew up with everything at our disposal," he continues. "We had the fancy schools, the expensive cars, the latest and greatest gadgets, but we never really had our dad's approval."

Ooof, that cuts deep. But still, not paying attention even though he's finally opening up like I've wanted.

Not falling for it.

I'm mad...

"When I started working for him, I thought that maybe that's when he'd tell me he was proud of me. Sure, graduating college didn't to do it, but maybe...just maybe working for him and him seeing my potential, that was going to do it. But as time went on, I started to see that winning his pride, winning his affection, was going to take more than just doing a good job." He clears his throat. "So, I worked harder. While Haisley took off and did her own thing and Hardy took over the almond business, I focused on following in my dad's footsteps. And with every passing year, with every new deal secured or idea that I saw come to life, it was never... good enough. Nothing has ever been good enough."

Crack.

Did you hear that?

That was me breaking, only slightly. But breaking just enough to pay more attention to what he's saying.

"Then I started to see who he really was as a man. Conniving. Deceitful. Ready to ruin someone's life for his own benefit, and I knew, I knew there was no way I wanted to be like him. I didn't want his approval. I didn't want him to be proud. I actually wanted him to be disgusted with me because I wasn't about to make the same deals he was. I wasn't about to put myself forward over everyone else. That's when Hardy and I broke off from our dad, when we contacted the Cane brothers and started a co-op. We invested, and we invested quickly. Luckily, so far, it's paid off, but I see the lasting impact my dad's business has had on the world, and I feel it's my responsibility to reverse that."

I rub my lips together, my heart sort of breaking for him.

"I know I'm chasing a dream that almost feels impossible, but with my dad hanging a lawsuit over our heads, trying to steal our business and take down his own sons, I feel this tremendous pressure to rise above and prove that you can create a successful business without destroying the people around you to do so."

He lets out a deep sigh. "Joining the Mayfair Club gets me closer to expanding the business, but also, it's…it's something my dad never did, despite wanting to be part of it. He wanted the status. He didn't care what the club values; he cared about the merit. And I know that because of that, he never received a member recommendation. So being there today, being able to do something my dad wasn't able to do, fuck, it felt good, Sloane. I felt like I was accomplishing something, and when it all fell apart, I just felt like I could hear my dad in the background. I felt like I could hear him laughing at me, and I lost it. I lost it on you, and I never should have. None of it was your fault. I'm sorry."

And there it is.

The apology.

A sincere apology.

One I feel like men in his position would never even think about offering to someone like me. And here he is willingly handing it over.

"I really am sorry."

He shifts on the bed, and I can tell he turns away toward his side.

Dammit.

Why does he have to do this to me? Why does he need to make me
feel empathy for him when that's the last thing I want to feel? I don't want
to have any emotions toward him, but ugh, I can't imagine the pressure
he goes through daily, knowing he has a powerful father hovering over
him, just waiting for him to make a mistake. The pressure must be so
incredibly heavy to shoulder.

I might know a thing or two about that. Jude has been the father figure
in my life, a strong one at that. I would be lost without him, but he also has
a hard time accepting me for who I am, for the person I've grown to be.

And even though I shouldn't feel this way toward Hudson, I don't
want him shouldering all of that. I don't want him having to worry alone.
I want him to be able to lean on me. To use me for an escape, to talk to me
about these things instead of letting them live inside himself and eating
him alive.

So I turn around and scoot toward him and tug on his shoulder, rolling
him to his back. I slide my hand over his thick, well-defined pecs and lean
on my elbow as I stare down at him. "I'm sorry, too."

He shakes his head. "No, don't apologize. This is not on you. It's on me."

"Hudson—"

"I'm serious, Sloane." He cups my cheek. "You're doing so fucking
great. You really are. I know how hard you're working. And I'm over here
being a dick to you because I'm frustrated with myself. I don't... Fuck..."
He looks away and then quietly says, "I don't want to be my dad."

"You're not," I say, even though I don't know his dad very well. I mean,

Reginald Hopper knows how to put on a show. When we were all in Bora Bora together, he played the loving father role, but I know that's not the real man that he is. I know from Jude that Reginald is a devious man, someone who, like Hudson said, would do anything to get his way, and we saw that clear as day when he manipulated the situation with Maggie and Brody. Hudson it not like that.

"I am," he says quietly.

I tip his chin, so he has to look at me. When his eyes meet mine, I shake my head. "You're not, Hudson. If anything, you're protective, overly protective. If you were like your father, do you think you'd make sure that I was comfortable, that I was able to help my sister purchase the house that we so desperately wanted to keep in our family? No, you probably would have turned me away for good." I run my finger over his forehead and down his cheek. "And if you were like him, instead of holding out and never kissing me, never fucking me, you would have taken what you wanted without any consideration of my feelings. That's not you."

"I could never take advantage of you or your body," he says softly. "Never."

"Exactly, Hudson. That's because you're not like your dad. You're nothing like him, and you can't think that way. You are so much better than him in all aspects. I know enough about him and I know enough about you to be confident that there's no comparison. None."

"How can you say those things?" he whispers. "After all the shit that I've put you through. How can you say that?"

"You haven't put me through anything I haven't agreed to," I answer. "This was my idea to get married. I agreed to being Sheridan's bridesmaid. What's going on between us has nothing to do with what you've put me through and everything to do with me knowing exactly what I decided to do." I lean in closer and whisper, "And I've agreed to this." Then I press a kiss to the tip of his nose and pull away.

"Fuck," he quietly whispers but then puts his arm around me. "Come here." He lowers me to his chest, where I rest my head, and he pulls me in tight, his arm circling me. His hand finds my thigh and then pushes my shirt up, leaving my hip bare to his palm.

A warm sensation spreads through my body as I rest against him, realizing that I haven't had this form of comfort, not ever really. Where human touch can lead to warmth. Where a clasped arm can lead to protection. This right here is new.

And I...I love it.

This isn't sex.

This isn't carnal attraction.

I thought I could have a physical relationship without it going deeper, but this is intimacy. This is so much more than I've ever had. And as much as I try to keep my walls up around this man, because he's kept his up, this moment, with him holding me tight, this could very well break down those walls.

"Thank you," he says.

"Thank you for what?" I ask as I feel so freaking comfortable resting on this man. *I may not want this to ever end.*

"Thank you for understanding me."

"You don't need to thank me for that," I say. "That's what being married is all about. We understand each other." I rest my hand on his bare stomach and let my thumb trail over his stacked abs.

He blows out a heavy breath and says, "Careful, any lower and you're going to turn me on."

"We wouldn't want that," I say as his hand slides up my side, pulling my shirt with it.

"No, we wouldn't," he says as his thumb connects with the side of my breast.

I roll my teeth over my lip as my hips move in closer to him. "Do that again and I might straddle you."

"Can't have that," he says. "Maybe you should, uh...roll over, face away from me."

"Maybe," I say. "Think it would be better?"

"Yeah." He lets out a short breath. "I do."

"Okay." I push off his chest and then stare down at his handsome face. I glance at his mouth and then back at his nose.

His tongue peeks out, wetting his lips, and I swear with one little movement, he has me panting, wanting more than he's been willing to give me.

I lower my mouth, mere inches from his face, and I wait a moment to see if he might break, to see if he wet his lips for a reason, but when he doesn't make a move, I kiss his nose one more time and then turn away from him. He follows my lead, scooting in behind me, and because he yanked my shirt up, he slides his hand over my midsection easily and pulls me into his nice warm body.

"You're not wearing underwear," he says.

"No, I'm not."

"Why not?" he asks, speaking closely to my ear.

"To torture us both."

"Well, you're doing a damn good job."

"Thank you. I will take that compliment with pride."

He chuckles and smooths his hand up my stomach. "Fuck, Sloane."

Two words.

Just two words and my entire body lights up.

"You want this, don't you?"

"More than you fucking know."

"Then just have me. Please, Hudson."

I feel him shake his head as his hand glides under my breast. "I can't."

"Then you can't feel me like that. You're making me wet."

"How wet?" he asks.

"Really wet." And then because I can't stand this push and pull, I move my fingers between my legs, slide them up my slit, then reach up and swipe them across his bottom lip.

"Fuck," he growls. "Fuck, you taste... Jesus, Sloane."

"Don't you want more? Don't you want to fucking bury your tongue between my legs and feast?"

"Don't," he says, his hand sliding across the underside of my breast again. "Fuck, please don't."

No, I'm over this.

I'm so over this restriction he's put on us. It's nonsense. We both want each other. Why not take it?

"Don't you want me between your legs, sucking your cock? Don't you hate knowing the last cock I ever sucked was Devin's?"

He pauses, and I know I struck a chord.

It's not a fair chord.

I played dirty, but come on!

Please, someone break this man.

When he doesn't move or say anything, I realize how much of a line I crossed.

"Hudson, I—"

"Don't."

"But, Hudson, I'm—"

"Don't," he says more firmly. "Just fucking don't." Then he reaches over me and tugs on the drawer of the nightstand.

"What are you doing?"

He moves back to his position and then hands me my vibrator. With our gazes connected, in a deep, growly voice, he says, "Fuck yourself."

"Wh-what?" I ask.

"You heard me. Fuck yourself." When I don't move, he adds, "Now."

Shaky but also so fucking turned on by being ordered around, I move the vibrator between my legs and turn it on, letting the vibrations buzz through me and relax my entire body.

"Fuck," I whisper as my eyes shut and I sink into the mattress.

Hudson's hand finds my stomach again and then glides up, under my shirt, and when I think he's about to touch my breasts, he doesn't. He slides his forearm between my breasts right before his hand clamps around my neck.

God, yes.

I love everything about the way he's commanding me, controlling me. His large palm, pressing down on my throat, owning me.

His lips lower to my ear as he says, "I might not be able to fuck you, and I might not be able to experience your mouth, but I sure as fuck am going to lie here and listen to you come."

My teeth roll over my lip, and I shift the vibrator so it's right against my clit. I know it will only take seconds in this position.

"That's right," he whispers. "Pretend it's my cock, sliding against your wet cunt." He breathes in sharply. "Pretend it's me, hovering over you." His thumb presses into the spot just below my ear.

"God, yes," I whisper as my body starts to climb.

"Pretend I'm so out of control from that slick pussy that I start thrusting over you, wishing that maybe just one thrust...one thrust would slip inside you."

"Fuck," I say as my pleasure starts to coil. "Hudson, I...I want you."

"Pretend, Sloane. Now with one taste, one thrust, I'd never be able to stop. I'd own your cunt. I'd claim it as mine, no one else's."

The vibrations send chills down my spine, my body starting to reach its apex.

"I want your cock. Give me your cock."

"No," he snaps. "But you will have my cum."

He sits up, pulls his cock out of his briefs—his long, thick cock that's pulsing for attention—and starts stroking himself. He sits on his knees, hovering over me as one hand returns to my neck and the other pleasures himself.

"That's it, you fucking filthy girl, fuck yourself. Let me hear you finish."

"Fuck," I gasp. "Touch me."

"No. Touch yourself."

Frustrated, I flip my shirt up to my neck, exposing my breasts to him and catch the absolute torture as he stares down at me, at my rock-hard nipples.

"Jesus fuck," he says as he wets his lips, his hand loosening on my neck.

"Touch them, Hudson. I know you want to."

He swallows, his Adam's apple bobbing.

"Pinch my nipples. The minute you do, I'm coming. Anything, Hudson. Please, anything."

"No," he says with such control that it makes me nuts. I drop the vibrator, lift up, and remove the shirt completely, leaving me totally exposed to him. I spread my legs and start shooting the vibrator in and out.

"I need your giant cock. I need you to give me what I need. Show me you'll be my best fuck ever. I know you will, but show me."

"Make yourself come, god dammit," he says, his breath losing control has he continues to stroke himself, now faster. "Fuck yourself...now, Sloane."

He's close—I can see it in his posture, in his tense muscles, in the veins rippling in his neck.

"Fuck," he shouts and then moves his cock closer to my mouth. I raise up only slightly and then when his eyes are shut, I drag my tongue over the tip.

His eyes blink open, his hand stops, and the look of utter torture falls over his expression.

"Delicious," I say.

Anger rolls through him, and he pins me down again by the neck, brings his cock right up to my mouth, and then starts pumping again. He stiffens and then starts coming as he shouts profanities.

"Motherfucker, take this cum. Take it."

His cum falls into my mouth and around my neck, and it's the most delicious and thrilling thing that's ever happened to me. It's so freaking erotic watching him come undone that in a matter of seconds, I'm shaking, convulsing, and calling out his name as I finish as well.

When I'm done, I turn off the vibrator and lie there, marked as his. *Again.*

And just like the night before, he presses his lips to my ear and growls, "Mine."

CHAPTER TWENTY
HUDSON

"SLOANE, BREAKFAST," I SAY AS I finish rolling the cart into the dining room area. I set our food on the table, and I'm about to call her again when she comes waltzing into the dining room completely and utterly naked.

Fuck.

Me.

I've never been so attracted to one single human before in my entire life, but here I am, becoming addicted to someone I have no right becoming addicted to.

The girl has curves, fucking gorgeous curves. She's not stick thin like other women I've dated. She has some meat on her bones—places I can hold on to. Her pussy is bare between her legs, her hips swell in the perfect way, and her tits, fuck me, they are gorgeous. Not perfectly round, just more than a handful with darker nipples that are hard as shit. Puckered, begging for my mouth.

I don't know how I've allowed this to happen, how she's so freely naked around me, but I'm finding it really hard to tell her to put some clothes on.

"Thank you for getting breakfast," she says as she smooths her hand over my chest before leaning over the table to check on the food.

This is going to require some epically strong willpower.

Like really fucking strong.

I take a seat in my chair and focus on the eggs in front of me—that is until she takes a seat on the table next to my plate, then my eyes shoot straight to her breasts.

Christ, they're so fucking perfect.

"Are you sure you want that for breakfast?" she asks. "Because I thought that maybe you would want something else." Then she slides my plate to the side and props her legs up on my shoulders, giving me a full view of her...

"Hudson. Hey, your phone is ringing."

"What?" I snap awake, feeling completely disoriented as I look around the bedroom, Sloane next to me in a T-shirt, me in my briefs. "What's happening?"

"Your phone is ringing," she says.

I look over my shoulder to my nightstand where my phone's lit up, Hardy's name scrolling across the screen. "Jesus, what time is it?"

"Three," Sloane mumbles and then flops back down on her pillow.

I grab my phone and answer it. "What?" I say, feeling like the wind has been snatched right from under me.

Christ, that dream. It felt so goddamn real.

"Hudson, we got the papers."

"What?" I ask, rubbing my eye with my palm as I get out of the bed and head into the living room, closing the bedroom door behind me.

"We've been served."

"Served what?"

"The lawsuit, Hudson. Jesus. From Dad."

That wakes me up. "Wait, seriously?"

"Yeah, seriously. And it's—fuck, it's not looking good."

"What do you mean it's not looking good? He has no leg to stand on. We didn't do anything wrong."

"That's not what he thinks. Apparently, there's a clause in our trust funds that states he's privileged to a percentage of income from anything we invest in while using our trust fund money. Meaning...the almond farm, Magical Moments by Maggie, and Brody's storefronts."

I feel all the blood drain from my face. "That can't be right."

"There is documentation that has been provided that says otherwise," Hardy says.

"So what the fuck does that mean?"

"It means he's suing us for negligence to pay and charging interest. He's also claiming rights to each business because we didn't discuss our investments with him first."

"He can't fucking do that," I nearly roar and then push my hand through my hair.

"I don't know, man, I sent it to the lawyers and they're combing through everything right now. It's not looking good."

"Have you spoken to Haisley?"

"No."

"Is he claiming rights over her business?"

"She's not mentioned, just us. And I think if this is correct, if he really has rights to everything we've created using the funds, that includes him having rights over the things we invested in with the Cane brothers."

"Fuck," I say again. "There's no way. There's no fucking way. We had our lawyers go through it all. We had them comb the documents to make sure we were doing everything correctly."

"They must have missed something," Hardy says, sounding just as lost as I feel in this moment. *How? We paid them to be thorough, to look at every fucking thing to do with our trust funds.* "Fuck, dude, I feel sick."

And that's Hardy.

He feels sick and I feel...mad.

Enraged.

How. Did. They. Miss. This?

I'm ready to blow a goddamn gasket.

"When are you going to hear back from the lawyers?"

"They said to give them forty-eight hours. They don't want to miss anything."

"Okay," I say as I pace the living room. "Forty-eight hours then. Call me if you hear more." I hang up the phone and throw it at the couch while shouting, "Fuck."

Thrumming with anger, I grab the bottle of scotch that's on the dry bar and I head out to the terrace, where I sit on one of the chairs and stare out at the crisp night while undoing the cap. I lift the bottle to my lips and take a long, full swig.

How can a father be so cruel? So vindictive? So fucking awful?

Why even have kids if you're going to treat them like this? If you're going to act like your children are your enemies rather than people to be proud of, people you can love and cherish and help grow in life?

Why the fuck have them?

I take another swig and lean my head back.

How could this happen? Everything we worked for, everything we've done, just snatched up, into the hands of the man who wants nothing more than to see our demise. To be able to point and laugh in our faces and tell us he told us so. That we are not good enough. That we are a disappointment. That we will never live up to his standards and expectations. That he will *always* win. Against us.

I take another swig.

And another swig.

And then one more just as the curtains from the living room blow with the wind, out into the terrace, revealing Sloane, standing there, looking so goddamn beautiful all sleep rumpled and in my shirt.

"Are you…are you okay?" she asks, looking tentative, scared.

I don't want her to be scared around me.

I don't want her to ever feel uncomfortable around me.

Never.

I set the bottle down and hold my hand out to her. She walks up to me, takes it, and I pull her down on my lap where she faces me and straddles my legs. I rest my hands on her waist and lean my head back, staring at her beautiful face.

Her hands smooth up my chest and she quietly asks, "What's going on? Why are you drinking at three in the morning?"

I slide her shirt up so my hands rest on her bare hips, and I drag my thumbs over her hip bones. I wet my lips, letting my eyes focus on her mouth.

"Hudson...talk to me."

That's the last thing I want to do. I don't want to talk. I don't want to think. I just want to act.

I reach over and grab the bottle of scotch and take a sip. Staring at her, I bring the bottle to her mouth. To my surprise, she takes it and tips it back. Cutely she shivers as the liquid flows down her throat. She hands back the bottle, and I take one more sip before setting it back down.

On a sigh, I take the hem of her shirt in my hands and tug it up and over her head, leaving her completely bare to me.

I know I shouldn't.

I really fucking shouldn't have her like this, but hell if I can stop myself.

Everything in my life is unbalanced. Nothing feels right. I'm about to lose everything, and the only reassurance, the only good thing I have going on for me right now, is this woman.

My wife. *My temporary wife.* But the woman I have shared far more with than anyone else. I gave her my fears, my darkness. But now, now I need her. Just her. "You don't want to talk, do you?" she asks, leaning forward.

"No," I say, moving my hands up her sides.

"Then use me," she says and presses a kiss to my neck.

"No," I say as her lips work up to my jaw.

"Use me, Hudson." Her fingers dig into my skin, and she rocks her pussy over my hardening length.

"I can't," I say as my hands round over her ass and squeeze.

Fuck.

She's so perfect.

Her body, her willingness, her need.

Her mouth moves up to my ear as her hand travels down between us and slips under the waistband of my briefs. I don't even get a second to stop her before she grips my cock and whispers, "Use. Me."

And just like that, my will snaps.

The issues with my dad.

The business I'm trying to hang on to.

My promise to Jude to protect Sloane.

It all fades to black because it's all going to implode anyway.

The business will be my father's; Jude and the Cane brothers will never be able to trust me again. The only thing I have is this woman, offering herself freely to me, so I allow myself to indulge.

To take.

To give in to what I've been holding back on for so long.

I grip the back of her head, pull her in close, and bring my mouth to her neck, where I kiss along the column, nibbling and tasting.

"Yes, baby," she says, her hand floating into my hair, where she tugs on the short strands. "Use me, Hudson."

That spurs me on as my mouth peppers kisses along her jaw to the spot just below her ear as she reaches down and starts to stroke me.

"Fuck," I grumble and lift her up out of the chair. Her legs wrap around my waist, and with my mouth doing a number on her neck, I carry her back into the hotel room and straight to the bedroom, where I toss her on the bed. Her hair fans out against the mattress as I push my briefs down and take my cock out. Staring at her, I start stroking myself as she spreads her legs and moves her hand over her pussy. She presses two fingers to her clit while pinching her nipple at the same time.

Her mouth falls open as she gasps and then smiles, because she knows she's driving me crazy. She knows I love watching her touch herself.

Eyes on me, she again says, "Use me." And then she spreads her legs wide, showing me that beautiful pussy.

My mouth waters.

I need a taste.

I've been wanting one for so goddamn long. And right now, what could I really lose? I'm losing it all anyway; I might as well enjoy myself. Especially with my beautiful and very willing wife in front of me.

I grip her ankles and pull her to the edge of the bed before I fall to my knees, spread her, and place my mouth right between her legs. I part her with my thumbs and slide my tongue along her slick clit.

"Oh my God," she yells as her chest lifts up.

"Jesus Christ," I mutter as her taste sits on my tongue. I look up at her, my mind going feral as I move back in and start lapping at her. "Fuck, you taste so good."

I stroke, letting her hard clit rub against my tongue.

I nibble with my lips, enjoying the way she thrashes against me.

I flatten my tongue, taking slow, steady strokes until I can feel her pulse against my mouth.

"Fuck...fuck," she says, her chest heaving, her hands finding my hair. She tugs on the short strands. "More, Hudson. Right there."

I take the point of my tongue and focus just on her clit, flicking back and forth in short strokes, soaking in every last second, not letting an ounce of her arousal slip past me.

"Fuck me. Oh my God, fuck, Hudson, ahhh, I'm...fuck. I'm close."

I've never heard a woman swear like her, and it's intoxicating. I love seeing her unravel. I love that she's unraveling because of me. That I'm the one doing this to her, causing her to feel such freedom.

"So close. Oh my God, right there. Right there, Hudson. Fuck..." Her mouth parts open, her body stills, and then with one more flick, she starts shattering beneath me, her body convulsing as she moans so loudly that I'm pretty sure the people in the lobby can hear us. "Oh fuck," she mumbles, and then slowly comes back down to earth.

I lean back and wipe at my mouth, loving that I can still smell her all over my face.

I stand from the floor and grip my cock and start pumping because, Jesus, I need relief. With her still on my tongue, I feel high as shit. She sits up on the bed, watching me, then wets her lips before pulling me down on the bed. She moves between my legs, forces me to let go of my dick, and then drags her palms over my thighs, spreading my legs wider.

My cock twitches in anticipation as she moves her mouth toward it, but instead of going straight to where I ache the most, she kisses my stomach, my legs, my inner thighs, and then her mouth moves to my balls where she lightly starts licking them.

"Fuuuuuuck," I drag out as precum graces the tip of my dick.

She tilts her head to the side, letting her hair fall over her shoulder, and slowly works her tongue up to the base of my shaft.

"Shit," I say, leaning back on my elbows.

She circles around the base, flicking her tongue, molding her lips along the tight skin, and works her way up, inch by inch, never giving me exactly what I need, just teasing me until I'm fucking crazy. She said she was good at this, but *good* is not the right adjective. She's phenomenal.

When she reaches the spot just at the base of the tip, she doesn't move any farther. She plays there, kissing, sucking the skin, flicking her tongue, driving me so fucking mad that my cock is twitching every time she makes a move.

"Baby, fuck . . ." My hips shift, my dick trying to find relief. "Suck me," I say in desperation.

A smile passes over her lips, and she rounds her tongue over the head.

Around and around, making my body feel fucking numb but never fully giving me what I crave.

"Jesus," I say as I thread my hand through her hair. "Suck me, Sloane." I tug on her hair, causing her to gasp, but then an even larger smile passes over her lips…as she disobeys and moves her mouth back down, right to my balls as she pulls them into her mouth. "Uhhhn, motherfucker," I say as I fall back to the bed. "Fuck." I press my hands to my face, my legs starting to shake. "Fucking suck me," I nearly yell.

She drags her tongue up my length, right to the tip, before bringing me deep into her mouth.

Fucking finally.

"Yesss, baby. Yes, suck me hard."

I look up and watch her cheeks hollow as she sucks me so goddamn hard that my eyes roll to the back of my head.

"Too good. Shit. Too fucking good."

I thrust my hips up just as she comes down over my cock, and I hit the back of her throat, making her gag. But like the good fucking girl that she is, she doesn't stop—she keeps sucking and sucking while her hand gently massages my balls.

It's the best fucking feeling, so damn good that I thrust up with her sucking, my hips out of control. I'm unable to stop. I want that release. I need that release and just as I feel my balls draw up, my orgasm right on the edge, she pulls away, letting my cock fall from her mouth to my stomach.

"Sloane," I say, out of breath. "Keep going."

She shakes her head and then moves up my body. "I said use me."

"I'm using your goddamn mouth."

She slides her hand up my stomach and whispers, "Use my cunt. If you want your release…then use me."

Growling out of frustration, I flip her to her back, push her up the bed, and move between her legs. I bring my cock to her entrance and her eyes immediately shut as her lips pull together, her tits jutted up.

"Eyes on me," I snap.

She gazes up at me as she says, "What?"

"I want those eyes on me when I enter you."

She nods, holds her breath, and brings her knees up to her chest, holding them as I position myself at her entrance. Her eyes stay on mine as, inch by inch, I enter her.

"Fuck," I growl at just how perfect she feels. The moment I get one hit, that's all it takes—I feel what it's like to be inside of her, and I know there's no way in hell I'm going back.

Ever. This is too fucking good.

Too warm.

Too tight.

Too goddamn amazing.

I slide in more and more until I'm all the way in, with nowhere else to go.

Her eyes are wide, her mouth parted, and she's struggling to breathe as she takes all of me.

"Deep breaths, Sloane. Deep breaths."

I breathe with her so she can sense the cadence, and when she matches her breath with mine, I cup her delicious tits for the first time, trying to get her to relax more, despite desperately needing to drive into her.

"These tits, fuck." I suck her nipple between my teeth.

"Oh my God," she says while squeezing her legs around me. "Yes, Hudson."

She tugs on my hair, and I move over to her other breast, getting lost in the feel, in how soft she is. How warm. How utterly perfect she is for my body.

I squeeze her breasts together and round my tongue around her nipples, then suck her nipples past my lips, causing her inner walls to contract around me.

"Yes, Hudson." Pleased, I release her breasts and slowly start pumping my hips. Her eyes connect with mine, and as I move in and out of her, a smile starts passing over her lips. "Harder," she says, clearly comfortable now. "Use me harder."

I grip her neck just tight enough as I piston my hips inside her. Her hands encircle my wrists, and she keeps me there, staring up at me, her beautiful lips parted.

At the sight in front of me, I lose control. I let loose. I hold nothing back as I pound into her. Stroke after stroke, getting lost in the feel of her tight pussy, sucking me in.

It's so fucking good.

Nothing has been better.

No one has been better.

It's everything I thought it would be with her, and with every thrust, I feel my body becoming more and more addicted. Needing another hit, begging for more.

"So tight." My eyes find hers. "This cunt is mine. Got it?"

She nods, wetting her lips.

"No one else. This cunt...is...mine."

I thrust my hips so hard, she scoots up the bed.

Another thrust, we're up to the headboard.

One more and I have to pin her in place by the neck a little more, but not too much that she can't breathe.

Her cries filter through the room, her heels dig into my back. "So close," she says and I can feel her tightening around me. "Right...there." And then, with her eyes set on me, she whispers, "Fill me with your cum."

It's what pushes me over the edge. It only takes a few more strokes before she cries out my name, shattering beneath me and convulsing around my cock. It takes me two more strokes as my limbs go numb and my cock swells right before I spill into her.

"Fuck...me!" I cry out as I dump into her. "Fuck." I breathe heavily and loosen my hold on her neck as I lean my head forward, pressing our foreheads together.

She grips my cheeks, looking into my eyes. And then, gently, she lifts and kisses me on the nose.

I let out a heavy breath and do the same, gently placing a kiss on her nose.

She stares up at me, those soulful eyes that weaken me, looking for so much more. And I know I shouldn't, I should pull away now, but fuck, I can't. Not when she's filled with me, not when we're this close…

I hover over her, my mouth lingering. I kiss her on the nose one more time and then lower my mouth to hers and, for the first fucking time since I've laid eyes on this woman, I match my lips with hers, kissing her gently.

She inhales, a sharp hitch in her breath before she sinks in and wraps her arms around my neck, pulling me in closer.

And I fall.

I fall into her embrace.

Into the way she works her mouth over mine.

Into the haze this woman puts me in.

I get lost.

I get high.

Within minutes, I feel the fissure form in my heart because this is different.

I've shared far more of myself with this woman than any other.

This is different than any kiss I've ever experienced before. *It feels so real. Deep. Meaningful.*

It brings comfort.

She does that.

And as she tightens her hold on me, I know for certain that nothing will ever be the same again.

There are too many feelings to label.

This moment, this is life-changing.

CHAPTER TWENTY-ONE
SLOANE

THE SOUND OF THE HOTEL door closes, waking me from my slumber. It takes a few seconds, but I blink my eyes open, letting them adjust to the light pouring in from the gauzy curtains where the sun is radiating a glow across the room. I shift my body, twisting toward the other side of the bed, looking for Hudson, but when I come up short, I sit up taller, feeling a wave of pain push through me.

Fuck, that hurts.

I glance around the room, looking for any sign of Hudson. When I can't see him, I let the blankets fall from my chest and reach for my shirt that for some reason is not on the edge of the bed. I slip it on over my head and head straight for the bathroom where I spend a few minutes brushing my teeth and using the bathroom.

When I'm washing my hands, I glance in the mirror, and I'm stunned when I find a lightly colored bruise traveling down the column of my neck. Shocked, I lift my shirt and look over the rest of my chest, taking in the marks that mar my skin.

Hudson was here.

Flashbacks to last night flit through my mind as I let my shirt down. I knew things would be different with him, but I never thought they would be like that. I never thought I'd feel a sense of being protected as he claimed me, marked me, possessively took control of me. He didn't shy away from what he wanted, what I wanted. He didn't hold back or treat me like I couldn't handle a more intense experience. It was as if he saw me as his equal for the first time, like he fully respected me, and that's a feeling I can't ever forget.

I straighten out my hair before heading to the living room, where I glance around, looking for him, but I come up short. Disappointment washes through me. Concern. Fear.

He left.

It's a red flag, a man disappearing after the night we shared. They should never leave and make you feel alone, lost, like you might have done something wrong. And yet I take a seat on the couch, attempting to tell myself that everything is okay.

That he's not running off.

That he's not regretting the night before.

That maybe he went for a jog or a workout…or that he needs to call his brother because he thinks this was the biggest mistake of his life, and now, he doesn't know how to handle it.

I walk back to the bedroom and slip on a pair of pajama bottoms, then return to the living room. I check the terrace, just in case I missed him out there, but nope, he's gone, and he took his phone with him.

No doubt he's making the call.

He's probably trying to figure out how to get out of this mess. Looking for help, assistance, anything to make him feel better about his choices.

I sit back on the couch and pull my legs into my chest as tears start to well in my eyes.

This is stupid. You shouldn't be crying over this. You said you weren't going to get invested, and here you are…investing.

No, you will not sit here and be sad.

I stand from the couch and find my sandals.

If anything, I'm allowing myself to be sad, but I will have coffee and a croissant while I'm sad.

I change out of my clothes in the bedroom—goodbye pajama pants I had on for a minute—and switch into leggings and a long-sleeved T-shirt. I pull on socks over my leggings and go to the bathroom, where I throw my hair up into a messy bun, pulling two strands from the side to frame my face.

Pleased, I snag my phone from the nightstand and head out of the hotel room to the elevator. I'm the kind of girl that keeps everything on her phone, credit cards, mobile hotel key. If I ever lost my phone, I'd be lost myself.

I half expect to see Hudson in the hallway for some reason, but when I don't, I keep my head held high. *You're fine.*

Everything is fine.

This is what he was afraid of, attachment. *So get it together, Sloane.*

When the elevator doors open, I get in and press the lobby button before leaning against the wall.

That kiss though, God—it was everything I expected and more. Soft and deep, like we were connecting on a different level, a higher level, one I never would have expected with him given how closed off he's been. And yet, he opened up last night. Something happened to him, something Hardy told him that made him open up. If I only knew what it was.

The elevator opens, and I'm about to get off when I realize I'm not at the lobby level. An older woman walks onto the elevator and smiles at me right before doing a double take.

"My goodness," she says, pressing her hand to her neck. "Are you okay?"

Shit…I forgot about the bruises.

"I am." I put on a smile. "Don't even ask, one of those incidents you wouldn't believe if you heard it." I chuckle. "Let's just say I'm never playing croquet again."

She laughs, thankfully. "Ah, a dangerous sport if not played properly."

"Tell me about it."

When we reach the lobby, I think about going back up to the room to cover up but then skip it because who cares. The croquet story worked; I'll use it again if I need to.

I head out of the lobby and across the street to Joe and the Juice. Before I can do so, the door opens and Hudson walks through with two cups of coffee in hand and a bag.

"Excuse me," he says, not even noticing me.

"Hudson," I say, surprised to see him.

He pauses and turns. When his eyes meet mine, they soften. "Sloane, what are you doing—fuck." He steps in closer and bends to look at my neck. "Fuck, did I do that?"

I clear my throat and nod. "Um, yes, but it doesn't hurt."

"Pardon me," a man says as he tries to get through the doors.

Hudson and I move to the side, the bustle of the city going by us as he looks more closely at my neck.

"Fuck, I'm sorry. I didn't know...I lost control."

"It's fine," I say and then meet my eyes to his. "I liked it."

"I shouldn't have been so rough."

I press my hand to his arm. "I liked it, Hudson. I liked it a lot."

He wets his lips and then nods. "I, uh, I came down here to grab you some coffee and a croissant, but they ran out, so I grabbed banana bread."

"You...you did?" I ask.

His brow knits together. "Why do you ask like that?"

"Because when I woke up and you weren't in the room, I thought that maybe you were, I don't know...regretting things."

He leans in close and says, "I fucking came inside you last night. I claimed you as mine. Do you think I would regret that?"

I shrug my shoulders. "It's been up and down with you."

"I know," he says softly and then sighs. "Want to go for a walk?"

"I'd love that," I say.

He hands me my coffee and the bread, and then drapes his arm over my shoulder and directs me down the street toward the Green Park. We don't say anything to each other, rather we just enjoy the moment. It's a beautiful day in London. Crisp morning air, blue skies dotted by white, cotton-like clouds, and the green of the grass is gorgeous, the leaves on the trees just starting to turn.

We reach a bench in the middle of the park, and he helps me down by holding my hand before taking a seat himself. He drapes his arm over the back of the bench and turns toward me. I do the same, moving in close so I can feel his body's warmth. He cups my cheek and drags his thumb over my jaw, a loving look in his eyes.

I went from being on the verge of tears this morning, thinking this man regretted everything about last night, to him lovingly cupping my face while we have coffee in a park in the middle of London together.

What a roller coaster.

"I, um...I kind of panicked this morning when I didn't see you," I say, wanting to be fully transparent with him. "I thought you regretted last night, which I know is not the case now, and I get sort of emotional, which I hate myself for—"

"Why?" he asks.

"Why what?"

"Why do you hate yourself for getting emotional?"

"Because this is casual, you know. Sure, we're married, but we're not married forever, and I don't want you thinking I'm catching feelings or anything. I think I was just embarrassed, and that embarrassment morphed into emotions. Like I said before, the only other guy who—"

"Do not say his name," Hudson says while taking a sip of his coffee. "Do not fucking say his name."

"Okay, well, he was the only other one I had a good time with, and I was nervous that, I don't know, something was wrong with me or I don't know. Just a lot of doubt."

A kid on a scooter zooms past us, startling me right before Hudson takes my hand in his. He brings my knuckles to his lips and gently kisses them. When he pulls away, he says, "I'm sorry I made you feel any less than what you are, which is perfect." He kisses my knuckles one more time. "In all honesty, I walked out this morning, looking to...hell, looking to put distance between us."

I knew it.

I felt it.

His energy was off last night.

"But when I got downstairs to the lobby, I felt this stab in my chest, like I was doing the wrong thing." His eyes meet mine. "You're not the problem. You're the release." He clears his throat. "So I got coffee instead to bring back to you and talk. And I'm sorry that you felt insecure or embarrassed. You have nothing to feel embarrassed about. Absolutely nothing."

"Okay." I stare down at my coffee mug. "So why were you going to leave then?"

"Because my life is fucked," he says softly.

"What do you mean?"

He drags his hand over his face, looking visibly distraught. "Last night I got a call from Hardy. Our dad is suing us."

"Suing you?" I say, my brows turning down. "Why exactly is he suing you again?"

"Because we started our own business, and he's not happy about it. He's not happy we left him. He's not happy that we're working with the Cane brothers and hates everything about our business model. And because he is not a normal human, he wants to take it out on us, and that's exactly what he did. The threat has been hanging over our heads for a while now, but yesterday, the papers were served."

"I'm so sorry." I press my hand to his leg, scooting in closer. "That's... that's really shitty, Hudson."

"That's not even the worst part." He shakes his head, laughing as if he can't believe it. "He actually might have partial ownership over everything we've done since leaving his business because there's apparently fine print about our trust fund money, that if we use it to invest in anything, he has part ownership."

"Wait, seriously?"

Hudson nods. "Yes, so everything Hardy and I and your brother have done up to this point basically will benefit my father."

"Oh my God, Hudson. That's terrible."

How could someone's father do that to them? Someone who is actually family? I mean, my parents were never in my life; we were raised by my grandma, and it is true we often felt like we were a burden to her, but I could not imagine growing up with someone who is supposed to love me and protect me just automatically trying to destroy everything I've built.

"What are you going to do?"

He shrugs, looking utterly defeated. "No idea. I guess just wait and see how fucked we are after the lawyers review everything."

"There isn't anything you can do?"

"I really don't know, Sloane. Honestly, I don't want to think about it."

"I can understand that."

He's silent for a moment, staring past my shoulder and sipping his coffee. After a few seconds, he asks, "Want to get lost today?"

"What do you mean?"

His eyes meet mine. "Let's get lost, forget about everything, and just...not think. Just see the sights. Explore."

"Don't we have dance lessons today?"

"I'll move them to tomorrow." He smooths his hand down my neck, over my bruise. "Get lost with me. Help me forget for just one day."

I swallow a sip of my coffee and realize that this could be the death of me, this minor request. Because I'm already bordering on feeling more for this man, but having him need me in this moment, having him lean on me, I know it will take its toll. Because I like to be needed.

I like to be needed by him.

I like the value I offer to him, especially since I've felt so lost, so unsure of myself. Seeing that I can have this kind of effect on someone, it brings me joy.

I know I will act like I'm not affected, even though deep down, being the person that helps him forget will only elevate this bubbling feeling inside me. It will elevate the attachment I already have. And that can be very dangerous because I said I wasn't going to grow attached.

But look at his face. Those pleading, tormented eyes. I can see the toll his father has taken on him. I can sense that he's teetering on breaking down, and I know that feeling all too well. I don't want him to feel that way, so even though I know this will possibly be my undoing, I know there is only one answer.

"I would love to."

Hand in hand, we make our way back into the lobby after a long walk through the Green Park and up the elevator to our room.

"I'm going to take a quick shower and get changed. I can be ready in about ten if you don't mind me going without makeup."

"You're beautiful either way," he says as the elevator doors part on our floor.

"Thank you," I say as he opens the door to our hotel suite. I let go of his hand and head to the bathroom. On the way, I strip out of my shirt and drop it to the floor before looking over my shoulder to watch him where he stands at the door, observing me. I reach behind me and undo my bra and drop that to the floor before pushing my leggings all the way to the floor as well and toeing them away, leaving me naked.

His eyes never leave me.

His gaze so intense.

Wanting that connection with him, the one that I felt last night so this void that I feel in the pit of my stomach is no longer there, I strut up to him and slip my hand under his shirt when I reach him.

His fingers travel over my neck, along my collarbone, and over my breasts where he marked them last night. I push his shirt up even farther until he allows me to take it off fully.

God, he's so hot.

How he has time to keep up with his physique, I have no idea, but I can't get enough of it. I bring my mouth to his chest and start kissing his pecs, dragging my tongue over his nipples, then I lower down to his abs, licking every single crevice until I'm eye level with his growing erection.

Smiling, I slip my fingers into the waistband of his joggers and pull them down, releasing his cock.

It's heavy in my palm as I start stroking it and watch it grow more and more with every stroke until he's fully hard, stretching toward my mouth, ready for me.

I love sucking cock so much.

I love the control it gives me.

I love seeing a man fall apart because of my mouth.

Gives me intense pleasure.

I gently nudge him backward until he's leaning against the wall and then help him out of his shoes, socks, and pants. When he's completely naked, I spread his legs farther and cup him. While I occasionally lick the tip of his dick, I massage his balls in my hand, prepping him, getting him worked up to the point that he's ready to burst.

"Fuck," he grumbles as he rests his head against the wall. "So fucking good."

Pleased, I continue to play with his balls while I bring my mouth to the root of his shaft and work my lips over it, kissing, sucking, licking, but staying in one centralized place. I know this drives him crazy from the way he tightens his hands into fists. Normally, the sensation of pumping up and down is what they want, but staying centralized, in one place—its stimulating and also drives them nuts wanting more.

"Sloane."

I release him from my hand and stand up, leaving him stretching up toward his stomach. When his eyes meet mine, I say, "Stay there."

I go to my nightstand where I grab my vibrator and my lube—thank God I thought of it—and bring it back to where Hudson is standing against the door to our hotel room. I take his hand and lead him over to the sitting area and stretch him out over the chaise lounge. I spread his legs and prop them up before I start lubing up the vibrator. Checking with him, I ask, "Can I?"

He wets his lips and nods his head.

Thrilled, I slowly insert the vibrator in his ass, letting him adjust, and when it's where I want it to be, I turn it on. He immediately moans, his legs falling open, and his cock springing forward.

Jesus Christ, that's so hot.

"Fuck...fuuuuuck," he says, his hips moving.

I might not even have to do anything—I might be hitting him in just the right spot.

"Uhhnn, fuck." His hands close into fists, his eyes squeeze shut, and I watch precum slip out of his tip and dribble down his stomach. "Baby... fuck...I...fuck."

I smile to myself because I don't think I've ever seen a reaction like this before. He's clawing at the couch, shifting his body, heaving his chest. His cock is twitching, his body thrumming, his balls tightening.

"Holy shit...fuck, baby...oh fuck."

My pussy throbs from the sight of him. My body tightening from seeing him fall apart like this.

And I'm unsure of what I want to do. I want to watch him. I want to see how long it takes before he comes, but God, I'm so hot right now, so hard up, in need of him.

"What do you want?" I ask as I play with his hard nipple.

"Fuck...I..." His jaw clenches together. "Your tight cunt. I want that fucking tight cunt."

Drenched and spiraling with lust, I straddle his lap and take his dick in my hand and position it at my entrance.

"Now, fucking now, Sloane."

I sit down on him, filling myself up with his erection, and I watch as the veins in his neck pulse from our connection.

"Mother...fucker." His hands fall to my hips, and before I even have a chance to gather myself, he starts lifting me up and pounding me down. "Fuck me...hard. Fuck me, Sloane."

Lust spiraling through me, I place my hands on his chest, and I dig my fingernails into him as I lift up and slam down on him.

"Fuck yes, baby. Just...like...that."

I do it again.

And again.

And again.

And with every time I push down, I squeeze around him. On the third one, my orgasm starts to pool around me, a numbing feeling crawling through my veins, a blank beat of euphoria pulsing at the base of my spine.

"Hudson, God, I'm...I'm close."

"Fuck me. Fuck me," he growls.

And I go feral. He's begging me, pleading. I've never heard anything sexier.

I pump over him. Unable to feel my feet, unable to catch my breath, I just focus on the pleasure coursing through me, on the sounds of him moaning, on the faint vibration I can feel until I feel him tense beneath me and then roar out in pleasure.

"Fuck!" he cries as I feel him spill inside me.

That's all it takes—my orgasm tips over the edge, and I'm coming around him, contracting my walls, prolonging his orgasm as well.

"Oh fuuuuuck," he groans as we both start to fade back down to reality. I fall on top of his chest, and he wraps his arms around me, keeping me close to him.

He holds me tightly, kissing my shoulder, kissing my neck, and when I lift up just a little, his lips find mine, and once again, we make out, letting our tongues dance and our mouths meld together.

When we pull away, I remove the vibrator and wash it in the bathroom, trying to regain my bearings. I turn around to find him standing in the doorway, leaning against it.

I turn back around and lean against the bathroom counter and watch his eyes in the mirror as they travel up and down my body before they fix back on my face.

"Where the fuck did you learn that?" he asks.

I shrug. "You know...places."

He walks up to me and lifts me up on the counter. He wraps his hand around the nape of my neck and holds me still. "I fucking blacked out."

"Good." I lean forward and kiss the marks I left on his chest from my fingers. "I'm glad."

"You can't do that to me, Sloane. I'm too old."

That makes me laugh as I look up at him. "I thought you said you were not that old."

"Blacking out during sex means I'm too goddamn old."

"Or it means you might finally be with someone compatible."

"That could not be more right." His hand travels down my back before he brings my leg up on the counter, exposing me. "I feel like I owe you more." He squats down in front of me and I chuckle.

"I'm not going to say no to that." And then he starts playing with me with his tongue, and I lean against the mirror, staring up at the ceiling, so grateful that I married this man.

CHAPTER TWENTY-TWO
HUDSON

"I SHOULD HAVE WORN A skirt today," Sloane says as she stands in front of Westminster Abbey. "The breeze could have blown it up, and I could have had a Marilyn Monroe moment." She does the classic pose, and I lower her phone from where I'm taking a picture.

"I would not have enjoyed that."

She playfully pouts. "Why not?"

"Because I don't want any more strangers seeing my wife's perfect ass."

She clutches her chest. "Aww, you called my ass perfect."

"Because it is," I grumble as I lift the camera again and take a picture of her posing in front of the majestically beautiful building.

We decided to ride on the big red buses for an on-and-off tour. Basically, you hop on and off at any stop for the whole day. Sloane was all about it, wanting to sit on the top level. I've never done it to be honest, too touristy for me, but experiencing it with Sloane, it's probably one of the most amusing things I've done in a long time. Because when she's not oohing and ahhing and pointing at things she wants me to look at, she's snuggled into my side, stroking my leg, whispering in my ear...

Fuck, this...this is very addicting.

My wife is addicting.

Her contagious smile.

Her flirty attitude.

Her need to touch me as her love language.

I like it. I like it too much.

Then again, at this point, who gives a fuck, right? The business is going down. Jude is going to be pissed at me anyway, might as well relish what I've been wanting to have for God knows how long. Let me have this fucking day.

Let me enjoy.

"Now we need one together. Oooh, I have an idea, you can pretend you're proposing to me in front of the Abbey, and I can act all shocked. We can get a round of applause and maybe a free tea and crumpet."

"That's not how it works."

"You never know. A local tea merchant might walk by and see us and offer us a free tea to celebrate. Oooh, that's what we should do. We should spend the day, you down on one knee, proposing in various places to see if we can get anything free."

"You realize I could purchase anything you might want, right?"

She rolls her eyes. "I know that, but it's more fun when you get it for free. An absolute thrill. Come on, it'll be fun. Plus, you never proposed to me, so this would be you making it up to me."

I eye her.

"Please." She tugs on my arm. "I promise to suck your dick for a solid twenty minutes when we get back to the hotel. You can set a timer."

I mean…having her mouth on my cock for twenty minutes, doubt I would last two minutes, but I'm not going to turn that down.

"Fine," I say, exasperated.

She chuckles and then whispers, "Sucker, I planned on sucking your dick for that long tonight anyway." She takes off her wedding ring, which I don't care for, and hands it to me. "You have to take yours off too or people are going to think you're an adulterer."

"I don't like you taking your ring off."

She rolls her eyes dramatically. "Okay, Mr. Possessive. Don't worry,

I'm going to say yes when you propose. You can slip it right back on." She nudges me. "Now come on, let's get free things."

She takes my phone from my hand and glances around, then she stops a person walking by and asks, "Could you take a video of us in front of the Abbey?"

"Of course," the woman says as she hands her water bottle to her friend.

As Sloane pulls me into position, I take my ring off and slip it into my pocket. This is the most ridiculous thing I've taken part in. Normally, this would not be something I would engage with, but right about now, pretty sure I give zero fucks about life, so I cozy up next to Sloane as she gives the camera peace signs.

She nudges me with my hand, so I turn toward her, get down on one knee, and she shrieks in fake surprise, covering her hand with her mouth. Her reaction is comical, overanimated, and absolutely ridiculous, but I go along with it.

Holding the ring up to her, I catch a crowd forming around us and I say, "Sloane, love of my life, I can't imagine a day going by without you by my side. Will you make me the happiest man and be my wife?"

She shrieks again, nods, and holds out her hand. I slip the ring onto her finger, and she leaps into my arms, knocking me to the ground while the small crowd that has formed around us cheers.

She grips both of my cheeks and kisses me on the lips while I bring us both to our feet. I hug her. She hugs me. And then she waves to the crowd like Miss America being carted around on a float.

The woman taking our video walks up to us with a huge smile on her face. "That was the sweetest thing I've ever seen. So beautiful."

"Thank you," I say.

"If you don't mind, could you take a few pictures of us posing?" Sloane asks.

"It would be my pleasure."

The lady steps back and starts working the angles while Sloane kisses me. Holds out her hand, showing off her ring. She even has me dip her while the crowd around us cheers. It's so fucking ridiculous, but also...I kind of like it.

When we're done, we thank the lady, thank the people around us who offer us a congratulations, and hand in hand, we head toward the bus stop.

"Sheesh," Sloane complains. "Not a single free item. Can you believe that?"

"I can," I say. "We were in the middle of a touristy area. If you want free, you can't be near a bunch of people who have nothing to offer that's free."

She pauses and looks up at me. "Oh my God, you're right. We need something more local, more intimate. Not so flashy." I can see that look in her eye.

"What the hell are you thinking?"

"Let's find one of those corridors, you know, a hidden alley where it opens up and there are businesses everywhere. That will guarantee us something free."

"If you say so..."

"Oh my God," Sloane whispers. "This is perfect. The bunting in the background, the cobbled stone. This place was made for proposals."

I glance around the small courtyard that is behind the Embassy of Japan. There is a cobbler's storefront, a pharmacy, and a Polish-Mexican fusion restaurant.

"Umm, this does not scream proposal."

"Of course it does. Look how cute that pharmacy is."

I take in the black storefront with gold lettering stating it's a pharmacy. "Yes, maybe they'll see us and offer some free allergy medication."

"Why, do you need some?"

"No," I say with annoyance. "This is ridiculous, Sloane. We don't need free things."

"I know we don't need them, but what an opportunity." She slips her ring off again and hands it to me.

"I don't like how easily you take that off."

"Dear God, man. We're married. It's not like every time I take it off, we get divorced."

"No, every time you take it off, I have to propose."

"Facts, but you like it."

"Maybe a little." I wink.

Smiling, she continues, "Okay, this time, maybe say something a little more personal in your speech."

"I don't need to be directed," I mutter. This is not how I intended the day to go.

"Now, ask that lady over there eating her pierogis to take a video. Maybe she'll give us some of her nachos as a congratulatory reward."

"Congratulatory reward?" I ask, eyebrow raised.

"You know what I mean. Now go, go."

Sloane pretends to take in the small courtyard while I go up to the lady who is enjoying her Polish-Mexican feast.

"Pardon me," I say, gathering her attention. "Um, I'm about to surprise my girlfriend over there with a proposal. Do you think you could film it for me? She thinks you're just taking pictures." She looks around at the location, looking a little surprised.

"Oh my gosh, of course," she coos, thankfully.

"Thank you."

I hand her the phone and walk up to Sloane. "She's going to take pictures for us," I say loudly. "Smile, babe."

Sloane cuddles in close, kicks her heel up, and throws up the peace sign. Then like last time, I step away and get down on one knee. Sloane goes through the routine of looking surprised. This time she even drums up some watery eyes while I take her hand in mine.

"Baby," I say, trying not to laugh at how stupid this is. "I love you more than anything. I knew it the day you almost clobbered me with a croquet mallet."

She clutches her chest.

"I need you in my life forever. Will you marry me?"

Hand clasped over her mouth, she nods and then leaps into my arms, knocking me flat on the ground again. The lady with the phone cheers while taking pictures from all different sort of angles. Tangled up in each other, I'm able to slip the ring on her finger and find her lips to kiss her.

There isn't much commotion in the courtyard, since it's pretty clear of people, but there are a few random claps here and there.

When we stand, the lady tells us to pose, so Sloane wraps my arms around her, like a classic prom picture and we take a few photos before the woman hands us the phone back.

"My goodness, this was such a joy to be a part of," she says.

"Thank you," I say as I glance around, not a soul in sight now. Sloane will not be happy.

"Why here?" The lady folds her arms in front of her, waiting for a grand story.

Sloane looks up at me and says, "Go ahead, sweetie, tell her."

Christ. Of course she's going to make me come up with something. I'm not good at this shit like she is. Not quite a talker like her.

I pull on the back of my neck and say, "Uh, this is where I ran into her for the first time, over there." I thumb behind me. "At the pharmacy. She was, uh, sick and I was looking for…"

"Condoms," Sloane interrupts. "But this silly American didn't realize that pharmacy didn't have any."

"Oh," the lady says, her face dropping in disapproval.

"Protection matters a lot to him," Sloane says, patting me on the chest, even though we have yet to use one condom. A conversation I need to have with her. "Anyway, I was dripping with snot, he was horny, and well, the rest is history."

How is the rest history with that?

"That's…uh, that's romantic."

"It is. What a dream of a story." Sloane lifts up on her toes and kisses my jaw. "Aren't I lucky?"

"Very." The lady nods. "Well, congratulations again and good luck with everything."

"Thank you," I say with a lift of my hand.

Then I loop my arm around Sloane and guide her toward the alleyway.

"Horny and dripping with snot?" I ask.

"I don't know. I was irritated that no one was around to give us something free and it just came out. What a bust."

"Aw, well, you're welcome for the proposal. Can't wait to spend an eternity with my blushing bride."

"We need to try again."

How did I know she was going to say that?

"We need somewhere more public, but something that might get us a free deal…" She pauses and then holds her finger up. "I know just the place."

Oh, I'm sure she does.

———

"Sloane."

"Hmm?" she asks with a smile.

"What the hell do you expect to receive by me proposing to you here?"

"Well, if we don't get free tea, then we for sure are going to get a free ride on the London Eye."

I stare up at the large Ferris wheel, which has a very long line.

"They are not going to give us a free ride."

"You don't know that. This is the perfect place to get something free. Just watch." She takes off her ring again and slips it into my hand. "We need to find someone who is going to take pictures who will make a big to-do about the proposal. Someone loud, preferably obnoxious."

She taps her chin and looks around as I pocket her ring.

"This is not going to work."

"With that attitude, it's not. Come on now. We have one goal today, to get something free."

"Pretty sure the goal today was to get lost in the city."

"Which we are, with a secondary goal of free things. Oooh, what about that lady over there in the pink leopard print? She would be perfect."

"If you think so," I say as I glance at the lady who is looking at a map of London.

"Ask her to record and remember, make the proposal personal."

"Yeah, yeah, I know." I move over to the lady holding the map and I clear my throat before saying, "Excuse me. I'm about to propose to my girlfriend over there and I was wondering if you could pretend to take a picture of us in front of the London Eye but really video the whole thing."

She snaps the map together, tosses it over her shoulder, thankfully someone grabs it before it blows away, and she takes my phone from my hand. "On it."

"Uh, thanks."

Unsure if this is the lady that we want, I head over to where Sloane is standing and wait for leopard print to follow, but when she doesn't, I grow concerned.

"Why is she looking around?" Sloane asks.

"Uh, I don't…oh fuck, she's taking off."

And in the blink of an eye, the lady in leopard bolts to the right, my phone clutched in her hand. The fucking audacity.

"Oh no," Sloane calls out just as I take off in a sprint after her.

Not on my fucking watch.

I dodge people left and right, calling out that she stole my phone. Tourists and onlookers watch as I chase her down the Queen's Walk, hoping and praying she doesn't decide to chuck my phone into the River Thames.

In a panic, she looks over her shoulder, seeing that I'm gaining on her. She tries to put it into high gear, but I've been running enough in my life that anything she does is not going to help, so she gives up, tosses my phone in the air out of desperation to escape and I attempt to dive and catch it, but miss by a fingertip, taking most of the blow from the impact and watching my phone skitter across the pavement.

Motherfucker.

Scraped-up clothes, a hole in my jeans now, I pick up my phone off the ground and welcome the new crack in the corner that splinters out from the center of my phone.

Yup, seems about right.

After a few seconds, I feel an arm on my shoulder and heavy breathing. I look behind me to see Sloane, bent over, gasping for air.

"Did…did you get it?" she asks.

"Yup." I flash her the screen. "In pristine condition."

She stands tall, hands on her hips, clearly in pain as she squints to look at the screen. "Oh boy, is that unfortunate."

I clench my jaw together. "Very."

She grips her side and winces. "You know, she seemed like an upstanding citizen. What a terrible misjudgment of character on my part." She motions back to the London Eye. "Shall we find someone else?"

"No," I say.

"No to the proposal or no to someone else? Because imagine how cute we would be with engagement photos in front of such a landmark."

"Sloane, I'm losing patience."

"I can see that." She lets out a deep breath. "Okay, so maybe this wasn't the right location. I can see how this is a tourist trap for theft. Maybe we go more intimate."

"We did intimate. No one was there."

"No, I have a good idea. I promise. We are getting something free this time, and no phones will be stolen. Follow me."

"Sloane, we're done," I say in a stern voice, causing her to snap out of her proposal extravaganza.

She nods and lets out a heavy sigh as she leans against the bridge wall behind her. "You're right, I'm sorry. Ugh, why did that lady have to ruin everything?" She helps me to my feet and dusts off my pants. "Are you okay?"

"Yeah, I'm fine."

"Okay." Smiling up at me, she says, "What do you want to do?"

I stare into those eyes of hers, the ones that captured me from day one, and I feel this overwhelming sense of needing to please her. Needing to make her happy. I honestly don't care what I want. I want what she wants.

"We can go to a museum. Is that something you might like to do?"

"I like museums," I say as I wrap my arm around her shoulders and pull her into a hug. Her arms wrap around my waist and immediately I feel comfort.

I don't know how she does it, how she is able to make me feel like nothing can happen to me when I'm in her arms, but fuck, that's exactly what it feels like.

I've never had that feeling of protection before, like someone is my shield, but Sloane gives me a piece of that well-being.

"Then let's do a museum."

"Okay," I answer, "but first...tea."

"How does this look to you?" I ask, staring up at the green awning of a café and tea shop just outside the Royal Mews.

"Looks darling."

"Perfect." I open the door for her and then walk in behind. The shop is quaint with uneven hardwood floors, white cottage shelving, and mismatched tables and chairs. Gold-framed art is on every inch of the wall, while fake flowers fill in the holes as decorations. It's charming, something you would find in a town in the English countryside, not a bustling city like London.

"Dear God, this is adorable," she says while turning toward me. "This was such a good find."

"Grab a seat wherever you want," the shop owner says.

"I'm going to run to the bathroom." Sloane kisses my chin. "I don't care where you pick."

"Sounds good," I say, and she takes off toward the back of the shop.

Out of sight, I turn toward the owner and say, "Could I have a word for a moment?"

"Of course. How may I help you?"

"Did you see that woman I was with who just took off to the bathroom?" The shop owner nods her head. "That's my wife. She has had me on a wild-goose chase all day, asking me to propose to her to see if we can—and I say this in a begrudging way—get something for free. Now, I'm not looking for anything free from you. She thinks that I'm irritated and over the whole thing, but now that we're here, I think it would be great to surprise her again. I know this is a really weird request, but if you will pretend to not only take pictures when I propose, but also pretend to give us something for free, I will pay you very well at the end of this."

She chuckles and nods. "Never had a request like that, but yes, I can accommodate. How much are you talking?"

"Name your price."

The shop owner smiles, and I know I'm about to be taken advantage of, but at this point, anything to earn me that smile from Sloane.

CHAPTER TWENTY-THREE
SLOANE

"I CAN'T BELIEVE YOU SURPRISED me with a fake proposal. I honestly didn't see that coming, almost felt like a real proposal," I say as I hang on Hudson's arm as we walk through Hyde Park. "It was so magical."

"Very magical," Hudson says.

"And they offered us so many free things. That's why you have to bring it down to a human level, you know? People who shop local, live local, not looking to capitalize on tourists but rather interact with them on a human level, those are the people you need to surround yourself with. They truly cared about our love in there."

"They really did. You could feel it."

"I'm glad they were the ones we could end this quest with." I sigh and lean my head against his shoulder. "And the tea set they gave us too? I mean the scones were great enough, but the addition of the tea set, that was unexpected."

"I think they just saw how committed we were to each other and thought it could be a celebratory tea set."

"Our anniversary set. We must drink tea from it every..." I pause and then laugh, because...duh, there is no anniversary. "Oh wait, we're not going to have an anniversary. Hmm, well, maybe every year we can get together on the day we divorce and cheers to a job well done."

Hudson grows tense next to me.

"That's unless you want to be married to me forever." I look up at his clenched jaw and poke it. "Hey, what's the tension for?"

"I just don't like it when you talk about divorce. It's not necessary."

"Okay," I say, caught off guard. "Didn't know that bothered you."

"You're my wife, Sloane, of course it fucking bothers me."

"But like...not a real wife."

"It's as real as it will ever get, and until it's not, I don't want to hear about divorce."

Yikes, okay. Once again, he could not be more confusing.

"I'm sorry, Husband. No more divorce talk. What do you want to talk about then?"

"Condoms."

"Uh, what?" I ask on a chuckle, totally not expecting him to say that.

"I want to talk about condoms."

"Okay. Interesting topic, but we can go there. When was the first time you ever tried to put one on?"

"Not like that," he says in exasperation. "We're not using them, Sloane."

"Ah, right, I have noticed your penis has been quite liberated in my vagina."

"Jesus Christ," he mutters, but I can see the humor on his lips.

"Tell me it's not true. Your old dilly dong has been running loose in there, filling me up with your strong seed." I fist pump the air, and he lowers my fist down with his hand.

"Can you, for the love of God, not say 'strong seed'?"

"Would you prefer 'milky white pearls'?"

"I would prefer none. Christ, Sloane." This time he chuckles. "Dealing with you feels like herding cats a lot of the time. It's hard to get you to focus and not act like a..."

"Like a what?" I ask, staring up at him.

"I don't know...an annoying asshole fresh from college."

"How dare you." I feign insult.

We both laugh, and he frees himself from my grasp but then wraps his arm around my shoulder. "Fuck, you're frustrating."

"Ahh, but you like it."

He shakes his head. "I do, which means there is something really wrong with me."

"It's called the Sloane Effect. I've sucked you in. Now you're trying to find a way to deal with it, but you're feeling all discombobulated. It's okay, you'll get there." I slip my hand around his waist as we slowly walk through the park, a light breeze dusting up the very few leaves that have fallen.

"Don't think I will, but back to the condoms."

"Right. Was there something particular you wanted to discuss or just point out that we're not using them because I'm well aware. Sex has never felt this good, and I was thinking about it earlier and whether it was because of the lack of condoms or if it was because of you, and I came to the conclusion that you have absolutely nothing to do with it and it's all about the condoms."

He stops and turns to look at me, that death look in his eyes that makes me laugh way too hard.

"God, the look on your face."

"Not funny, Sloane."

I chuckle some more and then fully turn toward him as he moves us to the side and out of the way. I press my hands to his chest, over his thick pecs, and say, "I'm kidding. I know the reason why I'm screaming your name at night is because of you, not the lack of condoms. All you."

"Why do you sound like you're kidding when you say that?" His hands smooth down my back and to my ass.

Oooh, yes please.

"I'm not kidding. I'm very serious. You rock my world, Husband."

"Mm-hmm, say it more seriously."

I slide my hand behind his neck and bring him in closer as I say, "I can't stop thinking about the way you make me feel when you're deep inside me, thrusting. When you hover over me, your abs firing off as your cock swells and you fill me with your cum. I crave it, Hudson. I need it. I know that no one will ever make me spiral into pleasure the way that you do. No one."

He wets his lips as he nods. "Good girl."

I smile and stand on my toes to kiss him. It's short, sweet, and nothing too deep because I know if I do anything more than that, we'll find ourselves in a predicament in the park.

"Call me that again and we're going to have to race back to the hotel."

"Patience," he says with a squeeze to my ass.

I kiss him one more time and then more seriously ask, "Why did you want to talk about condoms?"

He tucks a stray piece of hair that flies over my face behind my ear as he says, "Because we aren't using them, and I want to make sure you're protected, that you're okay with that."

I nod. "I'm on birth control if that's what you mean. And yes, I'm okay with that. I've been checked. You have nothing to worry about."

"You don't either," he says softly, dragging his thumb over my cheek as he stares lovingly down at me. "If you want me to use them, though, I can."

I shake my head. "I don't. I don't want anything between us."

"I don't want anything either."

"Good, glad we had this talk."

I kiss him one more time and we keep walking until we reach a bench. We both take a seat, and I slide in next to him, cuddling in close as he wraps his arm around me and places his hand on my hip.

"Despite your phone almost being stolen, this was a really fun day."

"Yeah, it was."

"I like you like this," I say as I play with the fabric of his shirt. "Loose, fun, willing to do things."

"I'm always like that."

I scoff...loudly. "Please, Hudson. Your general mood can be defined as uptight and rigid. Usually not pleasant to be around. But when you do have your moments of levity, like today, it's hard not to get attached to you, to not want to feed off your energy. I've had a lot of fun today, even when you were grumpy over the proposals."

"I mean, you can only do it so many times."

"I don't know, seems like a tradition was formed today."

"I'm not proposing again."

"You say that now, but when I make a slideshow of our pictures and videos, I know you're going to want to add to it."

"Not happening."

"Maybe you can propose at dance lessons tomorrow."

"Uh, no, we're supposed to be married at dance lessons."

"Oh, right." I chuckle. "Hard to keep up. I took my ring off so many times today, can't remember if I'm attached or not."

He gives me that *not so pleased* look.

"You know I'm kidding."

"You better be," he says, clearly unamused.

"You know it's okay to joke, right?"

"I'll joke when I find something humorous. You talking about whether we are married or not is not humorous to me."

"I see, and what exactly would be humorous to you? Because you didn't find the ripping of the pants and the poking of the bare balls in the club humorous either, but when I look back at it now, wow. What a sight. To be a fly on the wall for that ordeal."

"Still not funny."

"The split pants or the bare-balls poking?"

"Both."

"Hmm, shame. I feel like we could have gotten some good laughs out of it. Okay, if we can't find the humor in it just yet, what do you find funny?"

He thinks on it for a moment, and I watch his handsome face recollect his past, his jaw working back and forth. He really is such an attractive man, even when he's pensive.

"Most recently, I would have to say when Brody was scared shitless by the snake branch. I can still think about that and laugh."

"Same," I say on a chuckle. "That was good. The poor guy could not catch a break that entire trip."

"Also when he nearly got his dick speared off by my dad. That was good."

"Yes, and wasn't he high on seasickness medication?"

"Something like that." Hudson chuckles.

"See?" I say, patting his chest. "This is what I'm talking about. You can let your hair down and laugh."

"I know I can. I just choose to focus on more important things." He sighs and runs his hand over his shoulder. "Which seems pointless now that I think about it. What a waste of time and energy. All for what? For it to be snatched away. Money sure as fuck can't buy you happiness. It just buys you complications."

"Do you really think it's all going to be taken away from you?"

"I don't know," he answers, sounding hopeless. "If it is, there are a lot of people who are going to be fucked. You know, it's not just about me. It's about my brother, your brother, my sister, the Cane brothers, Maggie and Brody, Everly. There is so much connected to us that, if my father takes it over, I know he will destroy it out of spite."

I stare out at the park, wishing there was something I could do, something smart I could say, but I truly feel helpless in this moment. I don't feel like I have anything I can offer him of value and that makes me upset.

"What's the look on your face?" he asks.

"What look?"

"A disappointed look."

"Oh, I was just thinking about how I can't really help you in this situation. Like, I don't know what to say or do. I have zero advice, zero ideas. Feels kind of helpless, you know?"

"You're not, though." He links our hands together. "You're here, and that counts."

"Great. I'm here. That's reassuring."

He chuckles. "Do you know what I would be doing right now if I were alone and you weren't here?"

"No."

"I would be in my hotel room, not a single light on, drunk off my ass. No one would be able to get in touch with me. I wouldn't want to talk to anyone. I would sulk. I would destroy myself because that's how I would feel, like everything is collapsing around me and I would just let it happen." He tangles our fingers together. "But I'm not doing that, not with you here."

This feels intimate.

This feels much deeper than a marriage deal.

This feels like he's crossing over to something so much more.

And I shouldn't allow the conversation to keep going because that's not what we do, but I can't help it. I'm curious.

"Why not?" I ask.

His eyes meet mine. "Because I don't want you to see me like that."

"Why not?" I ask again, pushing him to give me the truth.

He glances away for a moment and then says, "Because I'm supposed to be the one protecting you, shielding you. Not the other way around."

"I would though," I say. "I would protect you, Hudson. I would help you, comfort you, be there for you. You don't always have to put on a front like everything will be okay. If you want to drink, if you want to sulk, I can be there for you. We don't have to be sitting in a park, fresh air all around us, trying to put on a happy face. If you want, I will be there for you for whatever mood you need to be in."

He shakes his head. "I don't want that."

"Then what do you want?"

"You," he says.

"All of me?" I ask.

He wets his lips and nods. "Yes, all of you." He's so confusing, but in this moment, I can only imagine he's not talking about forever. But for now, I can commit to him and only him.

"Well, I'm yours, Hudson."

"All of you?"

"All of me," I answer.

As long as I don't fall in love with you and give you my heart.

I walk out to the living room, fresh from the shower, wrapped in my robe as I look around the living room. Hudson took a phone call, so I told him I wanted to wash up from the day and took my time to give him privacy.

I listen intently to see if he's still on the phone, and when I don't hear him, I move through the suite until I notice the terrace door is partially open. I hesitate for a moment, waiting to see if he's on the phone, but when I don't hear anything, I walk outside to find him sitting on a chair, a glass of amber liquid in hand, staring off into the distance.

"Everything okay?" I ask.

He glances in my direction and shakes his head. "No."

"Is there anything I can do to help?"

"No," he answers again.

"Was that Hardy?"

He nods and holds his hand out to me. I take it and he pulls me down onto his lap. I straddle his legs, facing him while his hand smooths up my bare thigh.

"Any news?"

"Just that they've combed through the documents, and it says clear as day that he has partial ownership over whatever we invest in." Hudson drags his hand over his face. "I can't believe we missed that."

"That does seem odd, that you would miss that," I say. "I've seen you read over documents." I look off to the side. "What document is he referring to?"

"The trust documents that I had to sign when I took the money."

"And you looked through them?"

"Yes," he answers. "Hired my own lawyer as well."

"And those are the documents that the lawyer is looking at now?"

"He's looking through the papers that were sent to us, yes," he says, his voice questioning. "What are you after, Sloane?"

"Well, I feel like this is going to sound stupid, but you're looking over the documents he sent you. Did you consider looking at the document you signed?"

"It's the same, Sloane."

"Are you sure though?" I ask, feeling him grow tense. "I mean, I don't really know what I'm talking about, but what I do know is that your dad is not the best human. Wouldn't it be convenient if he just...tampered with things to go his way?"

"That's fraud."

I shrug, feeling stupid. "Sorry I brought it up. I just thought that maybe—"

He pulls his phone out of his pocket and punches around on it before bringing it up to his ear. Wanting to give him some privacy, I start to move, but he grips my hip, keeping me in place.

"Have you looked at our trust documents?" Hudson says, not even offering Hardy a hello.

I faintly hear him on the other line. "Yes, that's what we've been looking at."

"No, the ones that we signed, that we keep in the safety deposit box at the bank."

"No, just the ones that were sent over as reference."

"I need you to go to the bank and pull the ones that we signed and compare the documents."

"Why? Do you think they tampered with the agreement?"

"I don't know," Hudson says. "But I think it's worth checking. I think we would have flagged that kind of wording and tried to work around it."

"Okay, I can head over there when it opens."

"Call me immediately."

"Got it."

Hudson hangs up and sets his phone down on the ground before tilting his head back and pressing his hand into his eyes.

"Fuck," he roars, startling me.

I attempt to get off his lap again, but he keeps me in place. His eyes land on mine and I can see something dark behind his pupils. He's not the same man I was just with at the park or the man bouncing around London proposing.

This is the man who I would find in the office day in and day out, huffing and puffing about getting work done.

In a deep, husky voice, he says, "Strip."

"What?" I ask.

"I want you naked, Sloane. Strip."

The tone is dark, almost twisted. And if this was anyone else, I would get up right now and leave. But this is Hudson—no matter how angry he is, I know he's not going to hurt me.

He needs this.

He needs this release.

He needs a form of escape, and if that's me, I'm more than willing to give it to him.

I slip the knot of my robe loose and let it fall open.

Hudson brings his hands to my shoulders and slides the robe down, over my arms and off my body, leaving me naked on top of him.

He wets his lips and sits forward to pull his shirt up and over his head. He drops the fabric to the side and says, "Make me hard."

Accepting his challenge, I scoot off his legs—this time he lets me— and I undo his jeans. He assists me in taking them off by lifting up while I slide them down over his hips. Once he's free of them, I spread his legs and move up his body, my hands gliding over his thighs, up his stomach to his chest. I drag my breasts along the way, letting my hard nipples press against his skin. He bites on his lower lip as he stares down at me. I shift and take a seat on his lap, right over his already-hardening erection. With my back pressed against his chest, I slip my hand back behind me, around his neck and hold on as I slowly make circles with my ass over his lap.

"You're so big," I say as I feel him continue to grow. "I love how thick you are."

His hands find my hips, slowly guiding my motions, but I want more, so I take his hands in mine and slide them up to my breasts, stopping just under them. I don't let him touch them just yet; I just let the backs get brushed by them while I move over his cock.

"I want you inside me, Hudson. I want you filling me up."

His hand splays out over my stomach while he speaks directly into my ear. "I want to fuck you. Hard. Need this, Sloane. I need you."

Three words, they are my unraveling.

The pain I feel coming from him.

The aching for this nightmare he's living through to be over—it is set to the side as he finds solace in me.

And for someone who has never felt needed like this, it fills me to the point of feeling complete.

Whole.

"Good," I whisper. "Because I expect nothing less."

Then to my surprise, he pushes up and out of the seat, taking me with him. He turns us around, bends me over at the waist so my hands are resting on the seat he was just sitting in, and he slaps my ass, spanking me out of complete shock.

A gasp falls out of my mouth just as he does it again.

"Oh fuck," I cry, not expecting to be this turned on.

He smooths his hand over the sore spot and whispers, "You okay?"

"Perfect," I say.

"Good." And then he spanks me again before taking his cock out of his briefs and positioning it at my entrance. "You wet?"

"Drenched," I answer.

He rubs the tip of his cock over my arousal and growls when he finds out I wasn't lying.

"Such a good girl," he says as he spanks me again.

"Mmmmmm," I moan as my breath starts to hitch in my chest. "Again."

"That's my girl," he says as he spanks me one more time and slips his cock inside, in one solid thrust, feeling the way I contract from his hand to my ass. "Christ, this cunt." He grips my hips and digs his fingers into my ass as he leisurely pumps into me. "So tight. So perfect."

He slams in hard, then pulls out slow.

"I want to wreck you," he says, pulling out and slamming in again. "Destroy you." Slam, hitting me in that spot that will make me reach my orgasm faster. "Make you worthless to any other man." He thrusts so hard, the chair beneath my hands shifts.

I'm already worthless for other men.

Hudson pounds into me over and over again, making me so full that I can't do anything other than feel his cock slide in and out of me, pulsing, thrusting. It feels so good. So freaking good that every nerve ending in my body is shot, racing to the end goal, to the point of no return, where I break out into an acute sweat and the feeling of sweet bliss surges through me.

"Yes," I moan. "Yes, Hudson. More. Harder."

He spanks my ass again, eliciting a long moan from my lips. "Oh God. Again."

He listens so well, spanking me over and over until I'm crying out his name, my orgasm on the verge.

"I'm there. Oh God."

"Come on my cock," he roars, his hand finding my ass one last time before I tip over the edge and start convulsing around him while white-hot pleasure rips through me, nearly making my vision go black.

He pulls out of me and turns me around, where he forces me down to the chair. His hand rocking over his cock, he moves in close. "Suck me off."

Still in a daze, I bring my mouth to his tip and open wide, letting him thrust to the back of my throat.

"Jesus fuck," he roars as he holds my head and he does it again. I gag this time, and he loves it. He pulls out, giving me a second to breathe before he thrusts again and again and again. "So close. So goddamn close."

I take his balls in my hand and start massaging them as I watch his eyes roll in pleasure while I suck him in one more time before he stills, body trembling, and then he's coming in my mouth, groaning out in pleasure.

He pulls out and strokes his cock, letting the rest of his cum land on my breasts.

Once he's done, he lets out a deep breath.

"Go get in bed. I'm not done with you."

Excitement pulses through me because that's exactly what I wanted to hear. *Because I'm not done with you either, Husband.*

CHAPTER TWENTY-FOUR
HUDSON

"HUDSON, PUT YOUR PHONE DOWN," Sloane says, her hand moving up my chest as we lie in bed.

"I'm just checking to see if Hardy has found anything."

"You'll hear your phone if he has. Just…just relax for a moment. You're going to drive yourself insane waiting."

I set my phone down and blow out a frustrated breath. "Sorry. I'm just on edge."

"How can you possibly be on edge after what we just did?"

I smirk, thinking about how I just fucked Sloane up against the window of our hotel room, high off the fact that people could see us. "Just am."

"Okay, well, maybe we think of something else."

"Sure," I say, turning toward her. I slide my palm up her stomach to her breast. "Let's play."

"Slow down there, sir," she says, pushing my hand away. "You're going to need to give me a second or else you'll make me raw, and is that something you really want?"

"Raw?" I raise a brow. "Is that really a thing?"

"I have no idea," she answers. "But I can imagine it being a thing, so let's just…I don't know, talk."

"I'd prefer to have my face between your legs."

"Understandable. It's a great place to be. I often found my hand hanging out there before you came along, but I think we need to have a conversation."

"You want to have a conversation? Fine, how often was your hand between your legs?"

She rolls her eyes but props her head up with her hand. "Maybe every other night. I like to come, so I wasn't shy about it. There were times where I would use my hand because I enjoyed the challenge, but most of the time I used a vibrator. But I clearly don't need to worry about that with you around."

"You better not. If you want to come, you find me."

"What if you're in a meeting?" she asks with a smirk. "Should I just walk up to you and say, 'Mr. Hopper, your assistant needs to come'?"

"No."

She laughs. "That doesn't seem very adventurous."

"We are not fucking in the office."

"Where's the fun in that?" she asks.

"There's no fun in it."

"Wow, okay." She blows out a breath, causing a piece of her hair to fly up and then back against her cheek. "We might not even be married at that point though, so I guess it's fine."

The way she so casually talks about us not being together anymore grates on my goddamn nerves. I'd prefer that she doesn't think about the future when it comes to us. Because I don't know what the future entails, but there's one thing I know for certain, I'm not ready to let go just yet.

"Talking about divorce again, Sloane?" I ask with a dark tone in my voice.

"Uh…" She taps her chin. "No, I don't think so. Did it sound like divorce? I can't recall."

"It did," I answer, gripping her chin.

She smiles. "My mistake." Then she moves on top of my chest, her bare breasts pressing against my skin. I move my hand to her ass, where I possessively keep it. She drags her finger over my jaw. "You're so handsome."

"That's the kind of thing you should be saying."

"I'm serious. So handsome. I remember the first time I saw you in Bora Bora for Jude's wedding. I was awestruck."

"Awestruck, huh?"

She nods. "Very. I told Stacey how hot you were. I was pining hard, despite knowing I would never have a chance to be with you."

"And you went and got a job with me?"

"Well, I was desperate for the job. I needed something to gain experience, and I wasn't landing anything. Well, anything of substance, so yeah, I took the job with you."

I round my hand over her ass as she wets her lips.

"Did you ever think I was pretty?"

"I didn't let myself look at you," I answer honestly.

"You didn't?"

I shake my head. "No, because I got one look at you at the wedding, when you were at the reception, dancing with your sister, so fucking carefree, like not a thing in the world could hurt you, and I felt that freedom all the way to my soul. The joyous smile on your face, the happiness in your eyes—it was such a brief glimpse, but one that hit me in a way I've never felt before. And I knew you were trouble. Immediately knew it. So I kept my eyes down."

"Well, that's sad," she says with a pretend pout of her lips. "Because I worked hard picking out the outfits I wore to the office, and to hear they were wasted is upsetting."

"Trust me, they weren't wasted."

Her brow quirks up. "No? You snuck a peek every once in a while?"

"Yeah," I say on a sigh. "I would. Then I would chastise myself."

"Because you wanted me?"

I roll my teeth over the corner of my lip. "Yes, I did."

"Mm, I like knowing that. The pervy old man, watching over his assistant."

"Can you not call me that?"

She laughs, and I fucking love the sound, despite it being directed at me. "You know I'm kidding. I don't think you're pervy."

"Or old."

"Ehh, that's debatable."

"Pretty sure an old man wouldn't have been able to fuck you the way I did a few moments ago."

"Oh sure, it's not like you did much work. I was the one doing everything."

I pull away, blinking a few times, making her laugh even more. "I was holding you up and fucking you against a window. If I were an old man, I would have broken a hip."

"I did hear some cracking..."

"Shut the fuck up."

She laughs some more, and I try to move her away from me, but she hangs on tight and starts kissing my jaw. "No, don't push me away. I take it all back." She kisses some more and then works up to my nose where she kisses me there as well. "You're not old. You're young and spry and have a very delicious cock."

That sparks my interest. "Delicious?"

"Oh yes." She nods. "Very. Love having it in my mouth."

That's a fact. Anytime we start to get intimate, I always find her mouth between my legs, and I fucking love it.

"Well, I love that dirty mouth of yours." I drag my thumb over her lip.

"Have you ever had better head? And don't lie to me. If you have, tell me what she did."

I chuckle and shake my head. "No, babe, you're it."

"It as in...the only one who has ever given you head?"

I roll my eyes. "No. But the only one that I dream about fucking in the mouth day in and day out."

That brings a satisfied smile to her lips. "Oooh, that's a crown I like wearing."

"Good." I move my thumb over her cheek, her pretty eyes sparkling under the dim light.

"Now that we established that you're not old, possibly a little pervy with the mouth fucking, and that I'm the best that you've had your dick in, not to mention that you seem to enjoy calling me *babe* every now and again, I want to know more about you, like...what's your favorite band, music... Do you even listen to music?"

"No. Don't like music."

She raises herself up, her expression clearly disturbed. "What kind of psychopath are you? Who doesn't like music?"

I chuckle. "I'm kidding. I like pretty chill stuff."

"Okay." She blows out a heavy breath. "Jesus, that was going to be a problem. What do you mean by chill? Like Nora Jones? Maybe Kenny G?"

"Christ, who likes Kenny G?"

Her mouth falls open in shock as she fully pulls away and picks up the blanket to cover her breasts.

"Uh, I like Kenny G."

"Stop." I shake my head and attempt to pull on her blanket because I don't like her covering herself up, but she holds it close.

"I'm not kidding."

"Sloane. Be serious."

"I am being serious. Kenny G is a gift on the saxophone, an instrument that doesn't get enough credit anymore, I might add."

"Sloane..."

"Hudson..."

I stare at her, waiting for her to break, to tell me she's kidding, but when she holds steady, I slowly realize that maybe in fact she's not joking around.

"You really like Kenny G?"

"Yes, and I find it incredibly insulting that you think I was joking."

"Then prove it."

"Prove my love for Kenny G?" she asks.

"Yeah...babe...prove it."

Her eyes narrow and she crosses her arms, locking her blanket in place. "Okay." She clears her throat. "Kenneth Bruce Gorelick was born June 5, 1956, and despite his clearly old age, he has mastered the electric sound of the saxophone, which he started playing at the age of ten." *Oh shit, she was serious.* "Mr. G has sold over seventy-five million records globally, his 1992 album, *Breathless*, being his best seller, followed by his Christmas album, *Miracles*. Not only can he successfully blow air into a brass instrument and create music, but he's also a producer and most notably worked on soundtracks like *The Bodyguard*. Uh yeah, you heard that right, that Whitney Houston movie. He was an early investor in the Starbucks chain, is an aircraft pilot, and is an avid golfer with a handicap of +0.6."

I drag my hand over my cheek. "I think you know more about him than you do about me."

"Because he actually cares to share his life, unlike you, who says you like chill music but can't put a name to such chill music, therefore, not sharing a damn thing."

"Okay, okay." I rub her bare leg. "You're getting worked up."

"Yes, because you said you didn't believe that I loved Kenny G and I'm not lying. I love him. I like his curly hair and the way he feels the music he's playing and the sound of it. I love everything about him, and I wish more people would get their heads out of their asses and notice his talents, not just shuffle him away because he's a product of the early eighties. Did you know his net worth is over one hundred million? Yeah,

Hudson, one hundred million. That's nothing to put your nose up about. So…check your attitude."

"Okay, shhhh," I say, attempting to calm her down. "The attitude is checked."

"Is it though? I feel like you're just trying to be nice right now. You know what? We're going to listen to him, right here, right now." She reaches over to her nightstand, where she grabs her phone and starts tapping away on it. Then she looks me in the eyes and says, "This is 'Songbird,' and if you haven't heard this yet, you are dead to me. Your dick will never see the light of day in my mouth ever again."

Jesus Christ.

I perk up and pray that even if I haven't heard it, I can at least be convincing enough to fake it.

"And I'll know if you're lying."

She sets the phone between us and stares me down while the soothing sound of eighties smooth jazz filters into the room, instrumentals I cannot recognize for the life of me playing, making me panic. And then after a few seconds of intro, Kenny G comes in with his saxophone, a familiar tune that I've definitely heard before.

"Hey, I know this song."

"Do you really?" she asks skeptically.

"Yeah, I do." And then, to prove it to her, I hum along with the song, what little I do know, and I watch a smile creep over her lips before she tackles me on the bed and moves over the length of my body.

"Oh my God, I've never found you hotter than right now."

I laugh as I stare up at her.

"Fuck me. Fuck me hard, Hudson."

She doesn't have to ask me twice…

Our heads hang off the end of the bed, sheets rumpled around us, Kenny G still playing in the background.

I can barely catch my breath as Sloane pretends to smoke an imaginary cigarette.

Jesus.

Christ.

I...I can't feel my goddamn legs.

I don't even think I know where I am at the moment as the light starts to return to my eyes.

"That was the best sex of my life," Sloane says, breathless.

How she's even able to talk right now is beyond me—the girl put in the work.

"We will always have sex with Kenny G now."

When she puts it like that...

"No, Sloane." I turn to her, placing my hand on her stomach. "That was, fuck, that was amazing, but I'm not about to be triggered to arousal every time I hear Kenny G. Not fucking happening. It's bad enough that when I hear a saxophone, I'm going to think of your cunt coming all over my cock."

She smiles and cups my cheek. "Awww, are you really?"

"Yes."

"Then my work here is done." She hops out of bed as if I didn't just rail her a few seconds ago and moves into the bathroom where she cleans up.

I shift out of bed and check my phone, but there's nothing from Hardy, so I move toward the bathroom just as Sloane starts exiting.

"Oooh, hello there." She kisses my chest. "I'm starving. Can I order some room service?"

"Order whatever you want."

"Thank you, Husband."

To my displeasure, she slips on her robe and moves into the living room, where I hear her ordering soft pretzels. I clean up in the bathroom, splash some water on my face, then slip on a pair of boxer briefs before heading into the living room where Sloane is hanging up the phone.

"I ordered a few things. Hope that's okay."

I sit next to her and place my hand on her bare thigh. "That works."

"Will you eat with me?"

"As long as I can have you for dessert," I say.

"Says the guy who was gasping for air a few seconds ago."

"Babe, you fucked me while hanging on to the headboard and bouncing up and down. Your tits were, fuck, I'm going to get hard just thinking about it."

She chuckles. "I gave you a show, did I?"

"Yeah, you did."

"Well, looks like this wife knows what she's doing."

"She does." I lean in and press a sweet kiss on her lips. She lightly moans and cups the back of my neck and moves on top of my lap.

Christ.

I slip my hands inside of her robe, pressing them against her bare waist as her hands filter into my hair, kissing me harder.

When she pulls away, I feel drugged.

Light-headed. Although, I'm now doubting my intelligence for pushing her away physically for so long. *I feel fucking amazing.*

She kisses the tip of my nose and then slides her hands down to my pecs. "Tell me something about you."

"What do you want to know?" I ask, feeling like an open book.

"What did you want to be when you were growing up? And you can't say something like…take over your dad's business. Like what was the thing you wanted to be as a kid?"

"A deli worker."

"What?" She laughs, her smile stretching from ear to ear. "A deli worker?"

"Yeah, I was fascinated by the big meat slicers, and I thought it was cool. I wanted to be the one who sliced the meat."

"Oh my God, Hudson." She pats my chest. "That's the cutest thing I've ever heard. Did you ever get to slice the deli meat?"

"I did. I actually bought myself a meat slicer a few years ago and a giant turkey breast. I sliced it up and gave everyone two pounds."

"No, you didn't."

I nod slowly. "I did. This was during a time when I was bored out of my mind, not particularly challenged because my dad wasn't giving up control, and well...decided I'd live out a fantasy I thought I'd never see."

"Aww, that's kind of..."

"Sad?"

"Maybe a little," she says with a pinch to her fingers. "But also, sweet in a way. A thirty-year-old man handing out pounds of sliced meat. That's...nice."

"Is it though?" I ask with a wince.

"I mean, were you wearing an apron that said *meat delivery*?"

"No."

"Seems like a missed opportunity to me."

I chuckle. "Yeah, maybe it was." I squeeze her waist. "What about you, what did you want to be when you were younger? Can't possibly be the wife to your boss."

"Actually, when I was five, I announced to the world that if my boss didn't put a ring on my finger, then I'd burn everything to the ground."

"Wow, a very mature five-year-old."

"What can I say?" She shrugs. "I am special."

"You don't have to tell me."

She smiles sweetly. "But, you know, if I did end up burning things to the ground, I would have settled for being a geologist."

Now that surprises me. "Rocks?" I ask.

She nods. "Yup. Rocks. I was obsessed, well, still kind of am. I have a collection. It's not very big because did you know rocks can be expensive?"

"How? They're free."

"Not like…rocks you can find on the ground while taking a walk. Although I've found some pretty great ones that way, but more like rocks that are unique to other regions, the kind of rocks that you have to dig for or search to find. Like amethyst and malachite and fluorite. The rocks you see at rock stores that are all polished and pretty."

"Oh, okay. Did you have books on rocks?"

"I got this one from the library that I'd check out over and over until one day, the librarian gave it to me. Told me I was the only person who ever wanted to look at it, so she wanted to make sure it went to a good home. Funnily enough, it was one of very few personal items I brought with me to your house."

"You did?" I ask, feeling surprisingly touched.

"I did. It's sort of a comfort thing for me at this point. Anyway, yeah, rocks."

I rub my thumbs over her soft skin and tilt my head to the side as I say, "I find that incredibly adorable."

"Adorable?" Her nose scrunches up. "I don't think I want you thinking of me in that way. I only want you to think of me as sexy, hot, a temptress. Not adorable."

"Adorable is a good thing, makes you more human."

"Do you want me to find you adorable?"

"As long as you find me, that's all I care about."

"Such a smooth talker," she says. Although I don't think she realizes how honest I just was. I haven't sat and shared *stuff* like this with anyone… ever. There's never been time for talking when all I've thought about is business. Even when I've bedded women, they've known what they were there for, and it wasn't to talk. She's Jude's sister, so it makes sense that I find it easy to talk to her. But I also think it's because she's Sloane. *Sweet, sexy, and adorable Sloane.*

"So are you going to leave me some day to become a geologist?" I ask.

Her expression falls as she shakes her head. "I would need a plan of what I want to do with my life in order to leave, and unfortunately for me, I didn't go to school for geology."

"Why not?"

"Didn't know if it was something that could help my family. I majored in business and assumed that the career opportunities were vast, more chances at scoring a job."

"That makes sense. I can understand that feeling probably more than you would expect."

Just then, there's a knock at the door. Our food is here.

I carefully move her off me and say, "Cover up."

I open the door for in-room dining and allow them to roll the cart up to the couch, where Sloane has her legs tucked under her, not showing off a damn thing. Such a good girl.

I tip the server, thank him, and shut the door as Sloane lifts off the covers to the food.

Soft pretzels with cheese.

Truffle fries.

And...oddly a salad.

Wouldn't expect her to order a salad; then again, I could see her ordering it for me.

"Oh my God, these pretzels are incredible," Sloane says midchew. "I want to share, but also, I kind of don't."

I take a seat next to her and drape my arm along the back of the couch. "Yeah, you're going to have to share." I pluck one of the pretzels from the plate and dip it in the sauce. When I bring the pretzel up to my lips, I watch her act cutely shocked that I would take one of her pretzels. "Mmmm, delicious," I say after taking a bite.

"Wow, and here I thought you lived by the motto *happy wife, happy life*."

"I do. If I'm properly fed, I'll have the energy to properly pleasure you, which makes you happy."

"I don't know, I'm thinking this pretzel is better than sex right now."

"Yeah, I'm thinking this pretzel is better than your pussy."

She gasps, which makes me laugh.

"Don't shoot fire if you can't handle it coming right back at you," I say.

"You know, just for that, no more sex for you," she replies with a lift of her chin.

"Good luck keeping my cock out of your mouth."

"Hudson Hopper!" Her lips tilt up at the corners. "Sir, what has gotten into you? You're so lively and...and comedic."

"That's what happens when you tear down my walls."

"Aww." She presses her hand to her heart. "You saying you can be yourself around me?"

"Yeah...I think I can."

"I don't think we wore the right thing," Sloane whispers from the corner of her mouth.

I glance down at her leggings and crop top, and then to the ladies dressed in full Regency-style dresses with empire waistlines, pale hues, and lace.

"Um, yeah, I don't think we got the memo."

"We look like fools, especially you."

"You're the one showing midriff," I counter.

"And you're the one in joggers, a T-shirt, and a paisley floral ascot."

Which is nearly choking me to death.

"What was I supposed to say when the guy twice my age with the bushy eyebrows told me to wear it?"

"I don't know, tell him no?"

"I panicked," I say.

"Not a very Hudson Hopper thing for you to do."

"I panic all the time; I just don't show it."

"Well, it's showing in the form of a cravat today."

"Are we paying attention?" our instructor asks, snapping her fingers at us.

"Yes," I say, straightening up.

"Then please repeat what I just said."

Shit.

I can feel my cheeks flame at being caught red-handed not paying attention.

"Uh, to not step on each other's toes."

"Solid guess," Sloane whispers to me.

"No," Mary Beth snaps. "I said the first thing you do when the music starts is…"

She holds her hands out and the rest of the class—in unison I might add—says, "Bow and curtsy."

"Right," I say. "Sorry about that."

"Best pay attention," Mary Beth says with an evil eye directed at me specifically. "Now." She holds up her hands, both holding conductor sticks, and continues, "Curtsy, then promenade."

Sloane and I turn to each other, her lips twitching in humor as she curtsies and I bow to her. Then we move side by side and connect hands at each other's lower backs. She puffs her chest, I straighten up, and then we each slide a foot forward, then tiptoe on two. Slide, tiptoe. Slide. Tiptoe.

"Remember the day when you offered me up to Sheridan and Archie like a piece of meat, saying I could fill in as a bridesmaid?" Sloane asks.

"Yes," I say.

"Well, I hope you're happy. You did this to us."

I trip over my feet, losing the rhythm.

"Hudson," Mary Beth calls out. "Stay in time with the music."

"I'm trying," I say, but because Sloane keeps moving as well as everyone else around us, I can't seem to catch up, and Mary Beth ends up tapping her sticks on the lectern in front of her.

"Stop, stop, stop. We must start over. Positions."

"Christ," I mumble as we move back to where we started.

"It's not that hard, Hudson," Sloane whispers.

"Says the girl who keeps talking to me. Let me concentrate."

"As you wish, Husband," she says with a smirk.

"Everyone in position, and let's begin."

The music plays from the beginning again, and I reach for Sloane, but instead of her hand connecting with mine, my hand smacks into her head as she curtsies in front of me.

"You have to bow," Mary Beth yells from her perched position.

"Fuck, right," I say, dragging my hand over my mouth in frustration while Sloane rubs the side of her head.

"That was most unpleasant, my lord," Sloane says in a British accent.

"Can you not, please."

"Just getting into character."

"From the top," Mary Beth calls out while everyone grumbles. "Bow and promenade."

The music starts again, and I bow this time, then connect hands with Sloane, and together, we dance, shuffling around in a circle until we reach our original position. Christ, we did it.

"Keep going," Mary Beth shouts.

So we continue to shuffle and tiptoe, my goddamn calves burning as we move over the uneven slate flooring of the church turned dance studio.

"You're doing it. I'm so proud, my lord."

"Stop calling me that."

"You can say *my lady* if you want."

"Stop talking, Sloane." I concentrate on my footwork.

"Head up, Hudson," Mary Beth calls out.

"Nope," I shoot back to her as I stare at the ground, really concentrating.

"She doesn't like you."

"I couldn't care less," I say just as Mary Beth taps her stick on her lectern.

"Gather hands, everyone, and circle."

Sloane effortlessly parts from me, takes my hand and then moves toward the man behind her and takes his hand as well. Following her lead, I do the same.

And, boy oh boy, is this lady's hand moist.

The moist of all moist.

So moist that all I can think about is just how moist.

And warm.

So warm.

Bacteria-type warm.

Warm and moist.

"Move," Sloane says, but it's too late. The group piles in behind me while moist hand tugs on me, causing me to jolt forward, right into her back.

And like a domino effect, one right after the other, we all tumble forward, falling to the ground.

Pleated dresses rumple around.

Pressed suits crinkle.

And perfectly coiffed hairdos are tampered with while we all roll around together, trying to gain our bearings.

"What on earth?" Mary Beth shouts as we all struggle to stand.

"It was him," a man says, pointing at me.

"He's ruining everything," a woman says as she pushes down on her breasts, which are close to being exposed.

"He can't even bow."

"I can bow," I say defensively.

"Ehhh," Sloane says, not helping my case.

"Everyone, take a quick five while I have a conversation," Mary Beth says while moving away from her lectern.

I help up Sloane and attempt to help some other dancers, but they ignore me, sticking their noses up. Uh, I think they're failing to remember that everyone starts from somewhere and that at one point in their lives, they weren't these dancers with magical footwork.

It wouldn't hurt them to remember that.

Mary Beth ushers me and Sloane off to the side and turns her back to the group as she speaks. "You are not taking this seriously."

"Yes, I am."

"You are not. I can see it in your eyes that you think this is ridiculous," she accuses.

"Uh, I think it's ridiculous that we're not afforded any mistakes."

"This is not for beginners."

"This..." I pause and then turn toward Sloane. "What class is this?"

She shrugs. "I don't know. The Wimbachs signed us up. Although I seem to be picking it up just fine."

"You are quite lovely probably, given the experience Sheridan told me about," Mary Beth says to Sloane. "Hudson, on the other hand, you might need to sit out."

"I'm not sitting out. Just give me a second to learn and it will be fine."

Being bad at something, not what I enjoy.

If she would just give me a goddamn second, I can get ahold of this.

Mary Beth steps in closer and whispers, "The dancers are getting irritated."

"Yeah, I can sense that," I whisper back. "And as someone who is the CEO of a company, the people beneath you feed off your energy. So maybe instead of being irritated and hostile toward me, you encourage everyone around us to put on a freaking smile and help a guy dance with his wife."

From the corner of my eye, I can see Sloane smile. "It would mean so much to me if everyone cut Hudson some slack."

"This class is really for you, Sloane. He's not the one dancing in the wedding."

"Do you not believe in allowing couples to experience joy together?" I ask. "We're keeping the romance alive over here. I know I'm not involved in the wedding, but that doesn't mean I don't want to learn with my wife. You don't know us. Maybe this is something we want to do alone in our home when we get back to the States. Ever think about that?"

"Will you?" she asks.

"Yeah, my shoes with the buckles and my white tights are being shipped right now."

Her eyes narrow and her chin lifts. "This is not a joke."

I pinch the bridge of my nose. "Can you please just offer us some grace here? I know that Archie and Sheridan are probably forking out good money for this, meaning, I'm sure you're going to want a positive review."

Her eyes narrow further. "Are you threatening me?"

"I'm asking you for patience," I say, growing impatient myself.

"Fine." She turns away from us and claps her hands. "Everyone, we're going to start from the beginning and cover some of the basic steps. Our esteemed Hudson would like to keep the romance alive with his young wife. From the top."

Everyone groans and offers me looks of pure annoyance and hatred.

Grumbling under my breath, I say, "She is not getting a good review."

"She was not my favorite human," I say, breaking the silence in the car.

"I could tell," Sloane says. "You didn't say bye to her. Talk about a snub."

"She didn't deserve it. She was rude."

"I think it was because you kept forgetting to bow."

"Who needs to bow?" I nearly yell as the car pulls up to the club. "This isn't the eighteen hundreds. Why is bowing necessary?"

"Part of the culture and tradition, Husband."

"Yeah, well, it was ridiculous."

Our driver parks the car and then rounds to my side, where he opens up the door. I step out first and hold out my hand to Sloane, who changed into a light pink dress in the bathroom while I changed into a suit. *With* briefs.

We're meeting Archie and Sheridan at the club, as well as Terrance, Sheridan's dad. It was a last-minute request that I wasn't going to turn down. But now that I'm frazzled from Mary Beth, I feel uneasy. Also, I'm hating the time difference between me and Hardy right now because I'm dying to know what is going on with the lawyers.

I'm tense.

I'm unsure of everything.

And I'm irritated that dancing around in a circle was harder than I expected it to be.

Watch, Devin is probably some master at the footwork because he doesn't have anything better to do with himself than dance alone in his apartment, thinking about and yearning for Sloane.

"Hey," Sloane says, squeezing my hand. "You're really tense."

"I'm fine."

"You don't seem fine."

"Trust me, I'm—"

"Hey, you guys."

No.

Absolutely not.

No fucking way.

I lift my head just in time to see Devin walk up to us with a shit-eating grin and a pep in his stupid, unwelcoming step.

What the hell is he doing here?

"Hey, Devin," Sloane says as he walks up to her and kisses her on the cheek. This motherfucker.

I clench my hand into a fist at my side as he says hi to Sloane, then turns toward me for a handshake.

For a brief moment, I envision my fist plowing through his stomach, but I keep it together and shake his hand, pulling together one of the fakest smiles I've ever been able to muster.

"Dillon, good to see you."

"Devin. It's Devin," he says.

"Oh shit," I say on a playful laugh. "Sorry, man."

Actually, I'm not sorry.

Not sorry in the slightest.

"You headed to the club?" he asks, pointing behind us.

"Yes." I slip my arm over Sloane's shoulders. "Going to have dinner with Archie and Sheridan and her father."

"Yeah, me too," Devin says.

Uhhh…how the hell does that work?

I clear my throat and say, "Don't you need to be a member to be granted access? And don't you need to be married to be a member?"

"Terrance actually invited me, used one of his one-time passes."

"That was nice," I say through clenched teeth. A one-time pass would have been nice to know about, although that would have only granted me access once and to secure a deal, it isn't always about the first impression—it's about multiple impressions over time.

Devin pats his suit jacket and says, "Brought him some expensive cigars as a thank-you. Glad I can spend the evening with you guys as well. We can catch up, Sloane."

"We can," she says, but minus the joyful tone that's in his voice.

"Well, then, I guess we shouldn't make our hosts wait much longer for us." I gesture toward the doors. "Lead the way, Devin."

We enter the club, and because Devin is a guest, he's pulled into the welcoming room, while Sloane and I slip right in. I am sure to pull her toward the stairs and straight up to the bar where I know Archie and Sheridan are waiting.

"I can feel the anger pouring off you," Sloane whispers.

And because she's right, I pull her to the side, off in a corner, and whisper, "Where the fuck does he come off just...coming to the club, as if there aren't requirements to grant access?"

"It sounds like Terrance invited him."

"Why? He offers no value to society."

"Hudson, he's studying to be a surgeon."

"Doesn't make him a good person."

"Do you think this club is full of good people?" she asks. "Elite clubs like this are usually full of the opposite."

"This club was founded on philanthropy. But either way, he doesn't belong here, and why are you defending him?"

"I'm not defending him. I'm trying to get you to calm down."

"Getting me to calm down by suggesting his presence is not a big deal is not calming me down. You need to join in my anger."

"Okay." She clears her throat before her expression morphs into displeasure. "That motherfucker, showing up here, to our sacred spot where I poked your balls for the first time. How the fuck dare he? I demand he be kicked out. I demand he write us an apology letter. I demand he gets put on a plane and sent back to the States immediately because hell will freeze over before I share another breath of oxygen with that man. Freeze over!" She pumps her fist to the air, while I stare at her, completely unamused.

"The sarcasm isn't hitting."

"Really?" she says. "Because I thought I just slayed."

"There you two are," Sheridan says, walking up to us. "We were informed that you arrived."

We both plaster on smiles while we greet each other and then Sloane says, "Just talking dirty to each other over here in the corner."

Jesus Christ.

Sheridan smirks. "Oh?"

"Got to keep the romance alive, you know?"

"Very admirable. Um, not to change the subject, but how was the dance class today?"

"Good," Sloane answers. "Great actually. I think I only need about one more and I should be good to go. I can practice with the bridal party once everyone arrives."

"Really?" Sheridan asks, hopeful.

"Really," Sloane says.

Sheridan lightly claps her hands as Archie walks up as well. "This is so exciting." Sheridan lets out a low breath as Archie puts his arm around her and greets me with a nod. "To be honest, I've been kind of nervous about this entire situation. I mean, who really hires someone to be a bridesmaid? I've felt awkward and weird and at times embarrassed, but knowing you felt good about the dances today, that…that really gives me so much relief."

Sloane steps up and takes Sheridan's hand. Looking her in the eyes, she says, "I need you to not think that way…ever again. There is nothing awkward or embarrassing about having me in the wedding. Things happen, and your friend breaking her leg was unpredictable and unfortunate. I'm just glad I can step in and help. Trust me when I say this is an honor, to be a part of a day full of love and tradition. I'm grateful to be here in London with my husband, I'm grateful to have made a new friend, and I can't wait to watch you two celebrate the love you have for each other. Please, don't fret another moment over bringing me into the wedding party. This is a joyous occasion, let's keep it that way."

Wow.

Fucking wow.

That was...

Sheridan nods, tears filling her eyes before she pulls Sloane into a hug.

Archie smiles at me and then reaches out his hand. I shake it in greeting just as I hear, "This is the girl filling in as a bridesmaid?"

We all turn to find Terrance, standing there in a smoking jacket, his hand in the front pocket and his other hand twisting the end of his gray mustache.

"Papa," Sheridan says as she steps aside. "This is Sloane."

Not attempting to move, Terrance gives Sloane a brief once-over before saying, "Well, Sloane." He holds his arm out to her. "I think after that speech, you and I need to get to know each other better. Come."

Sloane slips her arm through Terrance's, and I watch them walk off toward the back deck that looks over the lawn while I stand there stunned.

Just fucking stunned.

Because my wife very well might have just helped me out more than she will ever realize.

CHAPTER TWENTY-FIVE
SLOANE

"THANK YOU," HUDSON WHISPERS INTO my ear for the tenth time since we sat on a love seat together after we shared an outdoor dinner with Archie, Sheridan, Terrance—my new best friend—and Devin.

He rubs his hand over my thigh, keeping me incredibly close to him.

I turn my head toward him and speak quietly. "You don't have to keep thanking me."

"I do," he says, and then to my surprise, he loops his finger under my chin and tugs me in close, placing a soft kiss on my lips, a lingering one, one that feels so freaking intimate that it sends a bout of butterflies through my stomach. When he pulls away, he whispers, "You helped me out so much."

"Well, that's what I'm here for."

"You shouldn't have to be."

"But I am. This is mutual."

"I don't know, seems like the scales are uneven and leaning in my favor."

I play with the collar of his dress shirt. "Then even them out tonight."

"Easy," he says.

"I was unaware you had such a brilliant wife," Terrance says while taking a seat across from us.

He spent the evening chatting with me while we were served dinner, essentially blocking everyone else out, even Hudson. We spoke about musicals, something he seems to be very passionate about. He is a big fan of the old-timey ones with the tap dancing. While I told him I was a die-hard fan of *Hamilton* and *Kinky Boots*.

He told me all about beef Wellington and the proper way to cook it.

I told him I had zero cooking experience but it was something I was hoping to get better at so I could make some fun meals for me and Hudson.

He asked if I had ever been to the UK before, and I told him I came from humble beginnings that prevented travel, and this time away, plus the trip to Bora Bora, were really the only big trips that I've been on.

We joked and shared stories, and when the meal was over, he went to go smoke a cigar while I snuggled into Hudson.

With the sun now set, pretty bulbed string lights hanging above us, and a whisper of people around us, Terrance has joined us again.

"I'm really glad you were able to meet her," Hudson says, then looks me in the eyes. "She's remarkable."

God, the way he says that combined with his expression, it almost feels like he absolutely means it. Like he cherishes me.

And excuse me if I don't freaking melt right on the spot.

How could I not with this man?

He's been such a closed-off, bossy, grumpy man who hasn't let me in an inch. But slowly and surely, with each passing day, he's warmed up to me. He's allowed me in to a part of his life, to help him. He's given me his trust. He's shared his insecurities. He's allowed me to support him. On top of that, he's seen me. He's made me feel valued, needed, like I actually have something to contribute.

And now, with that look, that kiss...I feel this connection to him that I've never felt with another human.

"She truly is," Terrance says, breaking my eye contact with Hudson. "Makes me wonder if I've misjudged you."

Hudson grows serious as he says, "I don't think I've given you the opportunity to get to know me better." Hudson presses his hand to his chest. "And that's on me, sir. I'll be honest with you. There were many times when I sat in my office and flipped a switch, turning on my business mode, and then forgot to turn it off. I'd get caught up in making the deal, in bettering the world. Moments like this, outside the office, where I get to spend an evening with new friends, in a beautiful city, with delicious food, I remember there is so much more than making the deal. So maybe you did judge me properly at first because it's all you truly knew about me."

I've always been impressed with Hudson Hopper. He's business savvy but kind. He has a good head on his shoulders, but this...this is another level.

This is him at peak performance.

"That's very commendable of you to say." Terrance leans back in his chair, studying us. "Can I be candid with you?"

"Please," Hudson says as his thumb rubs over my thigh.

"What happened with your father—from what I've heard, you and your brother betrayed him, claiming you wanted to run the business your way." He nods at Hudson. "What's your side of the story?"

Hudson shifts, but only slightly, indicating that he's uncomfortable but not too uncomfortable that he's going to skip the question.

"I'm not sure if you are aware, but my sister got married a little while ago in Bora Bora."

"Vaguely, congratulations."

"Thank you. It was a wonderful occasion, but during that time, we found out some things about our father that we couldn't align ourselves with. Of most concern, he was using a potential business partner to blackmail our sister into coming back to work under the Hopper umbrella. She left the family business years ago and built her own life. Dad was never happy about it and was doing everything he could to bring her back, to undermine her business, even by blackmailing and threatening others.

Haisley means everything to us." Hudson pauses, no doubt corralling his anger. "Hardy and I were not going to stand by and let our dad control her. That's when we dug deeper and discovered the inappropriate ways he was conducting business. We tried to discuss our concerns with him, but he wanted nothing to do with it, so we separated. We bought out the almond farm, a part of the business that he'd always found little value in, and we signed a few smaller businesses under the umbrella and joined together with the Cane brothers to work on more philanthropic projects."

He slowly nods. "And with the property here, your plans are legitimate?"

"Yes. We plan on creating low-income housing. It's what the Cane brothers started in San Francisco and have slowly been expanding throughout the US. We love the concept and feel passionate about extending this project outside the States. The opportunity with Archie arose, and well, I jumped on it because I have such respect for you both and would love the opportunity to work with Wimbach International on such a relevant and rewarding project."

"We could always use more low-income housing here," he says, still studying Hudson. He takes a second and then turns toward me. "Why did you marry Hudson? What do you see in him that I might not see?"

Why did I marry him?

Ummm...

So my sister and I could purchase our childhood home.

So Hudson could gain access to this club in order to talk to you.

So there was a very slim chance that I might be able to fall into bed with him, but that's neither here nor there.

I look up at Hudson's carved jaw, peppered in scruff, and I smile, thinking about how much I love the feel of that jaw moving between my legs. "It was an easy decision for me," I answer, which is not a lie. "He's unlike any man I've ever met." Also not a lie. "I have two siblings as well, a brother and a twin sister, and I saw in him what I see in myself, deep and genuine love for family. Dedication to family. It's what made me fall for him first. He's also incredibly smart. I started working for him and quickly noticed how intentional he was with his employees, during meetings, and even in emails. He wasn't demanding but respected everyone around him, and that impressed me and was an incredibly attractive trait. From there, I couldn't stop falling because of how he treated me, like I'm a queen. He made me feel seen. He made me feel valued. He made me feel like I had something to offer to this world." I shrug. "He's a one-of-a-kind man, and I'm grateful he chose me." Then I cup his cheek and press a light kiss to his lips that he returns.

"I can see that you two are very much in love, and I value those qualities too," Terrance says. "Qualities I haven't seen firsthand with your father."

"Maybe he'll get back to them one day," Hudson says.

"For your benefit, I hope so." He pats his leg. "Well, I just have one more thing to ask: What kind of wedding did you have? Because when I spoke to your father, he seemed unaware that you are married."

Oh.

My.

God.

I feel an immediate sweat break out on my upper lip as Hudson goes stiff next to me.

Terrance talked to Hudson's dad?

About us?

About our marriage.

No, this cannot be good. Did his dad talk to anyone else?

Hudson rubs his hand over his thigh as he clears his throat. I can see the distress in his eyes, in the way he carries himself, but it's hidden to everyone else. "Small, intimate. Just family, well, close family." He manages a small smile, but it's all for show, because behind those intense eyes of his, I know his mind is whirling.

"It was more about us," I add, trying to let him know that I'm here with him in this moment.

"With the intention of doing something later on down the road with family and friends," Hudson finishes. "But I wanted her as mine as quickly as I could make it happen."

"I can understand that. Do you plan on inviting your father?"

Jesus, this guy with the daddy issues. He already knows Reginald has been a dick to Hudson and he keeps pushing some sort of reconciliation. I hate that for Hudson.

"At the moment, I want to say yes, but we're battling a lawsuit he's filed against us. Maybe if we can get past the damage that he has done to our relationship, I will. The door is open to him to talk and make amends. I would love nothing more than to put this all behind us."

Such a diplomatic response, despite the war that Hudson's battling internally.

"I really hope you do. I couldn't imagine what it would be like if I weren't a part of my child's life. I shall encourage him from my end."

"That means a lot. Thank you." Hudson stands and reaches his hand out to me. "If you don't mind, Terrance, I promised my wife a dance out on the lawn."

"Of course, by all means." Terrance gestures for us to leave. I offer him a wave, and then hand in hand, we take off down the side steps that lead to the portable dance floor where a few couples are slow dancing under the stars.

"Are you okay?" I whisper.

"Just keep a smile on your face, he's going to watch us."

"Okay," I say as we make it to the floor where a string quartet is playing a beautiful rendition of "Rewrite the Stars."

Hudson pulls me in close, wraps his arm around my waist, while he connects his other hand to mine, holding it close to his chest. He lightly kisses my forehead and then connects our heads together while we slowly move to the music.

Whispering, I say, "Did you know your dad knew?"

"No fucking clue," he says stiffly.

"Any idea when he found out?"

"Nope," Hudson answers.

"Think he knows it's me?"

"No goddamn idea," Hudson mutters and then steps out and dips me. I stare up at him, and from the outside, I know it seems like we're probably in love and having a wonderful time, but I can see the panic in his eyes.

The worry.

The fear.

When he lifts me up, I ask, "What do you want to do?"

"I...I don't know. I need to talk to Hardy. I need to figure out what's—"

"Mind if I cut in?" a deep voice says, startling both of us.

Mother of God.

Now is not the time.

Hudson's head whips around and I know the minute he sees Devin because his nostrils flare and his grip on me grows tighter.

"I do mind," Hudson says, not a hint of sarcasm in his voice. "And I'd prefer it if you stop sniffing around my wife."

Oh boy.

Okay.

Tension is already high over here—better not let it get the best of us and do something stupid.

"I'm not sniffing around your wife."

"Please—"

"Hudson," I say, placing my hand on his chest. "Let me." Time to defuse. I turn to look at Devin and say, "Devin, it's been nice seeing you again and I wish you well with your education and everything you plan on doing with your life, but I don't think we should have any other interactions. You've made me feel uncomfortable."

His brows turn down.

"Oh, I didn't... I'm sorry. I didn't know. I was just trying to catch up with an old friend."

"I can understand that," I say. "But—"

"But fuck off," Hudson adds, causing me to wince.

"I think what Hudson means to say is that, since we have an intimate history, Hudson and I would both prefer if you and I kept our distance."

Devin looks between us and says, "I understand. I'm sorry if I made you uncomfortable. It was not my intention." He then looks Hudson in the eyes and adds, "You are lucky, remember that. Sloane is unique in every way. Hold on to her."

"I intend to," Hudson says, nearly growling. I'm surprised he doesn't chomp after Devin as he starts to walk away. When Devin is out of earshot, Hudson says, "Come on, we need to head back to the hotel."

The car is silent as we drive through Mayfair's heavily trafficked streets. Hudson's typing away on his phone, nowhere near me, clearly keeping his distance. I tell myself it's because he's in business mode and no other reason.

Although there's the fear in my heart that he's going to pull away, that his father knowing is going to make him freak out. And what if he did?

What if he did pull away?

This wasn't supposed to be forever, right?

So why do I feel my throat tightening over the thought of him distancing himself?

Before I start crying and getting far too emotional over this, I pull out my phone from my purse and text Stacey.

Sloane: Umm, things just got tricky here. Hudson's dad knows we're married, and we're trying to figure out if he has said anything. Have you heard from Jude?

Dumb question, because I know if she heard from Jude, she would have said something to me immediately. Night or day, she would have made sure I would have known.

My phone vibrates with a text back.

Stacey: Oh shit! That can't be good. No, I've heard nothing from Jude, and he came over last night with Haisley. I was asking him questions about replacing windows. He told me if we need new windows, that was the landlord's job. I kept my mouth shut and didn't say anything about us being the owners.

Sloane: God, I've completely forgotten about the house. Do we really need new windows? I'm such a shit sister. Things are getting complicated, and I'm dropping the ball.

Stacey: Um, things are complicated for sure, but you are the reason why we own the house, so please, don't feel bad about it. You're not a shit sister. But no, I don't think Jude knows or else he would have been furious.

Sloane: I guess that's a good thing. Do you think I should tell him?

Stacey: Now that, I don't know. Worst thing that could happen would be Hudson's dad tells Jude and then Jude has a stroke.

Sloane: That's what I'm afraid of too, but if I tell him and we don't finish what we're supposed to do out here, it could ruin everything for Hudson and I don't want that to happen either.

Stacey: Yeah, I'm going to offer no advice on this because I really don't want Jude coming up to me and saying 'Did you tell her not to tell me?'

Sloane: I mean, I did, and you didn't. You're already an accomplice. You were at the wedding.

Stacey: I'm choosing to ignore that.

Sloane: What a good sister. Ugh, Stacey, I'm in a pickle and I can feel Hudson pulling away, which probably shouldn't be a problem, but it feels like a problem, because...well...I think I might be having some feelings toward the man.

Stacey: NOOOOOOOOOO, Sloane, this is not what you were supposed to do.

Sloane: I know, okay. I don't need the lecture. It's just, he's so... he's so sweet and protective, and he fucks so well. Plus he's sensitive and opened up to me and I've just become attached and I know I shouldn't have but I did.

Stacey: Well, become unattached.

Sloane: It's not that easy.

Stacey: Sure it is. Just stop fucking him!

Sloane: Easy for you to say, you haven't sat on his penis.

Stacey: Thank God! Imagine the fallout. Seriously, Sloane, you need to take a step back, okay? This was supposed to be temporary. You both are getting what you need. After that, you can move on.

Sloane: I know, but I've been doing some thinking.

Stacey: This never ends well.

Sloane: Well, I've been struggling with what I want to do with my life and I think I sort of figured it out.

Stacey: How does this have anything to do with what we were talking about?

Sloane: Well, I thought about what would happen if maybe I stayed married to Hudson.

Stacey: Dear God.

Sloane: And how maybe we can use the house for good, rather than for us.

Stacey: Um...okay...

Sloane: Hudson does a lot of work with low-income housing and I thought, what if we turned the house into something of a safe house for families in need? Kind of pass the baton.

Stacey: That's, God, that's a really good idea.

Sloane: Right? I know nothing on how to make this work or where to get started, but I think it could be something great. And we can work on it together while still working our current jobs and who knows? We can really make it something and then maybe expand.

Stacey: Only problem with that plan is, where will we live?

Sloane: We can figure out those details later, but wouldn't this be…something great?

Stacey: It could be so great. Jude would really appreciate it. Oh, we could ask him for help! I bet he'd help us renovate and make it even more suitable for families.

Sloane: Oh, he would for sure.

Stacey: Now I feel like you marrying for money is turning into something even better than we planned.

Sloane: Look at me being a do-gooder with my pussy.

Stacey: The marriage didn't require you to show Hudson your pussy.

Sloane: I think we both knew it was going to happen.

Stacey: I know, but now you need to distance.

Sloane: Or I can tell him how I feel and see where it goes.

Stacey: That will not end well. He's a closed-off man. I don't think he's going to feel the same way, and I say that with love.

Sloane: I don't know, I think you could be wrong. He's different. I think he could be in the same headspace as me.

Stacey: Sloane, listen to me, no matter what, this is not going to end well. The least you can do is keep your heart out of it. Okay? Distance. Give yourself distance.

Talking about distance, Hudson has not looked at me once since we arrived back at the hotel. Not even when I asked him to unzip my dress and I let it fall to the floor, standing there in his ice-blue lingerie that he loves so much.

Nothing.

He has shut down completely as he sits out on the terrace, bouncing his leg up and down, his hand propping up his chin.

I can feel the nervous energy, can practically taste it. Something is brewing and I don't think it's going to work in my favor.

Not wanting to let him create too much distance, I head out toward the terrace in one of my matching pajama sets, which I know he's going to hate because he prefers me in his T-shirts. When I step out onto the terrace, he doesn't say anything, doesn't even look in my direction. His gaze remains fixed in front of him. So I move around his legs and take a seat on his lap. But when I sit down and balance myself on his leg, he doesn't put his arm around me, nor does he look at me.

Uh-oh.

Trying not to freak out because I can see where this is going, I loop my forearm around the back of his neck and remind myself that just an hour ago, he was holding me tightly on the dance floor. How much can really change in an hour?

"Hudson," I quietly say. "Are you okay?"

His leg that I'm not on bounces.

The tightness in his jaw looks like it could break a walnut.

And the angle of his brows, pointing down toward his nose, it's all I need to know to know he's not in a proper headspace.

I bring my hand to his cheek and carefully urge him to look at me. When he finally does, I don't see anger or sadness...I see nothing.

Like he's blanked out.

Become almost dead inside.

"What's going on?" I ask.

His tongue darts out, wetting his lips. "It could all be a fucking lie."

"What could?"

"The lawsuit," he says through clenched teeth.

"Oh, did you hear from Hardy?"

"Yes, he's just waiting to hear back from the lawyer, but he glanced at the documents and they don't match up."

"Oh my God. I mean, that's good news, right?"

His eyes find mine and I can see right away that this is not good news, at least not the kind of news Hudson wants to deal with.

"Do you see what he's trying to do, Sloane? He's trying to fuck over his two sons and lay claim to something he has no right laying claim to. It's undermining and deceitful, and it's coming from my fucking father."

God, I don't know what to say because what do you really say to something like that? *He's a dick? He's awful? You deserve better?*

Those are all things Hudson knows.

I don't feel like stating the obvious and I'm sure he doesn't want me stating the obvious.

But before I can decide on what to say, he lifts me off his lap and stands from his chair. Still wearing his dress shirt and pants from before, but now his shirt is undone and hanging open, he walks the length of the terrace, his hand in his hair, looking distressed and angry.

"Did he just think that we would roll over and give him what he wanted? It's fucking absurd."

Standing awkwardly, I clasp my hands in front of me and say, "I'm sorry, Hudson." Because what else is there to really say?

"Nothing was ever good enough for him, you know that?" he asks, looking me in the eyes. Is that rhetorical? Do I need to answer him? "And I did everything he fucking wanted. Everything. I worked as an intern in the mailroom. I sat through meeting after meaningless meeting taking notes for him, only for me to type them up and him to toss them in the trash the minute I handed them to him. He would use me when he needed, touting me around to family-oriented business partners, but would kick me to the curb when I wasn't useful. And then when I was finally put in charge of something, when I put in my time and did everything he asked, he undermined every decision I made. Never once said he was proud and often took credit for the ideas I came up with."

"Hudson—"

"And then when he tries to blackmail our sister, to hurt her business, we step out because we want nothing to do with him, only for him to retaliate with false information." He tugs on his hair hard. "Do you know how fucking worried I've been?"

I nod, realizing he just needs to vent in this moment.

"Terrified. Fucking terrified that I not only ruined my business but the businesses around me, attached to me. All for what? So that my dad can try to make me feel less than what I am? What a fuck!"

I'm about to say something when his phone rings. We walk over to where he was sitting, and he picks up the phone and says, "Yes?"

I can't hear who is on the other line, but I'm going to assume it's Hardy.

And as Hardy speaks, I can see the tension grow in Hudson's shoulders. I can see the anger start to billow out of him. Everything inside him is tightening.

"Countersue," Hudson says in a meaningful voice. "I don't give a fuck, Hardy. He wants to pull that bullshit, fucking call him out on it and sue him back."

He's silent for a second, his hand pulling out strands of his hair as he paces. "This is about us settling scores with our dad. He needs to realize he can't fuck with us." He moves toward the balcony of the terrace. "His lawyers should lose their licenses."

Wanting to calm him down, I walk up next to him and place my hand on his back, only for him to shrug away.

"Hold on a second," he says into the phone and then turns toward me. "Go to bed, Sloane."

"Huh?" I say, feeling like I got slapped in the face.

"Bed. Go to bed."

"I...I can wait for you."

"Don't." And then he turns away and heads down toward the opposite end of the terrace.

With his back to me, he folds in on himself, effectively disregarding me. I don't want to take it personally, but it does sting. I thought we were past that. But this distance feels like so much more than just space.

CHAPTER TWENTY-SIX
HUDSON

"I'M GOING TO LOSE IT," I growl into the phone as I sit.

"I know, but seriously, this was such a good find, Hudson. What were we thinking? We should have checked the original contract to begin with."

I slide my hand over my forehead. "Yeah, I think we've both been distracted."

"I can admit to that." He blows out a heavy breath. "I think we send the threat of a countersuit, have the lawyers list out all the damages, but then don't really press for action. I think the threat will scare him enough."

"I don't think so. I think he'll keep coming back."

"He has nothing on us," Hardy says. "And if we keep pressing and sue him back, it's only going to end poorly for us. We promised ourselves we would do things the right way, that we wouldn't sink to his level."

"So we're just going to let him walk all over us?" I nearly shout.

"No, we're setting the standard for how business will be handled moving forward. He will know not to fuck with us, but he won't be able to take any dirty laundry and air it out to potential business partners."

I'm about to shoot back when that last part sinks in. I hate to admit it, but he's right. If we were to countersue, he would make sure everyone in the business knew his boys were trying to sue him.

"Fuck, do you think that's what he was trying to do all along? Get us so fucking angry that we'd turn around and sue him and then use that against us?"

"Yeah," Hardy says. "I was talking to Everly about it, and she brought up the fact that this could have all been for show because he didn't have anything on us and was hoping we would countersue."

I grind my teeth together, thinking about the possible scenario. I lean back in my chair and drag my hand over my mouth. "I wouldn't put it past him."

"So I think we need to be level-headed about this. I think we need to put in a threat that will ensure he doesn't try to fuck with us again, but not be messy about it so he can use it to his advantage."

"Yeah, you're right. It's not what I want to do."

"Neither do I, trust me. I'm feeling really fucked in the head right now."

"Same," I say. "I was actually thinking about coming home, to wade through all of this legal bullshit."

"Oh, did the wedding happen already?"

"No." I shake my head, even though he can't see me. "But Sloane can stay here, and I can be back for the wedding. I just think I need to be there when we talk with the lawyers and decide how we handle everything."

There is a pause on the other line, and I can already tell that he doesn't agree with me.

"Is everything okay over there?"

No need to lie, he's going to call me out either way, so I say, "No, but that's not why I want to come back for a few days."

"Really? Because you haven't shown any sign of coming back. Hell, from the lack of communication between us, I could have sworn you were having a good time."

"I have been, and like I said, coming back is to make sure we are on the same page with the lawyers; hard to do that with an eight-hour time difference."

"Okay, so then why aren't things okay over there?"

I glance behind me to make sure Sloane isn't around. Hoping she's in bed, I say, "Things have gotten intense. Too intense."

"What do you mean...intense?"

"You know what I fucking mean, okay. She's just...she's different, and I'm different around her. It shouldn't be like this, but it is."

"Wow, I don't think I've ever heard a more evasive answer. That was rather impressive."

"Don't make me fucking say it." I drag my hand over my face.

"Yeah, I'm going to make you say it."

Grumbling, I say, "I like her. I shouldn't but I do, and I've become attached. And I shouldn't be attached. She talks about fucking divorce all the goddamn time, so I know she's not in the same mindset as I am, not that it matters because we're going to get divorced, we need to, because... well, fuck, Hardy."

"Oh God, what happened?"

I pause for a moment and then quietly say, "Dad knows."

"Dad knows what—wait, he knows about you and Sloane?"

"He knows I'm married. I don't know if he knows that it's Sloane. But Terrance was talking to Dad about me being married, and apparently Dad was surprised to hear about it. But if he finds out who it is, life is fucking over because you know he's not going to keep that to himself."

"Jesus Christ."

"Yeah, so another reason for coming back is to talk to Dad. To have that conversation with him, because I can't have him blowing up the marriage. Not when we're so close to making the deal and getting through the wedding. We just need a little bit more time, and I think I can get us that if I come home, talk to him about the lawsuit, and hopefully defuse the situation."

"You really think you can do that with Dad?"

"I don't know, but I would at least like to try. Not that I want to look that man in the eye, but in order to squash this, put it behind us, I would be willing to do that, especially if it means saving the relationship Jude has with Sloane."

"What about your relationship with him?"

I shake my head. "Hers is more important. She is more important."

"What are you doing?" Sloane says, sitting up in bed, looking all blurry eyed. She glances around. "Did you not sleep here last night?"

"I didn't sleep," I say as I stick my leather toiletry bag in my suitcase.

She rubs her eyes and asks, "Why are you packing? Should I be packing?"

"No," I answer, not wanting to look at her confused expression because if I do, this is going to be so much harder than I want it to be.

From the corner of my eye, I see her sit taller. "Where are you going?"

"Home for a few days."

"Home," she shouts as she gets out of bed. I zip up my suitcase, and I'm almost finished when she stops me and forces me to look at her. "What do you mean you're going home?"

"There are some things I need to resolve, Sloane."

"With the lawsuit? Let me come with you; I can help."

I shake my head. "I don't need your assistance." I finish zipping up my bag and set it on its wheels.

"Hold on a second," she says, stepping in again. "You can't just leave me here."

"I can. You have a fitting you have to go to for your dress. And you need to remain here in case Sheridan needs anything."

"But...but we were supposed to do this together. The dance lessons...the club..."

"I know, but you're ready for that. Plus, you will have my driver if you need to go anywhere."

"Wow, great, thanks. I'll have your driver. Seriously, Hudson, you can't leave me."

"I have to go back to San Francisco," I say in a sterner voice and grab my suitcase and head toward the front door.

"Hudson," she says, causing me to turn at the scared tone in her voice. Fuck.

Leaving would have been so much easier if she were asleep.

I face her, despite the war raging inside me, telling me to flee. When our eyes meet and I see just how terrified she is, a sick dread grows deep in the pit of my stomach.

"Wh-what is going on?" she asks, tears filling her eyes. "I thought…I thought everything was okay, but then last night you pushed me away and didn't sleep in the same bed—"

"I didn't sleep at all."

"You could have at least just lain with me, and now you're leaving. Were you going to leave without telling me?"

Yes.

If you didn't wake up, yes, I would have left, because that's the kind of coward I am.

"I have to catch my flight, Sloane."

Her lips grow tight and her arms fold in front of her. "Fine, go catch your flight, Hudson."

Fuck, sad to pissed in seconds.

Don't blame her though. Question is, how do I want to leave? It would be easier with her pissed off at me, since I need to keep my distance, but even though I am a coward, I can't do that to her, so I reach for her arm and tug her into my chest.

She's resistant at first but gives in and allows me to wrap my arms around her.

God, she smells so good.

She fits so perfectly in my arms.

I don't want to let this feeling go.

I kiss the side of her head and say, "It's only for a few days, then I'll be back. I need to finish this shit with my dad and be done with it."

"I could go with you," she says with hope.

"You know you can't," I say. "Sheridan needs you for the wedding, and that's why we're here, to be there for her, right? For the job." It's a subtle reminder for the both of us.

I take a step back and release her because I don't want to become too attached.

Those large eyes of hers connect with mine, confusion and pain running ramped through them. "Just tell me one thing, Hudson."

"What?" I ask.

"That you're not running away because of what happened yesterday."

"Nothing happened yesterday."

"Hudson, please," she says. "You can't tell me that things didn't change last night after we found out Terrance told your dad about us being married. I don't want you...running away from us. I don't want to handle this on my own. I can, but I don't want to."

"I'm not running away, Sloane. I'm trying to fucking fix things, okay?" When her eyes well up again, I sigh heavily. "I don't want you feeling sad or upset. I'm not running away. If I were, I wouldn't be coming back. Plus...Sloane, we shouldn't, we shouldn't be getting attached to each other like this."

And that does it.

That sentence right there.

Because my words set in as she takes a step back. And I can see the wheels in her head spinning, analyzing my comment before a mask of indifference falls over her features. That's all it took to snap out of this fantasyland we've been living in.

She wipes at her eyes and says, "You're right. I'm...I'm sorry." She wipes again. "I was just caught off guard. But you're so right." She exhales sharply and takes a step backward. "Um, have a safe flight."

I contemplate what to do next, because she just slammed a metaphorical door. She took what I said and sprinted with it. Which I should take as a blessing, because one sentence was all it took to remind us in this fucked-up situationship that we call a marriage, that it's all been a farce.

And yet, once again, things aren't settling well.

They don't sit right.

I want to tell her that I didn't mean it.

That she should expect me to call, text, FaceTime when I'm gone.

That I'm going to be thinking about her every second that I'm over in California.

But this is easier, better, right?

Having this distance?

She's setting the precedent right now by backing away.

This is business.

There shouldn't be texting when I'm gone.

There shouldn't be FaceTiming just so I can see her beautiful eyes. Or to catch a hint of her smile.

Nope, this is how it should be.

Cold.

Distant.

So I follow her lead.

I stick my hands in my pockets and say, "Thanks."

She takes another step back. "And if you need me to do anything, schedule meetings, whatever you need, just email me, I'll set it up."

"Don't worry about it—"

"I'm here for work, Hudson, and I'm your assistant, so you let me know what you need."

Yup, she's completely shut down, and before I say something stupid like...*you're not my assistant, you're my wife,* I nod.

"Okay, sounds good." I grab my suitcase handle and head toward the door. "Be back in a few."

"Yup. Safe flight."

I want to kiss her.

I want to hug her.

I want to strip her out of that stupid pajama set and fuck her so she will remember me when I'm gone.

But instead, I wheel my bag out of the hotel room and down the hall.

CHAPTER TWENTY-SEVEN
SLOANE

"HOW WAS DANCE CLASS?" MY driver, Harold, asks.

"Great, thank you," I say as I stare out the window.

"Would you like me to take you anywhere?"

"Just the hotel," I say while I cross one leg over the other.

"Mr. Hopper told me to take you wherever you wanted." He looks at me in the rearview mirror. "I can show you around."

I shake my head. "No, I have work to do. We can go back to the hotel. Thank you."

"As you wish," he says and puts the car in drive.

Dance class was actually boring and not fun at all. I wound up having to dance with Mary Beth, who couldn't be any drier. It was like dancing with a decade-old saltine. There was no humor, no laughter, and she was stiff as a board. Was she playing the part? Of course, but still, it was so much more fun with Hudson, especially when he forgot to bow before the dance started.

Today was just blah.

My phone beeps in my hand and hope surges through me as I pull it out of my purse in the hopes of hearing from Hudson, but when I see that it's from Sheridan, all that hope tumbles to the ground.

Not sure why I thought he might text me after the way he left, but I guess despite trying to act like him leaving didn't bother me, it bothers me immensely.

Tremendously.

He made me feel like nothing.

Like I didn't matter.

Like I was just a piece in his game.

And maybe I am.

Maybe I am a tool, and I was too stupid to realize it.

But why didn't it feel like I was utilitarian? Why did it feel like something so much deeper was developing between us? Why did it feel like he was ripping my heart out and taking it with him?

Then again, I should have known I never would have been more to him than just business.

Nothing like a good wake-up call to remind me where I stand.

I open the text from Sheridan and read it.

Sheridan: Hey, wanted to confirm the dress fitting tomorrow. Does that still work for you?

Feeling dead inside, I text her back.

Sloane: Yup, that works. I'll see you there.
Sheridan: Thank you! I appreciate you so much.

Well, at least someone appreciates me.

I set my phone down and stare out the window, my eyes not really focusing on anything as my mind flashes through this morning and the detached look in Hudson's eyes.

There is no doubt in my mind that if I didn't wake up, he would have left without saying bye. And what a shitty thing to do.

Awful actually.

It's bad enough that he's left me in a foreign country alone, but to do it without saying goodbye or leaving an explanation? What was I going to do, just wake up and be like...*Where's Hudson?* And then find out from the doorman, or the driver—no offense to Harold—that Hudson took off for America?

Jesus!

I bite down on the corner of my lip, trying to steady the emotions pulsing through me. I should have known this is what was going to happen. I should have been mentally prepared, but instead, I got caught up in the fanfare of "my wife" and the touching...and fucking.

God, I'm an idiot.

HUDSON

"Did you just get off the plane?" Hardy says when he walks into my office, looking surprised.

"Yeah," I answer as I wake up my computer.

"Why the hell are you here?"

"Why else would I be here?" I ask as I click on my email and watch my inbox fill with correspondence. Even though I was working on the plane, it looks like I've barely touched anything. That's the vicious cycle of emails though—the minute you answer one, two more come in.

"Don't you think you should get some rest first?"

"No," I answer, staring straight at my screen and skimming through an email from our lawyers.

"Dude, can I have your attention for two seconds?"

I sit back in my chair, fold my arms over my chest, and say, "What?"

"Don't you think we should talk about all of this? You look a little psychotic and the last thing we need is for you to make a mistake that you're going to regret later on. Not to mention, did you really leave—"

Knock, knock.

My eyes fly to the doorway of my office where Jude walks in. "Am I interrupting?"

From the sound of his voice, I can feel my balls crawl all the way up my throat.

"No," I say, my voice coming out squeaky. I clear it and repeat, "No. Come in."

He glances back at Sloane's desk and thumbs toward it. "I was hoping to catch my sister. I haven't heard from her in a bit and thought I'd treat her to dinner. Did she head home early?"

Jesus fuck, he has no idea she's in London right now. What the hell do I say?

Sweat immediately heats up my lower back as my mouth feels like glue, sticking together as I attempt to come up with something to say. Anything.

"Uhh…"

Nothing.

Not one goddamn thing comes to mind.

Because if I say that she's at home, he'll go there. Then he'll know I lied to him when he finds out that in fact she is not home.

Panic ensues.

More sweat forms.

And as he looks between us, I can watch his jovial expression slowly turn sour.

"Where is she?" he asks, looking none too pleased now.

Fuck.

Throat dry.

Hands clammy.

I look toward Hardy, who is trying to cut me in half with his eyes, begging me to say something, but I'm fucking lip locked.

Tired.

And I wasn't ready for this.

I watch Hardy roll his eyes and then turn toward Jude. "She's in London."

Jesus Christ!

Is he going to tell him the truth?

"London?" Jude's brows cinch together. "What the fuck is she doing there? And why didn't she tell me?"

Great question.

An obvious oversight on our end.

We were so worried about keeping the marriage a secret that we forgot about telling Jude that she was going there for work.

"She's a bridesmaid," Hardy says. "In the program."

"Oh." His brow knits together. "When did that start?"

"A little bit ago," I answer, finally finding my voice. "It's uh, it's for Sheridan and Archie Wimbach. They needed help, and she stepped up."

"Oh." He scratches the top of his head. "Why didn't she tell me?"

Because I married her.

Because she's been busy getting on her knees for me.

Because I'm the worst fucking business partner on the face of this earth.

"It happened pretty fast," I say.

He studies me for a moment and then says, "Weren't you in London?"

"Yup," I say, swallowing the lump of nerves that's forming in my throat. "Uh, just back here to deal with the lawsuit."

"What lawsuit?"

Fuck, we didn't even tell him about the lawsuit?

I look at Hardy, who winces. "We, uh, we weren't saying anything because we didn't want to worry anyone until we figured out exactly what we were going to do, but our dad finally served us with papers."

"What?" Jude asks, hands on his hips. "You should have fucking said something."

"Like Hardy said, we didn't want to worry anyone," I say, trying to remain calm. "And like I said, there's nothing to worry about because the lawsuit is erroneous. I'm going to speak to my father about it and put an end to this feud."

Jude looks between us, clearly not happy about any of the information he's received in the last five minutes. "So you came here to deal with the lawsuit and left my sister alone to fend for herself in London?"

Yup.

Because I'm an ass.

"She, uh, she said she was fine and could handle it," I answer, feeling my balls start to shrivel into dust.

"She's fine? She's not fucking fine, Hudson. She shouldn't be out there alone. Why the fuck would you just leave her there? She's never traveled to London before, and it's a big fucking city."

Hardy looks at me, eyes wide, clearly just as terrified as me.

"Look, man." I tug on my hair. "I appreciate how protective you are over your sister, Hardy and I are the same way with Haisley, but there is a time where you kind of have to let her do her own thing." Because Sloane is more than capable of doing things on her own. She's more than capable of taking care of herself. I've seen it firsthand.

"Don't tell me how to handle my sister." He points to his chest. "I'm the one who needs to protect her. She doesn't have parents—"

"Neither do we," I say, pointing to me and Hardy. "Sure, they exist and they're breathing, but they have no problem sitting back and watching us fail; they have no problem trying to destroy everything we've been able to create. I appreciate you and your need to protect your sister, but she chose to go to London for work. You told me to treat her like an employee, so I treated her like an employee."

The stress has gotten the better of me because I know and Hardy knows that's not entirely the truth. She didn't choose to be a bridesmaid; I forced it on her. Sure, she could have said no, but I made it hard for her to decline. And sure, she chose to go to London, but she also had to because that's where the wedding is and because I needed her to be at the club with me...after we got married. And yes, getting married was her choice, but I didn't stop it from happening, I went along for the ride because it benefitted me.

The whole thing is so convoluted. So wrong.

But given the amount of stress that I'm under, I can't seem to force myself to take any of the blame at the moment.

Jude looks off to the side and exhales. "Fuck, you're right. I did tell you that." He pushes his hand through his hair. "Sorry, I think I'm just bundling up my emotions and taking them out on you. Both of my sisters have kept me out of the loop on things. The other day I went by the house and saw a bunch of empty boxes and paint cans by the trash, and I wondered what they were doing and why the hell they didn't say anything to me or ask for my help. When I tried contacting Stacey, she didn't return my call. I feel like they're hiding something from me and...well, being in London was one of them. Not your problem though." He blows out another heavy breath. "Okay, I think I'll try contacting her. Thanks, man."

Fuck do I feel guilty.

I feel like the worst human on earth actually.

Because I know their silence has everything to do with me.

"Sure." I swallow down the lump forming in my throat.

"Okay, I'm headed out. I'll let Haisley know you two say hi."

"Thanks," Hardy and I say at the same time. Once we hear him leave, Hardy casually shuts the door and then turns toward me, sheer panic in his eyes.

"Dude."

"I know. I fucking know," I say, dragging both hands down my face. "Fuck, that was bad. That was really bad."

"You have me looped into this now. Like...if he finds out about you two, he's going to be livid, especially after having this conversation. He will murder the both of us."

"Christ, I know, Hardy!" I yell and then stand from my chair, my nervous energy getting the best of me. "Fuck." I tilt my head back and try to take calming breaths. After a few seconds, I say, "Let me get through these conversations with Dad, and then I can handle the Sloane situation."

"Think you can wait that long?"

I nod. "Sloane won't say anything. I know she won't. I just have to get through the next twenty-four hours and then I'll be able to handle the Sloane situation."

"Hudson," Hardy says, pulling my attention with the serious tone in his voice. "I'm counting on you, man."

"I know, Hardy. I know."

SLOANE

He's such a motherfucker.

Like the motherest of all fuckers.

Why?

Because he has not corresponded with me once.

For all I know, he could be floating around in the Atlantic Ocean, having never made it to California. The common courtesy would be to send a quick text to let me know that he landed. Maybe let me know that he's okay. I don't know…maybe check up on me and make sure that I wasn't run over by a cab because I was looking the wrong way while crossing the street.

But nothing.

Absolutely nothing.

And not only am I pissed about it, but, yeah, you guessed it, I'm hurt.

Yup. I cried.

I cried this morning.

I cried while going for a walk.

And I cried at my dress fitting, which by the way, I'm a saint for squeezing into that thing.

A corset? That was not part of the deal. No need for a plate at the wedding dinner, nope. I can just eat off my breasts, that's how propped up they were.

And if you're wondering if I've checked in on him, you know, since it goes both ways, the answer would be yes. I've sent precisely three text messages that have gone unanswered. I asked him if he landed. Checked in to see if he needed me to do anything for him. And the final one was to let him know I was fitted for the dress.

Nothing.

So, like I said, he is the motherest of all fuckers.

I take a seat on the couch, then lie down across it lengthwise and stare up at the ceiling. Nothing like the guy you like ignoring you to send you into a tailspin of self-doubt and loathing.

I skipped dinner, not interested in food, and I've opted to drown myself in water, because I'll be damned if the motherest of all fuckers causes me to be dehydrated. I know when we left, we both slipped into business mode, but there was a little piece of me that thought he might slip back into the man he was before he left—the man who joked around with me, held me, worshipped me, but I get it.

I see it now.

He doesn't care like I care.

Our eventual divorce is a given, and I need to accept that.

My phone beeps next to me, sending me into a jackknife flail, where I nearly roll off the couch as I reach for my phone. I fumble it to the ground, and in an embarrassing panic, reach for it, fumble it some more, and turn it over only to see Jude's name scroll across the screen.

Son of a bitch.

That was…humbling.

And humiliating.

Word to the wise, never become obsessed with a man; it leads to dark moments such as this where you think you're done with him, only to nearly fall off the couch from the possibility that he might be texting you back.

Unlocking the screen, I read Jude's message.

Jude: So…stopped by Hudson's office today.

"Oh dear God," I whisper as I sit up, my hands trembling, because what the hell?

Did Hudson tell him we were married?

Uh, that would have been good information to know.

Maybe a little heads-up would have been nice? A warning possibly.

And why isn't Jude reaching through the phone and attempting to lecture me?

Now, I've seen things like this play out before, where the person on the other side of the text thinks the person is talking about one thing when in reality they're talking about something else, only to divulge a secret.

Well, not me.

I'm better than that.

So I play it cool.

Sloane: Oh yeah? Give him a pat on the back? A solid hand-shake? Maybe brought him a French silk pie to share? Not sure if he even likes that, but what a nice treat for the both of you.

He texts back immediately.

Jude: What do you think I did at his office?

Okay, I don't like how evasive he's being. I need to play this right. So I take my chances and I text Hudson again.

Sloane: Hey, uh, my brother has texted me and said he stopped by your office. Any chance you want to let me know what you chatted about?

I send the message and wait a few seconds, hoping that maybe he will text me back right away, but unfortunately my husband is being very neglectful at the moment. So I text Jude.

Sloane: Umm, pretty sure I just said what I thought you did. Is that a no on the pie?

To my displeasure, Jude texts back right away.

Jude: Do I look like the type of person who shares pie?

This is very unlike my brother. He doesn't beat around the bush. He gets straight to the point, and the fact that he's not doing just that freaks me out. Makes me think that he possibly knows something that he shouldn't know.

And he's attempting to sweat me out.

Not going to happen.

Sloane: You've shared pie with me before.

The moment I send the text, the phone rings and for a moment, I think it's going to be Hudson to help a girl out, but instead, it's my brother, and I know I'm utterly fucked.

All I need to do is deny, deny, deny.

What's he going to do? Hop on a plane, travel across the Atlantic, and give me a stern talking-to? No, he won't do that. Worst-case scenario, he strangles Hudson, and I guess right now, better Jude than me, you know, since I'm his wife.

Clearing my throat, I answer the phone, "Hello, Big Brother."

"Hello, Sister who hasn't talked to me in a long time."

Okay, okay, his voice seems relatively normal. If he knew about me marrying Hudson, pretty sure there wouldn't be any pleasantries. So that's a nice observation to have.

"Yes, crazy, right? I've been pretty busy."

"So I've heard," he says.

What exactly has he heard?

"Oh yeah? What, uh, what have you heard around the streets?"

"I heard from your boss that you're in London."

Okay...he said *boss*. Not *husband*. That's a good sign.

"Why, yes, yes I am," I answer. "Having a little fun over here in the land of tea and Big Ben, and boy, is he big. Thick. Girthy."

"Sloane."

"Hmm?"

"Why didn't you tell me?"

"Why didn't I tell you I was in London?" I ask, just wanting to make sure we're on the same page.

"Yeah, why didn't you tell me?"

"Um, honestly, it all happened so fast. One minute I'm taking notes at a meeting and the next I'm signed up to be a bridesmaid in a Regency wedding."

"Regency?" he asks.

"Yeah, you know, like the olden times. I have to wear a corset, and I needed to learn dances. It was a whole thing. Anywho, yup, I'm in London."

"You still didn't answer my question: Why didn't you tell me?"

Because I was caught up in getting married.

Because I was afraid you would find out.

Because I'm terrified that the man I've been crushing on for a long time is the man who is currently breaking my heart.

"Because do I really need to tell you everything?" I ask. "You're married now, Jude."

"Just because I'm married, doesn't mean you should stop including me in your life. Stacey wouldn't even answer me, and when I went by the house the other day, I saw the trash and it looks like you're doing renovations. Renovations, Sloane." Crap. Forgot about that. "You know what my business is? Why would my sisters be conducting renovations without me? Without consulting? What are you two hiding?"

"We aren't hiding anything."

"Uh-huh, and why are you taking on a bridesmaid job? Is Hudson not paying you sufficiently? Because last I heard you were getting a decent salary."

Christ, this is why having a nosy and protective older brother is incredibly hard. You can't hide anything from him—at least not for long.

"What's going on, Sloane?"

"Nothing is going on," I say, remaining calm. "We're just doing some things around the house."

"What did I tell you about that? We made some changes when we were living there to make it homier, but we didn't invest a lot of money into it because it's not our house. If you're taking on another job to pay for whatever you're doing, that's just fucking stupid."

"It's not stupid—"

"It's a waste of your money. If you want to do renovations, then buy a place of your own."

"Jude, listen, it's—"

"I thought we talked about this," he continues, irritating me because it seems like he's having a hard time listening at the moment. "I know that house means a lot to us, but just because we had good memories there, doesn't mean we need to sink our hard-earned money into it."

"Jude, we aren't—"

"I just don't understand why you didn't talk to me about this. Taking on another job to renovate a house you don't own? That's not making smart choices, Sloane. You and Stacey know better than that. At least I thought I taught you better than that."

I don't know what comes over me.

Blame it on the emotions of not being able to connect with Hudson.

Or getting lectured by my older brother over something he has no idea about.

But I find myself blurting out a truth that I wasn't supposed to blurt out.

"We're not being stupid," I say. "We own the house."

The moment the words fall out of my mouth, I know it's a mistake because the phone practically goes dead as my brother processes this new information.

"Excuse me?" he says. "You what?"

Did you hear the tone?

Did it send a shiver up your spine?

Because my vertebrae are rattled.

With less bravado, I answer, "We, uh, we bought the house."

"You bought the house," he says, his voice so not convinced as to what I'm saying.

"Yes, we bought the house, together. Well, we're renting to own at the moment."

"What the fuck are you talking about, Sloane?"

Feeling like I need some help on this, I say, "Um, maybe I can merge Stacey in on a phone call, you know, have her explain it with me."

"You know what? Great idea," he says. "I'll merge her. Hold on."

The phone goes quiet and panic sets in as I turn my phone on speaker and then swipe up to get to my messages where I check my texts with Hudson.

Once again, nothing from him.

I'm offended. You can't tell me that he doesn't have his phone with him. This is intentional.

He's intentionally being an ass.

"Sloane, you there?" Jude says, coming back on the line.

"Yes," I answer.

"Stacey, you there?"

"Sure am," she says. "Hey, Sister. How's old London?"

"London-y," I answer, not wanting to get into too much because we can't be having anything slip.

"So to what do I owe the pleasure of this sibling conversation?"

"Jude and I were—"

"You bought the house?" Jude asks, interrupting me.

There's silence and then, "Uhhhhh, yeeeeeah." And then, "You told him?"

"Yes, but—"

"Yeah, she told me," Jude says. "Told me everything."

"Well, that's not—"

"Wow, really?" Stacey laughs. "And you're not marching over to Hudson's place to choke him with your bare hand?"

Oh fuck.

Oh fuck.

OH FUCK!

"Why would I be choking Hudson?"

"You wouldn't," I say quickly. "There would be no choking of Hudson."

"Stacey, why would I be choking Hudson?" His voice grows with an intimidating edge.

No, don't say it, Stacey.

Keep your mouth shut.

I fumble quickly to text her.

To warn her.

That's what I should have been doing instead of checking to see if Hudson texted me. That motherfucker.

I nearly black out as my fingers move across the phone.

"Stacey," Jude barks, scaring the phone right out of my hands.

"Um, did I say Hudson? I mean…uh, Hoo-done. Yeah, Hoo-done. It's uh, one of those young-people terms you wouldn't know. Anywho, um, what, uh what were we talking about?"

Jesus, Stacey.

Not even close to a good recovery.

"We're talking about why you bought a house and how that would be connected to Hudson."

"There's no connection," I say, bringing the phone close to my mouth so he can hear me loud and clear. "Yup, none, whatsoever. Don't know why she said that. I think, wait… Stacey, did you take one of those gummies you were talking about trying?"

"Yes, yes, that's right. Uh-huh, I took a gummy. Silly me. Should have waited until a little later. You know, I'm actually sort of not feeling well, so if I could just jump off this call, that would be great."

"You're not going anywhere," Jude growls. "Now, someone tell me what the hell is going on."

Wanting to jump in and make sure Stacey doesn't say anything, I quickly think of a reason and say, "I got a raise."

But to my dismay, Stacey says at the same time, "They're married."

Oh.

Dear.

Fucking.

Jesus.

My ass puckers and my stomach flops to the ground while the line goes dead. I look down at my screen to see if he hung up, but nope, he's still there, probably suffering through some sort of conniption.

Finally, very slowly, very deeply, he says, "What the fuck did you just say?"

I swallow the lump in my throat and answer, "Uh, he gave me a raise."

"Not you," he yells. "Stacey, what the fuck did you just say?"

I sink down on the couch, tears welling up in my eyes as my sister softly says, "They're married."

"Are you fucking kidding me right now?" Jude says, the anger of three Scottish clans billowing out of him. "You married Hudson?"

"Sloane, I'm sorry," Stacey says, her voice wobbling, no doubt she's crying and feeling like total shit.

"Stop talking, Stacey. Sloane, did you marry Hudson?"

I nod my head even though he can't see me and then with a weepy voice, I say, "Yes."

More silence.

And that's what kills me.

The silence.

Because he doesn't need to say anything for me to know how upset he is.

How angry he is.

How hurt he must be.

"I'm sorry, Jude. But—"

"Don't," he says. "Don't… Do not fucking talk to me."

Then he hangs up the phone, dropping the line between all three of us.

I toss the phone on the coffee table, cover my eyes, and sob.

CHAPTER TWENTY-EIGHT
HUDSON

I CLENCH MY HANDS AT my side, taking calming breaths as I ride the elevator up to my father's office.

He's expecting me.

I made sure of it.

I want him prepared. I want him wondering why I'm coming to talk to him.

I want him possibly shaking a little.

Hardy asked if I wanted him to come with me, but I told him I needed to do this myself. I need to face my father and have this conversation. I know Hardy has some things to work out with him, but that's on a different level. When it comes to business, that's between me and my dad.

He's always seen me as competition, as someone to disparage and insult, but not anymore.

It ends now.

Today.

The elevator doors part, and I lift my head to the ostentatiously decorated space with the wood paneling and gold accents everywhere. It… it feels embarrassing.

There's no need for such extravagance. My father followed the rule that people will want to work with you based on how you show your wealth, but Hardy and I don't have that same mindset. Neither do the

Cane brothers. You simply prove your worth by the way you invest in the projects presented to you.

I move through the space, a few heads popping up, eyes widening when they see me walk by. I nod, offer them a smile, because if anything, I'm not the dick in this building.

When I reach his receptionist, I don't even recognize her. Not surprised—my dad is unpleasant to work with. I nod my head and say, "Good morning. Hudson Hopper to see Reginald."

She fumbles with the phone when her eyes meet mine and she says, "Oh, right, um, please head in. He's expecting you."

"Thank you," I say and offer her a smile before I open the heavy door to my dad's office, dark and something you'd see on *Mad Men*.

My dad isn't sitting at his desk, twirling his mustache and waiting for me; instead, he's sitting in one of the chairs in his sitting area, a cup of coffee in hand, looking fresh and relaxed. Unlike me, who's still struggling to keep his eyes open from the lack of sleep and the stress this entire situation has placed upon me.

"Good morning," Dad says with a smirk derived from the devil himself.

"Good morning," I say as I unbutton my suit jacket and then take it off, wanting to keep things casual. "Can I have a seat?"

"Would love it," Dad says, acting far too nice at the moment. Almost... cocky. Little does he know what I'm about to present him with. "Can I get you a drink?"

"I'm okay," I say, even though an IV drip of caffeine would be ideal right now. Once I deal with this, I'm headed back to London on a red-eye to make the wedding. Just need to power through on this.

Leaning forward, Dad sets his coffee on the table in front of us and then crosses his ankle at his knee and opts for a more comfortable position. "How is the missus?"

"I'm not here to talk about that."

"So you don't want to talk about your wife that you never told me about?"

Remaining calm, I say, "She's off-limits."

He studies me for a moment and then asks, "Okay, so then to what do I owe the pleasure?"

I lean forward, my forearms on my thighs, and look my dad dead in the eyes. "We know you lied about the trust documents."

A master at the poker face, he casually says, "What are you talking about?"

"When we first got the papers from you, we wondered how we could have possibly missed such a detail. We were racking our brains over it. Honestly, we were disappointed in ourselves. That was until we pulled out the actual documents that we signed and saw how you tampered with them."

"I have no idea what you're talking about."

Normally, this would infuriate me and I would fly off the handle because we both know he's lying. We both know his naivete is not even remotely close to authentic, and I hate that he thinks he can get away with it, but I'm going to try for a different tactic this go-around. I'm going to remain calm.

I'm going to reason with him.

I sit back in my chair, taking a calming breath, and say, "Can I ask you something?"

"It's weak to ask if you can ask something. A strong man would just ask." His attempt at gaining control over the situation. Not going to trigger me.

"The greatest strength isn't about how hard you can steamroll a conversation but how you can understand the person you're conversing with. I know you like to have control; therefore, I'm giving you the ability to tell me yes or no."

His lips thin ever so slightly—not so much that someone who doesn't know my dad would notice but just enough that his son who has been studying him for years will notice.

"Just ask your question," he says in an annoyed tone, which gives me hope that maybe I'm breaking through the wall he clearly erected around himself.

"The lawsuit, when you were putting it together with your lawyers, dreaming up plans to sue your children, what was the end goal? Was it money? Was it because you were hurt and you thought it was the only way you could feel better? Was it to teach us a lesson in business? What was your end goal? I'm just genuinely curious, so I can understand you better."

"You don't need to understand people in business, Hudson. This is where you're going wrong. There is no understanding. There's the deal and if the deal will benefit you or not. The minute you start trying to understand people is the minute you show weakness."

"I don't see it that way," I say. "I see it quite the opposite, actually. When talking with the Cane brothers and making a deal with them, we sat down and had an honest conversation about our intentions, our goals, and the why behind it. It was the reason we were able to secure the deal with them. Working with Archie and Terrance in the UK, I know it's something you've been after, but sitting down with Terrance, offering him a chance to get to know me on a personal level, to understand my intentions, is what's securing me that deal." My dad's jaw grows tight. "Business might have been conducted differently when you were establishing yourself, and I'll be honest, it worked. You built an empire."

"One you don't want any part in," he says, drumming his fingers on the armrest of his chair.

"I didn't want any part in the way you were treating people, Dad," I say honestly, with a calm tone. "I'm in awe of the way you've been able to grow into different markets and establish a reputable brand, but I don't believe you need to walk over everyone to get there. That's why we left, not because we don't love you or because we don't believe in the hard work you've put into Hopper Industries."

This time, he looks to the side, toward the window that offers one of the better views of the bay that I've ever seen.

"You and I both know the documents your lawyer sent have been tampered with, and that's illegal. We're not going to countersue nor do we plan on making a counterattack. Hardy and I spoke, and we want there to be peace between us—peace in the family—but you're making that hard on us. And if you keep trying to deepen this divide, you're going to be absent for a lot of things. Jude and Haisley are going to start having a family soon. Do you really want to miss out on that? What about Hardy and Everly? We're moving on with our lives and entering different phases, and we want you and Mom to be a part of that, but only if you're going to drop the bullshit and stop coming after us. I know you're trying to hold on to us, to keep us working for you, but you're only driving us further and further away."

He presses his hand to his cheek, still looking out toward the bay. He sits there silently, not saying a thing, so I just let him continue to do so as I wait. I want him to say something; I want him to think this over.

Finally, after what feels like minutes, he says, "I spent years building a business that my family could take over, that could be handed down for generations." He meets my eyes. "You knew that, Hudson. You and Hardy both knew that. I was priming you; I was ready to retire and hand you the reins, and then you just left. You met up with a competitor and started something new. Do you know what kind of a slap to the face that was? Do you understand the embarrassment I've had to endure from such a careless decision?"

"It wasn't careless, Dad. I need you to understand that."

"You chose people you barely knew over me." He points to his chest. "You chose a lower-level employee over me."

"Because you were trying to blackmail your daughter," I counter. "You were trying to take away the one thing that Haisley built and grew on her own. The pride you have for Hopper Industries, that's the same kind of pride Haisley has for her rental business. And you were trying to take that away and own it."

"Because she left too!" he shouts. "You weren't supposed to leave. You weren't supposed to just take off. She was the first to go, and I could feel it. Hardy with the farms, he was the next to go, and it was only a matter of time before you took off as well. I built the business for you three, damn it," he says, slamming his fist into the chair, startling me. "I built it for you, and you just walked away."

He looks away again, and I know it's because, this time, he doesn't want me to see the emotion on his face. He doesn't want me to see his weakness, but I'm seeing it.

We are his weakness.

His family is his weakness, and I think he needs to know that, despite his decisions, we will always have love for him.

I stand from my chair, move his coffee to the side, and then sit on the table in front of him. I place my hands on his knees and say, "Dad, look at me."

When he doesn't at first, I wait.

After a few seconds, I repeat, "Please, look at me."

He takes a breath and turns toward me.

"Haisley built her business on her own because she had something to prove to herself. You treated her like the youngest, only girl in the family. She was your little sweet pea. Everything was handed to her, and she hated that. She wanted to prove that she could do something on her own, make something of herself that was separate from her family, and I don't blame her for that. Living in the shadow of her brothers growing up was not easy, especially with how much you focused on teaching Hardy and me the ways of the business. But Hardy, he wasn't going anywhere. He loved working on the farms. He loved the almond industry and the potential there. He was pulling away because that's what he wanted to focus on. Me, I had no intentions of doing anything other than following in your footsteps."

I press my hand on top of his aged fingers. He's stiff at first, unsure of what to do with the touch, but then he relaxes as he looks me in the eyes.

"I love you, and I respect what you've been able to do, but I was not going to sit by and let you hurt my sister, let you hurt others by making selfish business decisions. I have too much pride in our family name, so leaving was the only option. And I'm sorry that we hurt you, but we need you to know where we were coming from."

He glides his tongue over his teeth and says, "Well, thank you for letting me know where you stand."

Did I expect him to pull me into a hug and apologize for what he did? No.

I honestly thought he would have kicked me out a few minutes ago, but I'm still here.

So I take the moment to just keep my hand on his, and when he doesn't move, when he doesn't ask me to leave, I say, "I would love to get to a point in our lives again where we can spend a weekend together in the Hamptons or at one of the resorts and have family time, remind ourselves where we started. Have another Hopper Game competition, just get back to us. But we need you on board, Dad. We can't allow you back in our lives unless you understand where we are coming from and why we made the choices that we made. Not to hurt you or embarrass you but to show you that you raised three children with values and ethics and respect. So much so that we're going to hold our own father accountable for his actions."

I squeeze his hand and stand. He continues to look out the window while I gather my jacket and slip it back on.

Not sure I need to say anything else, I head toward the door just in time for him to call out, "Hudson?" I turn toward him and meet his weary eyes. "I'll have my lawyers drop the lawsuit."

As if he's doing me a favor. But it's probably the best I can get from him for now.

"Thanks, Dad."

I reach for the door and he says, "And maybe, when you're ready, you can tell me more about your wedding."

I feel my skin break out in needles as I think about Sloane and all of the unanswered and unread text messages I've allowed to just sit in my phone.

I glance over my shoulder. "Yeah, maybe, Dad. Have a good day."

Feeling like I have my head on straight, I let out a deep breath as my driver weaves through traffic.

That was...that was heavier than I thought it was going to be. I expected to go in there and lay down the hammer, scare my dad away, but then something inside me changed. I saw the anger in his eyes, but also...sorrow.

He could see it all in front of him, slipping away from him, his children creating that distance, and there was regret there.

Actual regret.

I didn't think I would ever see that from my father, but it was plain as day, and it's what made me switch the way I handled it. It's what made me change my mind.

It's what makes me feel like maybe the man does have a heart.

Relieved, I take my phone out of my pocket and open my text messages. I have four unread.

Four from one person.

Four that have gone unanswered.

Guilt consumes me as I stare down at the blue dot, letting me know that I have not touched them, haven't even looked at them. But I couldn't. I knew if I looked at them, I wouldn't have been able to be strong for my meeting with my dad.

I knew I wouldn't have my mind in the right place.

With Sloane, I've come to find that she weakens me, and not in a sense where it's a bad thing. She's weakened me in the sense that she's my Achilles' heel. Shit, just like my dad's weakness is his kids. That's a startling realization.

But where we differ is I know with Sloane, if I thought about her and the scared look in her eyes when I took off, I would have returned. I almost did when I was in the airport. I almost threw caution to the wind and turned right back around to hold her. To comfort her.

But responsibilities for the business, for protecting the people around me who count on me, that took precedence. I had to shut down the lawsuit, to move on, to make sure everyone else was taken care of.

And now that it's over, I can focus on her.

Sloane.

The woman who deserves all of my attention.

The woman that...fuck, that I'm falling for.

She's actually taught me so much about myself in the last few weeks. She's shown me that I don't have to be serious all the time. That I can speak of my past and not be ashamed. That I can find comfort in another human. That I can open my heart to someone other than my siblings...

And she's so goddamn smart. So intuitive, so much more mature than I've ever given her credit for. She's the reason why I've been able to carry on with this business dealing. She's the reason I've been able to remain grounded. She's the reason why I want to rush back to London, tell her that I patched everything up, that I...that I want to give us a chance. Because she's where I find peace. She's where I feel like myself the most, and she needs to know that.

I tap on her name and I skim over her messages, dread filling me with every word written by her.

Fuck.

I drag my hand over my face, feeling her fear in her texts. The panic. The worry.

The anger.

I...I hurt her.

I fucked up.

My stomach twists, tangles within itself as I start to type back a response, telling her that I'm so sorry, that I'm coming back, that I'll be there soon...but as I'm about to press send, I realize one thing—this is not good enough.

She deserves better.

She deserves so much more than a text message.

And that's what I'm going to give her.

CHAPTER TWENTY-NINE
SLOANE

"MORNING, MA'AM," THE DOORMAN SAYS as he opens the door
for me.

"Good morning," I say in a cheerful voice, despite feeling anything
but cheerful.

The only good thing I have going for me at this moment is the
smoothie in my hand and the croissant in my bag. After a long walk in
Hyde Park, where I lie under a tree, staring up at the leaves for far too
long, I stopped at Joe and the Juice for a smoothie, which, not to knock
England, but they are pretty liquidy. I'm used to a more frozen smoothie
from America. But, dare I say, they're maybe more delicious over here.

Either way, this drink is the only good thing I have going for me at
the moment.

Jude won't answer my texts or calls.

Stacey can't stop crying and apologizing.

I'm stuck in a freaking foreign country, pretending to be a bridesmaid
for someone I barely know.

And my husband refuses to text me back.

So this pink drink that is dangerously sloshing around as I enter the
elevator is the best thing in my life.

The only thing in my life.

My true love.

The elevator doors part, and I head to my room, pulling out my key card and unlocking the door. I push it open, walk in, take my shoes off, and head toward the couch, where I look up and find a man sitting on it.

"Mother of God!" I yell, tossing my smoothie and croissant in the air, only for it to splash on the ground and cover the entire living room in pink liquid. Hand clutched to my heart, I mutter, "You motherfucker."

Ignoring me, Hudson casually lifts the room phone up and calls for the front desk, where he asks for someone to help clean up in our room.

I'm leaning against the wall of our room, breathing heavily and staring down at the one good thing that was going on in my life. "What the hell are you doing here?"

"I told you I'd be back."

I stand taller and look him in the eyes. "Oh, right, how many days ago was that? Sorry, I assumed you were dead since I haven't heard from you."

I move into the bathroom, where I grab some towels and then carry them to the living room to start cleaning up.

"I have someone coming to do that."

"Yeah, me spilling my smoothie because my husband, who hasn't made contact with me in days, just decides to randomly show up and scare the living shit out of me does not constitute a *them* problem. I can clean up."

"Sloane, can we talk?"

"No," I say and continue to clean.

"Please, Sloane."

I look up at him and sit back on my feet, so I'm kneeling on the floor. "Do you think the use of the word *please* is going to change my mind? You have absolutely lost it, Hudson."

I continue to wipe the floor, so he reaches for one of my towels. I gather it to my chest, nearly snarling at the man. "Get your own towels."

"Sloane, can we please just stop for a second and talk?"

"No. You have two choices: you can jump off a cliff, which would be my preferred option, or you can finish cleaning this up and go get me a new smoothie, because it's the only thing I was looking forward to today, while I go take a shower because I have to get ready for a wedding you signed me up for. But like I said, finding a cliff is preferred." I stand and toss the towels on the ground and start to walk toward the bathroom when he grabs my arm to stop me.

I yank my arm away, but he follows…closely.

"Sloane, I was busy—"

"Do not give me that bullshit," I yell at him as I strip my shirt over my head, leaving me in a bra and shorts. I watch his eyes glance over me before meeting my expression. "I don't want to hear one goddamn excuse from you. There is no way you were so busy you couldn't at least text me back. People saying they're busy as an excuse as to why they didn't get in touch with someone is a fucking cop-out. It takes less than thirty seconds to text and let me know you landed. Just admit it, you had zero intention of talking to me."

He drags his hand over his face, looking distraught.

Well, welcome to my freaking world.

"Do you realize that I was here, alone, with no communication from you, wondering what the hell was going on, while my world was falling apart—"

"Why was it falling apart?" he asks, a pinch to his brow.

"Oh, so you care now?"

He growls in frustration. "Sloane, please—"

I hold up my hand and take a step back. "You know what your options are—a cliff or a smoothie. Either way, get the hell away from me."

And then I move into the bathroom where I slam the door, then slowly sink to the floor and cry.

"Pull harder…*Husband.*"

The last few hours have been tense to say the least.

He keeps trying to talk to me.

I keep telling him to fuck off.

He attempted to apologize—*attempt* being the key word.

I told him to find a cliff again.

He brought me a smoothie.

I drank it and thanked him because at least I have manners.

Now that I'm showered, makeup is done, hair is done thanks to the unfortunate hairdresser who had to come into this anger-filled room and do my hair, I'm forced to ask Hudson for help with my corset.

"I don't want to hurt you...*Wife*," Hudson says on a grunt.

"How could you possibly hurt me any more than you already have?" I counter, because, well, facts.

Growing frustrated, he lets go of the strings and takes a step back. Not sure why he's frustrated; he's the one who fucked up. He's the one who led me on, who protected me and made me feel cherished, only to flip the switch in a single night and take off to another country without any communication on his end.

I tried.

I tried to talk to him, but he was radio silent, and he just expects to walk back in here as if nothing happened?

Everything happened.

Everything!

My brother found out about us.

He hasn't spoken to me since.

And I've felt so alone.

So freaking alone in this entire thing all because of Hudson.

I can't think of that now, though.

I just need to get this day over and done with so I can go home and move on.

Which, God, what am I going to do when I get home?

Job one, divorce the motherfucker.

Job two, talk to my brother.

Job three, get my freaking life together.

On a deep breath, I say, "Hudson."

His eyes fall on me, and once again, they hungrily take me in, eating me up one once-over at a time.

A few days ago, I would have reveled in the way he's looking at me. I would have craved it. But now…now it irritates me.

"What?" he asks.

I pop a hip and say, "I need you to dress me."

His Adam's apple bobs, his hands clench at his side, and one more time, his eyes fall to my chest and then back up to my face where his eyes land on my mouth.

Seriously?

He's really thinking about that?

After everything?

Well, only one way to solve this…

"Or has your intent been to undress me this entire time?" I ask as I drop my corset to the ground, letting him feast.

And he does.

Like he hasn't eaten for months.

I close the space between us, push him back on the bed, and then kneel before him. I slide my hands up his thighs as he leans back on his hands, staring down at me.

"Sloane," he says, his voice gravelly. "Wh-what are you—"

I pass my hand over his cock, just a light swipe, enough to make him sweat. And when I see him relax, just for a moment, I say, "Do you really think I'm about to suck your cock, Husband?"

"I don't…I don't know what you're doing."

"I'm trying to make it through the next twenty-four hours so I can get the hell away from you, get back home, and hire a divorce attorney." I stand and pick my corset off the ground, shielding my breasts. "Now stop looking at me as if I'm yours because I'm not."

He stands and closes the space between us, and when I turn around to offer him my back so he can tie me up, he stops me and gently moves me against the wall so I have to face him.

"Don't," I say, shying away from him.

"Sloane, I'm—"

"He knows," I say, not wanting Hudson to try to apologize to me or change my mind about how I feel.

I feel him stiffen, pause, and then say, "What?"

My eyes meet his. "Jude. He knows."

He takes a step back. "Since when?"

"Oh, you're interested now in what's going on?" I drop the corset again and grab my robe off my bed. I slip it on and cinch it at the waist before turning toward him. "I tried telling you; maybe if you actually answered the text messages I sent you, you would know." Emotion catches in my voice as I say, "I've been out here, all by myself, Hudson, dealing with the fact that my brother is not talking to me, that my sister is crushed, and that I'm stuck here, fulfilling a favor to someone who doesn't even want to communicate with me." I gesture toward the couch. "You think my eyes are red for no reason? I've been sobbing on that couch, waiting for you. Fucking waiting for you, Hudson." My eyes well up and I try to will the tears away, but it's no use as they tip over and fall down my cheeks.

"Fuck." He grips his hair. "I...I'm sorry, Sloane."

"Don't bother." I start gathering my things. "I'm going to take my dress to the bridal suite and have them get me ready."

He attempts to stop me, but I pull my hand away.

"Don't fucking touch me," I yell, scaring him away just enough that he gives me space. Looking him in the eyes, I say, "Let's just get through the night looking like a happy couple. Then tomorrow, I'm flying home, and we're done."

HUDSON

"Sloane, please stay." I'm begging. Pleading. So fucking sick to my stomach over what I've done to her.

How I've neglected her.

This is so much worse than I thought it would be.

You fucking idiot.

"See you at the venue," she says as she shuts the door, leaving me in the hotel alone, just like I did to her.

I drop down to the couch and push my hands through my hair, frustrated with myself, because that's the only person I can be frustrated with.

The moment I read through her texts, I knew I fucked up. But her not even talking to me, letting me apologize, this is a level of anger I didn't see coming.

A level of anger I rightfully deserve.

And the fact that Jude knows and I wasn't here for her. Sick. I feel fucking sick.

He's known for a while, but the question is how long? Can't be any longer ago than when he was asking questions about Sloane in my office, unless that was all an act.

I think back to that day and how casual and surprised he was that his sister was in London.

No, there's no way he acted like he didn't know. He would have come into the office snarling. So he found out after that day, question is, how and what the hell is going through his head?

I grab my phone from my pocket and check the time. I hate that Sloane is heading off to the wedding by herself, but I need to figure some things out.

It's early over in California, but I'm going to need Hardy to wake up. I press his name and put the phone on speaker. It rings and rings and rings until his voicemail picks up.

Not going to do.

I call again.

And again.

Until on the fourth time, he answers the phone with a gravelly voice. "What?"

"I need you to wake the fuck up, man. Jude knows."

There's silence, then shuffling.

"Everything okay?" I hear Everly say in the background.

"Yeah, babe. Go back to sleep," Hardy says. Then more silence until, "What the fuck are you talking about?"

"Dude, I fucked up."

"Why does that seem to be a recurring theme with you?"

"I don't need the sarcasm, man. I hurt Sloane."

"Christ," he mumbles. "What did I say about all of this?"

"I know, okay. I fucking know. I'm an asshole. I thought I was doing the right thing and I wasn't, and I just got back to London, where Sloane informed me that Jude knows."

"What? For how fucking long?" Now he's sounding more awake.

"She wouldn't give me details. She won't talk to me. I, uh, I've really fucked things up with her."

"Not surprised," Hardy says and then grumbles, "Fuck. Has he contacted you?"

"No. I was wondering if he's been in touch with you."

"Not since he visited us in the office. Do you think he found out that day?"

"I'm assuming he did. He was looking for Sloane when he came into the office. My guess is that he called her, and then from there, he found out. Not sure how though. Fuck." I pinch the bridge of my nose. "Have you heard from him at all, even email?"

"Nothing, and he was supposed to get back to me about a possible project down by the pier."

"Shit."

"I told you this wasn't going to end well; I fucking told you, Hudson."

"I know. I know." I lean back on the couch and stare up at the ceiling. "Trust me when I say I'm living in hell." I clear my throat and say, "I, uh, I didn't really stay in contact with her while I was gone."

"What?" Hardy yells on the phone. "Why the fuck would you do that?"

"I was trying to focus on one thing at a time," I groan. "She...she's a weakness for me, and I didn't want to think about her out of fear that I wouldn't be able to handle Dad. You know the kind of control he has over us...over me. I was nervous, fucking worried over the fact that Dad knew and was going to let the cat out of the bag. I was...I was stressed, and I just...I just tried to go one step at a time."

"You're a fucking idiot. Business aside, that's shitty, man. After everything you put her through? That's shitty."

"I fucking know, Hardy. I know how shitty I've been. I can see it in her eyes; I can feel it in my chest. I knew the moment I read through her texts. I thought I was leaving her here strong, when in reality she was just putting on a front. And I've been trying to apologize, and she won't let me."

"Should I feel sorry for you?"

"No. I'm not asking you to feel sorry for me."

"Then what the hell are you asking?"

"Nothing. I'm just telling you everything that's happened."

"Well, it seems to me like everything you've done has been a massive mistake, starting with marrying her, then fucking her, then leaving her and not talking to her. I mean, Jesus Christ, if you are trying to be anything but Dad, you're failing miserably."

My mouth goes dry and my stomach flips upside down. "What did you just say?"

"You fucking heard me," Hardy yells. "You're treating her like a possession, not like a human. That's something Dad would do."

"I'm not treating her like a possession."

"Really? Because all I've seen you do is use her. Use her for business gain, use her for your own pleasure. What are you really doing for her? And no doubt she's pissed at you since she won't even let you apologize. Do you know what this is going to do to our business? Christ, Hudson. You thought me getting together with Everly was bad? This is a whole other level and could possibly fuck everything up for us." I can practically hear him shake his head as he adds, "Didn't talk to her, Jesus fuck, man."

"I'm...I'm sorry," I say somberly. I knew I was wrong, but labeling it a move Dad would make, that's a revelation I was not prepared for because he's right. He could not be more right. This is exactly how my dad would treat the situation. And here I am, walking into his office all high-and-mighty, when in reality, I'm just as bad as him. "I need to fix this."

"And how do you plan on doing that?" Hardy asks.

Swallowing my emotions, I say, "Putting her first for once."

Hardy is silent for a moment and then says, "Something you should have done from the beginning."

"I agree." I'm quiet for a second, thinking over what Hardy said. "I don't want to be like him. I don't want to be like Dad. He never put personal relationships ahead of business."

"Because he assumed if business was good, then everything else was good, and I think we're slowly starting to realize that if we put personal above business, then the business thrives."

"Yeah," I say softly. "I like Sloane, Hardy. I shouldn't, but I like her a lot."

He sighs on the other line. "Enough to risk everything?"

I press my palm to my eye, rubbing it. "Yeah."

"Then you're in the right frame of mind to fix things."

Beep.

"Hold on a second," I say and then look at my screen where I see an incoming call from Haisley. "Fuck."

"What?"

"Haisley is calling me."

"She knows."

"Yup."

"You have to answer," Hardy says. "Just remember who you're putting first, then everything else will fall into place."

"I sure as fuck hope so." I hang up with Hardy and answer Haisley's call. "Hey, Hais."

"You married Sloane?" she shouts.

I wince and sink farther into the couch. "Listen—"

"No, you listen. I have a husband who is ready to rip my brother's head off, and the only reason he hasn't yet is because I've stopped him, or else he'd be in London right now, tearing you apart." I don't know what to say to that, so I remain quiet. "What the hell were you thinking? You know how protective Jude is, you know he trusted you to make sure his sister was taken care of. Why would you do that?"

I blow out a heavy breath and say, "It was a mutual decision that benefitted both parties."

"What do you mean it benefitted—oh my God, Hudson, was this all done for business?"

I wince again and nervously say, "Yes, it was."

"I…I can't… Oh my God… Wait, is that where the money came from? Is that why they were able to buy the house?"

"Yes," I answer.

She's quiet. I swear I can hear a pin drop through the phone. And then, "Disgusting, Hudson. You bought her."

"It…it wasn't like that. And it's not currently like that"

"What do you mean… 'it's not currently like that'?"

"I…I like her, Hais. A lot."

There's silence.

More silence than I want there to be.

And after what feels like minutes, she says, "What?"

"I have feelings for her. And I know I've fucked this up and I know that Jude is pissed, but I can't deny the way I feel about her. Sloane means something to me."

"But...but you said it was for business."

"Started that way, but she's...she's made an impact on me, and I can't sit on these feelings and do nothing about it. I know Jude is pissed. I know he is not happy and is probably hurting from the betrayal he must be feeling. But I promise you, I will fix this. I promise."

"How, Hudson?"

"I don't know yet," I say quietly. "But I promise I will."

CHAPTER THIRTY
SLOANE

THIS IS EASILY THE WEIRDEST wedding I've ever been to.

And listen, I'm not here to judge, okay? I truly believe what you want to do on your special day is really up to you, but the only thing missing from the 1800s' gilded soiree in this nineteenth-century ballroom is body odor.

Let me paint you a picture.

A hand-painted ceiling sets the scene with flying, naked cherubs, cotton-like clouds, and intimate touching of index fingers. Polished pillars line the perimeter of the room and are highlighted by ambient uplighting. And a combination of white lilies and powder-blue ribbons dress up dramatically sized vases that are centered on each table.

Currently I'm stuffed into an empire-waist gown that has turned out to be itchier than I anticipated, a corset that has my boobs touching my chin, with my hair curled in tight, uncombed tendrils that frame my face. I'm wearing gloves that stretch all the way up to my bicep, flats that are cutting into the tops of my feet, and I'm engaged in a dance with a man who clearly had a shot or two before the wedding according to the scent seeping out of the corner of his mouth.

Meanwhile, the wedding guests flank the perimeter of the ballroom, watching intently as we perform the steps to live music coming from a string quartet playing on a balcony overlooking the room. The bride and groom are smiling widely, newly married, ready to embark on their exciting journey, while the rest of us parade around, hoping this nightmare will soon be over.

At least that's what is in my head.

I have already plotted my exit. I'm going to fake sick, clutch my stomach, and take off with a twiddle of my fingers and a pat on my back for a job well done, because why would I have to stay? I stood while the couple gave their vows, I swayed back and forth, hoping and praying the corset didn't cut off all circulation in my body, and I performed the dances.

Nothing else will be needed of me.

Sure, would I like to stay because the cake looks like something I would want to plow my face into and have a feast? Of course.

But no cake is worth this kind of torture.

The kind of torture where your lousy husband stands off in the corner, eyeing you the entire time, never letting his gaze stray. It's been like that since the moment I walked down the aisle. I could feel his eyes on me. It made my skin prickle and my heart rate accelerate, which of course sent me into a spiral of self-loathing.

This man has put me through a tumultuous time starting from "oh, she can be your bridesmaid" to "on your knees and suck me off" to "oops, forgot how to text," and here I am, practically panting because he's looking at me.

I hate him.

I want nothing to do with him.

And yet my nipples are ready to break through my corset to seek out his fingers.

The music ends and everyone claps while I turn to...uh...God, tall guy with alcohol breath, and curtsy while he bows.

Then the dancers start mingling with the crowd. Hudson is in the corner, a glass of liquid in his hand. I glance over to him, wondering if he wants me to come up to him or not, and well, it's going to be a *not*.

Leaving-early plan needs to commence.

I bring my hand up to my stomach, ready to hinge at the hips ever so slightly to exhibit pain just as there is a tap on my shoulder.

I turn to find Sheridan standing behind me, tears welling up in her eyes. Her dress is simple and white, with lace details. Her gloves are lace as well, and the florals in her hair complement her dress beautifully. And speaking of tendrils, I think she has at least five hundred all individually curled.

"Oh, Sloane, thank you so much." She pulls me into a hug that blows up my ability to act sick. "You did such a beautiful job and executed everything so well."

I slap on a smile as she pulls away, looking like I was the luckiest person to be chosen for such an event. "Are you kidding me? This was so much fun. I'm so glad I could be a part of it."

"Really? You had a good time?"

"The best. Can't wait to go home and tell my ballroom instructor that I took part in a cotillion. He will be so proud."

"Well, I'm glad we could add that to your dancing résumé."

"You surely did. And the wedding, it was so beautiful. The weather could not have been more perfect."

"Have you looked outside?" she asks. "It's pouring. We made it inside just in time. I heard it's good luck for it to rain on your wedding."

People just say that to cheer up the couple so they don't go into a tailspin about a soggy wedding.

"I heard the same thing," I say with joy I've mustered up out of the deep pit of my very soul. "Looks like it's going to be a long-lasting marriage."

She smiles softly and then glances over at Archie. "I think so too." She then takes my hand in hers and says, "Thank you again. You truly saved the day."

And now I feel bad for having bitchy thoughts in my head. I guess despite being uncomfortable, heartbroken, and just flat-out depressed due to my current state of events, I have to admit that it does feel good that I was able to help Sheridan out. I can only imagine how stressful it is to get married, and losing a vital person for the day can't be easy.

"It seriously was my pleasure," I say and then give her a hug. She squeezes me tight and waves bye to me.

Okay, so does that mean I'm relieved of my duties? Because boy would I love to slip out of this corset—

"You looked great out there." I turn to find Devin standing next to me, looking all proper in his ascot and velvet waistcoat. "Didn't know you could dance that well."

Neither did I, but if anything, I've learned to rise to the occasion.

"Thank you," I say as I catch him glancing at my breasts.

Jesus, Devin. Guess he didn't get the hint last time Hudson spoke to him.

"Save a dance for me later?"

"Do you really think that's a good idea?" I ask. "I think we know what happened last time."

"We can't dance as friends?" he asks.

"Would it really be dancing as friends?"

He wets his lips and then takes a step closer. "Do you really love him?"

"She does," Hudson says, as he slips his arm around my waist. In a low, terrifying tone, he continues, "And unless you want to lose your fucking life, stay away from her."

Then he guides me away from Devin and toward an open window that catches the breeze from the storm outside but is welcome because I need to cool off.

"You realize once we're divorced, you can't keep doing that."

His grip on me tightens as he says, "I will always protect you, Sloane."

I turn toward him, keeping up the appearance as if we're having an intimate conversation. "Really? Where were you the last few days then?"

"I don't want to do this here."

I chuckle. "What do you want to do, then? Pretend to be a happy couple and enjoy the evening?"

His eyes soften and he quietly says, "Dance with me."

Vulnerability laces his eyes, and it's not a look I see from him often. Usually when he's talking about his brother and sister but never in a business setting, and that's what this is. We're here on business.

"No."

"Can I ask why?"

Can he ask why? Can I ask why he's being so polite? Normally, he would demand I dance with him and stupid me would fall all over myself to agree to his command.

"Because the less I have to touch you, the better."

"You're my wife, Sloane," he says quietly.

"And this isn't actually the eighteen hundreds. I have a mind of my own and can make my own decisions, and my decision is to spend as little time with you as possible."

He sighs and those eyes of his plead with me. "The problem with that is we're in a situation where you can't ignore me. We have to put on a good show. Therefore, you can either stand here with me, hold my hand, and let me occasionally run my lips up your neck, or you can dance with me."

"You wouldn't."

He wets his lips, wraps his arm around me, and presses his hand to my lower back, pulling me in tight. Then with his other hand, he tilts my chin up and lowers his mouth only a few inches from mine.

"I would have no problem kissing you all goddamn night, Sloane."

I stare into his eyes, the same eyes that used to make me feel weak in the knees. "Don't, Hudson. Don't try to change my mind with...with this attention. What you did was wrong."

"I know that," he says quietly, still holding me softly. "I handled the entire situation so incredibly wrong, Sloane. There is no excuse for me other than I'm an asshole, and I'm sorry I put you through something you didn't deserve."

That's...uh...that's an apology that I wasn't quite expecting.

430 | MEGHAN QUINN

His hand smooths farther up my back. "You have put yourself out there for me, you've helped me, you've saved me in ways that I don't even think you know, and yet, I treated you like you meant nothing to me. You deserve so much better."

"I...I do," I say, a little shocked.

His nose rubs against mine before his cheek slides across mine and his lips find my ear. "When we get back, I promise you, I will make it up to you."

Still stunned, I stand there, unsure of where this is coming from. "Wh-why are you saying that?"

"I need to do right by you," he whispers.

And for some reason, that raises a red flag. What's with the quick change of heart? He doesn't talk to me for a few days, and then all of a sudden, he's here, holding me, saying he needs to do right by me.

That's not a sentence he would say.

It's almost like he's being forced to say it.

But who would force...?

I lean back and look him in the eyes. "You spoke with Jude."

"I didn't," he replies.

"Don't lie to me. You spoke to him, and that's why you're being nice to me."

"No, I didn't," he replies. "I tried to speak to you before I knew that Jude was aware of our marriage. But you wouldn't let me. This is what I've wanted to say; you're just listening now."

"I don't believe you," I say, my voice trembling.

"It's the truth."

"So you didn't speak to Jude...or Hardy...or Haisley."

His eyes dart to the side and that's all the information I need.

"Oh, so you did."

"I spoke to Haisley and Hardy," he says quickly. "But what I'm saying to you is what I meant to say to you when I got to the hotel."

"Spare me." I roll my eyes. I do not trust this man. I can't. He's too hot and cold and he's a damn good liar. So, no, I'm never going to trust him again. "God, you're such…you're such a manipulator, Hudson."

"I'm not manipulating you."

"Yes, you are," I say in a low tone so no one can hear me. "You know damn well I'm attracted to you, that I…that I have feelings for you—" I catch myself as the words fall out of my mouth.

"You what?" he asks, lifting away.

Oh shit.

Did I just say that?

God, why did I say that?

"Nothing," I say, shaking my head as a wave of nausea hits me all at the same time. "Just, just let me go."

"Sloane—"

"Let me go, Hudson, or I'm going to start screaming."

He slides his hand off me but leans into my ear and says, "We're not done talking about this."

Oh, yes we are.

"I'm so sorry," I say to Sheridan.

"Oh my gosh, don't apologize. I totally understand. This corset is cutting into me as well."

I smile, trying to keep my head above water and save face, even though I'm mentally and internally crumbling. "Thank you. I'm so happy for you, and please, keep in touch."

"Oh, this is not goodbye. This is see you later. After all, you'll be visiting the Mayfair Club."

If only she knew.

"That's so true. Pencil me in for another afternoon tea."

"You can count on it." She kisses me on the cheek, and then with a wave, I take off and head out of the ballroom, down the hall, and straight out the entrance of the building where a doorman flags down a cab for me.

"Hold up," I hear Hudson call out just as I step inside the cab.

Damn it.

"That's my wife," he says as he grabs the taxi door.

The doorman leans in and says, "Do you know this man?"

I glance at Hudson, and I'm so tempted to say no, but that will solve absolutely nothing other than make the situation worse, so I nod, and the doorman allows Hudson to join me.

Hudson gives the driver our address and sits back in the seat and rests his hand on my thigh.

We must look ridiculous in our wedding garb; then again, not sure how out of the ordinary it is. I wonder how many people have United Kingdom weddings, seeking out their *Bridgerton* dreams.

I don't say anything because what is there really to say? I thoroughly embarrassed myself in the ballroom, shocked the hell out of the man next to me, then bolted. Remember way back when Hudson said I wasn't mature enough to handle the situation we are currently in? I'm finding that to be incredibly true at the moment. This relationship with Hudson, it became too much. Feelings got involved. Emotions have been tangled and twisted. And now I just feel lost. I feel unsure. I feel like the man who was once by my side and who I connected with is a distant memory. All I want to do is climb into my most comfy sweatshirt, hold on to my childhood teddy bear, and wish all of this out of my life.

Our hotel isn't far from the club, and when we arrive, Hudson pays by card, then helps me out of the cab by taking my hand. Continuing to hold it, we make our way to the elevator, then ride in silence, him still holding my hand the entire time.

When we reach our room, he lets go of me to open the door with a key card. Once in the room, I book it straight to the bathroom, where I start undressing, because I don't want to be in this garment any longer than I need to be.

I feel his presence before I see him. And when I turn to face him, I find him leaning against the bathroom door, arms crossed, no longer wearing his suit jacket or ascot. Just his dress shirt, untucked and unbuttoned.

Knowing I need his help, I say, "Can you undo this corset for me?"

He pushes off the doorway, walks up behind me without a word, and starts undoing the strings. With every tug, the corset gives until it's fully undone. I keep it close to my chest, though, and move away from him and toward the closet, where I quickly change into a pair of leggings and a loose-fitting top. Then I grab my suitcase and place it on the ground, opening it so I can shove everything I need inside.

"What are you doing?" His gruff voice sounds out through the small space of the closet.

"I can't stay here tonight," I say. "I need to leave." I shove what I can in the suitcase and head into the bathroom, where I start gathering my toiletries, tears brimming, ready to fall over because I feel so incredibly embarrassed. So hurt. So out of my own body that I want to be alone.

He doesn't stop me; instead, he watches me pack, his eyes tracking my every movement. I feel like I'm the main event, the way he watches over me. It makes me uncomfortable and very aware of everything I'm doing.

"Can you not watch me?" I ask as a tear slides down my cheek.

Once again, without a word, he moves away and heads into the living room, giving me the space I need. I pause in my packing, pull my knees into my chest, and rest my forehead on my knees as I allow myself to cry.

Letting it all out.

This is not how I expected this trip to end. Honestly, I didn't have a clue *how* it would end, but one thing is for sure, it wasn't in tears. It wasn't feeling lost and so incredibly despondent. *What if Jude never speaks to me again? What if this whole farce destroys their business—the very thing we were trying to save? Why did I ever suggest this in the first place?*

I take a few minutes to gather myself, to wipe at my cheeks, and to take a few deep breaths. When I think I'm ready to leave, I sit on top of my suitcase, zip it up, lift it up, and drag it out into the living room, where I find Hudson sitting on the couch, leaning forward, his hands digging through his hair. He glances up with just his eyes, and I see the same pain I'm feeling reflected in his irises.

I swipe at my nose with the back of my hand and move over to my sneakers. I put them on, one by one, and then grab my purse from the hook next to the door. Unsure of where I'm going, I turn my back and head toward the door, just as I hear a very quiet, "Don't."

It's so faint, I almost just breezed right over it, but I heard it.

I glance over my shoulder, my eyes landing on Hudson, his hair sticking up in all different directions, his eyes heavy, his expression bleak.

Leave, Sloane.

Leave now.

Stop looking at him and just leave.

But my legs don't listen as I remain still.

"Please," he says, his voice shaking. "Please don't leave."

My lip trembles from the sound of his voice.

My stomach turns in knots from indecision.

My heart hammers drastically in my heart, begging me to move forward, to go to him.

He swallows and repeats, "Please...please stay with me."

CHAPTER THIRTY-ONE
HUDSON

I WAIT, PLEADING WITH MY eyes, my heart, my mind, my fucking soul for her not to leave. For her to stay here with me, to listen, to give me a chance that I don't fucking deserve.

I watch as tears fill her eyes again, and knowing I caused those absolutely destroys me.

Do you see what you've put her through?

You should just let her go.

Let her be.

But…but I fucking can't.

Being back here, seeing her, being in her presence, it's…it's calmed me. It's sent this pulse of soothing adrenaline through me, telling me that this is where I should have been the entire time. This is who I should have been with this entire time. I should have been leaning on her. I should have been relying on her. I shouldn't have been scared. I shouldn't have been hiding her. I should have been up front about my…fuck, about my feelings for her, but it wasn't until I realized that I lost a piece of her that I found out how I truly felt.

And now…now I'm just hoping that she stays in this room with me. I'm not going to force her. If she wants to leave, she can leave, but I have to at least try.

"Please, Sloane," I say, my voice breaking.

She squeezes her eyes shut and looks away, and for a moment, I think she's going to take off, that she's not going to at least hear me out, but then she drops her purse and walks over to the couch, giving me an ounce of hope.

She takes a seat, pulls her legs into her chest, but doesn't say anything, just stares at the coffee table in front of her.

I want to touch her, hold her, pull her in close, but I know there's no way in hell she's going to let me do that, so I turn toward her instead, closing the distance between us so there are only inches rather than feet keeping us apart.

I tug on my hair again, my nerves shot as I try to gather my words, to explain to her what's going on in my head.

"I...I'm sorry, Sloane. It feels so empty saying that, because they're just words, anyone can say I'm sorry, but fuck, I feel it. I'm not just saying it. I'm feeling it." Her eyes look up, giving me an ounce of her energy. "You have been so great on this trip. You've been incredible, making this deal actually plausible, and...and...I messed up, terribly. You opened my eyes, showed me that I could trust someone with my insecurities, with my worries. You gave me comfort when I didn't know I needed it. But when I found out that my dad knew about us, instead of leaning on you like I should have, I blacked out. I flipped into damage control. I thought I was protecting you, but instead, I was hurting you. I was caught up with my dad, with keeping our marriage a secret, with trying to figure this lawsuit out, and I pushed you aside. I was scared, and I hurt you." I shake my head. "I handled the situation so poorly and didn't keep you safe the way I said I would. I let fear enter your heart. I allowed you to question, to fret, to feel isolated." Tears fall down her cheeks. "And fuck, if I could do it all over again, I would not have left without you. I never should have left you."

She swipes at her cheeks.

"I know I hurt you, and I don't deserve for you to even give me this time, but fuck, I...I don't want you to leave."

"Please, Hudson." She shakes her head. "I can't...I can't—"

"I have feelings for you too," I say, cutting her off.

"No." She goes to stand but I press my hand to her leg. Her eyes meet mine in anger. In pain. "You don't have feelings for me, Hudson. Don't play with me like that."

"I would never fucking say something I didn't mean, especially when it comes to you," I say harshly. "I'm...I'm falling for you."

"No." She shakes her head again. More tears. "Please, please don't say that."

"Why?"

"Because I can't handle it. I don't believe you. You're, you're upset about Jude and Haisley, and you're saying that to save face with them."

"I'm not fucking lying," I say.

"I don't believe you," she yells back. "Because if you were falling for me"—her voice cracks—"you never would have treated me the way that you did."

"I was scared, Sloane," I shout back. "I was trying to save the business from my father's grasp. I was gearing up to face him, and I thought that if I focused on you, if I gave in to my feelings for you in that moment, I wouldn't have been able to stand up to my father. Because you're...you're my weakness."

"Is that supposed to make me feel better?"

"No." I shake my head. "But it's the truth. I didn't answer you because I was scared to think about you. I couldn't think about you out here by yourself. I couldn't think about the look on your face when I told you I was leaving. I had to block it out, and it wasn't the right way to handle it. I know that now. I know that I put business over you...again, and I fucked up. I've never felt like this before. I didn't know how to fucking react. I've never had a good example of love, and that seems like an excuse, but it's the reality of the situation. I fucked up what we had. I never told you how I was feeling when I should have because I was afraid of being weak, but I'm here now, telling you. Fucking telling you the truth."

Her lip trembles as she stares at me. What I wouldn't give to be in that head of hers. To hear her thoughts, to know what her next move is going to be because I've never been in a situation like this before. I've never confessed feelings for someone, let alone begged them to stay with me. The entire situation has my stomach in knots and my heart nearly beating out of my chest.

"Believe me, Sloane," I say. "Please. You've made me a stronger man. You've supported me; you've showed me that life isn't always about business but about having fun, joking, laughing. You opened my eyes, you helped me, giving me strength to face my father. You've changed so much so quickly, and I can't…" I gulp. "I can't have you leave. Please…stay."

She stares at me, almost dumbfounded. And for a second, I think that maybe I've gotten through to her, that she'll give me a chance, until she slowly stands and moves toward the door. I stand as well, my heart ripping out of my chest as she picks up her purse and grips her suitcase, closing the space between her and the door.

With one last effort, I walk up behind her, and as she opens the door, I press my hand to the cool wood, keeping it closed while my body lines up against her back.

"Please," my voice cracks. "Please don't leave me."

She looks over her shoulder at me. "Hudson."

"I'm not lying," I say in desperation. "I…I'm falling for you. Please don't leave me in pieces like I left you. I'm not as strong as you, Sloane. Please. I can't…I can't say goodbye to you. I can't stomach it. Stay. Hate me but stay."

Tears fall down her cheeks as she says, "I do, I hate you."

"I know, baby," I say quietly, causing more tears to fall from her eyes.

"I hate you so much." She turns more toward me, so I lift my hand to her cheek and swipe at her tears with my thumb.

"I know."

Then she drops her purse and buries her head in my chest, sobs wracking her small frame as she repeats "I hate you" over and over again.

And I take it.

I take every emotion behind her words.

I swallow them whole, wanting to steal this pain I've induced as I wrap my arms around her, letting her use me anyway she wants, as long as she doesn't leave.

"I'm so mad at you. I want to hurt you like you hurt me."

"Hurt me, Sloane. Be mad at me. Hate me. Do anything you want, just...just stay with me."

She pounds her fists into my chest and then pushes off me, taking a step back. Her eyes meet mine as she says, "I don't want to have these feelings for you, Hudson. I want to be able to leave this room without tears, not giving two shits about how you feel, but...I can't."

"I wish I was strong enough to let you. But I'm not."

"Fuck," she whispers before she wets her lips and then walks up to me, loops her hand to the back of my head, and pulls me down to her mouth, kissing me with all of the intensity of her words.

My hands fall to her hips as I spin us to the wall and press her up against the smooth surface. Her hands push my shirt off my shoulders and down to the ground before going to the hem of her shirt, where she pulls it up and over her head. My hands slide up her sides, finding her braless. I keep my thumbs just under her breasts as I grip her tightly, keeping her close while her hands find my pants and undo them. She pushes them down along with my briefs.

I step out of them, and while she keeps kissing me wildly, she shimmies out of her pants before looping her arms around my shoulders and hopping up.

I press her back to the wall and mash our mouths together, taking every ounce of her that she's willing to give. And with the way her tongue swipes against mine and how her hands dig into my hair, it seems like she's willing to give me everything.

Her center rubs against my length, so I move my hand between us, position my cock at her entrance, and let her take control as she lifts her hips and then slips me inside her. And it's the best fucking feeling of my life.

"I'm sorry," I say as I thrust inside of her. "I'm so fucking sorry."

I move my mouth over her neck, talking to her the entire time.

"I need you, Sloane. In my life." I kiss along her jaw. "In my arms." I thrust deeper, her legs clamped around my waist. "In my heart. Don't... don't fucking leave me." I find her mouth again and then slip my hand into one of hers, pressing it against the wall while I grip her hip with the other and thrust harder as she pants in between, her tongue dancing with mine. "Please don't leave me."

She groans and tightens around me.

"Please, baby."

I thrust harder, faster.

"Stay."

"God," she calls out, her head falling against the wall. "Fuck."

"Stay with me." I release her and slip my hands under her ass and thrust her up and down over my length, watching as she tenses, then, with one final thrust, falls apart, moaning out my name as I follow right behind her, spilling myself while she contracts around me.

As we both attempt to catch our breath, I bring my hands to her face, cupping her cheeks gently as I kiss her lips, her forehead...then her nose. When I pull away, more tears fall down her cheek as her eyes meet mine.

"You don't need to forgive me. I just ask, please, give me the chance to prove to you that I will be better. Please let me do better."

Her teeth roll over the bottom of her lip as she slowly nods her head.

Relief floods through me as I wrap my arms around her, pulling her into a hug.

"Fuck," I whisper. "Thank...thank you," I say, my voice choking up. "Thank you, baby. I promise, I'll be better. I promise..."

I run my fingers over Sloane's back, watching her breath rise and fall as she stays in a deep slumber.

Christ.

This woman.

How did it get to this point?

How did she slip into my cold fucking heart and bury herself there?

And how come it took me so long to realize it?

Maybe because I'm so fucking jaded from my father's behavior. Maybe because I've closed myself off from feeling this way, not wanting to get hurt again. But by doing that, I hurt her, and that's something I will never forgive myself for.

I glance down at the curve of her lips, the swoop of her nose, the length of her eyelashes... She's so goddamn beautiful, but that's not what I like the most about her. I'm addicted to her personality, to the way she has no problem standing up to me, to how she constantly challenges me, making me fucking laugh. How insightful she is, how she makes me think differently and forces me to be a better person. She's...she's the entire package, meaning I can't fuck this up again.

I drag my fingers down her back and back up. No, I need to do everything to keep this.

And I know where it starts.

I kiss the top of her head and slowly slip away from her and out of bed, making sure she stays asleep before I grab my phone off the nightstand and close the bedroom door before walking out to the terrace, naked.

I take a seat on one of the chairs and unlock my phone. The backlight of the screen nearly sears my eyes, but I sift through my contacts, and when I find Jude's name, I hit it before bringing the phone up to my ear.

I don't expect him to answer. I expect him to send me straight to voice-mail, which is fine—I have an idea of the kind of message I'm going to

leave him—but when he answers the phone, I can feel my entire body stiffen.

"What the fuck do you want?" he says as I put the phone on speaker.

"I need to talk to you."

"I'm sure you fucking do," he says and I'm sure if we were having this conversation in person, he'd be spitting venom.

"I'm sorry, man."

"Sorry for what?" he asks. "For marrying my sister? For not telling me about it? For leaving her in fucking London all alone?"

"Yes," I answer. "For all of it."

"I trusted you. I fucking trusted you. And then you pull this bullshit. How, how am I supposed to move forward from this? You broke our trust."

"I know," I say, shame filling me up. "I fucked up, Jude."

"Were you just using her?"

"At first, yes," I say, telling the truth. "It was mutual."

"So you bought her."

I wince, knowing how that sounds. "We made an agreement," I say. "But...it's different now."

"What do you mean it's different now?"

I pinch my brow and say, "I...I care about her."

"No," he says. I can practically feel his fist coming through the phone. "No, not fucking happening."

"Jude, I didn't—"

"Do you really think I want you, fucking *you*, Hudson, to have feelings for my sister?" I swallow the lump in my throat. "You have a better relationship with your office desk than your fucking family."

I don't want that to be a true fact, but given my track record...

"You're not trustworthy. You're more interested in the company than your family. And you go back on your word, so why would I ever want my sister to be with a man like you?"

His words hit harder.

Harder than I expected because there's a hint of truth to them. A truth that reopens a wound.

A wound that I thought I closed, patched up, only for him to rip it wide open.

I might like her, I might be falling for her, I might need her more than I ever thought I would need another human being in order to breathe easier, but do I deserve her? That's the question.

"This is how this is going to fucking play out," Jude continues as a numbness takes over my body. "You come home with my sister. You end this marriage and offer her a severance package to fucking leave with a solid recommendation so she can find another job, then we'll have a conversation about where and how the business is going to move forward from here. If that means you buy me out, we'll figure it out, but moving forward, you are my wife's brother, and that's it. Nothing more."

End it with her?

Bile rises up my throat from the mere thought of that.

"Did you hear me?" Jude shouts.

"Yes," I say, my voice cracking and my mind whirling with what it would be like to stop talking to her. To give her up. To let her walk away.

"You will stay away from her, understood? You stay fucking far away from her. I don't want to see you near her, talking to her, even looking at her. She's not yours. Get that through your fucking head: she's not yours. Do you fucking understand?"

I wet my lips and squeeze my eyes shut.

I don't want to agree.

I don't want to say goodbye.

But…he's right. She deserves so much more.

So is there really any other option than for me to let go? For me to suffer? *Even if it will rip my heart out of my chest.*

"Do you fucking understand, Hudson?"

"Yes," I answer, the one word feeling like razor blades falling out of my mouth.

"Good." And then he hangs up.

I lean back in the chair and stare up at the sky, my nerves twisting in knots, my breath shortened in my lungs.

How the fuck am I supposed to just walk away? After what we shared tonight? After the feelings we have? I'm just supposed to take her back to the States and be done with her?

I think back to earlier tonight, how she wanted to leave me. How she desperately wanted to shake me away.

How she repeated over and over again how much she hates me.

I'm...I'm not being fair to her. I'm playing with her emotions for my benefit.

Once again...something my father would do.

But I will not be him. I will not fucking act like him.

She will dictate how this relationship goes, and if that means I say goodbye to her tomorrow, then so be it. But at least I have tonight. One more night with her.

I stand from the chair and head back into the hotel room. I shut the terrace door behind me and make my way into the bedroom, where I find her curled up on her side of the bed. I plug my phone back in and slip under the covers, moving over to her side. I bring her warm body in close to mine, wrap my arm around her waist, and bury my head into her hair.

Mine.

She's fucking mine.

Not for long.

But she's mine for now.

CHAPTER THIRTY-TWO
SLOANE

I SLIP MY SWEATSHIRT OVER my head and adjust it on my shoulders and waist while I stare at Hudson sitting on the bed, watching every move that I make.

I heard everything.

Every bit of his conversation with Jude.

The moment he left the bed, I knew something was up, so I followed him and listened in.

I could hear the pain in Hudson's voice—I felt it all the way to my toes. And the anger coming from Jude, I've only seen that a few times, but those few times, it was scary. But last night, it wasn't scary.

It was…frustrating.

Infuriating.

Made me extremely upset with the one single man I've grown to count on my entire life.

How dare he?

How dare he think he can manipulate and control my life like that, without even talking to me?

Well, I'll tell you one thing, it's not going to happen.

I fluff out my hair and then walk up to Hudson and straddle his lap. He's been pretty quiet all morning, not saying much other than asking me if he could get me anything or help me with packing my bags properly, not like the manic way I did it last night.

But the silence ends here.

He cups my ass as I wrap my arms around his shoulders. I can see it in his eyes that he's counting down the minutes until he says goodbye. He's thinking that there isn't much time left, so he's going to soak it all in.

Not happening.

"Tell me what's going on in your head."

He wets his lips and whispers, "Just how lucky I've been to have you."

I run my fingers through his hair. "You say that as if it's past tense."

"Nah, just lucky."

"Mm-hmm," I answer and then get to the point. "Want to tell me about your phone call last night?"

His eyes meet mine; they seem so defeated. "You heard that?"

"Yes, I did."

He nods and then leans back on his hands, giving us a few inches of distance, but I don't let him get too far. "Your brother said some things that rang true in my head."

"Did he?" I ask. "So you're telling me after everything you said to me last night, after the way you begged and pleaded for me to stay, you're just going to allow my brother to step in and disassemble us like that?"

"It's complicated, Sloane."

"Doesn't seem complicated to me. Look me in the eyes right now and tell me you don't have feelings for me."

He looks me in the eyes, but he says, "You know that's not fucking true."

"Okay, so then why are you letting him control what happens between us?"

"I…I don't know." The defeated expression on his face nearly breaks me. "I want to do the right thing. I don't want to manipulate you. I want you to make the choice."

"Great. My choice is you."

"Sloane—"

"No, you listen to me. I'm your wife," I say with conviction. "It might have started off as an agreement, Hudson, but from the beginning, you have said that I'm yours and you're mine. We are married, and you've taken that very seriously, which means as your wife, my value in your life ranks higher than Jude's."

He drags his hand over his face. "Sloane, the things he said, they're so goddamn true."

"Like what?" I ask.

"That I have more of a relationship with my office desk than I do with my family. That I'm not trustworthy. That I go back on my word and that I'm more interested in business than I am in my morals. You deserve better. He knows it, and I know it."

"Well, I don't know it," I say. "And shouldn't my opinion matter the most? Shouldn't how I feel matter the most? Not to mention, none of that is true. You left your dad's business because you cared about your sister and your morals. You absolutely do not go back on your word. You chose to marry me, and you've taken that very seriously. Not to mention, you are trustworthy—"

"I left you in fucking London alone with no communication from me, Sloane. That's not necessarily reliable. That was me focusing on the job and hanging you out to dry."

I swallow the pain of the reminder because, yes, that was not his best showing, but I also know there was a reason he did that.

"Tell me this," I say. "Why did you leave London?"

"You know why."

"No, tell me. You never actually told me what happened."

He sighs and says, "I went to talk to my dad."

"About the lawsuit?"

"Yes."

"Anything else?"

He looks off to the side. "We hashed out our grievances."

"Uh-huh, and how did that go?"

He shrugs. "I mean, it seemed like it ended okay. Like there was possible room for him to make a difference, to change the way he approaches a relationship with us."

"And you came back here wanting to patch things up with me, correct?"

"Yes," he says.

"Why?"

"Why? Because I...because I didn't want to lose you."

"Why?" I ask again.

"Why did I not want to lose you?"

"Yeah, Hudson, why?"

"Because you...you make me feel...safe. Seen. Heard. You bring joy to my rather mundane life. You challenge me in ways I never thought I would be challenged. You make me come alive, and you're truly one of very few who have done that, the only other ones being Hardy and Haisley. And when you're near, I feel happiness, like I know everything is going to be okay because you're by my side."

God, I wasn't expecting to hear him say that.

But wanting to prove my point, I cup his cheek and say, "And you're going to throw that all away because of my brother?"

"It's not just your brother," he says. "It's a livelihood, many people's livelihoods. I can't choose happiness over that."

"And what about my happiness?" I ask. "What about yours?"

He shakes his head. "You will find someone better, Sloane. Someone younger. Someone you can relate to more. As for me, I've had a taste of joy because of you, and I'm going to savor it, but I can survive without it."

"Survive? Is that what you want? To survive through life, Hudson? That's really sad. Not to mention, I don't want anyone else. I want you." My hands fall to his chest. "I want you. I want us. I want this marriage."

"Don't...don't say that," he says, dropping his head.

I lift up his chin with my fingers and force him to look me in the eyes. "I mean that, Hudson. I mean that with everything in me. I want us. Twenty-four hours ago, I didn't want anything to do with you. But you showed me why we work well together. We push and pull, but we end up meeting in the middle. I thought I hated you because I felt so fucking hurt by your actions. But because you talked to me, shared what was actually happening inside your heart, I forgave you. I want this. I...I'm falling for you, and I'll be damned if I let my brother dictate whether or not I can be with you."

"Sloane—"

"Tell me you don't want me. Go ahead, say it and I will stop this conversation right now."

He shakes his head. "No."

"Tell me you want a divorce."

"No," he says again.

"Look me in the eyes and tell me you're done with me."

His beautiful eyes meet mine as he says, "Never."

I grip his cheeks, and he wraps his arms around me as our foreheads connect. "Tell me you want me."

"I want you," he says softly.

"Tell me you want this, us."

"I fucking want us," he says, his voice tortured.

"Tell me you have feelings for me."

"I fucking...I fucking love you, Sloane." And I feel the world stop spinning in this moment, with those three little words. "It's why, fuck, it's why I'm willing to give you up, to salvage your relationship with your brother."

"Don't," I say, my heart filling with joy, with nerves, with a flooding sense of energy that I've never felt before. "This is between us, not him." I wet my lips. "Tell me you want this marriage."

"I want it, baby." His hand slides into my hair. "I fucking want it."

"I want it too," I say and press my lips to his. He reciprocates the kiss, his hand cupping the back of my head, holding me in close.

The intensity of the kiss sets off a dull throb between my legs.

The way his tongue works over mine creates a wave of adrenaline that rushes over me.

And when he leans back onto the mattress, I lift my sweatshirt up and over my head. Then I reach behind me and undo my bra before I pull his shirt over his head. I kiss along his chest, over his pecs, and up his neck.

When I reach his ear, I whisper, "I love you too." And then kiss his jaw. "Don't let me go, Hudson. Don't give me up."

His grip on me grows stronger as he says, "I don't want to."

"Then don't." I lift up and look him in the eyes. "Then don't."

Hudson is asleep, looking incredibly peaceful in his first-class pod. Which I'm grateful for, because I need him to relax. After we made love, he changed our flight to a later one and then held on to me in bed. Tightly. He kissed my head every so often, murmured that he loved me, and glided his fingers up and down my back and arm. It was as if he was trying to soak in every last moment, despite me telling him not to let me go.

When we were in the airport, he looked sick to his stomach.

When we took off, I could practically see the anguish in his eyes.

And it occurred to me in that moment: he truly has no idea how to handle this.

With my phone hooked up to the Wi-Fi, I start a new text message and send it.

Sloane: Hey Hardy, it's Sloane. Not sure if you have my number. I know I've put you and Hudson in a hard spot and I'm sorry. I want to make it better and in order to do that, can I ask you something?

I wait for a response.

Everyone around us is either sleeping or watching the in-flight entertainment. I have my eyes on *The Fall Guy* with Ryan Gosling and Emily Blunt, but there is no way I'm going to be able to focus until I figure out what I'm going to do with Jude.

My phone buzzes, and a text comes through from Hardy.

> **Hardy:** It's not your fault, Sloane, but I appreciate you wanting to make it better. How can I help?

I look over at Hudson again to make sure he's asleep, then text Hardy back.

> **Sloane:** Growing up, has Hudson always shouldered the responsibility of everyone else's problems, trying to find solutions for them?
>
> **Hardy:** Absolutely.
>
> **Sloane:** Has he been the kind of big brother Jude is, where he will make sure his siblings are happy before him?
>
> **Hardy:** Hate to admit it, because it makes me look like a selfish ass, but yes.
>
> **Sloane:** Has anyone ever really stood up for him? Or has he just taken what's handed to him in order to make others happy?
>
> **Hardy:** Well, fuck, Sloane. Didn't think you were going to be asking these kinds of questions.
>
> **Sloane:** LOL, I'm sorry. I just want to make sure I understand him, since he's kind of in a weird state right now.
>
> **Hardy:** I don't think anyone has stood up for him, not even me. What's going on? Is he okay?
>
> **Sloane:** Yesterday was brutal. When he got back, I didn't allow him to apologize because I was so angry, then at the wedding, he attempted to apologize and I didn't let him. When

we got back, I tried to leave the hotel with my things, and he stopped me, pleaded with me to stay. We talked and well… he told me he loved me.

Hardy: What? He did? Jesus, I had no clue.

Sloane: Neither did I. This was after he had a conversation with Jude, which I overheard. He didn't know at the time that I was listening. Jude told him to basically give me up and that he was going to figure out what to do with the business. Hudson is in bad shape. He's clinging to me and I think he's still of the belief that he needs to let me go.

Hardy: Fuck, I wish he told me.

Sloane: Seems like he just shoulders everything and that's why I wanted to talk to you, because when we get back, I'm going to talk to Jude. If Hudson is always trying to put everyone first but himself, it's about time someone put him first.

Hardy: You're right, Sloane. You're absolutely right and I'm sorry I haven't done that. I'm grateful that you are.

Sloane: This isn't a slight against you, Hardy. Trust me when I say, as a younger sibling, I know what it means to be protected. It's rare to see a moment when the protector has to be protected. This is that moment and I want to be the one to be there for him.

Hardy: Thank you.

Sloane: You don't need to thank me. This is what I want.

Hardy: Can I ask you a question?

Sloane: Of course.

Hardy: Did you tell him you loved him back?

Sloane: Without a pause.

Hardy: Good. I didn't think I would ever see the day when Hudson fell in love, but here you are. From the sounds of it, it doesn't seem like you would, but please don't hurt him. He's been through enough. I don't think he could survive losing someone like you.

Sloane: I have zero intentions of hurting my husband.

CHAPTER THIRTY-THREE
HUDSON

I DON'T WANT TO LET her go.

I want her to stay with me, in our house, in our bed.

I want to cling to her, love her, spoil her, make her mine over and over until our bodies can't move anymore.

But the closer we get to the house, the more I realize that I might just have to say goodbye to her.

Our hands are linked as our driver makes his way down our street.

My stomach is in knots.

My head is pounding with a stress headache.

And I swear bile keeps rising in my throat from the thought of what the future might hold...or what it doesn't hold.

The driver pulls up to the side of the house and puts the car in park. He exits and starts unloading our suitcases while Sloane turns toward me.

When our eyes meet, a wave of dread hits me all at once.

"Can I borrow the driver?"

"W-why?" I ask.

Does she want to move her things back to her house?

"I need to go do something." She cups my cheek and whispers, "But I'll be back. I promise."

A lump grows in my throat, feeling like a rock, stuck and cutting off my airway. "Sloane, I don't think..." I swallow. "I don't think you should—"

She places her finger over my lips, cutting me off from finishing my sentence. "Tell me what you told me last night, what you told me this morning."

I look her in the eyes and say, "I love you."

"Good. Hold on to that."

She steps out of the car, and I follow behind her. When we're on the sidewalk and the driver is taking the suitcases up the steps to the front door, she moves in close to me and slides her hand up my chest before gripping the back of my neck. She tugs me down and kisses me softly.

My hands fall to her ass, and I hold her close as I revel in the way her lips move against mine.

I don't want this to be the end.

But why does it feel like it?

Why does it feel like this is all going to come crashing down around me?

I know she's asking me to fight for her, to stay with her, but fuck, what about Jude? What about the business? What about everything I've been able to establish with my brother? And now that I'm failing—once again—is my dad going to see it and break apart the very fragile bandage that was placed over the open wound between us?

"Stop," she says when she pulls away. She presses her hand to my brow, relaxing it. "Stop thinking."

"Sloane, I'm fucking…I'm fucking sick to my stomach."

"I know." She moves her hand up and down my chest. "Please, just go inside, relax, shower. I'll be back. I promise."

"He said—"

"I know what my brother said. And I don't care what he said. Trust me, please."

She stares up at me, pleading with me with her large eyes, and fuck, I can't say no to her. Ever. "Okay," I answer.

"Thank you." She kisses me again, and when she pulls away, she whispers, "I love you."

Those three little words—when she says them to me, it almost feels like the entire world tilts on its axis, stops rotating, and it's just me and her.

"I love you," I say back before she squeezes my hand and gets back in the car.

I stand there on the sidewalk as the driver gets in the car and takes off, feeling like this was the last time I am going to hear her say that to me, which makes my stomach churn all over again.

As much as she wants to say that it's going to be okay, I know for a fact that it's not.

SLOANE

I stand on the doorstep of my brother's house, not an ounce of nerves pulsing through me.

Not even a little.

Instead, I feel levelheaded.

I know what I want to say, and I'm not going to skip a beat while I say it.

The door opens, and Haisley is on the other side in a pair of red shorts and an oversized gray shirt with her hair piled on the top of her head.

"Sloane," she says, looking surprised.

"Hey, Haisley. Could I speak with my brother, please?"

She glances behind her and slowly works her way out onto the doorstep with me, shutting the door behind her. "He's not in a good headspace."

"I understand that, but it's not going to stop me from talking with him. This needs to happen before he starts creating scenarios in his head."

"I think that's already happened."

"Then there's even more reason to talk to him."

She pauses me and says, "I don't know what Hudson did—"

"I love him," I say, plain and simple. "And he loves me. There's nothing to say other than we're married and we plan on keeping it that way."

"Oh," she says, completely shocked. "I...I had no idea." She looks past my shoulder and then back to me. "You love him?"

"I do."

She nods. "He...he needs that."

"I know," I say softly.

"I think he needs it the most out of all of us."

"I've gathered that."

She sighs. "And you're here to defend him?"

"I am. I'm here to help my brother understand."

She nods and then a small smile creeps out over her lips. "You know, I wouldn't have put you two together, but if I think about it, I can see how you could be perfect for each other."

That makes me smile too because she's right. "We balance each other."

"I see it. And honestly, when I found out, I was more concerned about my husband and his reaction and how this might affect him. I never thought about my brother and that...that makes me sad. I don't think he ever lets people think about him and his feelings; he's always shouldering everyone else's burdens."

"He is, which is why I'm here. This is not his fight; this is mine. I want to be the one who stands up for him, who takes care of this. He needs someone being there for him, like he's there for you and Hardy."

Her lips turn up. "God, you're...you're going to make me cry." She pulls me into a hug and whispers, "Thank you." When she pulls away, she continues, "And I'm sorry that I came on strong. This is all brand-new, and I didn't take in the information the way that I should have."

"You also didn't know that feelings were involved either. I hate to admit it, but I've liked him for a while now, ever since Bora Bora at your wedding."

Her smile grows even wider now. "You know, I thought I caught you staring a few times."

"How could I not?"

"I mean, I can certainly see why not. He's my brother—"

"Yeah, and your brother is hot."

She laughs now and squeezes my arm. "Okay, please spare me the details."

"Oh, just like you spared Stacey and me the details about you and Jude?" I give her a look. "I think I owe you way more details about me and Hudson."

"How about you go talk to your brother instead?"

"That's not going to get you out of what I owe you though," I tease and reach for the door, but Haisley stops me.

"Two things. Thank you for loving my brother. I can't wait to see you together and see how you make him happy. I honestly look forward to it."

"Thank you."

"Secondly, I would tread carefully with Jude. Also, I will back you up if you need me."

"I appreciate that, but I think this is something I need to do on my own."

"I understand." She pulls me into a hug again and then whispers, "Good luck. He's out back."

"Thanks."

I slip inside the house and head to the backyard.

I find him in a lounge chair, his back toward me, staring out toward the bay.

With my confidence intact, I walk right up to him and take a seat in the lounge chair next to him.

"Who was—" He pauses when he makes eye contact with me. "Sloane, what are you doing here?"

"We need to talk," I say and watch his entire body grow tense.

"There is nothing that you and I need to talk about. This is between me and Hudson."

"Actually, it's not. It's between you and me." He goes to talk, but I press my hand to his arm and say, "Please, please let me get this out. I need you to understand before you make a judgment regarding what happened between me and Hudson."

"There's nothing to understand. He took advantage of you."

"I took advantage of him," I say, causing him to shake his head. "Please, Jude. Please just listen."

His tongue slides over his teeth before he turns toward me and says, "Fine, talk."

Here goes nothing.

"The moment I met Hudson in Bora Bora, I thought he was beautiful."

"Christ," Jude mutters.

"I did, and when you helped me get a job with him, well, I took it very seriously. I was incredibly grateful, but the more time I spent with him, the more I started to like him."

"Jesus, Sloane."

"I'm sorry, but it's true. But I never acted on anything, ever, and he wouldn't give me the time of day either. He took the boss-assistant relationship very seriously. So nothing happened."

"Okay," he says, letting me continue.

"Then we had a meeting at Maggie's, and that's where things got tricky. Sheridan and Archie were meeting with Maggie to discuss needing another bridesmaid for their wedding because one of theirs broke her leg. They assumed I was for hire and said I was perfect. Hudson said I could do it, but you could tell he immediately regretted it after. Either way, Hudson gave me the opportunity to back down, and I didn't take it."

"Why not?"

"I knew he needed the help. But I think it was also because that day when I went home to talk to Stacey about it, we'd gotten a letter from our landlord, saying that he was going to sell the house. He gave us the option to rent to own, but we needed a down payment and neither of us had the money." His eyes grow angry, but I keep going. "We didn't want to lose the house; it has meant so much to us over the years, and well, I came up with a plan. During that meeting Hudson had, he found out that he needed access to the Mayfair Club to get close to Terrance, and to become a member, you have to be married, so I proposed that I would marry him if he gave me a down payment for the house."

"Jesus fuck, Sloane. Are you kidding me right now?"

I shake my head. "I'm dead serious. And...oh shit, I forgot, after the meeting at Maggie's, he fired me."

"He what?" Jude roars.

"It was deserved, I was being insubordinate, and I didn't take it well. But when I saw the letter from the landlord, I panicked and asked him to marry me. He said no. Several times. For days. He said he would never do that to you, to me. But I kept pressing until I wore him down."

Jude rubs his hand over his forehead. I can only imagine what is going through his mind. "Sloane, when I got you this job with him, I was expecting you to act professionally, not take advantage of my business partner."

"I did, I was acting very professional, but I don't know, panic set in and we didn't want to ask you for help. We wanted to do it on our own—"

"By selling yourself?" he nearly roars.

I hold back my wince and stay strong. "The arrangement benefitted both parties, and I refuse to feel bad about it. I refuse to feel bad about any of it because after we got married and went to London, something changed between me and Hudson. We had both been harboring feelings, but in London we got closer, got to know each other better, and those feelings developed." Jude lifts his brow. "And then we fell for each other."

"What?" he says, looking confused. "You fell for each other?"

"Yes," I answer. "I love him, Jude, simple as that."

"Hold on." He blinks, trying to comprehend. "You...you barely know him. How could you love him?"

"I know him better than you do. I know the kind of man he is outside of the conference room. I know that he'd do just about anything for me, that he's protective and sweet and funny. He can let loose, and when he needs to, he is protective and will hurt anyone who comes near me. He takes our relationship very seriously, and he's one of the best *and* imperfect men I've ever met. I know that he was willing to give me up, despite not wanting to, in order to make you happy, in order to make everyone else happy but himself. And I refuse to let it happen. I refuse to let you dictate what happens in our lives."

"Sloane," he says, pinching the bridge of his nose. "You don't know what love is. You're too—"

"Do not say *young*," I say, growing stern with my brother. "I'm not too young. I know exactly what love is. I feel it when I'm with him, and no one else makes me feel that way. No one. I feel joy when I'm with him. I feel comfort. Ease. He makes me happy, makes me feel special, and I know it's the same feeling you get when Haisley is in the room because you've told me about it. You've gone into detail about how Haisley makes you feel. It's the same thing, Jude." He starts to shake his head again, but I place my hand on his and say, "You need to stop thinking of me as the little girl that you protected when we were growing up and start seeing me as the woman I've become." His eyes meet mine and I continue, "I love you, Jude. You've given me so much in this life, and I'm so grateful for it, but I need you to recognize that if you can't grow with me, then I'm going to have to leave you behind."

"What?" he asks, looking offended.

"It's not fair for you to keep me in this box you created many years ago, a box where you believe you're keeping me safe. You might be protecting me, but you're not letting me grow, you're not letting me find my way in this world—"

"Because you don't have a way."

"I do," I say, growing frustrated. "And Hudson is one of the people who helped me realize what I am passionate about. I want to do good. I want to help those who were in a situation like us growing up. Stacey and I talked, and we are turning the house into a safe haven. We're going to start small, but we plan on growing once we have the right funding and business plan. But the house, that's the beginning. So please don't insult me, don't insult us, by saying we don't know what we're doing. You need to trust that you helped us grow into the resilient women we are today and that we're making good decisions, even if in an unconventional way."

He sits back and clears his throat. "You want to make a safe haven?"

"Yes," I answer, hoping that he's starting to ease up. "I was watching what Hudson and Hardy were doing, offering more affordable housing, and it made me realize we had the opportunity to do something too, you know? Stacey loves the idea, although we need to find her a place to live once we get the house ready and find a family to host—"

"What about you?"

I sigh and look my brother in the eyes. "I'm living with Hudson, Jude. We're married, and I don't plan on changing that."

He works his jaw to the side, clearly not happy about my response but also not as angry as he was before.

"You...you love him?"

I nod. "I love him."

"And he loves you."

"He was the first one to say it."

He smooths his hand over his jaw now, thinking about it. "Why didn't you think you could tell me?"

"Oh, I don't know, maybe because I was afraid of how you were going to react."

"You could have talked me through it."

"There is no way you would have sat and listened."

"I did today."

"Today is different," I say. "You already found out and have had days to get used to it. This was me cooling you down and letting you know you can't treat Hudson the way you did on the phone, which I happened to overhear. He deserves so much better than to have you threaten him like that. He's a good man, and I know you know this. Deep down, you know that he will protect me, take care of me, love me, never hurt me. You know this, or else you never would have gone into business with him."

He looks down at the ground, seeming to think that over.

"You are a man of morals, Jude. Your loyalty runs deep, and you don't associate with people who do not share the same values. So if you were to pick anyone to take care of your sister, wouldn't it be the person who you trust with your livelihood as well?"

He sighs and seems to wrestle with the idea. After a few seconds, he asks, "You really love him?"

"I really do."

"Christ." He drags his hand over his face. "When the hell did you grow up?"

I chuckle and place my hand on his knee. "When you were falling in love with Hudson's sister."

Cue Haisley, who comes up to us and sits down next to Jude. She rubs her hand over his thigh, and he wraps his arm around her.

Softly, Haisley says, "He needs love, Jude. And Sloane is the one offering him the type of love I don't think he thought he would ever have or ever deserve. Please don't take that away from my brother."

"Hell," he groans and then looks between us. "Ganging up on me like this…not fair."

"Do I need to bring in Stacey? Really make it unfair?"

"No."

Haisley and I chuckle and then I place my hand on his arm again. "Can you please accept this? Accept us?"

He twists his lips to the side, takes a moment, and then lightly nods his head. "Yeah, I can."

HUDSON

Silence.

It's an eerie feeling, especially when everything in your head feels chaotic. Unsettled. Out of control.

She's been gone over two hours. Two fucking hours.

And I know she said she was coming back, but why did it feel like she was actually saying goodbye? And shouldn't I be happy about that? That she's making the split between us easier?

I probably should, but I'm not.

I'm actually fucking gutted.

I can't…fuck, I can't even think—

The front door opens, and I spin around from where I'm pacing in the living room to see Jude walk through. Every nerve in my body seizes and a spike of adrenaline shoots up my spine.

Fuck.

But he's not alone—Haisley and Sloane walk in behind him.

What the hell is going on?

"Told you I'd be back," Sloane says casually as she walks up to me, places her hand on my chest, and then stands on her toes to kiss me on the cheek.

Jesus, what is she doing? Trying to get me killed?

"It's okay," she says. "He's not here to hurt you."

So she thinks.

Jude looks between the two of us. I can see him trying to understand, attempting to find approval. I feel like I should say something to him, but I don't quite know what to say. Do I apologize? Do I tell him I love her? Do I ask him what's going on?

"Can I have a second with Hudson?" Jude says.

Okay, so he does plan on harming me. That's fine. I deserve it.

Sloane points at Jude and says, "Be nice."

Then she and Haisley go off to the kitchen, where they pretend to get drinks, even though I know they're trying to listen in.

Jude closes the space between us, and I remain standing as I wait for his next move.

He places his hands in his pockets and looks me in the eyes. "She told me you love her. Is that true?"

Keeping my gaze set on his: "That's true."

"That the marriage was her idea?"

"That's also true."

"That you are protective and take care of her."

"Yes," I answer.

"And that you plan on staying married to her?"

I swallow and nod. "That's what I want."

His tongue presses into the side of his cheek as he slowly nods. "She's a part of my heart, my soul. I can't have anything happen to her."

"You have my word that I would never let something happen to her. Ever."

He nods again. "Good answer." He then stretches his hand out to me, and I take it. He pulls me in close and whispers, "Hurt her and I hurt you, understood?"

"I wouldn't expect anything less," I answer, surprised by this conversation. What the hell did Sloane do?

"Good." He pulls away just enough to look me in the eyes. "I'm sorry about the way I treated you, threatening our business relationship like that. It was wrong."

"I'm sorry I even put you in that position."

He curtly nods. "Give me a second to soak this all in. We can catch up Monday."

"Okay," I answer as he steps away.

"Haisley, you ready?" he calls out.

"Yup," she says but quickly walks up to me and gives me a hug. "I'm happy for you, Hudson. You deserve her."

Then together, they take off, leaving me in a state of confusion alone with Sloane. She seems to find the whole thing funny as she walks up to me with a huge smile on her face.

"What...what just happened?"

She pushes me down on the couch and then straddles my lap. "I had a talk with my brother. Told him everything and said that he was not allowed to treat you the way that he did."

"You did?" I ask.

"Yup. I told him that we love each other and that we planned on staying married. That he needs to trust the fact that I know what I'm doing and trust that you are going to love me the way that I deserve."

"You...you stood up for me?"

She moves her hand over my cheek and says, "Of course I did. Someone needs to, and if anything, it should be your wife." She leans forward and presses a kiss to the tip of my nose. "I am still your wife, right?"

"Y-yeah," I say, stunned. "Unless you planned on getting that divorce like you said you were going to."

She shakes her head. "No, the sex is too good. I think I want you to stick around."

I chuckle but then grow serious because I need to know the truth. "You really want this? Me?"

"I do."

"Are you sure?"

"Yes," she answers. "I want all of you, Hudson. I want the good, the unsure, the hesitant, the bossy, the asshole, the dreamer, the achiever, the protector. I want every single piece of you. There was a reason I was attracted to you from the moment I saw you, and it wasn't just the carved jawline." My lips tilt up. "It was because I felt a connection when you looked me in the eyes for the first time. I knew there was something there; I just couldn't figure it out quite yet. But now that I have, I never want to let it go. Please tell me you feel the same."

"I do," I answer. "I want this, you and me. I want this feeling I have when I'm around you to last forever and I never want to lose it. You... you make me feel something I've never truly felt before. You make me feel seen, comforted, loved."

She smiles and connects our foreheads together. "I want you to always feel that way around me. Always."

"Keep loving me and I will."

She smirks and then kisses me on the lips, deepening the connection by opening her mouth and swiping her tongue against mine.

I melt into the couch and let her take charge, letting her love me, letting her comfort me.

Never in a million years did I think I would ever find someone like her. I was dead set on building a business and nothing else, but then Sloane came along and changed everything.

She gave me joy.

She became my rock, even though I didn't know I needed that.

She gave me a reason to rely on someone other than myself.

She made me a husband by becoming my wife, and that's a title I will forever cherish.

EPILOGUE
HUDSON

"THE PLACE LOOKS BEAUTIFUL," SLOANE says as we take in the event space that Maggie and Everly have transformed into a baby shower paradise.

"Thank you," Maggie says, looking very pleased with herself. "I really hope Jude and Haisley will like it."

"I know they will," Sloane says.

"Well, help yourself to some signature mocktails. They should be here anytime now."

With my hand in hers, I bring Sloane over to the bar, where we read the list of drinks that Maggie and Everly spent a lot of time curating.

It wasn't very long after Sloane and I got back from London that Jude and Haisley found out they were expecting. We were vaguely aware they were trying to start a family, but we didn't think it was going to be that quick for them, and I don't know that they expected it either. I can still remember the day they told us. Jude was still a little icy toward me but warming up. We were all at Stacey and Sloane's house helping paint the walls, when Haisley painted on the wall that they were expecting. She asked us to check on the color in the bedroom, and when we walked in and saw they were pregnant, the entire place erupted.

It was needed, badly. It thawed Jude out completely. I can still remember the hug he gave me that day. It was a hug that lasted longer than it probably should have. It was tighter than expected, and when he pulled away, I saw a hint of tears welling up in his eyes as he said, "I'm going to be a dad."

I knew in that moment that he was letting down his guard fully and letting me in again because he was going to need the help and support. And I've been that man for him day in and day out. I've been by his side as he's learned everything he needed to about being a dad, and I've even helped him set up the baby's room when Haisley has been too tired and too sore to help.

"Your dad is here," Sloane whispers as she brings her drink up to her lips.

I glance toward the door, where my dad walks in with my mother. Normally, he would be wearing a suit, because that's all he really wears, but today, he's wearing a pair of slacks and a simple polo shirt. Very understated for him, which I appreciate.

Ever since I had that talk with him, he's been...trying.

It's taken some time, but slowly, he's been asking Hardy and me out to lunch just to chat. We don't talk about business, don't mention our goals or our plans; instead, we reminisce. We talk about sports, we find commonality in shows we are watching, and of course, we talk about our wives.

And those monthly meetings started turning into biweekly meetings, then a dinner here and there during the week, which turned into a family dinner on Sundays. By no means are we perfect, and there is still a hint of animosity between all of us that we're slowly but surely shedding since deep-rooted anger takes a while to heal, but we are at least making the attempt to do so.

Dad spots us and heads in our direction.

"Place looks great," Mom says as she places a kiss on my cheek and turns to Sloane. "You look stunning." She places her hand on Sloane's growing belly. "Not much longer for you either."

My beautiful wife places her hand on her stomach and smiles up at me. "Just a few more months."

My dad gives me a firm handshake, then kisses Sloane on the cheek. "Will the house be ready before you give birth?"

"Yes, Stacey said only a few more weeks, and then we will be opening our second location."

Dad genuinely smiles. "That's excellent, Sloane. You should be proud, especially after that article I read about Twin Haven and how it's changing the rental landscape of San Francisco."

"Thank you. We're really thrilled about the growth we've seen. And of course, we couldn't have done it without your donation."

Dad waves her off. "It was my pleasure." He then looks at me and says, "I learned that if I'm going to invest my money, then I need to start investing in the right things, with no strings attached."

I smile at my dad as a lump grows in my throat. Had you told me a year ago that my dad would be saying such a thing to me, I would have told you, you were crazy. I never thought he'd have a change of heart, that he would take on some of the values that Hardy and I have instilled in our business, but he has. He's made a significant change in how he conducts himself. And it's been a learning curve for him. He's taken a hit here and there and has had to learn how to deal with it, but he's taken it in stride.

And when did I see that real change start to happen? When he realized his kids' lives were moving on, and if he didn't change, they'd move on without him.

Clearing my throat, I say, "Help yourself to some drinks. I think Jude and Haisley are going to be here soon."

"Thanks," Dad says and makes his way over to the bar.

"Seems like your dad is proud of you," Sloane says as she leans into my shoulder.

I wrap my arm around her and hold her tight, keeping her as close to me as I can. "Seems like he's proud of you."

"I think he's proud of both of us." She stands on her toes and kisses my chin before she yelps.

"Are you okay?" I ask, concern etching my brow.

She grips the side of her stomach and says, "Yes, this bugger of a son of yours keeps kicking me."

"Do you want to go sit down?"

She nods, and I take her over to a couch, where I take a seat and then pull her down on my lap. I lightly place my hand on her stomach and wait for our son to kick.

The day she told me she was pregnant is etched into my brain. She had been feeling off for what felt like weeks. She was telling me that everything was hurting, that she was sick, and we thought that maybe it was exhaustion from renovations or the stress of Twin Haven and the rapid growth they were seeing, but when she wasn't getting better, I told her to see the doctor. That night, she came home and had this ghostly white look on her face. When I asked her what was wrong, she reached into her purse and pulled out a folded piece of paper. I unfolded it and read the two words, written in black Sharpie.

I'm Pregnant.

When I looked up at her for confirmation, all she did was nod her head yes.

She then told me that she must have gotten pregnant when she was switching her birth control. We were using condoms, but it seems as though those didn't hold out. At first, we were surprised, scared, flat-out spiraling, but then we realized that having a baby was what we wanted. Sure, he was coming sooner than expected, but it was what we wanted.

From then on out, it's felt like we've been in a blissful state. Not to mention, it's helped that Haisley and Jude have been a month and a half ahead of us, so we've seen what to expect and even been able to go to some of the classes with them.

"You are going to be such a good dad," she whispers as she plays with the hairs on the back of my neck.

My eyes connect with hers. "You are going to be the best fucking mom."

She smirks and then leans forward and kisses me on the lips. "I couldn't have asked for anyone better to go on this journey with."

"Same, baby," I answer.

"Hey," Archie says as he walks up with Sheridan. "How are you feeling?"

After their honeymoon, Archie and Sheridan came back to San Francisco to settle some of their business and we became pretty close with them. It started with Sheridan and Sloane being friends, which then lead to me and Archie hanging out more, and from there, they became part of the group. They're headed back to London shortly, but we have plans to visit soon.

And if you were wondering, yes, Archie closed on the deal with us, thanks to Terrance's approval. We've been back and forth to London a few times, working on the contracts and grants to start on renovations, and every time we've been back, Sloane and I have made our way to the Mayfair Club, where we've avoided croquet but spent many nights on the terrace, looking up at the stars.

"Feeling good," Sloane says. "Feeling really good."

"We saw the article about Twin Haven. You must be so proud," Sheridan says.

"They did a wonderful job on it." Sloane looks me in the eyes. "We were very happy with how it came out."

"They're coming," Maggie says. "Everyone in their places."

We remain seated while everyone crowds around together with little sticks that say *surprise* on them.

"Are you going to want a surprise baby shower?" I ask Sloane.

She shakes her head. "I've been surprised enough for one lifetime. I'll pass."

"What have you been surprised about?" I ask.

"Well, the way you fuck, that's for sure."

That makes me laugh out loud, drawing attention from the crowd.

She then whispers in my ear, "Saying I do in your office, never thought that would happen."

"True," I say.

"Then poking your balls in a posh, upscale club."

"Very much a surprise."

"Then falling in love with a guy thirteen years my elder."

"Can you not say *elder*? Jesus."

She laughs. "And then finding out we're pregnant. Kind of over the surprises at this point."

"But the last one, that was the best one."

She shakes her head. "No, falling in love with you was the best one."

ABOUT THE AUTHOR

New York Times, #1 Amazon, and *USA Today* bestselling author, wife, adoptive mother, and peanut butter lover. Author of romantic comedies and contemporary romance, Meghan Quinn brings readers the perfect combination of heart, humor, and heat in every book

Website: authormeghanquinn.com
Facebook: meghanquinnauthor
Instagram: @meghanquinnbooks